Limitless

Alan Glynn was born in 1960. He studied English Literature at Trinity College and has worked in magazine publishing in New York and as an EFL teacher in Italy. His second novel, *Winterland*, was published in 2009, and will be followed by *Bloodland* in 2011. He is married with two children and lives in Dublin.

Praise for *Winterland*:

'The crime novel really has become the state-of-the-nation fiction . . . *Winterland* is a book that speaks to absolutely now.' Val McDermid, *Sunday Independent* (Ireland)

'*Winterland* is a page-turner in the best sense of the word, a novel filled with clearly drawn, morally ambiguous characters . . . The plot never lets up for a moment and the three set-pieces of the story are as good as anything I have read in contemporary crime fiction. The great achievement of the novel, however, is the creation of Gina Rafferty herself.' John Boyne, *Irish Times*

'A fast-moving, tightly-plotted, exciting read from the bright new star of Dublin noir crime fiction.' *Irish Independent*

'An enthralling and addictive read.' *Observer*

'A gripping tale of a world of greed and secrets.' Laura Wilson, *Guardian*

'A dark edgy thriller packed with genuine suspense and a real sense of danger, diving into a world of crime, corruption and violence that is all too convincing.' *The Times*

'Glynn keeps his narrative exuberant and fleet-footed . . . The real crimes in Glynn's provocative and richly textured novel are not necessarily the killings, but the unfettered exercise of greed and political self-interest.' *Independent*

D0964403

LIMITLESS

ALAN GLYNN

faber and faber

First published as *The Dark Fields* in 2001
by Little Brown & Company
This paperback edition published in 2011
by Faber and Faber Limited
Bloomsbury House
74–77 Great Russell Street, London WC1B 3DA

Printed in England by CPI Bookmarque, Croydon

A CIP record for this book
is available from the British Library

ISBN 978–0–571–27334–8

2 4 6 8 10 9 7 5 3 1

For Eithne

I wish to thank the following people for their help and support, both moral and editorial:Eithne Kelly, Declan Hughes, Douglas Kennedy, Antony Harwood, Andrew Gordon, Liam Glenn, Eimear Kelly, Kate O'Carroll and Tif Eccles.

He had come a long way to this blue lawn, and his dream must have seemed so close that he could hardly fail to grasp it. He did not know that it was already behind him, somewhere back in that vast obscurity beyond the city, where the dark fields of the republic rolled on under the night.

F. Scott Fitzgerald, *The Great Gatsby*

PART ONE

[**1**]

IT'S GETTING LATE.

I don't have too sharp a sense of time any more, but I know it must be after eleven, and maybe even getting on for midnight. I'm reluctant to look at my watch, though – because that will only remind me of how little time I have left.

In any case, it's getting late.

And it's *quiet*. Apart from the ice-machine humming outside my door and the occasional car passing by on the highway, I can't actually hear a thing – no traffic, or sirens, or music, or local people talking, or animals making weird nightcalls to each other, if that's what animals do. Nothing. No sounds at all. It's eerie, and I don't really like it. So maybe I shouldn't have come all the way up here. Maybe I should have just stayed in the city, and let the time-lapse flicker of the lights short-circuit my now preternatural attention span, let the relentless bustle and noise wear me down and burn up all this energy I've got pumping through my system. But if I hadn't come up here to Vermont, to this motel – to the Northview Motor Lodge – where would I have stayed? I couldn't very well have inflicted my little mushroom-cloud of woes on any of my friends, so I guess I had no option but to do what I did – get in a car and leave the city, drive hundreds of miles up here to this quiet, empty part of the country . . .

And to this quiet, empty motel room, with its three different but equally busy décor patterns – carpet, wallpaper, blankets – vying, *screaming*, for my attention – to say nothing of the shopping-mall artwork everywhere, the snowy mountain scene over the bed, the *Sunflowers* reproduction by the door.

3

I am sitting in a wicker armchair in a Vermont motel room, everything unfamiliar to me. I've got a laptop computer balanced on my knees and a bottle of Jack Daniel's on the floor beside me. I'm facing the TV set, which is bolted to the wall in the corner, and is switched on, tuned to CNN, but with the sound turned right down. There is a panel of commentators on the screen – national security advisers, Washington correspondents, foreign policy experts – and although I can't hear them, I know what they're talking about . . . they're talking about the situation, the crisis, they're talking about Mexico.

Finally – giving in – I look at my watch.

I can't believe that it's been nearly twelve hours already. In a while, of course, it will be fifteen hours, and then twenty hours, and then a whole day. What happened in Manhattan this morning is receding, slipping back along all those countless, small-town Main Streets, and along all those miles of highway, hurtling backwards through time, and at what feels like an unnaturally rapid pace. But it is also beginning to break up under the immense pressure, beginning to crack and fragment into separate shards of memory – while simultaneously remaining, of course, in some kind of a suspended, inescapable present tense, set hard, *un*breakable . . . more real and alive than anything I can see around me here in this motel room.

I look at my watch again.

The thought of what happened sets my heart pounding, and audibly, as if it's panicking in there and will shortly be forcing its way, thrashing and flailing, out of my chest. But at least my head hasn't started pounding. That will come, I know, sooner or later – the intense pin-prick behind the eyeballs spreading out into an excruciating, skull-wide agony. But at least it hasn't started yet.

Clearly, though, time is running out.

So how do I begin this?

I suppose I brought the laptop with me intending to get everything down on a disk, intending to write a straightforward account of what happened, and yet here I am hesitating, circling over the material, dithering around as if I had a couple of months at my disposal and some sort of a reputation to protect. The thing is, I don't have a couple of months – I probably only have a couple of hours – and I don't have any reputation to protect, but I still feel as if I should be going for a bold opening here, something grand and declamatory, the kind of thing a bearded omniscient narrator from the nineteenth century might put in to kick-start his latest 900-pager.

The broad stroke.

Which, I feel, would go with the general territory.

But the plain truth is, there was nothing broad-stroke-ish about it, nothing grand and declamatory in how all of this got started, nothing particularly auspicious in my running into Vernon Gant on the street one afternoon a few months ago.

And that, I suppose, really *is* where I should start.

[2]

VERNON GANT.

Of all the various relationships and shifting configurations that can exist within a modern family, of all the potential relatives that can be foisted upon you – people you'll be tied to for ever, in documents, in photographs, in obscure corners of memory – surely for sheer tenuousness, absurdity even, one figure must stand towering above all others, one figure, alone and multi-hyphenated: the ex-brother-in-law.

Hardly fabled in story and song, it's not a relationship that requires renewal. What's more, if you and your former spouse don't have any children then there's really no reason for you ever, *ever* to see this person again in your entire life. Unless, of course, you just happen to bump into him in the street and are unable, or not quick enough, to avoid making eye contact.

It was a Tuesday afternoon in February, about four o'clock, sunny and not too cold. I was walking along Twelfth Street at a steady clip, smoking a cigarette, heading towards Fifth Avenue. I was in a bad mood and entertaining dark thoughts about a wide range of subjects, my book for Kerr & Dexter – *Turning On: From Haight-Ashbury to Silicon Valley* – chief among them, though there was nothing unusual about that, since the subject thrummed relentlessly beneath everything I did, every meal I ate, every shower I took, every ball-game I watched on TV, every late-night trip to the corner store for milk, or toilet-paper, or chocolate, or cigarettes. My fear on that particular afternoon, as I remember, was that the book just wouldn't hang together. You've got to strike a delicate balance in this kind of

6

thing between telling the story and . . . *telling the story* – if you know what I mean – and I was worried that maybe there *was* no story, that the basic premise of the book was a crock of shit. In addition to this, I was thinking about my apartment on Avenue A and Tenth Street and how I needed to move to a bigger place, but how that idea also filled me with dread – taking my books down off their shelves, sorting through my desk, then packing everything into identical boxes, forget it. I was thinking about my ex-girlfriend, too – Maria, and her ten-year-old daughter, Romy – and how I'd clearly been the wrong guy to be around that situation. I never used to say enough to the mom and couldn't rein in my language when I was talking to the kid. Other dark thoughts I was having: I smoked too much and had a sore chest. I had a host of companion symptoms as well, niggly physical things that showed up occasionally, weird aches, possible lumps, rashes, symptoms of a condition maybe, or a network of conditions. What if they all held hands one day, and lit up, and I keeled over dead?

I thought about how I hated the way I looked, and how I needed a haircut.

I flicked ash from my cigarette on to the sidewalk. I glanced up. The corner of Twelfth and Fifth was about twenty yards ahead of me. Suddenly a guy came careering around the corner from Fifth, walking as fast as I was. An aerial view would have shown us – two molecules – on a direct collision course. I recognized him at ten yards and he recognized me. At five yards we both started putting the brakes on and making with the gestures, the bug-eyes, the double-takes.

'*Eddie Spinola.*'

'*Vernon Gant.*'

'How *are* you?'

'God, how long has it *been*?'

We shook hands and slapped shoulders.

Vernon then stood back a little and started sizing me up.

'Jesus, Eddie, pack it on, why don't you?'

This was a reference to the considerable weight I'd gained since we'd last met, which was maybe nine or ten years before.

He was tall and skinny, just like he'd always been. I looked at his balding head, and paused. Then I nodded upwards. 'Well, at least I still have some choice in the matter.'

He danced Jake La Motta-style for a moment and then threw me a mock left hook.

'Still Mr Smart-ass, huh? So what are you up to, Eddie?'

He was wearing an expensive, loose-fitting linen suit and dark leather shoes. He had gold-rimmed shades on, and a tan. He looked and smelt like money.

What was I up to?

All of a sudden I didn't want to be having this conversation.

'I'm working for Kerr & Dexter, you know, the publishers.'

He sniffed and nodded yeah, waiting for more.

'I've been a copywriter with them for about three or four years, text-books and manuals, that kind of thing, but now they're doing a series of illustrated books on the twentieth century – you know, hoping to cash in on an early boom in the nostalgia trade – and I've been commissioned to do one about the design links between the Sixties and the Nineties . . .'

'Interesting.'

'. . . Haight-Ashbury and Silicon Valley . . .'

'*Very* interesting.'

I hammered it home, 'Lysergic acid and personal computers.'

'*Cool.*'

'It's not really. They don't pay very well and because the books are going to be so short – only about a hundred pages, a hundred twenty – you don't have much latitude, which actually makes it more of a challenge, because . . .'

I stopped.

He furrowed his brow. 'Yeah?'

'. . . because . . .' – explaining myself like this was sending unexpected stabs of embarrassment, and contempt, right through me and out the other side. I shuffled from one foot to the other. '. . . because, well, you're basically writing captions to the illustrations and so if you want to get any kind of angle across you have to be really on top of the material, you know.'

8

'That's great, man.' He smiled. 'It's what you always wanted to be doing, am I right?'

I considered this. It was, in a way – I suppose. But not in any way *he'd* ever understood. Jesus, I thought, *Vernon Gant*.

'That must be a trip,' he said.

Vernon had been a cocaine dealer when I knew him in the late 1980s, but back then he'd had quite a different image, lots of hair, leather jackets, big into Tao and furniture. It was all coming back to me now.

'Actually I'm having a hard time with it,' I said, though I don't know why I was bothering to pursue the matter.

'Yeah?' he said, pulling back a little. He adjusted his shades as though he were surprised to hear what I'd said, but was nevertheless ready to start doling out advice once he'd nailed down whatever the problem might be.

'There are so many strands, you know, and contradictions – it's just hard to work out where to start.' I settled my gaze on a car parked across the street, a metallic-blue Mercedes. 'I mean you've got the anti-technology, back-to-nature Sixties, the *Whole Earth Catalogue* – all that shit . . . windchimes, brown rice and patchouli. But then you've got the pyrotechnics of rock music, sound-and-light, the word *electric* and the very fact that LSD itself came out of a laboratory . . .' I kept my gaze on the car. '. . . and also that – get this – the prototype version of the Internet, the Arpanet, was developed in nineteen sixty-nine, at UCLA. *Nineteen sixty-nine.*'

I stopped again. The only reason I'd come out with this, I suppose, was because it was on my mind and had been all day. I was just thinking out loud, thinking – what angle *did* I take?

Vernon clicked his tongue and looked at his watch. 'What are you doing now, Eddie?'

'Walking down the street. Nothing. Having a smoke. I don't know. I can't get any work done.' I took a drag from my cigarette. 'Why?'

'I think I can help you out.'

He looked at his watch again and seemed to be calculating something for a moment.

I stared at him in disbelief and was on the verge of getting annoyed.

9

'C'mon, I'll explain what I mean,' he said. 'Let's go for a drink.' He clapped his hands. '*Vamos.*'

I really didn't think my heading off with Vernon Gant was such a good idea. Apart from anything else, how could he possibly help me with the problem I'd just outlined to him? The notion was absurd.

But I hesitated.

I'd liked the sound of the second part of his proposition, the going for a drink part. There was also, I have to admit, a slight Pavlovian element to my hesitation – the idea of bumping into Vernon and heading off spontaneously to another location stirred something in my body chemistry. Hearing him say *vamos*, as well, was like an access-code or a search-word into a whole phase of my life that had been closed off now for nearly ten years.

I rubbed my nose and said, 'OK.'

'Good.' He paused, and then said – like he was trying it out for size – '*Eddie Spinola.*'

We went to a bar over on Sixth, a cheesy retro cocktail lounge called Maxie's that used to be a Tex-Mex place called El Charro and before that had been a spit-and-sawdust joint called Conroy's. It took us a few moments to adjust to the lighting and the décor of the interior, and, weirdly, to find a booth that Vernon was happy with. The place was virtually empty – it wouldn't be getting busy for another while yet, not until five o'clock at least – but Vernon was behaving as though it were the small hours of a Saturday morning and we were staking our claim to the last available seats in the last open bar in town. It was only then, as I watched him case each booth for line of vision and proximity to toilets and exits, that I realized something was up. He was edgy and nervous, and this was unusual for him – or at any rate unusual for the Vernon I'd known, his one great virtue as a coke dealer having been his relative composure at all times. Other dealers I'd been acquainted with generally behaved like adverts for the product they were shifting in that they hopped around the place incessantly and talked a lot. Vernon, on the other hand, had always been quiet and businesslike, unassuming, a good listener – maybe even a little too passive sometimes, like a dedicated weed smoker adrift in a sea of coke-fiends. In fact, if I hadn't known better, I might have thought that Vernon – or at least this person in front of me – had done his first few lines of coke that very afternoon and wasn't handling it very well.

We settled into a booth, finally, and a waitress came over.

Vernon drummed his fingers on the table and said, 'Let me see – I'll have a . . . Vodka Collins.'

'For you, sir?'

'A whiskey sour, please.'

The waitress left and Vernon took out a pack of ultra-lite, low-tar, menthol cigarettes and a half-used book of matches. As he was lighting up a cigarette, I said, 'So, how's Melissa?'

Melissa was Vernon's sister; I'd been married to her for just under five months back in 1988.

'Yeah, Melissa's all right,' he said and took a drag from the cigarette. This involved drawing on all the muscle power in his lungs, shoulders and upper back. 'I don't see her that often, though. She lives upstate now, Mahopac, and has a couple of kids.'

'What's her husband like?'

'Her husband? What are you, jealous?' Vernon laughed and looked around the bar as if he wanted to share the joke with someone. I said nothing. The laughter died down eventually and he tapped his cigarette on the edge of the ashtray. 'The guy's a jerk. He walked out on her about two years ago, left her in the shithouse.'

I was certainly sorry to hear this, but at the same time I was having a bit of a problem working up a plausible picture of Melissa living in Mahopac with two kids. As a consequence, I couldn't really make a personal connection to the news, not yet at any rate, but what I *could* picture now – and vividly, intrusively – was Melissa, tall and slender in a creamy silk sheath dress on our wedding day, sipping a Martini in Vernon's apartment on the Upper West Side, her pupils dilating . . . and smiling across the room at me. I could picture her perfect skin, her shiny straight black hair that went half-way down her back. I could picture her wide, elegant mouth not letting anyone get a word in edgeways . . .

The waitress approached with our drinks.

11

Melissa had been smarter than anyone around her, smarter than me, and certainly smarter than her older brother. She'd worked as the production co-ordinator of a small cable TV guide, but I'd always pictured her moving on to bigger and better things, editing a daily newspaper, directing movies, running for the Senate.

After the waitress had gone, I lifted my drink and said, 'I'm sorry to hear that.'

'Yeah. It's a shame.'

But he said it like he was referring to a minor earthquake in some unpronounceable Asian republic, like he'd heard it on the news and was just trying to make conversation.

'Is she working?' I persisted.

'Yeah, she's doing something, I think. I'm not sure what. I don't really talk to her that much.'

I was puzzled at this. On the walk to the bar, and during Vernon's search for the right booth, and as we ordered drinks and waited for them to arrive, I'd been having photo-album flashes of me and Melissa, and of our little slice of time together – like that one of our wedding day in Vernon's apartment. It was psychotronic, skullbound stuff . . . Eddie and Melissa, for example, standing between two pillars outside City Hall . . . Melissa doing up lines as she gazes down into the mirror resting on her knees, gazes down through the crumbling white bars at her own beautiful face . . . Eddie in the bathroom, in various bathrooms, and in various stages of being unwell . . . Melissa and Eddie fighting over money and over who's a bigger pig with a rolled-up twenty. Ours wasn't a cocaine wedding so much as a cocaine marriage – what Melissa had once dismissively referred to as 'a coke thing' – so, regardless of whatever real feelings I may have had for Melissa, or she for me, it wasn't at all surprising that we'd only lasted five months, and maybe it was surprising that we'd even lasted that long, I don't know.

But anyway. The point here and now was – what had happened with *them*? What had happened with Vernon and Melissa? They had always been very close, and had always played major roles in each other's lives. They had looked out for each other in the big bad city, and been each other's final court of appeal in relationships,

12

jobs, apartments, décor. It had been one of those brother-sister things where if Vernon hadn't liked me, Melissa probably would have had no hesitation in just dumping me – though personally, and if *I'd* had any say in the matter, as the boyfriend, I would have dumped the older brother. But there you go. That hadn't been an option.

Anyway, this was ten years later. This was now. Things had obviously changed.

I looked over at Vernon as he took another Olympic-sized drag on his ultra-lite, low-tar, menthol cigarette. I tried to think of something to say on the subject of ultra-lite, low-tar, menthol cigarettes, but I just couldn't get Melissa out of my head now. I wanted to ask him questions about her, I wanted a detailed up-date on her situation, and yet I wasn't sure what right I might have – if any – to information here. I wasn't sure to what extent the circumstances of Melissa's life were any of my business any more.

'Why do you smoke those things?' I said finally, fishing out my own pack of unfiltered Camels. 'Isn't it just a lot of effort for almost no return?'

'Sure, but it's about the only aerobic exercise I get these days. If I smoked those things,' he said, nodding at my Camels, 'I'd be on a life-support machine by now – but what do you want, I'm not going to give up.'

I decided I would try and get back to talking about Melissa later on.

'So, what have *you* been doing, Vernon?'

'Keeping busy, you know.'

That could only mean one thing – he was still dealing. A normal person would have said *I work for Microsoft now* or *I'm a short-order cook at Moe's Diner*. But no – Vernon was keeping busy. Just then it struck me that maybe Vernon's idea of helping me out was going to be an offer of some cut-price blow.

Shit, I should have known.

But then, had I really not known? Wasn't it nostalgia for the old days that had prompted me to come here with him in the first place?

I was about to make some wisecrack about his obvious aversion to respectable employment, when he said, 'Actually, I've been doing some consultancy work.'

'What?'

'For a pharmaceutical corporation.'

My eyebrows furrowed and I repeated his words with a question mark at the end.

'Yeah, there's an exclusive product range coming on-stream at the end of the year and we're trying to generate a client base.'

'What is this, some sort of new street language, Vernon? I've been out of the scene for a long time, I know, but . . .'

'No, no. Straight up. In fact' – he looked around the bar for a moment, and then went on in a slightly lower tone – 'that's what I wanted to talk to you about, this . . . creative problem you're having.'

'I—'

'The people I work for have come up with an amazing new substance.' He reached into his jacket pocket and took out his wallet. 'It's in pill form.' From the wallet he produced a tiny plastic sachet with an air-lock seal across the top. He opened it, held the sachet with his right hand and tapped something out into the palm of his left hand. He held this hand up for me to see. In the centre of it was a tiny white unmarked tablet.

'Here,' he said. 'Take it.'

'What is it?'

'Just *take* it.'

I opened my right hand and held it out. He turned his left hand over and the little white pill fell into my palm.

'What is it?' I said again.

'It doesn't have a name yet – I mean it's got a laboratory tag, but that's just letters and a code. They haven't come up with a proper name for it yet. They've done all the clinical trials, though, and it's FDA-approved.'

He looked at me as though he'd answered my question.

'OK,' I said, 'it doesn't have a name yet and they've done all the clinical trials and it's FDA-approved, but what the fuck *is* it?'

He took a sip from his drink and another hit from his cigarette. Then he said, 'You know the way drugs fuck you up? You have a

14

good time doing them but then you get all fucked up afterwards? And eventually everything in your life . . . falls apart, yeah? Sooner or later it happens, am I right?'

I nodded.

'Well, not with this.' He indicated the pill in my hand. 'This little baby is the diametric opposite of that.'

I eased the pill from the palm of my hand on to the surface of the table. Then I took a sip from my drink.

'Vernon, *please* – come on, I'm not some high-school kid here looking to score my first dime bag. I mean, I'm not even—'

'Believe me, Eddie, you've never done anything like this. I'm serious. Just take it and see.'

I hadn't done any drugs in years, and for the exact reasons Vernon had given in his little sales pitch. I did have longings now and again – cravings for that taste in the back of the throat, and for the blissful hours of rapid-fire talk, and for the occasional glimpses of a godlike shape and structure to the conversation of the moment – but none of that was a problem any more, it was like a longing you might have for an earlier phase in your life, or for a lost love, and there was even a mild, narcotic feeling to be had by just entertaining these thoughts, but as for actually trying something new, getting back into all of that, well – I looked down at the tiny white pill in the centre of the table and said, 'I'm too old for this kind of thing, Vernon—'

'There are no physical side-effects if that's what you're worried about. They've identified these receptors in the brain that can acti- vate specific circuits and . . .'

'Look,' I was becoming exasperated, 'I really don't—'

Just then a phone started ringing, a cellphone. Since I didn't have one myself, I figured it had to be Vernon's. He reached into a side pocket of his jacket and pulled it out. As he was opening the flap and searching for the right button, he said, nodding down at the pill, 'Let me tell you, Eddie, that thing will solve any problems you're having with this book of yours.'

As he raised the phone to his ear and spoke into it, I looked at him in disbelief.

'Gant.'

He really had changed, and in a way that was quite curious. He was the same guy, clearly, but he appeared to have developed – or grown – a different personality.

'When?'

He picked up his drink and swirled the contents of the glass around a bit.

'I know, but *when*?'

He looked over his left shoulder and then, immediately, back at his watch.

'Tell him we can't do that. He *knows* that's out of the question. We absolutely can't do that.'

He waved a hand in the air dismissively.

I took a sip from my own drink and started lighting up a Camel. Here I was – look at me – pissing the afternoon away with my ex-brother-in-law. I'd certainly had no idea when I left the apartment an hour or so before, to go for a walk, that I'd be ending up in a *bar*. And certainly not with my ex-brother-in-law, Vernon fucking Gant.

I shook my head and took another sip from my drink.

'No, *you* better tell him – and *now*.' He started getting up. 'Look, I'll be there in ten, fifteen minutes.'

Straightening out his jacket with his free hand, he said, 'No way, I'm telling you. Just wait, I'll *be* there.'

He turned off the phone and put it back into the side pocket of his jacket.

'*Fucking* people,' he said, looking down at me and shaking his head, as if I'd understand.

'Problems?' I said.

'Yeah, you better believe that.' He took his wallet out. 'And I'm afraid I'm going to have to leave you here, Eddie. I'm sorry.'

He took a business card from his wallet and placed it carefully down on the table. He put it right beside the little white tablet.

'By the way,' he said, nodding down at the tablet, 'that's on the house.'

'I don't want it, Vernon.'

He winked at me. 'Don't be ungrateful now. You know how much those things cost?'

16

I shook my head.

He stepped out of the booth and took a second to shimmy his loose-fitting suit into position. Then he looked directly at me. 'Five hundred bucks a pop.'

'*What?*'

'You heard me.'

I looked down at the tablet. Five hundred dollars for *that*?

'I'll take care of the drinks,' he said and wandered over towards the bar. I watched him as he paid the waitress. Then he indicated back in the direction of our booth. That probably meant another drink – compliments of the big man in the expensive suit.

On his way out of the bar, Vernon threw me a sidelong glance that said, *Take it easy, my friend,* paused, and then added, *and make sure you call me now.*

Yeah, yeah.

I sat there for a while pondering the fact that not only did I not do drugs any more, I didn't drink in the afternoons any more either. But here I was, doing just that – at which point the waitress arrived over with the second whiskey sour.

I finished up the first one and started in on the new one. I lit another cigarette.

The problem I suppose was this: if I was going to be drinking in the afternoon, I would have preferred it to be in any of a dozen other bars, and sitting *at* the bar, shooting the breeze with some guy perched on a stool just like myself. Vernon and I had chosen this place because it was convenient, but as far as I could see it didn't have any other redeeming features. In addition, people had started trickling in now, probably from surrounding offices, and were already getting noisy and boisterous. A party of five took the next booth up from mine and I heard someone ordering Long Island Iced Teas. Don't get me wrong, I had no doubt that Long Island Iced Teas were good obliterators of work-related stress, but they were also fucking lethal and I had no desire to be around when that gin-vodka-rum-tequila thing started kicking in. Maxie's wasn't my kind of bar, plain and simple, and I decided to finish my drink as quickly as possible and get the hell out of there.

Besides, I had work to do. I had thousands of images to pore over and select – to order and re-order and analyse and deconstruct. So what business did I have being in a Sixth Avenue cocktail lounge in any case? None. I should have been at home, at my desk, inching my way through the Summer of Love and the intricacies of micro-circuitry. I should have been scanning all those magazine spreads I had from the *Saturday Evening Post* and *Rolling Stone* and *Wired*, as well as all the photocopied material that was stacked on the floor and on every other available surface in my apartment. I should have been huddled in front of my computer screen, awash in a blue light, making silent, steady progress on my book.

But I wasn't, and despite these good intentions I didn't seem to be showing any signs of making a move to leave either. Instead, giving in to the numinous glow of the whiskey and letting it over-ride my impulse to get out of there, I went back to thinking about my ex-wife, Melissa. She was living upstate now with her two kids, and doing . . . what? *Something*. Vernon didn't know. What was *that* all about? How could he not know? I mean, it made sense that I wasn't a regular contributor to the *New Yorker* or *Vanity Fair*, or that I wasn't an Internet guru or a venture capitalist, but it didn't make any sense at all that Melissa wasn't.

The more I thought about it, in fact, the stranger it seemed. For my part, I could easily retrace my steps back through the years, through all the twists and turns and taste atrocities, and still make a direct, plausible link between the relatively stable Eddie Spinola sitting here in this bar, with his Kerr & Dexter book contract and his monthly health plan, and, say, some earlier, spindlier Eddie, hung-over and vomiting on his boss's desk during a presentation, or raiding his girlfriend's underwear drawer looking for her stash. But with this domesticated, upstate Melissa that Vernon had sketched, there didn't seem to *be* any connection – or the connection had been broken, or . . . something, I don't know.

Back then, Melissa had been akin to a force of nature. She'd had fully worked-out opinions about everything, from the origins of the Second World War to the architectural merits, or demerits, of the new Lipstick Building on Fifty-third Street. She would defend these opinions vigorously and always talked – intimidatingly, as if she were wielding a blackjack – about going back to first principles. You didn't mess with Melissa, and she rarely, if ever, took prisoners.

On the night of the Black Monday stock market crash, for instance – 19 October, 1987 – I was with her in a bar down on Second Avenue, Nostromo's, when we got talking to a party of four depressed bond-salesmen doing shots of vodka at the next table. (I actually think Deke Tauber might have been one of them, I seem to have a clear picture of him in my mind, at the table, glass of Stoli clenched tightly in his fist.) But in any case, the four of them were all shell-shocked and scared and pale. They kept asking each other how it had happened, and what it meant, and went on shaking their heads in disbelief, until finally Melissa said, 'Shit, fellahs, don't let me hold you back from the window-ledge there or anything, but couldn't you see this thing *coming*?' Sipping a frozen margarita and pulling on a Marlboro Light, she then launched – ahead of all the newspaper editorials – into a rapid-fire Jeremiad which deftly attributed Wall Street's collective woes, as well as the country's multi-trillion-dollar debt, to the chronic infantilism of Dr Spock's Baby Boomer gener-ation. She bludgeoned the four guys into an even deeper depres-sion than they'd probably bargained for when they agreed, back in the office, to go for a quick drink – for a quick, innocent little post-crash post-mortem.

I sat staring into my own drink now, wondering what had happened to Melissa. I was wondering how all of that bluster and creative energy of hers could have been channelled so . . . narrowly. This is not to denigrate the joys of parenthood or anything, don't get me wrong . . . but Melissa had been a very ambitious person.

Then something else occurred to me. Melissa's way of looking at things, her kind of informing, rigorous intelligence was exactly what *I* needed if I was going to be whipping this Kerr & Dexter book into shape.

Needing something, however, and being able to acquire it were of course two different things. Now it was *my* turn to be depressed.

Then suddenly, like an explosion, the people in the next booth all

19

started laughing. It went on for about thirty seconds and during it that numinous glow I had in the pit of my stomach flickered, sputtered and went out. I waited for a while, but it was no use. I stood up, sighing, and pocketed my cigarettes and lighter. I eased my way out of the booth.

Then I looked down at the small white pill in the centre of the table. I hesitated for a few moments. I turned to go away, and then turned back again, hesitating some more. Eventually, I picked up Vernon's card and put it in my pocket. Then I picked up the pill, put it in my mouth and swallowed it.

I made my way over to the door, and as I was walking out of the bar and on to Sixth Avenue, I thought to myself, well, *you* certainly haven't changed.

[**3**]

OUTSIDE ON THE STREET it was noticeably cooler than it had been. It was also noticeably darker, though that sparkling third dimension, the city at night, was just beginning to shimmer into focus all around me. It was noticeably busier, too – a typical late afternoon on Sixth Ave, with its heavy flow uptown out of the West Village of cars and yellow cabs and buses. The evacuation of offices was underway as well, everybody tired, irritable, in a hurry, darting up and down out of subway stations.

What was really noticeable, though, as I made my way through the traffic and over to Tenth Street, was just how quickly Vernon's pill – whatever the hell it was – appeared to be taking effect.

I had registered something almost as soon as I left the bar. It was the merest shift in perception, barely a flicker, but as I walked along the five blocks to Avenue A it gathered in intensity, and I became acutely focused on everything around me – on minute changes in the light, on the traffic crawling by to my left, on people coming at me from the other direction and then flitting past. I noticed their clothes, heard snatches of their conversations, caught glimpses of their faces. I was picking up on everything, but not in any heightened, druggy way. Rather it all seemed quite natural, and after a while – after only maybe two or three blocks – I began to feel as if I'd been running, working out, pushing myself to some ecstatic physical limit. At the same time, however, I knew that what I was feeling couldn't be natural because if I *had* been running I would be out of breath, I would be leaning against a wall and panting, gasping for someone to call an ambulance. Running? Shit, when was

21

the last time I'd done that? I don't think I'd run any distance at all at any time over the last fifteen years, never had occasion to, and yet that's how I felt – no head stuff, or buzz, or tingling, or racing heart, or paranoia, no particular awareness of pleasure, I simply felt alert and well. Certainly not like I'd just had two whiskey sours, and three or four cigarettes, and a cheeseburger and fries at lunchtime in my local diner – not to mention all the other unhealthy options I'd ever taken, options flicking backwards now through my life like a greasy deck of cards.

And then in the space of what, eight, ten minutes, I am suddenly *healthy*?

I don't think so.

It's true that I respond pretty quickly to drugs – everyday medicines included, be it aspirin or paracetamol or whatever. I know straightaway when something's in my system, and I go all the way with it. For instance, if it says on a packet 'may cause drowsiness', then that usually means I'll find myself slipping into something like a mild coma. Even at college I was always first out of the hatch with hallucinogenics, always the first one to come up, to detect those subtle, rippling shifts in colour and texture. But this was something else again, this was a rapid chemical reaction unlike anything I'd ever experienced.

By the time I reached the steps outside my building, in fact, I strongly suspected that whatever I'd ingested was already close to operating at full tilt.

I entered the building and walked up to the third floor, passing buggies and bicycles and cardboard boxes on the way. I didn't meet anybody on the stairs, and I'm not sure just how I would have reacted if I had, but neither did I detect in myself any sense of wanting to avoid people.

I got to the door of my one-bedroom apartment and fumbled for the key – fumbled because suddenly the idea of avoiding people, or of not avoiding people, or of even having to consider the question one way or the other, was making me feel apprehensive, and vulnerable. It also occurred to me for the first time that I had no idea how this situation was going to develop, and that potentially it could develop in *any* direction. Then I was thinking to myself, oh shit, if something weird happens here, if anything goes wrong, if bad stuff happens, if things get ugly . . .

But I stopped myself short and stood motionless for a while, staring at the brass inset on the door with my name on it. I tried to gauge how I was reacting to all of this, tried to calibrate it in some way, and I decided pretty quickly that it wasn't the drug at all, it was me. I was just panicking. Like an idiot.

I took a deep breath, put the key in the lock and opened the door. I flicked on the light-switch and gazed in for a few seconds, gazed in at the cosy, familiar, slightly cramped living space I'd occupied for more than six years. But in the course of those few seconds something in my perception of the room must have shifted, because all of a sudden it felt *un*familiar, *too* cramped, a little alien even, and certainly not a place that was very conducive to work.

I stepped inside and closed the door behind me.

Then, with my jacket barely off and draped on a chair, I found myself taking some books down from a shelf above the stereo system – *a shelf where they didn't belong* – and putting them on to another shelf, one where they did belong. Next, I was surveying the room, feeling edgy, impatient, dissatisfied about something – though what exactly I didn't know. I soon realized that I was looking for a starting point, and I eventually found one in my collection of nearly four hundred classical and jazz CDs, which were strewn everywhere about the apartment, some out of their cases, and of course in no particular order.

I alphabetized them.

In one go, in one uninterrupted burst. I gathered them all on to the floor in the middle of the room, divided them into two separate piles, each of which I then subdivided into further categories, such as swing, be-bop, fusion, baroque, opera and so on. I then put each category into alphabetical order. Hampton, Hawkins, Herman. Schubert, Schumann, Smetana. When that was done I realized that there was nowhere for them all to fit, no one place that would hold four hundred CDs, so I set about re-arranging the furniture.

I moved my desk over to the other side of the room, creating a whole new storage area where I could put boxes of papers that had previously occupied shelf space. I then used this space to house the CDs. Next, I repositioned various free-standing items, a small table I used as a dining area, a chest of drawers, the TV and VCR unit. After that, I reshelved all of my books, weeding out about a hundred and fifty: cheap-edition crime, horror and science-fiction novels that I would never read again and could easily get rid of. These I put into two black plastic sacks, which I got from a cupboard out in the hallway. Then I took another sack and started going through all of the papers on my desk, and in the drawers of the desk. I was fairly ruthless and threw out things I'd been keeping for no good reason, stuff that if I died my unfortunate executor would have no hesitation in throwing out either, because what was he going to do with it . . . what was he going to do with old love letters, pay slips, gas and electric bills, yellowed typescripts of abandoned articles, instruction manuals for consumer durables I no longer possessed, holiday brochures the holidays of which I hadn't gone on . . . *Jesus*, it occurred to me – as I stuffed all of this garbage into a bag – the *shit* we leave behind us for other people to sort out. Not that I had any intention of dying, of course, but I did have this overwhelming impulse to reduce the clutter in my apartment. And in my life too, I suppose, because I then set about organizing my work materials – folders full of press cuttings, illustrated books, slides, computer files – the underlying idea being to get the project moving in order to get it *finished*, and finished in order to make room for something else, something more ambitious maybe.

When my desk was all tidied up, I decided to go into the kitchen for a glass of water. I was thirsty and hadn't had anything to drink since I got in. It didn't occur to me at that point that I rarely drank water. In fact, it didn't occur to me at that point that the whole set-up was odd – odd that the kitchen hadn't been my first port of call on arriving home, odd that there wasn't already a can of beer in my hand.

But neither did it occur to me as odd that on my way across the living-room floor I should stop briefly to re-align the couch and the armchair.

24

Anyway, when I pushed the kitchen door open and switched on the light, my heart sank. The kitchen was long and narrow, with old-style Formica-and-chrome cupboards and a big refrigerator at the back. Every available space, including the sink, was covered with dishes and dirty pots and empty milk cartons and cereal packets and crushed beer cans. I hesitated for about two seconds and then got down to the job of cleaning it all up.

As I was putting the last scrubbed pot away I glanced at my watch and saw what time it was. I felt like I hadn't been home that long – maybe what, thirty, forty minutes? – but I now realized that I'd actually been back here in the apartment, and working busily, for over *three and a half hours*. I looked around the kitchen, barely recognizing it any more. Then, feeling increasingly disoriented, I wandered back into the living-room and stood gazing in shock at the extent of the transformation I'd wrought there, too.

And something else – in the whole three and a half hours I'd been back I hadn't smoked a single cigarette, which was unheard of for me.

I went over to the chair where I'd left my jacket. I took out the pack of Camels from the side pocket and held it in my hand to look at. The familiar pack, with the eponymous desert beast in profile, suddenly seemed small, shrunken, unconnected to me. It didn't feel like something I lived with every day, didn't feel like a virtual extension of myself, and that's when things really started seeming odd, because this was already the longest period of my waking life, probably since the late 1970s, that I had gone without a cigarette – and I still, as yet, had absolutely no desire to smoke. I hadn't eaten anything either, since lunchtime. Or pissed. It was all very weird.

I put the pack of cigarettes back where I'd found them and just stood there, staring down at my jacket.

I was confused, because there was no doubt that I was 'up' on whatever Vernon had given me, but I couldn't get a handle on what kind of a hit it was supposed to be. I had been abstemious and had tidied my apartment, OK – but what was *that* all about?

I turned around, went over to the couch and sat down very slowly. The thing is, I felt normal . . . but that didn't really count, did it, because I was a natural slob so my behaviour, to say the least of it, was clearly uncharacteristic. I mean, what *was* this – a drug for people who wanted to be more anal-retentive? I tried to remember if I'd heard of anything like it before, or maybe read about it, but nothing came to mind and after a couple of minutes I decided to stretch out on the couch. I put my feet on the armrest at the far end and burrowed my head in against a cushion, thinking that perhaps I could take this thing in some other direction, shift the parameters, float a little. Almost immediately, however, I began to detect something – a tense, prickly sensation, an acute feeling of discomfort. I swung my legs back off the couch at once, and stood up.

Apparently, I had to keep busy.

Navigating the choppy waters of an unknown, unpredictable and more often than not proscribed chemical substance was an experience I hadn't had in a long time, not since the distant, bizarre days of the mid-1980s, and I was sorry now that I had so casually – and stupidly – allowed myself open to it again.

I paced back and forth for a bit, and then went over to the desk and sat down in the swivel-chair. I looked at some papers relating to a telecommunications training manual I was copywriting, but it was tedious stuff and not really what I wanted to be thinking about right now.

I paused, and swivelled around in the chair to survey the room. Everywhere my eyes rested there were reminders of my book project for Kerr & Dexter – illustrated tomes, boxes of slides, piles of magazines, a photograph of Aldous Huxley pinned to a noticeboard on the wall.

Turning On: From Haight-Ashbury to Silicon Valley.

Although I was fairly sceptical about anything Vernon Gant might have to say, he *had* been adamant that the pill would help me overcome any creative problems I was having, so I thought, OK, why not try focusing some attention on the book – at least for a while anyway?

I switched on the computer.

Mark Sutton, my superior at K & D, had thrown me the proposal about three months before and I'd been tossing the idea around ever since – circling over it, talking it up to friends, pretending to be doing it, but looking at the notes I'd made on the computer, I realized for the first time just how little actual work on it I'd done. I had lots of other work to do, proof-reading, copywriting, and I was busy, sure, but on the other hand this was exactly the kind of work I'd been nagging Sutton for since I'd started with K & D in 1994 – something substantial, something with my name on it. I saw now, however, that I was in serious danger of blowing it. To do the job properly, I was going to have to write a ten-thousand-word introduction and about another ten to fifteen-thousand words in extensive captions, but as of now, judging by these notes, it was clear that I had only the vaguest notions about what I wanted to say.

I had accumulated plenty of research material, though – biographies of Raymond Loewy, Timothy Leary, Steve Jobs, political and economic studies, design source-books for everything from fabrics to advertising to album-covers to posters to industrial products – but how much of it had I actually read?

I reached over to a shelf above the desk for the Raymond Loewy biography and studied the photograph on the cover – a dapper, moustachioed Loewy posing in his very modern office in 1934. This was the man who had led the first generation of designer-stylists, people who could turn their hands to almost anything, Loewy himself having been responsible for those sleek Greyhound buses of the 1940s, and for the Lucky Strike cigarette pack, and for the Coldspot-Six refrigerator – all of which information I had gleaned from the blurb on the inside flap of the book as I stood in the shop on Bleeker Street trying to decide whether or not to actually buy it. But that information had been enough to convince me that I needed the book, and that Loewy was a seminal figure, someone I'd better bone up on if I intended to be serious.

But had I boned up on him? Of course not. Wasn't it enough that I shelled out $35 for the damn book in the first place? Now you want me to read it as well?

I opened *Raymond Loewy: A Life* at the first chapter – an account of his early days in France, before he emigrated to the US – and started reading.

A car alarm went off in the street and I endured it for a moment or two, but then looked up – waiting, hoping for it to stop, and soon. After a few more seconds it did and I went back to my reading, but as I refocused on the book I saw that I was already on page 237.

I'd only been reading for about twenty minutes.

I was stunned, and could not understand how I'd gotten through so many pages in such a short space of time. I'm quite a slow reader and it would normally take me three or four hours to read that much. This was amazing. I flipped back through the pages to see if I recognized any of the text and to my surprise I actually did. Because again, in normal circumstances I find that I retain very little of what I read. I even have a hard time following complicated plots in novels, never mind technical or factual stuff. I go into a bookshop and look at the history section, for instance, or the architecture section, or the physics section, and I despair. How is any one person ever again going to be able to come to grips with all of the available material that exists on any given subject? Or even on a specialist area of a subject? It was crazy . . .

But *this* – by contrast – this shit was *amazing* . . .

I got up out of my chair.

OK, ask me something about Raymond Loewy's early career.

Like what?

Like – I don't know – like, how did he get started?

Very well then, how did he get started?

He worked as a fashion illustrator in the late 1920s – for *Harper's Bazaar* mostly.

And?

He broke into industrial design when he was commissioned to come up with a new Gestetner duplicating machine. He managed to do it in five days flat. That was in May of 1929. He went on from there and ended up designing everything from tie-pins to locomotives.

I was pacing back and forth across the room now, nodding sagely and clicking my fingers.

Who were his contemporaries?

Norman Bel Geddes, Walter Teague, Henry Dreyfuss.

I cleared my throat and then continued, aloud this time – as if I were delivering a lecture.

Their collective vision of a fully mechanized future – where everything would be clean and new – was showcased at the World's Fair in New York, in 1939. With the motto 'Tomorrow, Now!', Bel Geddes designed the biggest and most expensive exhibit at the fair, for General Motors. It was called Futurama and represented an imagined America in what was a then-distant 1960 – a sort of impatient, dream-like precursor to the New Frontier . . .

I paused again, unable to believe that I'd taken so much of it in, even the obscure stuff – details, for example, about what was used as fill for the enormous land-reclamation scheme in Flushing Bay, where the fair had actually taken place.

Ash and treated garbage.

Six-million cubic yards of it.

Now how did I remember *that*? It was ridiculous – but at the same time, of course, it was fantastic, and I felt extremely excited.

I went back over to the desk and sat down again. The book was about eight hundred pages long and I reckoned that I didn't need to read the whole thing – after all, I'd only bought it for background information and I could always refer to it again later on. So I just skimmed through the rest of it. When I'd finished the last chapter – and with the book closed in front of me on the desk – I decided to try and summarize what I had read.

The most relevant point I extracted from the book, I think, was about the Loewy style itself, which was popularly known as streamlining. It was one of the first design concepts to draw its rationale from technology, and from aerodynamics in particular. It required that mechanical objects be sheathed in smooth metal casings and pods, and was all about creating a frictionless society. You could see it mirrored everywhere at the time – in the music of Benny Goodman, for instance, and in the swank settings of Fred Astaire movies, in the ocean liners, nightclubs and penthouse suites where he and Ginger Rogers moved so gracefully through space . . .

I paused for a moment and glanced around the apartment, and over at the window. It was dark and quiet now, or at least as dark and quiet as it can get in a city, and I realized in that instant that I was utterly, unreservedly *happy*. I held on to the feeling for as long as possible – until I became aware of my own heartbeat, until I could hear it counting out the seconds . . .

Then I looked back at the book, tapped my fingers on the desk, and resumed.

OK . . . the shapes and curves of streamlining created the illusion of perpetual motion. They were a radical new departure. They affected our desires and influenced what we expected from our surroundings – from trains and automobiles and buildings, even from refrigerators and vacuum cleaners, not to mention dozens of other everyday objects. But out of this an important question arose – which came first, the illusion or the desire?

And that was it, of course. I saw it in a flash. That was the first point I would have to make my introduction. Because something similar – with more or less the same dynamic at work – was to happen later on.

I stood up, walked over to the window and thought about it for a few moments. Then I took a deep breath, because I wanted to get this right.

OK.

The influence . . .

The influence on design later in the century of sub-atomic structures and microcircuitry, together with the quintessential Sixties notion of the interconnectedness of everything was clearly paralleled here in the design marriage of the Machine Age to the growing pre-war sense that personal freedom could only be achieved through increased efficiency, mobility and velocity.

Yes.

I went back over to the desk and keyed in some notes on the computer, about ten pages of them, and all from memory. There was a clarity to my thought processes right now that I found exhilarating, and even though all of this was alien to me, at the time it didn't feel in the least bit odd or strange, and in any case I simply couldn't stop – but then I didn't *want* to stop, because during this last hour or so I had actually done more solid work on my book than I had in the entire previous three months.

So, without pausing for breath, I reached over and took another book down from the shelf, a study of the 1968 Democratic National Convention in Chicago. I skimmed through it in about forty-five minutes, taking notes as I went along. I also read two other books, one about the influence of Art Nouveau on 1960s design and one about the early days of the Grateful Dead in San Francisco.

Altogether, I took about thirty-five pages of notes. In addition, I did a rough draft of the first section of the introduction and worked out a detailed plan for the rest of the book. I did about three thousand words, which I then reread a couple of times and corrected.

I started to slow down at around 6 a.m., still not having smoked a cigarette, eaten anything or gone to the bathroom. I felt quite tired, a little headachy perhaps, but that was all, and compared to other times I'd found myself awake at six o'clock in the morning – grinding my teeth, unable to sleep, unable to *shut up* – believe me, feeling tired and having a mild headache was nothing.

I lay down on the couch again and stretched out. I gazed over at the window and could see the roof of the building opposite, as well as a section of sky that had a tinge of early morning light slowly filtering through it. I listened for sounds, too – the lurching dementia of passing garbage trucks, the occasional police-car siren, the low, sporadic hum of traffic from the avenues. I turned my head in against the cushion and eventually began to relax.

This time there was no unpleasant prickly sensation, and I remained on the couch – though after a while I realized that something *was* still bothering me.

There was a certain untidiness about crashing out on the couch – it blurred the dividing lines between one day and the next, and lacked a sense of closure . . . or at least that was my line of reasoning at the time. There was also, I was pretty sure, a lot of actual untidiness lurking behind my bedroom door. I hadn't been in there yet, having somehow managed to avoid it during the frantic compartmentalizing of the previous twelve hours. So I got up off the couch, went over to the bedroom door and opened it. I'd been right – my bedroom was a sty. But I needed to sleep, and I needed to sleep in my bed, so I set about getting the place into some kind of order. It felt more like work than before, more of a chore than when I'd done the kitchen and the living-room, but there were definitely still traces of the drug in my system and that kept me going. When I'd finished, I had a long, hot shower, after which I took two Extra-Strength Excedrin tablets to stave off my headache. Then I put on a clean T-shirt and boxer-shorts, climbed under the covers and fell asleep within, I'd say, about thirty seconds of my head hitting the pillow.

[4]

HERE IN THE NORTHVIEW MOTOR LODGE everything is drab and dull. I glance around my room, and despite the bizarre patterns and colour schemes there's nothing that really catches the eye – except of course the TV set, which is still busily flickering away in the corner. Some bearded, bespectacled guy in a tweed suit is being interviewed, and immediately – because of the central casting touches – I assume he is a historian, and not a politician or a national security spokesman or even a journalist. I am confirmed in my suspicion when they cut to a still photograph of bandit-revolutionary Pancho Villa, and then to some very shaky old black-and-white footage from, I'd guess, about 1916. I'm not going to turn the sound up to find out, but I'm pretty sure that the spectral figures on horseback riding jerkily towards the camera from the middle of what seems like a swirling cloud of dust (but is more probably the peripheral deterioration of the actual film stock itself) are incursionary forces all riled up and hot on Pancho Villa's tail.

And that *was* 1916, wasn't it?

I seem to remember knowing about that once.

I stare at the flickering images, mesmerized. I've always been something of a footage junky, it never failing to strike me as astonishing that what is depicted on the screen – *that* day, *those* very moments – actually happened, and that the people in them, the extras, the folks who passed fleetingly before a camera and were captured on film, subsequently went on about their daily lives, walked inside buildings, ate food, had sex, whatever, blissfully unaware that their jerky movements, as they crossed over some city street, for instance, or got off a tram, were to be preserved for decades, and then aired, exposed and re-exposed, in what would effectively be a different world.

How can I care about this any more? How can I even be thinking about it?

I shouldn't let myself get so distracted.

Reaching down for the bottle of Jack Daniel's on the floor here beside my wicker chair, it occurs to me that drinking whiskey at this time is probably not such a good idea. I lift the bottle up anyway and take a long hit from it. Then I stand up and walk around the room for a while. But the dreadful hush, underscored by the humming of the ice machine outside and the violent colours now swirling all around me, have a distinctly disorienting effect and I judge it best to sit down again and get on with the task in hand.

I must keep busy, I tell myself, and not get distracted.

OK – so, I fell asleep fairly quickly. But I didn't sleep very well. I tossed and turned a lot, and had weird, disjointed dreams.

It was after eleven-thirty when I woke up – which was only about what, four hours? So I was still very tired when I got out of bed, and although I suppose I could have held on for another while longer, trying to get back to sleep, I knew I would have just lain there, wide awake, replaying the previous night over and over in my mind, and of course putting off the inevitable, which was to go into the living-room, switch on the computer and find out whether or not I had imagined the whole thing.

Looking around the room, though, I suspected that I hadn't. Clothes were folded neatly on a chair at the foot of the bed and shoes were lined up in perfect formation along the floor beneath the window. I quickly got out of bed and went into the bathroom to take a leak. After that I threw cold water on my face, and plenty of it.

When I felt sufficiently awake, I stared at myself in the mirror for a while. It wasn't the usual bathroom mugshot. I wasn't bleary-eyed or puffy, or dangerous-looking, I was just tired – as well as all the other things that hadn't changed since the day before, the fact that I was overweight, and jowly, and badly in need of a hair-cut. There was another thing I needed, too, but you couldn't tell it from looking at me in the mirror – I needed a cigarette.

I tramped into the living-room and got my jacket from the back of the chair. I took the pack of Camels out of the side pocket, lit one up and filled my lungs with rich, fragrant smoke. As I was exhaling, I surveyed the room and reflected that being untidy was less a lifestyle choice of mine than a character defect, so I wasn't about to argue with *this* – but I also felt quite strongly that *this* wasn't what counted, because if I wanted tidy, I could pay for tidy. What I'd keyed into the computer, on the other hand – at least what I remembered keying in, and hoped now I was remembering accurately – was definitely something you couldn't pay for.

I went over to it and flicked on the switch at the back. As it booted up and hummed into life, I looked at the neat pile of books I had left on the desk beside the keyboard. I picked up *Raymond Loewy: A Life* and wondered how much of it I would actually be able to recall if I were put on the spot. I tried for a moment to conjure something up from memory, a couple of facts or dates, an anecdote maybe, an amusing piece of designer lore, but I couldn't think straight, couldn't think of anything.

OK, but what did I expect? I was tired. It was as if I'd gone to bed at midnight, and now I was up at three in the morning trying to do the *Harper's* Double Acrostic. What I needed here was coffee – two or three cups of java to reboot my brain – and then I'd be fine again.

I opened the file labelled 'Intro'. It was the rough draft I'd done for part of the introduction to *Turning On*, and I stood there in front of the computer, scrolling down through it. I remembered each paragraph as I read it, but couldn't have anticipated, at any point, what was going to come next. I had written this, but it didn't feel like I had written it.

Having said that, however – and it would be disingenuous of me not to admit it – what I was reading was clearly superior to anything I might have written under normal circumstances. Nor, in fact, was it a rough draft, because as far as I could see, this thing had all the virtues of a good, polished piece of prose. It was cogent, measured, and well thought out – precisely that part of the process that I usually found difficult, even sometimes downright impossible. Whenever I spent time trying to devise a structure for *Turning On*, ideas would flit around freely inside my brain, OK, but if I ever tried to box any of them in, or hold them to account, they'd lose focus and break up and I'd be left with nothing except a frustrated feeling of knowing each time that I was going to have to start all over again.

Last night, on the other hand – apparently – I had nailed the whole goddamned thing in one go.

I stubbed out my cigarette and stared in wonder at the screen for a moment.

Then I turned and went into the kitchen to put on some coffee.

As I was filling the percolator and preparing the filter, and then peeling an orange, it struck me that I felt like a different person. I was self-conscious about every movement I made, as if I were a bad actor doing a scene in a stage drama, a scene set in a kitchen that was improbably tidy and where I had to make coffee and peel an orange.

This didn't last for very long, though, because there was an incipient old-style mess in the trail of breakfast spoor I left behind me across the work-top spaces. Ten minutes saw the appearance of a milk carton, an unfinished bowl of soggy Corn Flakes, a couple of spoons, an empty cup, various stains, a used coffee filter, bits of orange peel and an ashtray containing the ash and butt-ends of two cigarettes.

I was back.

Concern about the state of the kitchen, however, was merely a ploy. What I didn't want to think about was being back in front of the computer. Because I knew exactly what would happen once I was. I would attempt to move on to the rest of the introduction – as though this were the most natural thing in the world – and of course I'd freeze up. I wouldn't be able to do anything. Then in desperation I'd go back to the stuff I'd done last night and start picking at it – *pecking* at it, like a vulture – and sooner or later that, too, would all come apart.

I sighed in frustration and lit up another cigarette.

I looked around the kitchen and considered tidying it again, returning it to its pristine state, but the idea stumbled at the first post – the soggy bowl of cereal – and I dismissed it as forced and unspontaneous. I didn't care about the kitchen anyway, or the arrangement of the furniture, or the alphabetized CDs – all of that was sideshow stuff, collateral damage if you like. The real target, and where the hit had landed, was inside there in the living-room, right in the middle of my desk.

I extinguished the cigarette I'd lit only moments earlier – my fourth of the morning – and walked out of the kitchen. Without looking over at the computer, I crossed the living-room and went into the bedroom to get dressed. Then I went into the bathroom and brushed my teeth. I came back into the living-room, took the jacket I'd left draped on a chair and searched through the pockets. I eventually found what I was looking for: Vernon's card.

Vernon Gant – it said – consultant. It had his home and cellphone numbers on it, as well as his address – he lived on the Upper East Side now, go figure. It also had a tacky little logo in the top right corner. For a moment I considered phoning him, but I didn't want to be fobbed off with excuses. I didn't want to take the risk of being told he was busy or that I couldn't meet him until the middle of next week – because what I wanted was to see him immediately, and face to face, so I could find out all there was to know about this, I suppose, smart drug of his. I wanted to find out where it came from, what was in it, and – most important of all – how I could get some more.

[5]

I WENT DOWN TO THE STREET, hailed a cab and told the driver
Ninetieth and First. Then I sat back and gazed out of the window.
It was a bright, crisp day and the traffic, as we cruised uptown, wasn't
too heavy.

Since I work at home and hang out with people who mostly live
in the Village and the Lower East Side and SoHo, I don't often have
occasion to go uptown, and especially not uptown on the East Side.
In fact, as the cross streets flitted past and we moved up into the
Fifties, Sixties and Seventies, I couldn't actually remember the last
time I'd been this far north. Manhattan, for all its size and density
of population, is quite a parochial place. If you live there, you establish your territory, you pick out your routes, and that's it. Certain
neighbourhoods you just might never visit. Or it might be that you
go through a phase with a neighbourhood – which could depend on
work, relationships, food preferences even. I tried to think when it
had been . . . maybe the time I went to that Italian place with the
bocce court, Il Vagabondo, on Third and something – but that'd been
at least two years ago.

Anyway, as far as I could see, none of it had changed that much.

The driver pulled up at the kerb just opposite Linden Tower at
Ninetieth Street. I paid him and got out. This was Yorkville, old
Germantown – old because there wasn't much trace of it left, maybe
a few businesses, a liquor store, a dry cleaner's, a delicatessen or
two, certainly quite a few residents, and *old* ones, but for the most
part, or so I'd read, the neighbourhood had been Upper East-Sided
over with new apartment buildings, singles bars, Irish 'pubs' and

38

theme restaurants that opened and closed with alarming frequency.

At a quick glance, I could see that it certainly looked that way. From where I was standing I was able to pick out an O'Leary's, a Hannigan's, and a restaurant called the October Revolution Café.

Linden Tower was a dark red-bricked apartment building, one of the many built over the past twenty or twenty-five years in this part of town. They had established their own unarguable, monolithic presence, but Linden Tower, like most of them, was out-sized, ugly and cold-looking.

Vernon Gant lived on the seventeenth floor.

I crossed over First Avenue, took the steps down on to the plaza and went over towards the big revolving glass doors of the main entrance. By the looks of it, this place had people going in and out of it all the time, so these doors were probably always in motion. I looked upwards just as I got to the entrance and caught a dizzying glimpse of how high the building was. But my head didn't make it back far enough to see any of the sky.

I walked right past the reception desk in the centre of the lobby and turned left into a separate area where the elevators were. A few people stood around waiting, but there were eight elevators, four on either side, so no one had to wait for very long. An elevator went *ping*, its doors opened and three people got out. Six of us then herded into it. We each hit our numbers and I noticed that no one besides me was going higher than the fifteenth floor.

Based on the people I'd seen coming in, and on the specimens standing around me now in the elevator car, the occupants of Linden Tower seemed like a varied bunch. A lot of these apartments would be rent-controlled from a long way back, of course, but a lot of them would also be sub-let, and at exorbitant rates, so that would create a fair bit of social mix right there.

I got out on the seventeenth floor. I checked Vernon's card again and then looked for his apartment. It was down the hall and around the corner to the left, third door on the right. I didn't encounter anyone on the way.

I stood for a moment at his door, and then rang the bell. I hadn't thought much about what I was going to say to him if he answered,

39

and I'd thought even less about what I was going to do if he didn't, if he wasn't home, but standing there I realized that either way I was extremely apprehensive.

I heard some movement inside, and then locks clicking.

Vernon must have seen that it was me through the spyhole because I heard his voice before he'd even got the door fully open.

'Shit, man, that was fast.'

I had a smile ready for when he appeared, but it fell off my face as soon as I actually saw him. He stood before me wearing only boxer shorts. He had a black eye and bruises all down the left side of his face. His lip was cut, and swollen, and his right hand was bandaged.

'What ha—'

'Don't ask.'

Leaving the door open, Vernon turned around and motioned back at me with his left hand to come in. I entered, closed the door gently and followed him down a narrow hallway and into a large open living-room. It had a spectacular view – but then, in Manhattan, virtually anywhere with a seventeenth floor is going to have a spectacular view. This one looked south, and took in the city's horror and glory in about equal measure.

Vernon flopped down on to a long, L-shaped, black leather couch. I felt extremely uncomfortable, and found it hard to look directly at him, so I made a show of glancing around.

The room was sparsely furnished, given its size. There was some old stuff, an antique bureau, a couple of Queen Anne-type chairs, a standard lamp. There was also some new stuff, the black leather couch, a tinted-glass dining table, an empty metal wine-rack. But you couldn't exactly call it eclectic, because there didn't seem to be any order or system to it. I knew Vernon had been big into furniture at one time, and had collected 'pieces', but this seemed like the place of a person who had given up collecting, who had let his enthusiasm wane. The pieces were odd and mismatched, and seemed left over from another time – or another apartment – in their owner's life.

I stood in the middle of the room now, having seen everything there was to see. I looked down at Vernon, in silence, not knowing where to begin – but eventually *he* managed to say something. Through the pained expression on his face and the ugly distortion of his features, of his normally bright greenish eyes and high cheek-bones, he cracked a smile and said, 'So, Eddie, I guess you *were* interested after all.'

'Yeah . . . it was *amazing*. I mean . . . really.'

I blurted this out, just like the high-school kid I'd invoked sarcas-tically the previous day, the one looking to score his first dime bag, and who was now coming back for another one.

'What did I tell you?'

I nodded my head a few times, and then – unable to go on without referring again to his condition – I said, 'Vernon, what *happened* to you?'

'What do you think, man? I got in a fight.'

'Who with?'

'You don't want to know, believe me.'

I paused.

Maybe I didn't want to know.

In fact, thinking about it, he was right, I didn't want to know. Not only that, I was also a little irritated – part of me hoping that this business of his having had the shit kicked out of him wasn't going to get in the way of my scoring from him.

'Sit down, Eddie,' he said. 'Relax, tell me all about it.'

I sat down on the other side of the couch, got comfortable and told him all about it. There was no reason not to. When I'd finished, he said, 'Yeah, that sounds about right.'

I immediately said, 'What do you mean?'

'Well, it works on what's there, you know. It can't make you smart if you're not smart already.'

'So what are you saying, it's a smart drug?'

'Not exactly. There's a lot of hype about smart drugs – you know, enhance your cognitive performance, develop rapid mental reflexes, all of that – but most of what we call smart drugs are just natural diet supplements, artificial nutrients, amino acids, that kind of thing – designer vitamins if you like. What you took was a designer *drug*.

41

I mean, you'd have to take a shitload of amino acids to stay up all night and read four books, am I right?'

I nodded.

Vernon was enjoying this.

But I wasn't. I was on edge and wanted him to cut the crap and just tell me what he knew.

'What's it called?' I ventured.

'It doesn't have a street-name and that's because, as yet, it doesn't have any street profile – which is incidentally the way we want it to stay. The boys in the kitchen are keeping it low-key and anonymous. They're calling it MDT-48.'

The boys in the kitchen?

'Who are you working for?' I asked. 'You said you were doing consultancy for some pharmaceutical outfit?'

Vernon put a hand up to his face at that point and held it there for a moment. He sucked in some air and then let out a low groan.

'Shit, this hurts.'

I leant forward. What should I do here – offer to get him some ice in a towel, call a doctor? I waited. Had he heard my question? Would it be insensitive to repeat it?

About fifteen seconds passed and then Vernon lowered his hand again.

'Eddie,' he said eventually, still wincing, 'I can't answer your question. I'm sure you can understand that.'

I looked at him, puzzled. 'But you were talking to me yesterday about coming on-stream with some product at the end of the year, and clinical trials, and being FDA-approved. What was that all about?'

'FDA-approved, that's a laugh,' he said, snorting with contempt and side-stepping the question. 'The FDA only approves drugs that are for treating illnesses. They don't recognize lifestyle drugs.'

'But—'

I was about to pull him up here and say, 'Yeah, but you *said* . . .' when I stopped myself short. He *had* said it was FDA-approved, and he *had* talked about clinical trials, but then had I really been expected to believe all of that?

OK, what had we got here? Something called MDT-48. An unknown, untested, possibly dangerous pharmaceutical substance scammed out of an unidentified laboratory somewhere, and by an unreliable person I hadn't seen in a decade.

'So,' said Vernon, looking directly at me, 'you want some more of this?'

'Yes,' I said, 'definitely.'

With that established, and in the hallowed traditions of the civilized drug deal, we immediately changed the subject. I asked him about the furniture in the apartment, and if he was still collecting 'pieces'. He asked me about music, and if I still listened to eighty-minute symphonies by dead Germans at full volume. We chatted about these things for a while, and then filled each other in on some details about what we'd been doing for the last few years.

Vernon was fairly cagey – as he had to be in his line of work, I suppose – but as a result I couldn't make much sense of what he was saying. I did get the impression, however, that this MDT business had been occupying him for quite some time, and possibly even for a number of years. I also got the impression that he was anxious to talk about it, but since he wasn't sure if he could trust me yet, he kept stopping himself in mid-sentence, and any time he seemed on the point of revealing something he would hesitate and then quickly revert to a kind of pseudo-scientific sales patter, mentioning neurotransmitters, brain-circuits and cell-receptor complexes.

He shifted quite a bit on the couch as well, continually raising his left leg and stretching it out, like a football player – or maybe a dancer – I couldn't decide.

As he spoke, I sat relatively still and listened.

For my own part, I told Vernon how in 1989 – soon after the divorce – I'd had to get out of New York. I didn't mention the fact that he himself had done his bit to drive me out, that his all-too-reliable supply of Bolivian Marching Powder had led to some severe health and money problems – drained sinuses, drained finances – and that these in turn had cost me my job as the production editor of a now defunct fashion and arts magazine, *Chrome*. But I did tell him about the miserable year I'd spent unemployed in Dublin, chasing some elusive, miasmal notion of a literary existence, and about the three years in Italy teaching and doing translations for an agency in Bologna, as well as learning interesting things about food that I'd never known . . . like, for instance, that vegetables weren't necessarily designed to be available all year round, Korean deli-style, but had their seasons, and came and went in maybe a six-week period, during which time you furiously cooked them in different ways, such as – if it was asparagus, say – asparagus risotto, asparagus with eggs, fettuccine with asparagus, and that two weeks later you didn't even think about asking your greengrocer for asparagus. I was rambling here, and could see that Vernon was getting restless, so I moved things on and told him about how I'd eventually come back from Italy to find the technology of magazine production utterly transformed, making any skills I might have acquired in the late '80s more or less redundant. I then described the last five or six years of my life, and how they'd been very quiet, and uneventful, and had drifted by – flitted by – in a haze of relative sobriety and comfort eating.

But that I had great hopes for this book I was currently working on.

I hadn't meant to bring the conversation so neatly back around to the matter in hand, but Vernon looked at me and said, 'Well, you know, we'll see what we can do.'

This irked me a little, but the feeling was simultaneously muted and exacerbated by the realization that he actually could do something. I smiled at him and held my hands up.

Vernon then nodded at me, slapped his knees and said, 'OK, in the meantime, you want some coffee, or something to eat?'

Without waiting for an answer, he pulled himself forward and struggled up out of the couch. He walked over to the kitchen area in the corner, which was separated from the living-room by a counter and stools.

I got up and followed him.

Vernon opened the refrigerator door and looked in. Over his shoulder I could see that it was almost empty. There was a Tropicana orange juice carton, which he took out and shook and then replaced.

44

'You know what?' he said, turning around to face me. 'I'm going to ask you to do me a favour.'

'Yeah?'

'I'm in no shape to go out right now, as you can see, but I do have to go out later . . . and I need to pick up a suit at the dry-cleaner's. So could I ask you to run down and pick it up for me? And maybe while you're there you could pick us up some breakfast, too?'

'Sure.'

'And some aspirin?'

'Sure.'

Standing there in front of me, in his shorts, Vernon looked skinny and kind of pathetic. Also, up close like this, I could see lines in his face and grey streaks in the hair around his temples. His skin was drawn. Suddenly, I could see where the ten years had gone. Doubtless, looking at me, Vernon was thinking – with suitable variations – the same thing. This gave me a sinking feeling in my stomach, and was compounded by the fact that I was trying to ingratiate myself with him – with my *dealer* – by agreeing to run down and pick up his suit and get him some breakfast. I was amazed at how quickly it all slotted back into place, this dealer-client dynamic, this easy sacrificing of dignity for a guaranteed return of a dime bag or a gram or an eightball or, in this case, a pill that was going to cost me the best part of a month's rent.

Vernon walked across the room to the old bureau and got his wallet. As he was going through it – looking, presumably, for money and the dry-cleaning stub – I noticed a copy of the *Boston Globe* lying on the tinted-glass dining table. Their lead story was Defense Secretary Caleb Hale's ill-advised comments about Mexico, but why – I asked myself – was a New Yorker reading the *Boston Globe*?

Vernon turned around and walked towards me.

'Get me a toasted English with scrambled eggs and Swiss, and a side of Canadian bacon, and a regular coffee. And whatever you want yourself.'

He handed me a bill and a small blue stub. I put the stub in the breast pocket of my jacket. I looked at the bill – at the sombre, bearded face of Ulysses S. Grant – and handed it back to him.

'What, your local diner's going to break a fifty for an English muffin?'

'Why not? Fuck 'em.'

'I'll get it.'

'Whatever. The drycleaner's is on the corner of Eighty-ninth and the diner's right beside it. There's a paper store on the same block where you can get the aspirin. Oh, and could you get me a *Boston Globe* as well?'

I looked back at the paper on the table.

He saw me looking at it and said, 'That's yesterday's.'

'Oh,' I said, 'and now you want today's?'

'Yeah.'

'OK,' I said and shrugged. Then I turned and went along the narrow hallway towards the door.

'Thanks,' he said, walking behind me. 'And listen, we'll sort something out when you get back up, price-wise. Everything is negotiable, am I right?'

'Yeah,' I said, opening the door, 'see you in a few.'

I heard the door close behind me as I made my way down the hall and around the corner to the elevators.

On the ride down I had to resist thinking too much about how bad all of this was making me feel. I told myself that he'd had the shit kicked out of him and that I was just doing him a favour, but it brought me back to the old days. It reminded me of the hours spent waiting in various apartments, pre-Vernon, for *the guy* to show up and of the laboured small talk and of all the nervous energy invested in holding things together until that glorious moment arrived when you could hit the road, split . . . go to a club or go home – eighty bucks lighter, OK, but a whole gram heavier.

The old days.

Which were more than ten years ago.

So what the *fuck* was I doing now?

I left the elevator car, walked out through the revolving doors and on to the plaza. I crossed Ninetieth Street and headed in the direction of Eighty-ninth. I came to the paper store about half-way along the block and went inside. Vernon hadn't said what brand he wanted, so I asked for a box of my own favourites, Extra-Strength Excedrin. I looked at the newspapers laid out on the flat – Mexico, Mexico, Mexico – and picked up a *Globe*. I scanned the front page for anything that might give me a clue as to why Vernon was reading this paper, and the only possible item I could find related to an upcoming product liability trial. There was a small paragraph about it and a page reference for a fuller report inside. The international chemical corporation, Eiben-Chemcorp, would be defending charges in a Massachusetts court that its hugely popular anti-depressant, Triburbazine, had caused a teenage girl, who'd only been taking the drug for two weeks, to kill her best friend and then herself. Was this the company Vernon had said he was working for? Eiben-Chemcorp? Hardly.

I took the paper and the Excedrin, paid for them, and went back out on to the street.

Next, I headed for the diner, which I saw was called the DeLuxe Luncheonette and was one of those old-style places you find in most parts of the city. It probably looked exactly the same thirty years ago as it did today, probably had some of the same clientele, as well, and was therefore, curiously, a living link to an earlier version of the neighbourhood. Or not. Maybe. I don't know. In any case, it was a greasy spoon and being around lunchtime the place was fairly crowded, so I stood inside the door and waited for my turn to order.

A middle-aged Hispanic guy behind the counter was saying, 'I don't understand it. I don't understand it. I mean, what is this all about? They don't have enough problems here, they've got to go down there making more problems?' Then he looked to his left, '*What?*'

There were two younger guys at the grill speaking Spanish to each other and obviously laughing at him.

He threw his hands up.

'Nobody cares any more, nobody gives a damn.'

Standing beside me, there were three people waiting for their orders in total silence. To my left, there were some other people sitting at tables. The one nearest to me had four old guys at it drinking coffee and smoking cigarettes. One of them was reading the *Post* and I realized after a moment that the guy behind the counter was addressing his remarks to him.

'Remember Cuba?' he went on. 'Bay of Pigs? Is this going to turn into another Bay of Pigs, another fiasco like that was?'

'I don't see the analogy,' the old guy reading the *Post* said. 'Cuba was because of Communism.' He didn't take his eyes off the paper during this, and he also spoke with a very faint German accent. 'And the same goes for US involvement in Nicaragua and El Salvador. In the last century there was a war with Mexico because the US wanted Texas and California. That made sense, strategic sense. But this?'

He left the question hanging and continued reading.

Very quickly the guy behind the counter wrapped up two orders, took money for them and some people left. I moved up a bit and he looked at me. I ordered what Vernon had asked for, plus a black coffee, and said that I'd be back in two minutes. As I was going out, the guy behind the counter was saying, 'I don't know, you ask me, they should bring back the Cold War . . .'

I went to the dry-cleaner's next door and retrieved Vernon's suit. I lingered on the street for a few moments and watched the passing traffic. Back in the DeLuxe Luncheonette, a customer at another table, a young guy in a denim shirt, had joined in the conversation.

'What, you think the government's going to get involved in something like this *for no reason*? That's just crazy.'

The guy reading the *Post* had put his paper down and was straining to look around.

'Governments don't always act in a logical way,' he said. 'Sometimes they pursue policies that are contrary to their own interests. Look at Vietnam. Thirty years of—'

'Aw, don't bring that up, will you?'

The guy behind the counter, who was putting my stuff in a bag now – and seemed to be talking *to* the bag – muttered, 'Leave the Mexican people alone, that's all. Just leave them alone.'

I paid him and took the bag.

'Vietnam—'

48

'Vietnam was a mistake, all right?'

'A mistake? Ha. Eisenhower? Kennedy? Johnson? Nixon? Big mistake.'

'Look, you—'

I left the DeLuxe Luncheonette and walked back towards Linden Tower, holding Vernon's suit up in one hand and his breakfast and the *Boston Globe* in the other. I had an awkward time getting through the revolving doors and my left arm started aching as I waited for the elevator.

On the ride back up to the seventeenth floor I could smell the food from the brown paper bag, and wished that I'd got something for myself besides the black coffee. I was alone in the elevator and toyed with the idea of appropriating one of Vernon's strips of Canadian bacon, but decided against it on the grounds that it would be too sad, and – with the suit on a wire hanger – also a little difficult to manoeuvre.

I got out of the elevator, walked along the corridor and around the corner. As I approached Vernon's apartment, I noticed that the door was slightly open. I edged it open further with my foot and stepped inside. I called out Vernon's name and went along the hallway to the living-room, but even before I got there I sensed that something was wrong. I braced myself as the room came into view, and started back in shock when I saw what a complete mess the place was in. Furniture had been turned over – the chairs, the bureau, the wine-rack. Pictures on the wall were askew. There were books and papers and other objects tossed everywhere, and for a moment it was extremely difficult to focus on any one thing.

As I stood there in a state of paralysis, holding up Vernon's suit and the brown paper bag and the *Boston Globe*, two things happened. I suddenly locked on to the figure of Vernon sitting on the black leather couch, and then, almost simultaneously, I heard a sound behind me – footsteps or a shuffling of some kind. I spun around, dropping the suit and the bag and the newspaper. The hallway was dark, but I saw a shape moving very quickly from a door on the left over to the main door on the right, and then out into the corridor. I hesitated, my heart starting to beat like a jack-hammer. After a moment, I ran along the hallway and out through the door myself. I looked up and down the corridor but there was no one there. I rushed on as far as the end and just as I was turning the corner into the longer corridor I heard the elevator doors sliding closed.

Partly relieved that I wasn't going to have to confront anyone, I turned and walked towards the apartment, but as I did so the figure of Vernon on the couch suddenly flashed back into my head. He was sitting there – what . . . pissed off at the state of his living-room? Wondering who the intruder was? Calculating the cost of having the bureau repaired?

Somehow none of these options sat easily with the image I had in my mind, and as I got closer to the door I felt a stabbing sensation in my stomach. I went in and made my way down to the living-room, pretty much knowing at this stage what I was about to see.

Vernon was there on the couch, all right, in exactly the same position as before. He was sitting back, his legs and arms splayed out, his eyes staring directly ahead of him – or rather, appearing to stare, because clearly Vernon wasn't capable of staring at anything any more.

I stepped closer and saw the bullet-hole in his forehead. It was small and neat and red. Despite having always lived in New York City I'd never actually seen a bullet-hole before, and I paused over it in horrified fascination. I don't know how long I stood there, but when I finally moved I found that I was shaking, and almost uncontrollably. I simply couldn't think straight, either, as though some switch in my brain had been flipped, causing my mind to deactivate. I shifted on my feet a couple of times, but these were false starts, and led nowhere. Nothing was getting through to the control centre, and whatever it was that I should have been doing I wasn't doing – which meant, therefore, that I was doing nothing. Then, like a meteor crashing to earth, it hit me: of course, call the fucking police, you idiot.

I looked around the room for the telephone and eventually saw it on the floor beside the upturned antique bureau. Drawers had been removed from the bureau and there were papers and documents everywhere. I went over to the phone, picked it up and dialled

50

911. When I got through to someone I started babbling and was quickly told, *Sir – please . . . calm down*, and was then asked to give a location. I was immediately put through to someone else, someone in a local precinct presumably, and I babbled some more. When I finally put the phone down, I *think* I had given the address of the apartment I was in, as well as mentioning my own name and the fact that someone had been shot dead.

I kept my hand on the receiver of the phone, clenching it tightly, possibly in the mistaken belief that this was still actually doing something. The thing was, I had a lot of adrenalin to deal with now, so after a bit of rapid reflection I decided that it would be better to keep busy, to do something requiring concentration, and that pointedly *not* looking at Vernon's body on the couch would probably be a help as well. But then I realized that there was something I had to do in any case, regardless of my mental state.

I started shuffling through the papers around the upturned bureau and after a couple of minutes found what I was looking for, Vernon's address book. I flicked it open to the M section. There was one number on this page, and it was Melissa's. She was Vernon's next of kin.

Who else was going to tell her?

I hadn't spoken to Melissa in I couldn't remember how long – nine, ten years – and here now in front of me was her telephone number. In nine or ten seconds I could be talking to her.

I dialled the number. It started ringing.

Shit.

This was all unfolding a bit too quickly.

Rinnnnnggg.

Click.

Hum.

Answering machine. Fuck, what did I do?

The next half minute of my life was as intense as anything I could remember in the previous thirty-six years. First, I had to listen to what was undeniably Melissa's voice saying, *I'm not here right now, please leave a message*, though in a tone I found disconcertingly unfamiliar, and then I had to respond to her recorded voice by recording my own voice saying that her brother – *who was here with me in the room* – was dead. Once I'd opened my mouth and started speaking, it was too late, and I couldn't stop. I won't go into the details of what I said to her, mainly because I can't remember what I said, not exactly anyhow – but whatever . . . the point is that when I'd finished and had put the phone down, the strangeness of it all hit me suddenly and I was overwhelmed for a few moments by an uneasy mix of emotions . . . shock, self-disgust, grief, heartache . . . and my eyes filled up with tears . . .

I took a few deep breaths in an effort to control myself, and as I stood at the window, looking out over the city's blur of architectural styles, one thought kept running through my mind: at this time yesterday I hadn't even bumped into Vernon yet. Until that very moment on Twelfth Street I hadn't spoken to him in nearly ten years. Neither had I spoken to his sister, or really thought that much about her – but now here I was in the space of less than a day getting myself re-entangled in her life and in a period of my own life that I thought had gone for ever. It was one of those imponderables of existence that months, even years, can go by without anything significant happening, and then suddenly a cluster of hours comes along, or even of minutes, that can blow a hole in time a mile wide.

I turned away from the window – flinching at the sight of Vernon on the couch – and walked over towards the kitchen area. It had been ransacked as well. The cupboards had been opened and gone through, and there were broken plates and pieces of glass all over the floor. I looked back at the mess in the living-room, and my stomach sank yet again. Then I turned and went along the hallway to the door on the left, which led into the bedroom, and it was the same in there – drawers had been pulled out and emptied, the mattress had been upturned, there were clothes everywhere, and a large cracked mirror lay on the floor.

I wondered why it had been necessary to make such a mess, but in my confused state – and obvious as it was – it still took me a couple of minutes to get it . . . of course, the intruder had been looking for something. Vernon must have opened the door to him

52

– which also meant he'd known him – and when I came back I must have interrupted him. But what had he been looking for? I felt a quickening of my pulse even as I formed the question.

I reached down and lifted up one of the emptied drawers. I stared into it and flipped it over. I did the same with the other drawers, and it wasn't until I was going through some shoe-boxes on a high shelf in the closet a couple of minutes later that I realized two things. First, I was leaving my finger-prints all over the place, and second, I was actually searching Vernon's bedroom. Neither of these things was a good idea, not by any stretch of the imagination – but the question of leaving finger-prints in the bedroom was especially worrisome in the short term. I had given the cops my name and when they arrived I fully intended telling them the truth – or at least most of the truth – but if they found out that I'd been poking around in here, my credibility would surely be undermined. I could be charged with disturbing a crime scene maybe, or with evidence-tampering, or I might even be implicated in the crime itself, so I immediately began retracing my steps, using the sleeve of my jacket to wipe over as many of the objects and surfaces I had touched as possible.

Standing in the doorway a few moments later, I looked back into the room to check that I hadn't missed anywhere. For some reason which I can't explain, I then looked up at the ceiling – and in doing this I noticed something quite odd. The ceiling was a grid of smallish square panels and one of them, directly above the bed, seemed to be slightly out of alignment. It looked as if it had recently been disturbed.

At the same time as I noticed this, I heard a police siren in the distance, and I hesitated for a moment, but then I went over to the bed, stood on it and reached up to the loose panel. I pushed it out of position and peered into the dimness above, where I could just barely make out pipes and ducts and aluminum casing. I stuck my hand up and felt inside and around the edges. My fingers came into contact with something. I reached in further, straining my arm muscles, and grabbed whatever it was, pulling it down out of the square hole. It was a large, brown padded envelope, which I let fall on to the upturned mattress.

Then I paused and listened. There were two sirens wailing now, maybe three, and they were definitely in the vicinity.

I reached back up to the ceiling and repositioned the loose panel as best I could. Then I got down off the bed and picked up the envelope. I quickly ripped it open and tossed the contents out on to the mattress. The first thing I saw was a little black notebook, then a thick roll of bills – I think they were all fifties – and, finally, a large plastic container with an air-lock seal across the top, a bigger version of the one Vernon had produced from his wallet in the bar the previous afternoon. Inside it were – I don't know – maybe three hundred and fifty, four hundred, *five hundred* of the tiny white pills . . .

I stared down at them, with my mouth open – stared down at what was possibly as many as five hundred doses of MDT-48. Then I shook my head and started doing rapid calculations. Five hundred, say, by five hundred . . . that was, what . . . $250,000? A mere three or four of these things, on the other hand, and I could have my book finished in a week. I looked around me, acutely aware all of a sudden that I was in Vernon's bedroom, and that the sirens – which had been getting louder as I opened the envelope – were now winding down, and in unison.

After another moment of hesitation I gathered all the stuff up off the mattress and put it back into the envelope. Carrying it under my arm, I went into the living-room and over to the window. Way down at street level I could see three police cars clustered together, their blue lights rotating. There was a buzz of activity now as uniformed officers appeared out of nowhere, as passers-by stopped to look and comment, and as the cross-street traffic on Ninetieth began clogging up.

I rushed over to the kitchen and searched for a plastic bag. I found one from the local A & P and stuffed the envelope into it. I went down the hallway and out the main door, making sure that I left it open. At the far end of the corridor – in the opposite direction from the elevators – there was a large metal door I'd seen earlier, and I ran towards it. The door opened on to the emergency stairs. To the left of the stairs, there was a small area where the garbage chute was located, and a concrete alcove with a broom and some boxes in it. I dithered for a second, before deciding to run up the stairs to the next level, and then up to the next level again. There were four or five unmarked cardboard boxes stacked in the alcove. I put the plastic bag in behind these boxes, and without looking back I ran down the stairs again, taking the steps two or three at a time. I stumbled out through the metal door, still running, and back into the corridor.

With a couple of yards to go, I heard the elevator doors opening, and then a rising tide of voices. I got to the door of the apartment and slipped in. I went as fast as I could down the hallway and into the living-room – where of course at the shock of seeing Vernon again my heart lurched violently sideways.

Totally out of breath now, I stood in the middle of the room, panting, wheezing. I put my hand on my chest and leant forward, as though trying to ward off a coronary. Then I heard a gentle tap on the door outside and a circumspect voice saying, 'Hello . . . hello,' – a pause, and then – 'police.'

'Yep,' I said, my voice catching a little between breaths, 'in here.'

Just to be busy, I picked up the suit I'd dropped earlier, and the bag with the breakfast in it. I placed the bag on the glass table and the suit on the near side of the couch.

A young cop in uniform, about twenty-five years old, appeared from the hallway. 'Excuse me,' he said, consulting a tiny note-book, '. . . Edward Spinola?'

'Yes,' I said, feeling guilty all of a sudden – and compromised, and like a bit of a fraud, and a low-life – 'yes . . . that's me.'

[6]

OVER THE NEXT TEN OR FIFTEEN MINUTES, the apartment was invaded by what seemed like a small army of uniformed officers, plainclothes detectives and forensics technicians.

I was taken aside – over to the kitchen area – and quizzed by one of the uniforms. He took my name, address, phone number and asked me where I worked and how I knew the deceased. As I answered his questions, I watched Vernon being examined and photographed and tagged. I also watched two plainclothes guys hunkering down beside the antique bureau, which was still on its side, and sifting through the papers on the floor all around it. They passed documents and letters and envelopes to each other, and made comments that I couldn't hear. Another uniform stood by the window talking into his radio, and another one again was in the kitchen looking through the cupboards and the drawers.

There was a dream-like quality to the way the whole process unfolded. It had a choreographed rhythm of its own, and even though I was in it, standing there answering questions, I didn't really feel a part of it – and especially not when they zipped Vernon up in a black bag and wheeled him out of the room on a gurney.

A few moments after this happened, one of the plainclothes detectives came over, introduced himself to me and dismissed the uniformed officer. His name was Foley. He was medium height, wore a dark suit and a raincoat. He was balding and overweight. He fired some questions at me, stuff about when and how I'd found the body, which I answered. I told him everything, except the part about the MDT. As evidence to back up what I'd been saying, I pointed at the dry-cleaned suit and the brown paper bag.

The suit was laid out flat on the couch and was just up from where Vernon's body had been. It was wrapped in plastic film, and looked eerie and spectral, like an after-image of Vernon himself, a visual echo, a tracer. Foley looked at the suit for a moment, too, but didn't react – clearly not seeing it the way I saw it. Then he went over to the glass table and picked up the brown paper bag. He opened it and took out the items inside – the two coffees, the muffin, the Canadian bacon, the condiments – and laid them out along the table in a line, like the fragments of a skeleton displayed in a forensics laboratory.

'So, how well did you know this . . . Vernon Gant?' he asked.

'I saw him yesterday for the first time in ten years. Bumped into him in the street.'

'Bumped into him in the street,' he said, nodding his head and staring at me.

'And what line of work was he in?'

'I don't know. He used to collect and deal furniture when I knew him.'

'Oh,' Foley said, 'so he was a *dealer*?'

'I—'

'What were you doing up here in the first place?'

'Well . . .' I cleared my throat at this point, '. . . like I said, I ran into him yesterday and we decided to meet up – you know, chew over old times.'

Foley looked around. 'Chew over old times,' he said, 'chew over old times.' He obviously had the habit of repeating lines like this, under his breath, half to himself, as though he were mulling them over, but it was clear that his real intention was to question their credibility, and to undermine the confidence of whoever he was speaking to at the time.

'Yes,' I said, letting my irritation show, 'chew over old times. Anything wrong with that?'

Foley shrugged his shoulders.

I had the uneasy feeling that he was going to circle around me for a while, pick holes in my story, and then try to extract a confession of some kind. But as he spoke, and fired more questions at me, I noticed that he'd begun eyeing the coffee and the wrapped-up muffin on the table, as though all he wanted or cared about in the world was to sit down and have some breakfast, and maybe read the funny papers.

'What about family, next of kin?' he said, 'you have anything on that?'

I told him about Melissa, and how I'd phoned and left a message on her answering machine.

He paused and looked at me. 'You left a *message*?'

'Yes.'

He actually did mull this one over for a moment and then said, 'The sensitive type, huh?'

I didn't respond, although I certainly wanted to – wanted to *hit* him. But at the same time I could see his point. Even from the remove of a mere thirty or forty minutes, what I'd done by leaving that message now seemed truly awful. I shook my head and turned away towards the window. The news itself was bad enough, obviously – but how much worse was it going to be for her hearing it from *me*, and on an answering machine? I sighed in frustration, and noticed that I was still shaking a little.

I eventually looked back at Foley, expecting some more questions, but there weren't any. He had taken the plastic lid from the regular coffee and was opening the foil wrapper on the toasted English muffin. He shrugged his shoulders again and threw me a look that said, *What can I tell you? I'm hungry.*

After another twenty minutes or so, I was led out of the apartment and taken in a car to the local precinct to make an official statement. No one spoke to me on the way, and with different thoughts vying for space in my mind, I paid very little attention to my immediate surroundings. When I next had to speak I was in a large, busy office, sitting across a desk from another overweight detective with an Irish name.

Brogan.

He went over the same ground as Foley had, asked the same questions and showed about as much interest in the answers. I then had to sit on a wooden bench for about half an hour while the statement was being typed up and printed out. There was a lot of activity in the room, all sorts of people coming and going, and I found it hard to think.

I was eventually called back over to Brogan's desk and asked to read and sign the statement. As I went through it, he sat in silence, playing with a paper clip. Just before I got to the end of it, his telephone rang and he answered it with a *yeah*. He paused for a few seconds, said *yeah* once or twice more and then proceeded to give a brief account of what had happened. I was very tired at this point and didn't really bother to listen, so it wasn't until I heard him utter the words *Yes, Ms Gant* that I jolted up and started paying attention.

Brogan's matter-of-fact report went on for a another few moments, but then all of a sudden he was saying, 'Yeah, sure, he's right here. I'll put him on to you.' He held the phone out and signalled me to take it. I reached over, and in the two or three seconds it took to position the handset at my ear, I felt what I imagined to be untold quantities of adrenalin entering my bloodstream.

'Hi . . . Melissa?'

'Yeah, Eddie. I got your message.'

Silence.

'Listen, I'm really sorry about that, I was in a panic – I . . .'

'Don't worry. That's what answering machines are for.'

'Well . . . yeah . . . OK.' I looked over at Brogan, nervously. 'And I'm really sorry about Vernon.'

'Yeah. Me too. Jesus.' Her voice was slow and tired-sounding. 'But I'll tell you one thing, Eddie, it didn't surprise me that much. It was a long time coming.'

I couldn't think of anything to say to *that*.

'I know it sounds hard, but he was involved in some . . .' She paused here, and then went on, '. . . some *stuff*. But I suppose I'd better keep my mouth shut on *this* line, right?'

'Probably be a good idea.'

Brogan was still playing with the paper clip, and looked like he was listening to an episode of his favourite serial on the radio.

'I couldn't believe it when I heard your voice, though,' Melissa went on, 'and I almost didn't get the message. I had to replay it twice.' She paused, and for a couple of beats longer than seemed natural. 'So . . . what were you doing at Vernon's?'

'I ran into him on Twelfth Street yesterday afternoon,' I said, practically reading from the statement in front of me, 'and we agreed to meet earlier today at his apartment.'

'This is all so weird.'

'Is there any chance we could meet up? I'd like to—'

I couldn't finish the sentence.

Like to what?

She let the silence hang there between us.

Eventually, she said, 'I reckon I'm going to be very busy over the next while, Eddie. I'm going to have to arrange the funeral and God knows what else.'

'Well, can I help you with any of that? I feel—'

'Don't. You don't have to feel anything. Just let me give you a call when . . . when I have some time. And we can have a proper conversation then. How about that?'

'Sure.'

I wanted to say more, ask her how she was, keep her talking, but that was it. She said, 'OK . . . goodbye,' and then we both hung up.

Brogan flicked the paper clip away, leant forward in his chair and nodded down at the statement.

I signed it and gave it back to him.

'That it?' I said.

'For the moment. If we need you again, we'll call you.'

Then he opened a drawer in his desk and started looking for something.

I stood up and left.

Down on the street I lit a cigarette and took a few deep pulls on it.

I looked at my watch. It was just after three-thirty.

This time yesterday none of this had started yet.

Pretty soon I wasn't going to be able to entertain that thought any more. Which I was glad about in a way, because every time I did entertain it I fell into the annoying trap of thinking that there might be some kind of a reprieve available, almost as if there were a period of grace in these matters during which you could go back and undo stuff, get a moral refund on your mistakes.

I walked aimlessly for a few blocks and then hailed a cab. Sitting in the back seat, and going towards mid-town, I rewound the conversation with Melissa in my head and played it over a few times. Despite what we'd been talking about, the tone of the conversation had at least felt normal – which pleased me inordinately. But there *was* something different in the timbre of her voice, something I'd also detected earlier when I listened to the message on her answering machine. It was a thickness, or a heaviness – but from what? Disappointment? Cigarettes? Kids?

What did *I* know?

I glanced out of the back-seat window. The numbers on the cross-streets – the Fifties, Forties, Thirties – were flitting past again, as though levels of pressure were being reduced to allow me to re-enter the atmosphere. The further we got from Linden Tower, in fact, the better I felt – but then something struck me.

Vernon had been into some stuff, Melissa had said. I think I knew what that meant – and presumably as a direct consequence of this stuff he had been beaten up and later murdered. For my part, while Vernon lay dead on a couch, I had searched his bedroom, found a roll of bills, a notebook and five hundred tablets. I had hidden these items and then lied to the police. Surely that meant *I* was now into some stuff, too.

And could also be in danger.

Had anyone seen me? I didn't think so. When I got back up from the diner to Vernon's apartment the intruder had been in the bedroom and had fled immediately. All he could have seen was my back, or at most caught a glimpse of me when I turned around, as I had of him – but that had just been a dark blur.

He or anyone, however, could have been watching from outside Linden Tower. They could have spotted me coming down with the police, followed me to the precinct – *be following me now*.

I told the driver to stop.

He pulled over on the corner of Twenty-ninth and Second. I paid him and got out. I looked around. No other car – or cars – appeared to have stopped at the same time as we had, although I suppose I could have missed something. In any case, I walked briskly in the direction of Third Avenue, glancing over my shoulder every few seconds. I made my way to the subway station on Twenty-eighth and Lexington and took a 6 train down to Union Square and then an L train west as far as Eighth Avenue. I got out there and caught a cross-town bus back over to First.

I was going to take a taxi from here and loop around for a bit, but I was too close to home, and too tired – and I honestly didn't believe at this point that I *had* been followed – so I just gave in, dropped below Fourteenth Street and walked the remaining few blocks to my building.

[7]

BACK IN MY APARTMENT, I printed out the notes and rough draft of the introduction I'd written for the book. I sat down on the couch to read through them – to check again that I hadn't been imagining it all – but I was so exhausted that I fell asleep almost at once.

I woke up a few hours later with a crick in my neck. It was dark outside. There were loose pages everywhere – in my lap, on the couch, spread out on the floor around my feet. I rubbed my eyes, gathered the pages up and started reading them. It only took a couple of minutes to see that I hadn't been imagining anything. In fact, I was going to be sending this material to Mark Sutton at K & D the next morning, just to remind him that I was still doing the project.

And after that, after I'd read all of the notes, what then? I tried to keep busy by sorting through the papers on my desk, but I couldn't settle down to it – and besides, I'd already done a perfectly good job of sorting through the papers on my desk the previous night. What I had to do – and clearly there was no point in pretending I could avoid it, or even put it off – was go back to Linden Tower and pick up the envelope. I was fairly apprehensive at the prospect, so I started thinking about some form of disguise – but what?

I went into the bathroom, took a shower and shaved. I found some gel and worked it into my hair for a while, flattening it and forcing it straight back. Then I searched through the closet in my bedroom for something unusual to wear. I had one suit, a plain grey affair, which I hadn't worn in about two years. I also took out a light grey shirt, a black tie and black brogues. I laid them all on the bed. The only problem I could see with the suit was that the trousers

63

mightn't fit me any more – but I managed to squeeze into them, and then into the shirt. After I'd done up the tie and put on the shoes, I stood and inspected myself in front of the mirror. I looked ridiculous – like some overfed wiseguy who's been too busy eating linguine and clipping people to update his wardrobe – but it was going to have to do. I didn't look like me, and that was the general idea.

I found an old briefcase that I sometimes used for work and decided to take it with me, but passed on a pair of black leather gloves that I came across on a shelf in the closet. I checked myself one more time in the mirror by the door, and left.

Down on the street, there were no cabs in sight, so I walked over to First Avenue, praying that no one I knew would see me. I got a cab after a couple of minutes and started in on the journey uptown for the second time that day. But everything about it was different – it was dark now and the city was lit up, I was wearing a suit and carrying a briefcase in my lap. It was the same route, the same trip, but it seemed to be taking place in an alternative universe, one where I felt unsure of who I was and what I was doing.

We arrived at Linden Tower.

Swinging my briefcase, I walked briskly into the lobby area, which was even busier than it had been earlier on. I skirted around two women carrying brown-paper grocery bags and went over to the elevators. I stood waiting among a group of about twelve or fifteen people, but I was too self-conscious to really look at any of them closely. If I was walking into anything here, a trap or an ambush, then that's just what was going to happen – I would walk right into it.

On the way up in the elevator, I could feel the rate of my pulse increasing. I had pressed the button for the twenty-fifth floor, intending to take the stairs back down to the nineteenth. I was also hoping that after a certain point I might be left alone in the elevator car, but it wasn't to happen. When we arrived at the twenty-fifth floor there were still six people left and I found myself getting out behind three of them. Two went to the left and the third one, a middle-aged guy in a suit, went to the right. I walked behind him for a few steps and willed him to go straight on, willed him not to turn the corner.

But he did turn the corner, so I stopped and put my briefcase down. I took out my wallet and made a show of going through it, as though I were looking for something. I waited a moment or two, then picked up my briefcase again. I walked on and turned the corner. The corridor was empty and I breathed a sigh of relief.

But almost immediately – behind me – I heard elevator doors opening again, and someone laughing. I walked faster, eventually breaking into a run, and just as I was going through the metal door that led to the emergency stairs, I looked back and caught a glimpse of two people appearing at the other end of the corridor.

Hoping I hadn't been seen, I stood still for a few seconds and tried to catch my breath. When I felt sufficiently composed, I started walking down the cold, grey stairs, taking them two at a time. On the landing of the twenty-second floor I heard voices coming from a couple of flights below me – or thought I heard voices – so I slowed my pace a little. But when I heard nothing else, I picked up speed again.

At the nineteenth floor I stopped and put my briefcase down on the concrete. I stood looking at the stack of unmarked cardboard boxes in the alcove.

I didn't have to do this. I could just walk out of the building right now and forget the whole thing – leave this little package for someone else to find. If I did go ahead with it, on the other hand, nothing in my life would ever be the same again. I knew that for sure.

I took a deep breath and reached in behind the cardboard boxes. I pulled out the plastic A & P shopping bag. I checked that the envelope was still inside it and that the stuff was still inside the envelope. I then put the plastic bag into the briefcase.

I turned around and started walking down the stairs.

When I got to the eleventh floor, I decided it was probably safe enough to go out and take an elevator the rest of the way down. Nothing happened in the lobby or out on the plaza. I walked over to Second Avenue and hailed a cab.

Twenty minutes later I was standing outside my building on Tenth Street.

Back upstairs, I immediately took the suit off and had a quick

65

shower to wash the gel out of my hair. I changed into jeans and a T-shirt. Then I got a beer from the fridge, lit a cigarette and went into the living-room.

I sat at my desk and emptied the contents of the envelope on to it. I picked up the tiny black notebook first, deliberately ignoring the drugs and the thick wad of fifty-dollar bills. There were names and phone numbers in it. Some of the numbers had been crossed out – either completely or with new numbers written in directly above or below them. I flicked backwards and forwards through the pages for a few moments, but didn't recognize any of the names. I must have seen Deke Tauber's name, for instance, and a few others that should have been familiar, but at the time none of them registered with me.

I put the notebook back into the envelope, and then started counting the money.

Nine thousand, four hundred and fifty dollars.

I took six of the fifties and put them into my wallet.

After that, I cleared a space on the desk, pushing the keyboard of my computer to one side, and started counting the tablets. I put them into little piles of fifty, of which there were nine when I'd finished, with seventeen loose ones left over. Using a folded piece of copy paper, I shovelled the 467 tablets back into the plastic container. I sat staring into it for a while, undecided, and then counted out ten of them again. These I put into a small ceramic bowl on a wooden shelf above the computer. I replaced the rest of the cash and the container of tablets in the large brown envelope and took it with me into the bedroom. I put the envelope into an empty shoe-box in the bottom of the closet, and then covered the shoe-box with a blanket and a pile of old magazines.

After this, I toyed with the idea of taking one of the tablets and of getting down to some work straightaway. I decided against it, however. I was exhausted and needed to rest. But before I went to bed, I sat on the couch in the living-room and drank another beer, all the time looking up at the ceramic bowl on the shelf above the computer.

66

PART TWO

[8]

ALTHOUGH THINGS BEGAN to get a little blurry later on, looking back now – from my wicker armchair in the Northview Motor Lodge – I can remember the next day, which was a Thursday, and the two days after it, as just that . . . days – distinct entities of time that had beginnings and endings . . . you got up and then *x* number of hours later you went to bed. I took a dose of MDT-48 on each of these mornings, and my experience of it was pretty much the same as it had been during the first session, which is to say that I came up on it almost immediately, remained in my apartment the whole time and worked productively – *very* productively – until its effects wore off.

On the first day, I fielded a couple of invitations to go out with friends, and actually cancelled something I'd had on for the Friday evening. I finished the introduction – a total of 11,000 words – and planned out the remainder of the book, in particular the approach I was going to take with the captions. Naturally, I couldn't write these until I had a clear idea of which illustrations I'd be using, so I decided to get the laborious process of selecting the illustrations out of the way as well. This took me several hours to do. It should have taken me about four to six weeks, of course, but at the time I thought it best not to dwell on such matters. I gathered the relevant material – cuttings, magazine spreads, album covers, boxes of slides, contact sheets – and arranged it all on the floor in the middle of the room. I started sifting through it and made a sustained series of confident, resolute decisions. Before long I had a provisional list of illustrations and was in a position to start writing the captions.

But when I'd got that done, it suddenly occurred to me – and I didn't envisage it taking more than another day – wouldn't I then have the whole book done? A complete draft, and in only something like two days? OK, but I'd been thinking about it for months, gathering the material, turning it over in my mind. I'd devised a scheme for it – of sorts. I'd done a certain amount of research. I'd thought of the title.

Hadn't I?

Maybe. But there was no getting around the fact that for an endomorphic slug like me – central to whose belief system was the notion that a severe lack of discipline was somehow a thing to be cherished – accomplishing this much in two days was extraordinary.

But why fight it?

On the Friday morning I continued writing the captions and by about lunchtime I could see that I was indeed going to get them finished that day, so I decided to phone Mark Sutton at Kerr & Dexter to tell him what stage I was at. The first thing he wanted to know about was the telecommunications manual I was supposed to be copywriting.

'How's it coming along?'

'It's almost done,' I lied. 'You'll have it on Monday morning.'

Which he would.

'Great. So what's on your mind, Eddie?'

I explained about the status of *Turning On,* and asked him if he wanted me to send it over.

'Well—'

'It's in good shape. Possibly needs a little editing in parts, not much, but—'

'Eddie, the deadline on that's not for another three months.'

'I know, I know, but I was thinking that if there are any other titles in the series up for grabs, maybe I could do . . . another one?'

'Up for grabs? Eddie, they've all been assigned, you know that. Your one, Dean's, Clare Dormer's. What *is* this?'

He was right. A friend of mine, Dean Bennett, was doing *Venus,* a most-beautiful-women-of-the-century thing, and Clare Dormer, a psychiatrist who'd written a few popular magazine articles about celebrity-associated disorders, was doing *Screen Kids*, about the way children were portrayed on classic TV sit-coms. There were three others in the pipeline, as well. *Great Buildings*, I think, was one. I couldn't recall the others.

'I don't know. What about phase two?' I asked him. 'If these things do well—'

'No plans for phase two yet, Eddie.'

'But if these do well?'

I heard a quiet sigh of exasperation at this point. He said, 'I suppose there *could* be a phase two.' There was a pause, and then a polite, 'Any suggestions?'

I hadn't actually thought about it, but I was anxious to have another project on hand, so cradling the receiver on my shoulder I cast an eye over the bookshelves in my living-room and started reeling off some ideas. 'How about, let me see . . .' I was staring at the spine of a large grey volume on a shelf above the stereo now, something Melissa'd given me after a visit to a photography thing at MoMA, and a fight. 'How about one on great *news* photos? You could start with that amazing shot of Halley's Comet. From 1910. Or the Bruno Hauptmann picture – remember . . . at the execution? Or the train crash in Kansas in 1928?' I had a sudden flash of the mangled railway carriages, the dark billowing clouds of smoke and dust. 'Also . . . what else? . . . there's Adolf Hitler sitting with Hindenburg and Hermann Goering at the Tannenberg Monument.' Another flash, this time of a distracted Hermann Goering holding something in his hands, gazing down at it, something that looks curiously like a laptop computer. 'And then you've got . . . stick bombs over Paris. The D-Day landings. The kitchen debate in Moscow, with Khrushchev and Nixon. The napalm kid in Vietnam. The Ayatollah's funeral.' Still staring directly at the book's spine, I could literally *see* these images now, and vividly, one after the other, scrolling down as they would on a microfiche. I shook my head and said, 'There must be thousands of others.' I looked away from the bookshelves and paused. 'Or, I don't know, you could do *anything*, you could do movie posters, advertisements, twentieth-century gadgets like the can opener or the calculator or the camcorder. You could do automobiles.'

As I threw out these suggestions – reaching over to the desk at the same time to steady myself – I also became aware of a second tier of ideas forming in my mind. Up until that point I'd only ever been concerned about my own book. I hadn't thought about the series as a whole, but it struck me now that Kerr & Dexter were really being quite slapdash about it. Their twentieth-century series was probably only a response to a similar project that was being done by a rival publishing house – something they'd gotten wind of and didn't want to be trounced on. But it was as if once they'd decided to do it, they felt that was it – they'd done the work. To survive in the marketplace, to keep up with the conglomerates – as Artie Meltzer, K & D's corporate vice-president, was always saying – the company needed to expand, but off-loading a project like this on to Mark's division was just paying lip-service to the idea. Mark didn't have the resources, but Artie knew he'd take it anyway, because Mark Sutton, who was incapable of ever saying no, took everything. Then Artie could forget about it until the time came to apportion blame after the series had flopped.

What Artie was missing out on here, however, was the fact that the series was actually a good idea. OK, others would be doing similar stuff, but that was always going to be the case. The thing was to do it first, and better. The material – the iconography of the twentieth century – was there, after all, ready-made and waiting to be window-dressed, but as far as I could see Sutton had only managed to put together half a package, at best. His ideas lacked any focus or structure.

'Then you've got, I don't know, great sporting moments. Babe Ruth. Tiger Woods. Fuck, the *space* programme. There's no end to it.'

'Hhmm.'

'And shouldn't all of these books have similar titles?' I went on. 'Something identifiable – mine for instance is *Turning On: From Haight-Ashbury to Silicon Valley*, so Dean's could be, instead of just *Venus*, it could be . . . *Shooting Venus: From . . . Pickford to Paltrow*, or *From Garbo to Spencer*, something along those lines. Clare's, if she confined it to boys, could be . . . *Raising Sons: From*

Beaver to Bart. I don't know. Give it a formula, make it easier to sell.'

There was a silence on the other end of the line, and then, 'What do you want me to say, Eddie? It's Friday afternoon. I've got deadlines *today.*'

I could picture Mark in his office now, lean and geeky, struggling to stay on top of his workload, an un- or half-eaten cheeseburger on his desk, a secretary he was in love with ritually humiliating him every time their eyes met. He had a windowless office on the twelfth floor of the old Port Authority Building on Eighth Avenue, and spent most of his life there – including evenings, weekends and days off. I felt a wave of contempt for him.

'Whatever,' I said. 'Look Mark, I'll talk to you on Monday.'

When I got off the phone I started making some notes on a possible shape for the series and within about two hours had come up with a proposal for ten titles, including a brief outline and a list of key illustrations for each one. But then – what was the next step going to be? I needed to be commissioned to do this. I couldn't just work in a vacuum.

Mark's attitude and lack of interest was still bugging me, so I decided to call up Meltzer and put the idea to him. I knew Mark and Artie didn't get along too well and that Artie would be happy for an opportunity to lean on Mark, but as to whether Artie would actually go for the proposal itself or not was another question.

I got through to him straightaway and started talking. I don't know where it all came from but by the end of the conversation I practically had Meltzer restructuring the whole company, with the twentieth-century series the centrepiece of its new spring list. He wanted to meet me for dinner, but he and his wife had been invited to the Hamptons for the weekend, and he couldn't get out of that – his wife would kill him. He seemed agitated, though, unwilling to hang up, as if he felt this great opportunity was already beginning to slip out of his hands . . .

Next week, I said, we'll meet next week.

I spent the rest of the day copywriting the telecommunications manual for Mark and expanding on the notes for Artie – without seeing any contradiction in this, without giving any thought to the fact that perhaps, just maybe, by my actions, I might have endangered Mark Sutton's job.

In terms of the MDT hit itself, though – on that Thursday and Friday – there was nothing markedly different about it, no particular pleasure thing going on, but there was – as before – what I can only describe as this unrelenting fucking *surge* of having to be busy. There was nothing for me to do in the apartment, because all of that had been done – unless of course I wanted to redecorate the place, change the furniture, paint the walls, tear up the old floorboards, which I didn't – so I had no choice but to channel all of my energy into the copywriting and notes. And you must bear in mind what that kind of work normally involves. It might, for instance, involve watching *Oprah*, or sitting idly on the couch with a magazine, or even being in bed, asleep. Work did get done, eventually, but not in any way that you'd notice if you were only around for a day or two, observing.

I slept five hours on the Thursday night, and quite well too, but on the Friday night it wasn't so easy. I woke at 3.30 a.m., and lay in bed for about an hour before I finally surrendered and got up. I put on a pot of coffee and took a dose of MDT – which meant that by 5 a.m. I was back in full gear, but with nothing concrete to do. Nevertheless, I managed to stay in all day and occupy myself. I pored over the Italian grammar books I'd bought but never studied when I lived in Bologna. I'd picked up enough Italian to get by on, and even enough to get away with doing simple translations, but I'd never studied the language in any formal way. Most Italians I'd known wanted to practise their English, so it had always been easy to skate along with minimal skills. But I now spent a few hours picking through the tense system, as well as other key grammatical stuff – the subjunctive, comparatives, pronouns, reflexives – and the curious thing was, I recognized it all, realized I knew these things, found myself continually going *Yeah, of course,* that's *what that is.*

I did a series of advanced exercises in one of the books and got them all right. I then dug out an old number of a weekly news magazine I had, *Panorama*, and as I scanned the snippets about local politicians and fashion designers and soccer managers, and went through a lengthy article on Viagra, I could feel whole glaciers of passive vocabulary shifting loose and floating up to the forefront of my conscious mind. After that, I took down a copy of Alessandro Manzoni's classic novel *I promessi sposi* that I'd bought with the best of intentions but had never tackled, never even opened. I wouldn't have had a hope of understanding it in any case, much like an elementary student of English trying to read *Bleak House*, but I started into it regardless, and was soon surprised to find myself enjoying its remarkably vivid reconstruction of early seventeenth-century life in Lombardy. In fact, when I put the book down after about 200 pages, I barely noticed at all that I'd been reading in a foreign language. And the reason I stopped wasn't because I'd lost interest, but because I was continually being distracted by the notion that my spoken Italian might now be on a par with *this* – with my new level of reading comprehension.

I paused for a few moments and then took out my address book. I looked up the phone number of an old friend of mine in Bologna and dialled it. I checked the time as I waited. It would be the middle of the afternoon over there.

'*Pronto.*'

'*Ciao Giorgio, sono Eddie, da New York.*'

'*Eddie? Cazzo! Come stai?*'

'*Abbastanza bene. Senti Giorgio, volevo chiederti una cosa . . .*' – and so on. It wasn't until we were about half an hour into the conversation – and had discussed the Mexico situation in some depth, and Giorgio's marriage break-up, and this year's spumante – that Giorgio suddenly realized we were speaking in Italian. We'd nearly always spoken in English, with whatever conversations we might have had in Italian being about pizza toppings or the weather.

He was amazed, and I had to tell him I'd been taking intensive lessons.

When I got off the phone with Giorgio, I continued reading *I promessi sposi* and had it finished by midday. After that I plundered a book on Italian history – a general survey – and got caught up in a trail of references and cross-references about emperors, popes, city states, invasions, cholera, unification, fascism . . . This, in turn, led me to a series of more specific questions about recent history, most of which I couldn't answer because I didn't have the relevant reading material – questions about Mussolini's deal with the Vatican in 1929, CIA involvement in the elections of 1948, the P2 Masonic lodge, the Red Brigades, Aldo Moro's kidnapping and murder in the late 1970s . . . Bettino Craxi in the '80s, Di Pietro and *tangentopoli* in the '90s. I had a visceral sense of the huddled, eventful centuries rapidly succeeding one another, then toppling like pillars, crashing helplessly down towards the present and breaking up into the anxious, fevered decades, years, months. I could feel the webs of conspiracy and deceit – the stories, the murders, the infidelities – spindling back and forth across time, spindling back and forth, virtu-ally, across my skin. I was convinced, too, that with an intense enough concentration of will all of this could be held together in the mind, and understood, perceived as a physical entity with an identifiable chemical structure . . . *seen* almost, and touched, even if only for a fleeting moment . . .

By early on Saturday evening, however, as I sensed the MDT beginning to wear off, it has to be said that my zeal for understanding the complex polymers of history became somewhat muted. So I took another tablet. But by doing this, of course, I changed the dynamic of the whole thing and fragmented any sense of time or structure I had in my life at that point. Taking the drug again without a break also seemed to have the effect of increasing its intensity, with the result that I soon realized I couldn't stay in the apartment any longer and simply had to go out.

I phoned Dean and met him an hour later at Zola's on MacDougal. It took me a while to modulate my voice, to modulate the rate at which I was producing labyrinthine syntax, to modulate *myself*, basi-cally – because apart from the couple of telephone conversations I'd had, this meeting with Dean was my first serious encounter with anyone since I'd started taking the MDT, and my first face-to-face encounter, so I wasn't sure how I was going to feel, or how I'd be coming across.

Over drinks we quickly got on to discussing Mark Sutton and Artie

Meltzer, and I threw out my ideas for the expanded twentieth-century series. But I could see Dean looking at me oddly. I could see his eyebrows furrowing, as doubts about my current state of mental well-being formed in his mind. Dean and I were both freelancers at K & D, having met there a couple of years earlier. We had a healthy disrespect for everything about the company and shared a kind of slacker work ethic, so this talk on my part of editorial proposals and sales projections was unusual to say the least of it. I backed off somewhat, but then found myself expounding paranoid theories about Italian politics to him, and with a little more passion and detail than he would have been used to receiving from me on any subject. The other thing I saw him catching me out on – but which I think prevented him from accusing me of being coked up to my eyeballs – was the fact that I wasn't smoking. I then decided to add to his confusion by taking a cigarette from him, but just one.

After a while, a few friends of Dean's arrived and we all had dinner together. There was a middle-aged couple I'd met once before, called Paul and Ruby Baxter, who were both architects, and a young Canadian actress called Susan. Over dinner, we discussed lots of subjects, and it quickly became apparent to everyone present, myself included, that elaborate, scarily articulate views on just about everything were going to be emanating from my end of the table. I got into a protracted argument with Paul about the relative merits of Bruckner and Mahler. I gave them my '60s spiel, including a brief aside on Raymond Loewy and streamlining. I followed this with further ruminations on Italian history and the nature of time, which in turn developed into a lengthy expostulation on the inadequacies of Western political theory in the face of rapid global change. Once or twice – and it was as though from outside my body, as though from *above* – I became acutely aware of myself sitting at the table, talking, and for those fleeting moments, as I went on hacking a path through the knotty thickets of syntax and Latinate vocabulary, I had no real sense of what I was saying, no real idea if I was being coherent. Nevertheless, it all seemed to go down quite well – whatever it was – and despite being a bit worried that I was coming on too strong, I detected in Paul the same thing I'd detected earlier in Artie Meltzer, a kind of agitated need to keep talking to me, as though I were buoying him up somehow, empowering him, supplying him with regenerative energy waves. Neither was it my imagination, a bit later, when Susan started flirting with me, casually brushing her arm against mine, holding my gaze. I was able to side-track her by returning to the Bruckner-Mahler debate with Paul – though don't ask me why, because I was certainly getting bored with that subject, and she was strikingly beautiful.

After dinner, in any case, we went to a string of nightclubs – first to the Duma, then to Virgil's, then to the Moon and later to Hexagon. I don't remember exactly when, but I took another dose of MDT in a bathroom somewhere. What I do remember is that harsh, neon-bright *toilety* atmosphere, people reflected in mirrors all around me, some locked into teeth-grinding, out-of-focus conversations, others slumped up against white tiles, staring at themselves – drunk, wired, bewildered – as though they'd accidentally fallen out of their own lives.

I remember feeling electric.

An increasingly bewildered Dean went home some time after two, as did Susan. Other friends of Paul and Ruby's arrived, followed a while later by friends of *theirs*. Then Paul and Ruby dropped out. Another hour or two passed and I found myself in a huge apartment on the Upper West Side with a bunch of people I'd never met before. They were all sitting around a glass table doing lines of coke – but still, I was the one out-talking them. Standing up and walking around at a certain point, I caught sight of myself in a large ornate mirror that was hanging above a fake marble fireplace, and realized that I was the centre of attention, and that whatever I was talking about – and God knows it could have been anything – everyone in the room, without exception, was listening to me. At around five o'clock in the morning, or five-thirty, or six – I don't remember – I went with a couple of guys to a diner on Amsterdam for breakfast. One of them, Kevin Doyle, was an investment banker with Van Loon & Associates and seemed to be saying that he could throw some information my way, good information, and that he could help me set up a portfolio. He kept insisting that we meet during the week, in his office, for lunch, even for coffee, any day that suited.

The other guy just sat there the whole time staring at me.

Eventually – because sooner or later everyone had to go to bed – I found myself alone again. I spent the day criss-crossing the city, mostly on foot, looking at stuff I'd never really paid that much attention to before, like those mammoth apartment buildings on Central Park West, with their roof-towers and Gothic cornices. I wandered down to Times Square, over to Gramercy Park and Murray Hill. I went back in the direction of Chelsea and then down to the Financial District and Battery Park. I did the Staten Island Ferry, standing out on the deck to let the fresh, invigorating wind cut right through me. I caught a subway back uptown, and went to museums and galleries, places I hadn't been to in years. I went to a recital of chamber music at Lincoln Center, ate brunch at Julian's, read the *New York Times* in Central Park and caught two Preston Sturges movies in a revival theatre in the West Village.

Later on, I hooked up with a few people back in Zola's and got home to bed, finally, some time in the early hours of Monday morning.

[9]

AFTER THAT, THE FOLLOWING three or four weeks fused into one another, into one long stretch of . . . *elasto*-time. I was permanently . . . what? Up? High? Stoned? Out of it? Tripping? Buzzed? Wired? Chillin'? None of these terms is appropriate, or adequate, to describe the experience of being on MDT. But – regardless of what term you use – I was a certified MDT *user* now, taking one, sometimes two, doses of the stuff a day, and just about managing to snatch the odd hour of sleep here and there. I had a sense that I – or, rather, my life – was expanding exponentially and that before long the various spaces I occupied, physical and otherwise, were not going to be sufficient to contain me, and would consequently be put under a great deal of strain, maybe even to breaking point.

I lost weight. I also lost track, so I don't know over what period of time I lost the weight exactly, but it must have been about eight or ten days. My face thinned out a little, and I felt lighter, and trimmer. It's not that I wasn't eating, I was – but I was eating mostly salads and fruit. I cut out cheese and bread and meat and potato-chips and chocolate. I didn't drink any beer or sodas, but I did drink lots of water.

I was active.

I got my hair cut.

And bought new clothes. Because it was as much as I could bear to go on living in my apartment on Tenth Street, with its musty smells and creaky floorboards, but I certainly didn't have to put up with a wardrobe that made me feel like an extension of the apartment. So I took out two thousand dollars from the envelope in the closet and wandered over to SoHo. I checked out a few stores, and then took a cab up to Fifth Avenue in the Fifties. In the space of about an hour, I bought a charcoal wool suit, a plain cotton shirt and an Armani silk tie. Then I got a pair of tan leather shoes at A. Testoni. I also got some casual stuff at Barney's. It was more money than I'd ever spent on clothes in my entire life, but it was worth it, because having new, expensive things to wear made me feel relaxed and confident – and also, it has to be said, like someone else. In fact, to get the measure of myself in the new suit – the way you might test-drive a car – I took to the streets a couple of times, and walked up and down Madison Avenue, or around the financial district, weaving briskly in and out through the crowds. On these occasions, I would often catch glimpses of myself reflected in office windows, in dark slabs of corporate glass, catch glimpses of this trim-looking guy who seemed to know precisely where he was going and, moreover, precisely what he would be doing when he got there.

I spent money on other things, as well, sometimes going into expensive shops and seeking out pretty, elegantly dressed sales assistants, and buying things, randomly – a Mont Blanc fountain pen, a Pulsar watch – just to have that infantile and vaguely narcotic-erotic sensation of being wrapped in a veil of perfume and personal attention – *Would sir like to try* this *one?* With men I would be more aggressive, getting into detailed questions and information-swapping, such as the time I bought a boxed-set of Beethoven's nine symphonies recorded live on original instruments, and locked the assistant into a debate about the contemporary relevance of eighteenth-century performing practice. My behaviour with waiters and barmen, too, was uncharacteristic. When I went out to places like Soleil and La Pigna and Ruggles – which I'd started doing fairly regularly now – I was an *awkward* customer . . . there's no other word for it. I'd spend an unconscionable amount of time poring over the wine list, for example, or I'd order stuff that wasn't on the menu, or I'd invent some complicated new cocktail, on the spot, and expect the barman to mix it for me.

Later, I'd go to sets at Sweet Basil and the Village Vanguard and

81

start chatting with people at adjoining tables, and while my extensive knowledge of jazz usually ensured that I came out ahead in any conversation, it would also sometimes get people's backs up. It's not that I was being obnoxious, exactly, I wasn't, but I engaged with everyone, and in a very focused way, on whatever level, about whatever subject, squeezing each encounter for its last possible drop of what might be on offer – intrigue, conflict, tedium, trivia, gossip . . . it didn't matter. Most people I came across weren't used to this, and some even found it quite unnerving.

Increasingly, too, I was aware of the effect I was having on certain women I met – or sometimes not even *met* but just saw . . . across a few tables, or a crowded room. There appeared to be this curious, wide-eyed attraction that I couldn't really account for, but which led to some intimate, revealing conversations, and occasionally, too – because I was unsure of the parameters here – some fairly fraught ones. Then one time, during a Dale Noonan gig at Sweet Basil, this pale, thirtyish redhead I'd noticed came over between numbers and sat at my table. She smiled, but didn't say anything. I smiled back and didn't say anything either. I summoned a waiter and was about to ask her what she'd like to drink when she shook her head slightly and said, '*Non.*'

I paused, and then asked the waiter for the check. As we were leaving, with the frenetic Dale Noonan just starting up again, I saw her glancing back at the table she'd originally been sitting at. I glanced back as well. Another woman and a man were at the table, looking towards us, perhaps gesturing uncertainly, and in this fleeting tableau of body language I thought I detected a rising sense of alarm, maybe even of panic. But as soon as we got outside, the red-haired woman took me by the arm, almost pushing me along the street, and said, 'Oh my God' – in a very strong French accent – 'that screaming brass shit, I couldn't stand it any longer.' Then she laughed and squeezed my arm, drawing me towards her, as though we'd known each other for years.

Her name was Chantal and she was here on vacation, from Paris, with her sister and brother-in-law. I tried to speak to her in French, not very successfully, which seemed to charm her no end, and after about twenty minutes I felt as though I *had* known her for years. As we walked along Fifth Avenue towards the Flatiron Building, I gave her the 23 Skidoo spiel, tales of cops shooing away young men who used to gather on Twenty-third Street to see passing women's skirts billowing up in the gusts of wind. These gusts were caused by the narrow angle at the building's northern end, an explanation which then degenerated into a lecture on wind-bracing and early skyscraper construction, just what you'd imagine a girl in such circumstances would want, but I somehow managed – apparently – to make talk of K-trusses and wall-girders interesting, funny, compelling even. At Twenty-third Street she stood in front of the Flatiron Building herself, waiting for something to happen, but there was barely a breeze that evening and about the only thing detectable in the folds of her long navy skirt was a gentle rippling movement. She seemed disappointed and looked as if she was about to stamp her foot.

I took her by the hand and we walked on.

When we got as far as Twenty-ninth Street, on Fifth Avenue, we turned right. A moment later she told me that we'd arrived at her hotel. She said that she and her sister had been shopping all day, and that that would explain the bags and boxes and tissue paper and new shoes and belts and accessories strewn about the place. When I looked slightly puzzled, she sighed and said I wasn't to mind the mess up in her room.

The next morning we had breakfast in a local diner, and after that we spent a few hours at the Met. Since Chantal had another week left in New York, we agreed to meet again, and again – and, inevitably, again. We spent one entire twenty-four hour period together locked in her hotel room, during which time, among other things, I took French lessons. I think she was amazed at how much of the language I managed to learn, and how quickly, because by the time of our last encounter, in a Moroccan restaurant in Tribeca, we were speaking almost exclusively in French.

Chantal told me that she loved me and was prepared to give up everything in order to come and live with me in Manhattan. She'd give up her flat in Bastille, her job with a foreign aid agency, her whole Parisian *life*. I really enjoyed being with Chantal, and hated the thought of her leaving, but I had to talk her out of this. Never having had it so easy in a relationship, I didn't want to push my luck. But I also didn't see how our relationship could plausibly be sustained in the wider context of my burgeoning MDT habit. In any case, the way we'd met had been fairly unreal – an unreality which had been further compounded by the personal details I'd given her about myself. I'd told her that I was an investment analyst devising a new market forecasting strategy based on complexity theory. I'd also told her that the reason I hadn't taken her to see my apartment on Riverside Drive was because I was married – unhappily, of course. The parting scene was difficult, but it was nevertheless nice to be told – through tears, *and in French* – that I would live for ever in her heart.

There were a couple of other encounters, too. One morning I went to my friend Dean's place on Sullivan Street to pick up a book, and as I was leaving the building I got talking to a young woman who lived on the second floor. According to the bullet-point profile of his neighbours Dean had once reeled off, she was a single-white-female computer-programmer, twenty-six, non-smoker, interested in nineteenth-century American art. We'd passed each other on the stairs a few times before, but in the way of things in New York City apartment buildings, what with alienation and paranoia, not to mention endemic rudeness, we'd completely ignored each other. This time I smiled at her and said, 'Hi. Great day.' She looked startled, studied me for a nanosecond or two, and then replied, 'If you're Bill Gates. Or Naomi Campbell.'

'Well, maybe,' I said, pausing to lean back against the wall, casually, 'but hey, if things are that bad, can I buy you a drink?'

She looked at her watch and said, 'A *drink*? It's ten-thirty in the morning – what are you, the crown prince of Toyland?'

I laughed. 'I might be.'

She was holding an A & P shopping bag in her left hand and

under her right arm she had a large hardcover volume, lodged tightly so it wouldn't slip. I nodded at the book.

'What are you reading?'

She released a long sigh, as if to say, *Fellah, I'm busy, OK . . . maybe some other time*. The sigh then tapered off and she said, wearily, 'Thomas Cole. The works of Thomas Cole.'

'*View from Mount Holyoke*,' I said automatically. '*Northampton, Massachusetts, after a Thunderstorm – The Oxbow*.' It was as much as I could do to resist continuing with, 'Eighteen thirty-six. Oil on Canvas, fifty-one-and-a-half inches by seventy-six inches.'

She furrowed her eyebrows and looked at me for a moment. Then she lowered the shopping bag and put it down at her feet. She eased the large book out from under her arm, held it awkwardly and started flicking through it.

'Yeah,' she said, almost to herself. '*The Oxbow* – that's the one. I'm doing this . . .' She continued flicking distractedly through the book. 'I'm doing this paper for a course I'm taking on Cole and . . . yeah,' she looked up at me, '*The Oxbow*.'

She found the page and half held it out, but for us both to look at the painting properly we had to move a little closer together. She was quite short, had dark silky hair and was wearing a green headscarf inset with little amber beads.

'Remember,' I said, 'the oxbow is a yoke – a symbol of control over raw nature. Cole didn't believe in progress, not if progress meant clearing forests and building railroads. Every hill and valley, he once wrote – and in a fairly ill-advised foray into poetry I might add – every hill and valley is become an altar unto Mammon.'

'Hhm.' She paused to consider this. Then she seemed to be considering something else. 'You know about this stuff?'

I'd been to the Met with Chantal a week earlier and had absorbed a good deal of information from catalogues and wall-mounted copyblocks and I'd also recently read *American Visions* by Robert Hughes, as well as heaps of Thoreau and Emerson, so I felt comfortable enough saying, 'Yeah, sure. I wouldn't be an expert or anything, but yeah.' I leant forward slightly, and around, and studied her face, her eyes. She met my gaze. I said, 'Do you want me to help you with this . . . paper?'

'Would you?' she said in small voice. 'Can you . . . I mean, if you're not busy?'

'I'm the crown prince of Toyland, remember, so it's not like I have a job to go to.'

She smiled for the first time.

We went into her apartment and in about two hours did a rough draft of the paper. About four hours after that again I finally staggered out of the building.

Another time I was in the offices of Kerr & Dexter, dropping off some copy, when I bumped into Clare Dormer. Although I'd only met Clare once or twice before, I greeted her very warmly. She'd just been in with Mark Sutton discussing some contractual matter, so I decided to tell her my idea about confining her book to boys, starting with *Leave it to Beaver* and taking it as far as *The Simpsons* and then calling it *Raising Sons: From Beaver to Bart*. She laughed generously at this and slapped the back of her hand against my jacket lapel.

Then she paused, as though something she hadn't realized before was suddenly dawning on her.

Twenty minutes later we were down in a quiet stairwell together on the twelfth floor, sharing a cigarette.

I kept reminding myself in these situations that I was playing a role, that the whole thing was an act, but just as often it would occur to me that maybe I wasn't playing a role at all, and that maybe it *wasn't* an act. When I was in the throes of an MDT-induced episode, it was as if my new self could barely make out my old self, could just about see it through a haze, through a smoky window of thick glass. It was like trying to speak a language you once knew but have now largely forgotten, and much as I might have wanted to, I couldn't simply revert or switch back – at least not without an enormous concentration of will. Often, in fact, it was more comfortable not even to bother – why *would* I bother? – but one result of this was that I had a slightly less easy time of it with people I knew well, or rather with people who knew *me* well. Meeting and impressing a total stranger, assuming a new identity, even a new name, was exciting and uncomplicated, but when I met up with someone like Dean, for instance, I always got these *looks* – these quizzical, probing *looks*. I could see, too, that he was struggling with it, wanted to challenge me, call me a poseur, a clown, an arrogant fuck, while simultaneously wanting to prolong our time together and spin it out for all it was worth.

I also spoke to my father a couple of times during this period, and that was worse. He was retired and lived on Long Island. He phoned occasionally to see how I was, and we'd chat for a few minutes, but now all of a sudden I was getting caught up in the kind of conversations with him that he'd always craved to have with his son – and the kind that his son had always ungraciously denied him – idle banter about business and the markets. We talked about the tech stocks bubble and when it was going to burst. We talked about the Waldrop CLX merger that had been in all the papers that morning. How would the merger affect share prices? Who would the new CEO be? At first, I could detect a note of suspicion in the old man's voice, as though he thought I was making fun of him, but gradually he settled into it, seeming to accept that this, finally – after all the arid years of bleeding-heart, tree-hugging *crap* from his boy – was the way things were meant to be. And if it wasn't quite that, it wasn't a million miles off it either. I did get involved, and perhaps for the first time ever I spoke to him just as I would speak to any other man. But I was careful at the same time not to go overboard, because it wasn't like messing with Dean's head. This was my father on the other end of the line, my *father* – getting animated, working things out, permitting long dormant hopes to sprout in his mind, and almost audibly . . . *pop!* – would Eddie get a proper job now? – *pop!* – make some real money? – *pop!* – produce a grandchild?

I'd get off the phone after one of these sessions with him and feel exhausted, as if I somehow *had* produced a grandchild, unaided, spawned some distant, accelerated version of myself right there on the living-room floor. Then, like in a nature documentary time-lapse sequence, the *old* me – twisted, cracked, biodegradable – would shrivel up suddenly and disintegrate, making the struggle to recover any meaningful sense of who I really was even more difficult.

* * *

But moments of anxiety like this were fairly rare, and my abiding impression of the period is of how right it felt to be so busy all the time. I wasn't idle for a second. I read new biographies of Stalin, Henry James and Irving Thalberg. I learnt Japanese from a series of books and cassette tapes. I played chess online, and did endless cryptic puzzles. I phoned in to a local radio station one day to take part in a quiz, and won a year's supply of hair products. I spent hours on the Internet and learned how to do various things – without, of course, actually having to *do* any of them. I learned how to arrange flowers, for example, cook risotto, keep bees, dismantle a car engine.

One thing I did want to do for real, though, and had always wanted to do was learn how to read music. I found a website that explained the whole process in detail, rapidly deconstructing for me the mysteries of treble and bass clefs, chords, signatures and so on. I went out and bought a stack of sheet music, basic stuff, a few well-known songs, as well as more challenging stuff, a couple of concertos and a symphony (Mahler's Second). Within a matter of hours I'd worked my way through everything except the Mahler, which I then approached with caution, not to say reverence. Being so complex, it took me a good deal longer, but I eventually managed to find my way through its magnificent swirl of aching melodies and horror-show fanfares, its soaring strings and stirring chorales. At about two o'clock in the morning, in the eerie silence of my living-room, as I reached the mighty E-flat climax – *Was du geschlagen, Zu Gott wird es dich tragen!* – I felt one of those goosebump shivers rippling through my entire body, and tears welled up in my eyes.

The next step from this was to see if I could *play* music, so I headed off to Canal Street and bought myself a relatively inexpensive electric keyboard and then set it up beside the computer. I followed an online course and started practising scales and elementary exercises, but this wasn't at all easy and I very nearly gave up. After a few days, however, something seemed to click and I started being able to pick out a few decent tunes. Within a week, I was playing Duke Ellington and Bill Evans numbers, and soon after that I was actually doing my own improvisations.

For a while, I envisaged club dates, European tours, rain showers of record-executive business cards, but it didn't take me long to realize something crucial: I was good, but I wasn't *that* good. I could play 'Stardust' and 'It Never Entered My Mind', passably, and would probably be able to play both books of 'The Well-Tempered Clavier' if I worked at it non-stop for the next 500 hours – but the question was, did I really *want* to spend the next five hundred hours practising the piano?

For that matter, I suppose, just what *did* I want to do?

It was around this time, therefore, that I started feeling restless. I came to realize that if I was going to go on taking MDT, I would need some kind of focus and structure in my life, and that flitting from one interest to another wasn't going to be enough. I needed a plan, a credible course of action – I needed to be working.

I also had a more immediate question to deal with. What was I going to do with the 450 or so tablets? Some of them could be sold at $500 a piece, so the obvious thing I considered doing was, well . . . *dealing* them – and dealing them myself. But how, exactly, was I going to do this? Hang out on the street corner? Hawk them around nightclubs? Try and shift them in bulk to some scary guy with a gun in a hotel room? There were too many complications, and too many variables. Besides, it didn't take me long to see that even if I did get full price for even half of the tablets, $120,000 at the end of the day was nothing compared to the potential gains there could be from just ingesting them, and using them creatively, judiciously. I had more or less finished *Turning On*, for instance, and could easily knock off others in a series like that.

So what else could I do?

I sketched out possible projects. One idea was to withdraw *Turning On* from Kerr & Dexter and develop it into a full-length study – expand the text and cut back on the illustrations. Another idea was to do a screenplay based on the life of Aldous Huxley, focusing on his days in LA. I considered doing a book on the economic and social history of some commodity, cigars maybe, or opium, or saffron, or chocolate, or silk, something that could be tied in, later on, to a lavishly produced TV documentary series. I thought about putting out a magazine, or starting a translation agency, or setting up a film production company, or devising a new Internet-based service . . . or – I don't know – inventing and patenting an electronic gadget that would become indispensable, achieve world-wide brand-recognition in six months to a year and establish my place in the great twentieth-century pantheon of eponyms – Kodak, Ford, Hoover, Bayer . . . Spinola.

But the drawback with all of these ideas was that they were either too unoriginal or too quixotic. They'd each take a lot of time and capital to set up, and there was no guarantee in the end – regardless of how fucking smart I was – that any of them would work, or have enough appeal to be marketable. So the next thing I considered was the possibility of going back to school to do a post-graduate course. With a prudent use of MDT I could accumulate credits fairly quickly and shortcut my way to a belated career in . . . something, but the problem was – in *what*? Law? Architecture? Dentistry? Some branch of science? Even listing these options was enough to take me back twenty years and start my head spinning. And did I really want to get into all of that shit again – exams, term papers, dealing with professors? The mere thought of it was enough to make me throw up.

So what, then – I asked myself – was I left with?

Well, what do you think? Making money.

Making money . . . *how*?

By making telephone calls.

Hhn?

The stock market, stupid.

90

[10]

It seemed like the obvious thing. I'd been reading the financial sections every day in the newspapers, having those chats with the old man, even spinning elaborate stories to strange women about being an investment analyst, so the next step was surely to get involved for real, and in some practical way – by day-trading on my PC at home maybe, in options, futures, derivatives, whatever. It would be better than any job I could find, and of course playing the markets had the added attraction of being the new rock-and-roll. The only problem was that I didn't have a clear enough understanding of what options, futures and derivatives actually were – not enough, in any case, to start trading in them. I could bluff my way through a conversation, sure, but that wasn't going to be much use when it came to putting some real money on the table.

What I needed was an hour or two with someone who could explain in detail how the markets worked and then show me the mechanics of day-trading. I thought of Kevin Doyle, that guy I'd had breakfast with a couple of Sundays back, the one who worked for Van Loon & Associates, but as I remembered he was fairly intense and the kind of Wall Street suit who'd probably scoff at the notion of day-trading on a PC. So I phoned around some business journalists I knew and put it out that I was doing a section for a new K & D book on the whole day-trading phenomenon. I got a call back from one of them saying he could set up an interview for me with a friend of his who'd been day-trading online for the past year and would be more than willing to talk about it. The arrangement was that I'd go to this person's apartment, chat, take notes and watch him in action.

The guy's name was Bob Holland and he lived on East Thirty-third and Second. He greeted me in boxer shorts, led me down a hallway into his living-room and asked if I wanted a hit of espresso. The room was dominated by a long, mahogany table that had three computer terminals on it and a Gaggia espresso machine. There was an exercise bike between the far end of the table and the wall. Bob Holland was about forty-five, lean and wiry, and had thinning grey hair. He stood in front of one of the terminals, staring at the screen.

'This is the lair of the beast, Eddie, so you'll have to, er . . .' He pulled distractedly at his boxers with one hand, simultaneously keying something in to the computer with the other, '. . . you'll have to excuse the dress-code.' Still distracted, he pointed to the Gaggia and half whispered the word *espresso*.

I busied myself with the coffee machine and looked around as I waited for him to speak again. Apart from the table and the immediate space around it, the room had a neglected feel. It was dark and musty and looked like it hadn't been vacuumed in a while. The furniture and décor, as well, were more than a little fussy – too fussy, I thought, for this Spartan and focused warrior of the Nasdaq.

I figured that he'd probably been divorced in the last three to six months.

Suddenly, after a long bout of intense concentration and intermittent key-stroking – during which I sipped my espresso – Holland started speaking. 'Many people believe that when you buy a share of stock you are buying a proportional share in a business.' He spoke slowly, as though delivering a lecture, but continued to stare at the screen. 'Consequently, to figure out how much any proportional share is worth, you have to determine how much the business is worth. It's known as "fundamental" analysis, and it's where you look at the company's basic financial health – growth potential, projected earnings, cash flow, that kind of thing.' He paused, stroked a few more keys and then went on. 'Others look at the numbers only, with almost no regard for the underlying business or its current valuation. These are quantitative analysts, or "quants". Number crunchers. They consider judgements about things like management expertise and market potential to be too subjective. They buy and sell on a purely quantitative basis, using sophisticated algorithms to find minute price discrepancies in the markets.' He glanced at me briefly. 'Yeah?'

I nodded.

'Then you've got technical analysis. That's where you study price-and-volume patterns and basically try to understand the psychology surrounding a stock.'

He continued looking at the screen as he spoke, and I continued nodding.

'But trading is not an exact science, Eddie. I mean, the stock market can't be pinned down to any one system, which is why you get fuzzy talk of "irrational exuberance", and people trying to explain market behaviour in terms of psychiatry, biology, and even *brain* chemistry. I'm not kidding you – there were actually suggestions recently that investor caution was being inhibited by the high percentage of brokers and dealers on Prozac. So,' he shrugged his shoulders, 'given that no one knows anything, it's not surprising that most investors use a combination of the three basic approaches I've outlined to you.'

Over the next hour or so, still standing at the table – and looking like he'd just stepped in from a vigorous game of tennis – Bob Holland expanded on these ideas and also went into the minutiae of options, futures, derivatives, as well as bonds, hedge funds, global markets and so on. I took a few notes, but when I heard the explanations I realized that in a general way I *did* understand these terms, and that furthermore, just by thinking about this stuff, a large store of knowledge was being unlocked in my brain, knowledge that I had probably accumulated unconsciously over the years.

When he'd done with the big picture – how the investment banks and fund managers operated – he started in on day-trading.

'Then you've got guys like me,' he said, 'the new pariahs of Wall Street. Ten years ago it was the LBO types, the Gordon Gekkos. Now it's the geeks in baseball caps who sit in front of computers at home and trade thirty or forty times a day, picking off eighths, sixteenths, even thirty-seconds of a point per share, and then closing out their positions before the end of trading.' He looked away from the screen and directly at me, for maybe the second or third time since I'd arrived. 'We're accused of distorting the markets and causing volatility in share prices, but that's bullshit. It's what they said in the Eighties about the takeover guys. We're just the new wave, Eddie – electronic day-trading is the spawn of technology and regulatory change. It's that simple, it's flux, it's the nature of things.' He shrugged his shoulders again and turned back to the screen.

'I mean, come here – look at this.'

I stepped over quickly and stood behind him. On the middle screen, the one he was working at, I could see tightly packed columns of figures and fractions and percentages. He pointed to something on the screen – ATRX, a stock symbol for a biotech company – and said, 'This one opened at around sixty dollars a share and has just pulled back a little so its bid is now $59^{3}/_{8}$ . . . and its offer . . .' he pointed to another part of the screen, 'is $59^{3}/_{4}$ – that's a $^{3}/_{8}$ spread. Now the thing is, thanks to the latest software, and to regulatory changes introduced by the Securities & Exchange Commission, I can trade *within* that spread, and right here in my living-room.'

He highlighted the row of figures after the ATRX symbol and stared at it for a while. He checked something on one of the other screens, came back to the first one and keyed something in. He waited for a couple of moments and keyed something else in. He waited again – one hand held up in mid-air – and then said, quietly, '*Yes.*'

He turned around to me and explained what he'd done. Using that new trading programme, he'd discovered that there were three market-makers on ATRX's bid and two on the offer. Reckoning that ATRX would rebound, he took advantage of the wide spread by bidding $59^{7}/_{16}$ for 2,000 shares, which was $^{1}/_{16}$ over the best market-maker bid. Having topped this bid, Holland then got first in line to execute an order. The first 2,000 shares for sale at market went to him at $59^{7}/_{16}$. Very soon after this he offered to sell for $59^{11}/_{16}$, which was still lower than the ask price posted by the big market-makers. Holland had guessed right, and the stock was taken off his hands almost immediately. In just fifteen seconds and a few strokes of the keyboard he had netted over $500 and cut the spread by $^{1}/_{8}$ of a point.

I asked him how many trades like this he made every day.

Holland smiled for the first time. He said he made about thirty trades each day, mostly in lots of 1,000 or 2,000 shares, and rarely held a stock for more than ten minutes.

He smiled again and said, 'OK, they're not *all* like that one, but a lot of them are.' He paused. 'It's about identifying ripples in the charts and then reacting quickly.'

'You mean, it's not just about who has the most information?'

'Shit no. With all the indicators that are available these days, you just end up with conflicting signals. *Shit* no.'

Now that I had his attention, I bombarded him with more questions. How much preparation did he do for each trading day? How many positions did he keep open at any one time? What kind of commissions did he pay?

As Holland answered each of my questions, he gradually pulled himself away from the computer screens on the table. Then he started making himself an espresso, but by the time it was ready and he was drinking it, he seemed to have become sufficiently detached from his work to notice again that he was wearing nothing but boxer shorts, and to be self-conscious about it. He knocked back the remainder of the espresso, excused himself and wandered off down the hall into what I assumed was a bedroom.

In his absence, I went over to look at the computer screens again. It was amazing . . . he had made $500 – the price of one hit of MDT – in just fifteen seconds! I definitely wanted to learn how to do this, because if Bob Holland could execute thirty orders in a day, I was sure that I could manage a hundred, or more. When he came back, wearing jeans and a T-shirt, I asked him how I should go about learning. He told me that the best way to get into day-trading was to just do it – *trade*, and that most of the online brokers facilitated this by giving free access to simulated trading games and by conducting live tutorials.

'Simulation games', he said, in a tone that was becoming increasingly stilted, 'are an excellent way of developing your skills, Eddie, and of gaining confidence in placing trades but without actually having to take any risks.'

I got him to recommend some online brokers and software trading packages, and as I wrote this stuff down I kept firing questions at him. Holland answered everything I asked him, and comprehensively, but I could see that he was becoming slightly alarmed, as if the rate and nature of my questions was perhaps more than he'd bargained for – as if he felt that by answering them, by passing on this information, he might be unleashing some kind of Frankenstein monster into cyberspace, some desperate, hungry individual capable of who-knew-what financial atrocities.

It had taken a while, but Holland was completely focused on me now. In fact, he appeared more concerned with each new question and started introducing a cautionary note into his answers.

'So look, start *small*, start by trading hundred-share lots for the first month or so, or at least until you find your feet . . .'

'Hhm.'

'. . . and don't get too excited if you have a good day – one good day's trading doesn't mean you're Warren Buffet. The next trade you make could just as easily blow your account out . . .'

'Hhm.'

'. . . and when you enter a trade, make sure you have an idea of how you expect it to behave, because if it acts counter to that – get out!'

My impulse was to go *Yeah, yeah, yeah* to all of this, and Holland could see that. But the reason he wasn't getting through to me was because the more he warned me about the potential dangers of daytrading, the more excited I could feel myself becoming at the prospect of actually getting home and doing it.

As I was slipping my notebook into my jacket pocket, and then putting the jacket on to go, Holland upped the pace a little.

'Trading can get pretty intense, you know.' He paused, and then said all at a rush, 'Don't ever borrow money from family or friends, Eddie – I mean to trade, or to get yourself out of a trading crisis.' I looked at him, slightly alarmed myself now. 'And don't start *lying* to hide your losses either.'

There was a hint of desperation in his voice. I got the impression that he wasn't so much talking *to* me as *about* himself. I also got the impression that he didn't want me to leave.

I did, however, and badly – but I hesitated. I stood in the middle of the room and listened as he told me how he'd left his job as a marketing director to start day-trading and how within six months his wife had left *him*. He told me that he got restless and irritable whenever he couldn't trade – like on Sundays, for example, or in the middle of the night – and that trading had effectively become his entire life. He went on to say that he was incapable of accumulating cash in his account and often didn't even bother to open his brokerage statements.

'Because you don't want to face up to the extent of your losses?' I said.

He nodded.

Then he went deeper into confessional mode and started talking about his addictive personality and how if it hadn't been one thing in his life it had been another . . .

During all of this, the only thing I could think of was how sublime, how like a brief but intricate jazz solo that little fifteen-second passage of electronic commerce had been. Pretty soon, I couldn't even make out what Holland was saying any more, not clearly, because I was gone, lost in a sudden, intoxicating reverie of possibilities. Holland, I realized, had been stumbling around in the dark, shaving off the occasional sixteenth of a point here or there, quite obviously getting it wrong more often than he was getting it right. But this wasn't going to be the case with me. *I* would know what to do instinctively. *I* would know what stocks to buy, and when to buy them, and why.

I would be good at this.

When I eventually got away and returned to Tenth Street, my head was still reeling. But then, when I opened the door of the apartment and stepped into the living-room, I immediately felt oppressed, felt outsized – like Alice, like I'd soon be curling an arm round my head and sticking an elbow out of the window, just to *fit* in the place. I began to feel somewhat aggrieved, too, as though impatient that I hadn't already made lots of money from day-trading – aggrieved and in desperate visceral *need* of things . . . another new suit, a couple of new suits, and shoes, several pairs of them, as well as new shirts and ties, and maybe other new stuff, a better hi-fi system, a DVD player, a laptop, proper air-conditioning, and just more rooms, more corridor space, higher ceilings. I had the nagging sense that unless I was moving forward, moving up, unless I was transmuting, transmogrifying, morphing into something else, I was probably going to, I don't know, *explode . . .*

I put on the scherzo from Bruckner's Ninth and marched around the apartment, like a one-man panzer division, muttering to myself, weighing up the options. How was I to move forward? How was I to get started? But I soon realized that I didn't have too many options, because the money in the closet had dwindled to a few thousand dollars, which was about as much as there was in my bank account – and since, let's face it, a few thousand dollars plus a few thousand dollars is still, for all intents and purposes, a few thousand dollars, all I had in the world, then, apart from a credit card, was a few thousand dollars.

Taking what was left in the closet in any case, I went out shopping again. This time I headed for Forty-seventh Street and bought two fourteen-inch TV sets, a laptop computer and three software packages – two for investment-analysis and one for online trading. Disregarding Bob Holland's idea that too much information led to conflicting signals, I bought the *Wall Street Journal*, the *Financial Times*, the *New York Times*, the *Los Angeles Times*, the *Washington Post* and the latest issues of *The Economist, Barrons, Newsweek, The Nation, Harper's, Atlantic Monthly, Fortune, Forbes, Wired, Variety* and about ten other weekly and monthly titles. I also got a handful of foreign-language newspapers, ones I'd at least be able to take some kind of a stab at – *Il Sole 24 Ore* and *Corriera della Sera*, obviously – but also *Le Figaro, El Pais* and *Frankfurter Allgemeine Zeitung.*

Back in my apartment, I phoned a friend who was an electrical engineer and had him instruct me over the phone about how to splice the wires from the two new TV sets into my existing cable connection. He was very uncomfortable about it and wanted to come round and do it himself, but I insisted that he just *explain* it to me, goddammit – explain it to me over the phone and let me take notes. It was an entirely different matter, OK, from what I might have ventured to do under normal circumstances – change a plug, say, or replace a fuse – but I nevertheless managed to carry out his instructions, rapidly, and to the letter, and as a result I soon had the three TV sets operating side-by-side in the living-room. After that, I hooked up the new laptop to the computer on my desk, installed the software and went online. I did some research into Internet stockbrokers, and used my credit card and a bank transfer to open an account with one of the smaller companies. I then took the newspapers and magazines I'd bought and carefully spread them out around the apartment. I put reading material, open at relevant pages, on to every available surface – desk, table, chairs, shelves, couch, floor.

The next few hours flitted by in what felt like a couple of seconds. I spent them hovering anxiously in front of the five screens, absorbing information – and at a rate that made my previous efforts seem positively glacial. The three TV sets were beaming out different news and financial-service transmissions – CNN, CNNfn and CNBC – different tributaries into the one great global flood of information, analysis and opinion. The online broker I'd registered with – The Klondike Index – provided real-time quotes, expert commentary, news updates and hyperlinks to a variety of research tools and simulation games. On the other computer screen, I visited sites like Bloomberg, The Street.com., Quote.com, Raging Bull and The Motley Fool. I also occasionally took time out to dive-bomb over the acres of newsprint I'd accumulated, and read articles about anything and everything . . . Mexico, naturally, but also about genetically modified foods, peace talks in the Middle East, Britpop, the downturn in the steel industry, Nigerian crime statistics, e-commerce, Tom Cruise and Nicole Kidman, Basque separatists, the international banana trade . . .

Whatever.

Of course, I had no real idea of what I was doing here, there was no coherent strategy, it was all random, but I'd gravitated to this notion that the more data there was stored in my brain – and wide-ranging data – the more confident I would be when the time actually came to take some of those fabled split-second decisions.

And – come to that – what *was* I waiting for? I didn't have much latitude, financially, but if I'd really wanted to, I could have been trading online within a matter of seconds. To place an order, all I had to do was select a stock, enter data about the type of transaction and number of shares required, and then click the Send Order button on the screen.

I resolved to begin the following morning.

Turning around in my swivel-chair at 10 a.m., I paused to survey the apartment. It seemed to have mutated severely in the previous twenty-four hours. Less recognizable than before, less identifiable as a living space, it was now, to use Bob Holland's word, like the lair of some deranged obsessive. Too far into this to be getting squeamish, however, I swivelled back around to the two computer screens on the desk and set about looking for some suitable stocks to buy. I waded through endless pick lists, insider lists, Street-beater lists, but eventually went with my gut instinct and fixed on a medium-sized software company in Palo Alto called Digicon that I figured to be well placed for some short-term action. It had just gone through a lengthy period of trading within a very narrow price range, but seemed now to be on the point of breaking out of that. In fact, in the space of time it took me to consider Digicon, and to run some relevant data through the analysis programmes, the company's share price went up by half a point. The account I'd opened with Klondike had steep brokerage fees and charged high interest rates, but they did allow up to 50 per cent leverage on opening deposits. So I sent off an order to buy 200 shares in Digicon, at $14 per share. Over the next half an hour I bought a total of 500 shares in six other companies, using up all my available funds, and then spent the rest of the day tracking these companies, looking for likely sell signals.

During the course of the late morning and early afternoon, all but one of the seven stocks I'd chosen went up in price, and by widely varying degrees. I made quick decisions about which ones to offload. Digicon, for instance, went to $17^3/8$, but I didn't think it was going to go any higher, so I sold it and cleared a profit of more than $600 – less the commission and transaction fee, of course. Another stock rose from $18^{1}/_{2}$ points to $24^{3}/_{4}$, and another from 31 to $36^{7}/_{16}$. By offloading each of these stocks at the right time, I managed to increase my basic fund from about $7,000 to nearly $12,000, and in the last two hours of trading I sold off everything except US-Cova. This was the one stock that hadn't moved all day, despite signals that an uptrend was imminent. I felt irritated by this, because when I'd been choosing these stocks something almost physical had happened to me . . . a vague, tingling sensation in the pit of my stomach – or so it had seemed at the time. In any case, all of the other stocks had shifted, and I didn't understand why this one wasn't complying.

Undeterred, I placed an order for an extra 650 shares in US-Cova, at $22 per share. About twenty minutes later there was a blip on the screen and US-Cova started moving. It went up by two points, then by another three points. I watched as the share price just kept climbing upwards. When it reached $36 I typed in a sell order, but still held out for another increase, and only sent in the order when the share price had hit $39, an increase of $17 in little over an hour.

At close of trading on that first day, therefore, I had more than $20,000 in my account. Take away the initial $7,000 and fees, and that meant I had made somewhere in the region of $12,000 profit in a single day. It was small potatoes on the stock market, obviously, but it was still more than I'd often made in half a year as a free-lance copywriter. This was of course amazing, but it also hit me what an incredible run of luck I'd had: seven picks and seven winners, and on an average day of trading where the market had closed only twelve points up. It was extraordinary. So how had I done it? *Had* it been luck? I tried to go back over the whole thing, to retrace my steps and see if I could identify what signals I'd picked up on, what prompts had led me to these relatively obscure, low-profile stocks in the first place, but it proved an impossibly labyrinthine task. I checked through dozens of trend-lines again, re-ran analysis programmes and at one point found myself crawling across the floor of the apartment over the open pages of broadsheet newspapers and glossy magazines, in search of some article I vaguely remembered reading and that *may* have suggested something – or sparked off an idea, or led in some other direction, or *not*. I simply didn't know. Perhaps I'd heard something on TV, an off-the-cuff remark made by any one of a hundred investment analysts. Or come across something in a chat-room, or on a message-board, or in a webzine.

Trying to reconfigure my mental co-ordinates at the exact moments I'd chosen those stocks was like trying to stuff toothpaste back into a tube, and I soon gave up. But the one conclusion I could draw from this was that I'd probably used fundamental and quantitative analysis in about equal measure, and even though I might not get the proportions exactly the same on the next occasion, and could never recreate the conditions of that particular day, I was certainly on the right track. Unless, of course – intolerable thought – it *had* all been some kind of a fluke, an epic stroke of beginner's luck. I didn't believe that it had been, really, but I still needed to know for sure and was therefore anxious to get trading again the next day. Which meant keeping up the preparatory in-take of data, and – naturally – of MDT-48.

I got three or four hours' sleep that night, and when I woke up – which was pretty suddenly, thanks to a car-alarm going off – it took me quite a while to work out where, and indeed *who*, I was. Before the alarm jolted me awake, I'd been in the middle of a particularly vivid dream set in Melissa's old apartment on Union Street in Brooklyn. Nothing much happened in the dream, really, but it had a guided, virtual-reality feel to it, with tracking shots and detailed close-ups, and even sounds . . . the evocative whine of the radiators, for example, doors slamming down the hall, kids' voices rising up from the street below.

The eye of the dream – the POV, the *camera* – glided low along the pitch-pine floorboards, through the different rooms of this railway apartment, taking in everything, the grain of the wood, each swirling line and knot of it . . . clumps of dust, a copy of *The Nation*, an empty bottle of Grolsch, an ashtray. Then, moving slowly upwards, it took in Melissa's right foot, which was bare, and her crossed legs, which were bare, and the navy silk slip she was wearing, which

102

crumpled as she leant forward, half revealing her breasts. Her long shiny black hair was draped on her shoulders and arms, and partially covered her face. She was sitting in a chair, smoking a cigarette, brooding. She looked fabulous. I was sitting on the floor, looking – I imagined – slightly less fabulous. Then, after what might have been a few seconds, I rose up to my feet, and the point-of-view – dizzyingly – rose up with me. As I turned, everything turned, and in a kind of hand-held pan of the room I took in the mounted black-and-white photographs on the wall, the photographs of old New York that Melissa had always liked so much; I took in the stone mantelpiece of the disused fireplace, and above it, the mirror, and *in* the mirror – fleetingly – *me*, wearing that old corduroy jacket I'd had, and looking so thin, so young. Still moving round, I saw the open doors that connected this room to the bedroom at the front, and then, standing framed between the doors I saw Vernon, all hair and smooth skin and in a leather jacket he'd always worn. I got a really good look at him, at his bright green eyes and high cheekbones, and for a couple of seconds he seemed to be talking to me. His lips were moving, though I couldn't hear anything he was saying . . .

But then suddenly it was all over, the car-alarm was wailing plaintively down on Tenth Street and I was swinging my legs out of bed – taking deep breaths, feeling as though I'd seen a ghost.

Inevitably, the next image to take up residence inside my head was another one of Vernon, but it was a Vernon of ten or eleven years later – a Vernon with hardly any hair, and with facial features that were disfigured and bruised, a Vernon splayed out on the couch of another apartment, in another part of town . . .

I stared down at the rug on the floor beside my bed, at its intricate, endlessly replicating patterns, and shook my head very slowly from side to side. Since I'd starting taking the MDT pills a few weeks before, I had hardly given any real thought to Vernon Gant – even though, by any standards, my behaviour towards him had been appalling. After finding him dead I'd as good as ransacked his bedroom for God's sake, and then stolen cash and property belonging to him. I hadn't even gone to his funeral service – convincing myself, on no evidence whatsoever, that that was the way Melissa had wanted it.

I stood up from the edge of the bed and quickly walked into the living-room. I took two pills from the ceramic bowl on the wooden shelf above the computer – which I'd been refilling every day – and swallowed them. It was surely the case, too, that the stuff I'd taken rightly belonged to Vernon's sister now – and whatever about the drugs, Melissa probably *could* have used that nine grand.

With a knot in my stomach, I reached behind the computers to switch them on. Then I glanced at my watch.

It was 4.58 a.m.

I'd easily be able to give her double that amount now, though – and maybe even a lot more if my second day of trading went well – but wouldn't that be like paying her off in some way?

All of a sudden I felt sick.

This certainly wasn't how I'd ever envisaged renewing my acquaintance with Melissa. I rushed into the bathroom and slammed the door behind me. I lowered myself to the floor and into position over the rim of the toilet bowl. But nothing happened, I couldn't throw up. I remained there for about twenty minutes, breathing heavily, holding my cheek against the cold, white porcelain, until eventually the feeling passed – or, rather, feelings . . . because the weird thing was, when I stood up again to go back into the living-room and start work at my desk, I no longer felt sick – but I no longer felt guilty either.

Trading that day was brisk. I chose myself another little portfolio of stocks to work on, five middle-sized companies plucked from obscurity, and more or less cleaned up. Earlier on, over coffee, I'd seen references in several newspaper articles – and later, innumerable references on innumerable websites – to US-Cova and its extraordinary performance in the markets the previous day. Digicon and one or two others also got brief mentions, but no coherent picture emerged that could explain what had gone on, or that could link, in any way at all, the various companies concerned. A resounding *Go figure* appeared to be the general consensus of opinion, so even though the odds against someone randomly picking seven straight winners in a row were truly astronomical, it was still possible at that point, and in the absence of any other evidence, that my initial flush of success *had* just been a question of luck.

It soon became apparent, however, that something else was at work here. Because – just as on the previous day – whenever I came upon an interesting stock, something happened to me, something physical. I felt what I can only describe as an electric charge, usually just below the sternum, a little surge of energy that quickly rippled through my body and then seemed to spill out into the room's atmosphere, sharpening colour definition and sound resolution. I felt as though I were connected to some vast system, wired in, a minute but active fibre, pulsating on a circuit board. The first stock I picked, for instance – let's call it V – started moving up five minutes after I'd sent off the buy-order. I tracked it, while at the same time nosing around the various websites for other things to buy. With growing confidence, therefore, I found myself surfing stocks throughout the early part of the morning, leap-frogging from one to another, selling V at a profit and immediately sinking all of the proceeds from it into W, which in turn got sold off at just the right moment to finance a foray into X.

But as I grew confident, I also grew impatient. I wanted more chips to play with, more capital, more leverage. By mid-morning I had inched my way up to nearly $35,000, which was fine, but to make a proper dent in the market I'd probably need, as a starting point, at least double – but probably three or four times – that amount.

I phoned Klondike, but they didn't provide leverage of more than 50 per cent. Not having much of a history with my bank manager, I didn't feel like trying *him*. Neither did I imagine that anyone I knew would have $75,000 to spare, or that any legitimate loan company would shell out that kind of money over the counter – *so*, since I wanted the money now, and was fairly confident about what I could do with it, there appeared to be only one other course of action left open to me.

[11]

I PUT ON A JACKET and left the apartment. I walked along Avenue A, past Tompkins Square Park and down towards Third Street to a diner I often used. The guy behind the counter, Nestor, was a local and knew everything that went on in the neighbourhood. He'd been serving coffee and muffins and cheeseburgers and tuna melts here for twenty years, and had observed all of the radical changes that had taken place, the clean-ups, the gentrification, the sneaky encroachment of high-rise apartment buildings. People had come and gone, but Nestor remained, a link to the old neighbourhood that even *I* remembered as a kid – Loisaida, the Latino quarter of store-front social clubs, and old men playing dominoes, and salsa and merengue blaring out of every window, and then later the Alphabet City of burned-out buildings and drug pushers and homeless people living in cardboard shelters in Tompkins Square Park. I'd often chatted to Nestor about these changes, and he'd told me stories – a couple of them pretty hair-raising – about various local characters, old-timers, storekeepers, cops, councillors, hookers, dealers, loansharks. But that was the thing about Nestor, he knew everyone – even knew *me*, an anonymous single white male who'd been living on Tenth Street for about five years and worked as some kind of journalist or something. So when I went into his place, sat at the counter and asked if he knew anyone who could advance me some cash, and fast – extortionate interest rates no obstacle – he didn't bat an eyelid, but just brought over a cup of coffee and told me to sit tight for a while.

When he'd served a few customers and cleared two or three tables, he came back to my end of the counter, wiped the area around where

I was sitting and said, 'Used to be Italians, yeah? Mostly Italians, until . . . well . . .'

He paused.

Until what? Until John Gotti took it in the ass and Sammy the Bull went in the Witness Protection Program? *What?* Was I supposed to *guess*? That was another thing about Nestor, he often assumed I knew more than I did. Or maybe he just used to forget who he was talking to.

'Until *what*?' I said.

'Until John Junior took over. It's a fucking mess these days.'

I was close.

'And now?'

'The Russians. From Brighton Beach. They used to work together, them and the Italians, or at least didn't work *against* each other, but now things are different. John Junior's crews – *apparently* – couldn't turn over a cigar stand.'

I never had the measure of Nestor: was he just a fly on the neigh-bourhood wall, or was he connected in some way? I didn't know. But then, how *would* I know? Who the fuck was *I*?

'So lately, round here,' he went on, 'there's this guy, Gennady. Comes in most days. He talks like an immigrant, but don't let that fool you. He's tough, just as tough as any of his uncles that came out of the Soviet gulags. They think this country is a joke.'

I shrugged my shoulders.

Nestor looked directly at me. 'These guys are crazy, Eddie. I'm telling you. They'll cut you around the waist, peel your skin – peel it all the way up to over your head, tie a knot in it and then let you fucking *suffocate*.'

He let that one sink in.

'I'm not kidding you. That's what the mujahedin did to some of the Russian soldiers they captured in Afghanistan. Stuff like that gets passed on. People learn.' He paused, and did a little more wiping. 'Gennady comes in, Eddie, I'll talk to him, but just make sure you know what you're doing.'

Then he stood away from the counter a little, and said, 'You been working out? You look terrific.'

I half smiled at him, but didn't say anything. Clearly puzzled, Nestor moved on to another customer.

I sat there for about an hour and drank four cups of coffee. I glanced at a couple of newspapers, and then spent some time trawling through the expanding database I had between my ears, picking out stuff I'd read about the Russian mafia – the Organizatsiya, Brighton Beach, Little-Odessa-by-the-Sea.

I tried not to think too much about what Nestor had told me.

At around lunch-time, the place got busy and I began to consider the possibility that I was wasting my time, but just as I was about to get up and leave, Nestor nodded to me from behind the counter. I looked around discreetly and saw a guy in his mid-twenties coming in the door. He was lean and wiry and wore a brown leather jacket and sunglasses. He went and sat in an empty booth at the back of the diner. I stayed where I was and watched out of the corner of my eye as Nestor brought him down a cup of coffee and chatted for a few moments.

Nestor came back up to the front, collecting some plates on his way. He put the plates on the counter beside me and whispered, 'I vouched for you, OK, so go and talk to him.' Then he pointed a finger at me and said, 'Don't fuck up on me, Eddie.'

I nodded and swivelled around on my stool. I strolled down to the back. I slipped into the booth opposite Gennady and nodded *hello*.

He'd taken the sunglasses off and left them to one side. He had very striking blue eyes, a carefully maintained stubble and was alarmingly thin and chiselled. Heroin? Vanity? Again, what did I know? I waited for him to speak.

But he didn't. After a ludicrous pause, he made a barely perceptible gesture with his head that I took to mean *I* could speak. So I cleared my throat and spoke. 'I'm looking for a short-term loan of seventy-five thousand dollars.'

Gennady played with his left ear-lobe for a moment and then shook his head *no*.

I waited – waited for him to say something else – but that was obviously it. 'Why not?' I said.

He snorted sarcastically. 'Seventy-five thousand dollars?' He shook his head again and took a sip from his coffee. He had a very strong Russian accent.

'Yeah,' I said, 'seventy-five thousand dollars. Is that such a problem? *Jesus.*'

If it came to it, I knew this guy would probably have no qualms about sticking a knife in my heart – and if Nestor was right that'd only be for starters – but I found his attitude irritating and didn't feel like playing along.

'Yes,' he said, 'a *fucking* problem. I don't see you before. And I don't *like* you already.'

'*Like* me? What the fuck has *that* got to do with anything? I'm not asking you out on a date here.'

He flinched, *moved* – was maybe even going to reach for something, a knife or a gun – but then he thought the better of it and just looked around, over his shoulder, probably pissed now at Nestor.

I decided to push it.

'I thought all you Russians were big shots – you know, tough, in control.'

He looked back, widening his eyes at me in disbelief. Then he collected himself, and for some reason made up his mind to respond.

'What – I *not* in control? I turn you down.'

Now *I* snorted sarcastically.

He paused. Then he snarled, 'Fuck you. What *you* know about us anyway?'

'Quite a bit, actually. I know about Marat Balagula and the gas tax scam, and that deal with the Colombo family. Then there's . . . Michael . . .' I paused and made a show of trying to get the name out. '. . . Shmushkevich?'

I realized from the look on his face that he wasn't entirely sure what I was talking about. He would probably only have been a kid when the so-called daisy-chain of dummy oil companies had been in full swing in the '80s, trucking gas in from South America and forging tax receipts. And anyway who knew what these younger guys talked about when they got together – probably not the great scams of a previous generation, that was for sure.

'So . . . *what*?' he said. 'You a cop?'

'No.'

When I didn't add anything, he started to get up to leave.

'Come *on*, Gennady,' I said, 'lighten up, would you?'

He stepped out of the booth and looked down at me, clearly debating in his head whether or not he should kill me right here, or wait until we got outside. I couldn't believe how reckless I was being, but I somehow felt I was safe, that nothing could touch me.

'Actually, I'm researching a book on you guys,' I said. 'I'm looking for a focus, though – somebody whose point of view I can use to tell the story . . .' I held off for a couple of beats, and then went for it. ' Somebody like you, Gennady.'

He shifted his weight from one foot to the other, and I knew I had him.

'What kind of book?' he said in a surprisingly small voice.

'A novel,' I replied. 'It's really just taking shape at the moment, but I see it as a story with an epic dimension to it, triumph over adversity, that kind of thing. From the gulags to the . . .' I trailed off here, faltering for a moment, aware that I might be losing him. 'I mean, if you think about it,' I went on quickly, 'the guineas have had it all their own way up to now, but that five-families, men-of-honour, badda-bing badda-boom shit has become clichéd. People want something new.' As he considered what I was saying, I decided to hammer it home, 'So my agent thinks the movie rights on this will almost certainly be snapped up as well.'

Gennady hesitated for a moment, and then sat back down into the booth, waiting for more.

On the hoof, I managed to outline a vague plot centring on a young second-generation Russian who finds himself moving up through the Organizatsiya. I threw in references to the Sicilians and the Colombians, but with a repeated wave of the hand I also kept deferring, in anticipation, to Gennady's superior grasp of the details. Managing to flip the axis, I soon had *him* doing most of the talking – albeit in his fairly mangled English. He agreed with some suggestions I made and dismissed others, but he'd got the whiff of glamour into his system now and couldn't be stopped.

I hadn't planned any of this, of course, and as I was doing it I didn't really believe I'd get away with it either, but the boldest stroke was yet to come. After he'd agreed to do consultancy on 'the project' and we'd established a few ground rules, I managed to edge the conversation back around to the loan. I told him my advance on the book had already been spent and that the 75K was a gambling debt I had to pay off – and had to pay off *today*.

Yeah, yeah, yeah.

This matter was now a minor distraction to Gennady. He took out his cellphone and had a quick conversation with someone in Russian. Then, still on the phone, he asked me a series of questions. What was my social security number? Driver's licence number? What were the names of my landlord and my employer? Where did I bank and what credit cards did I hold? I took out my social security card and driver's licence, and read out the relevant numbers. Then I gave him the names and the other stuff he wanted while he relayed the information in Russian to the person on the other end of the line.

With that taken care of, Gennady put away his phone and got back to talking about the project. Fifteen minutes later his phone rang. As before, he spoke in Russian, at one point covering the mouthpiece with his hand and whispering, 'That OK, you cleared. So – what? Seventy-five? You sure? You want more? A hundred?'

I paused, and then nodded *yes*.

When he'd finished on the phone, he said, 'Will be ready in a half-hour.'

Then he put the phone away and placed his hands down flat on the table.

'OK,' he said, 'so who we going to cast in this thing?'

Half an hour later, on the nose, another young guy arrived. Gennady introduced him as Leo. He was skinny and not unlike Gennady, but he didn't have Gennady's eyes, didn't have what Gennady had – looked, in fact, like he'd had whatever it was Gennady did have surgically removed. Maybe they were brothers, or cousins, and maybe – I started thinking – maybe I *could* make something out of this. They spoke in Russian for a moment and then Leo pulled a thick brown envelope out of his jacket pocket, put it on the table, slid out of the booth and left without saying a word. Gennady shoved the envelope in my direction.

'This a knockdown, OK? Short term. Five repayments, five weeks, twenty-two-five a time. I come by your place each . . .' He paused, and stared at the envelope for a moment. '. . . each Friday morning, start two weeks from today.' He held the envelope up in his left hand. 'This no joke, Eddie – you take this now . . . you *mine*.' I nodded. 'I go into other stuff?'

I shook my head.

The other stuff being, I presumed – at the very *least* – legs, knees, arms, ribs, baseball bats, switchblades, electric cattle-prods maybe.

'No.' I shook my head again. 'It's OK. I understand.'

I was anxious to get away now that I had the cash, but I could hardly appear to be in too much of a hurry. It turned out, however, that Gennady himself had to go, and was already late for another appointment. We'd exchanged phone numbers, so before he left we agreed that in a week or so we'd make some arrangement to meet again. He'd check up on some stuff, and I'd work a little more on shaping – maybe even expanding – the central character of what had somehow mutated, during the course of our conversation, from a novel into a screenplay.

Gennady put on his Ray-Bans and was ready to go. But he paused, and reached over to shake my hand. He did this silently, solemnly.

Then he got up and left.

I called Klondike from the payphone in the diner. I explained the situation and they gave me the address of a bank on Third Avenue where I could deposit cash that would immediately be credited to my account.

I thanked Nestor for his help and then took a cab to Sixty-first and Third. I opened the envelope in the back of the cab and fingered the wads of hundred-dollar bills. I'd never seen this much cash before in my life and I felt dizzy just looking at it. I felt even dizzier handing it over at the bank and watching the teller count it.

After that, I took another cab back to Tenth Street and got settled down to work again. In my absence, the stocks I was holding had increased dramatically in value, bringing my base capital up to $50,000. This meant that with Gennady's contribution I now had almost $150,000 at my disposal, and with only a couple of hours' trading time left – and consequently very little time for research – I just jumped right into it, tracking valuations, schlepping stocks around, buying, selling, sprinting back and forth across the various rows of figures on the computer screens.

This process gathered considerable momentum and peaked late in the afternoon with two big scores – let's call them Y and Z – high-risk, high-yield stocks, each on a rapid upswing. Y carried me as far as the $200,000 mark, and Z carried me considerably beyond it, to just over a quarter of a million. It was a tense, sometimes harrowing few hours, but it gave me a real taste for the thrill of facing down the odds, and also for large quantities of adrenalin, a substance I could almost feel being secreted into, and moving through, my system – almost the way share prices themselves shifted and moved through the markets.

Despite my success rate, however, or maybe because of it, a sense of dissatisfaction began to creep over me. I had the feeling that I could be doing a lot more than just trading at home on my PC, and that being a guerrilla market-maker wasn't going to be anywhere near enough to keep me happy. The fact is, I wanted to know what it would be like to trade from the inside, and at the highest levels . . . what it would be like and how it would feel to buy *millions* of shares at a time . . .

I phoned Kevin Doyle, therefore – the investment banker I'd gone for breakfast with a few Sundays before – and arranged to meet him for drinks at the Orpheus Room.

The last time we met he'd been very intent on giving me advice about setting up a portfolio of stocks, so I thought I could maybe pick his brains a little and get some tips on how to move into the big league.

Kevin didn't recognize me at first when he arrived at the bar. He said I'd changed and was considerably slimmer than when we'd met at Herb and Jilly's.

He wanted to know where I worked out.

I looked at him for a moment. *Herb and Jilly's?* Then I realized that whoever Herb and Jilly were, it must have been at their place on the Upper West Side that I'd ended up that night.

'I don't work out,' I said. 'Working out is the new lunch, it's for wimps.'

He laughed, and then ordered an Absolut on the rocks.

Kevin Doyle was around forty, forty-two, and fairly trim himself. He was wearing a charcoal suit and a red silk tie. I couldn't remember much of what I'd told him at Herb and Jilly's, or afterwards in that diner on Amsterdam Avenue, but one thing I did remember clearly was that *I'd* done most of the talking, and Kevin – apart from trying to turn me on to some stock tips – had hung on my every word. It'd been that thing again, that wanting-to-impress-me, wanting-to-be-my-best-friend thing that I'd had with Paul Baxter and Artie Meltzer. I tried to analyse what this was, and could only conclude that maybe a combination of my being enthusiastic and non-judgemental – *non-competitive* – might have struck some kind of a chord in people, especially in people who were stressed out and on their guard all the time. At any rate, these days I had the talking thing a bit more under control, so I decided to let Kevin take the lead. I asked him about Van Loon and Associates.

'We're a small investment bank,' he began, 'about two hundred and fifty employees. We do venture capital, fund management, real estate, that kind of thing. We've brokered some fairly big entertainment deals recently. We did the MCL-Parnassus purchase of Cableplex last year, and Carl Van Loon himself is currently in talks about something else to Hank Atwood, the Chairman of MCL.' He paused, and then added, as though telling me he'd just been picked for the soccer team, 'I'm a managing director.'

But when he elaborated on this a bit, explaining that he was one of seven or eight managing directors in the company who babysat their own deals and then came out with huge commissions, I realized for the first time that Kevin wasn't just some Wall Street schmoe. From what he was telling me, I quickly reckoned that he probably cleared about two or three million a year.

Now *I* was impressed.

'What about Van Loon? Is he . . .' I asked, not even having a real question here, obviously succumbing a little to the magnetic pull of celebrity that still surrounded Kevin's boss.

'Carl's all right. He's mellowed a lot, you know. Over the years. But he still works as hard as ever.'

I nodded, thinking *How hard could that be?*

'The firm wouldn't be what it is today without him.'

This was a man who probably cleared about two or three million a *week*.

'Hhn.'

'So . . . how have *you* been?'

'Me? Fine.'

I didn't remember much of our previous encounter, but I was pretty sure I'd mentioned my book, and probably without saying that it was part of a cheesy series for a second-rate publisher – so, at least as far as I knew, Kevin thought I was a writer of some kind, a commentator, someone with their finger, so to speak, on the pulse of the *Zeitgeist* . . . someone he could have an intelligent, self-congratulatory but non-threatening conversation with, and about stuff like the new economy and megatrends and digitalization.

But I got to the point fairly fast.

'What do you make of all this electronic day-trading, Kevin?'

He thought for a second. 'It's just noise. These guys aren't spec-ulators, or even investors, they're *gamblers* – or else sorry geeks who think they've democtratized the markets.' He made a face. 'When this bubble pops, let me tell you, there's going to be a lot of blood spattered on the walls.'

He took a sip from his drink.

I lifted my glass. 'I've been doing it at home on my PC, using a software trading package I bought on Forty-seventh Street. I'm up about a quarter of a million in two days.'

Kevin looked at me in horror for a few seconds, taking in the information. But he was also confused, and obviously didn't know what to say. Then it registered.

'*A quarter of a million?*'

'Hmm.'

'*In two days?* That's pretty good.'

'Yeah, I think so. But I find I'm weirdly – how can I put this? – *dissatisfied* with it. I feel constricted. I need to expand.'

As he tried to come to terms with what I was telling him, Kevin shifted on his stool and maybe even squirmed a little. He was a confident guy, clearly very successful, and it was odd to see him mired in uncertainty like this.

'Ehm . . . perhaps . . .' he scratched his nose, 'you could . . . why don't you try one of those day-trading firms?'

I asked him what difference that would make.

'Well, you're not isolated, you're in a room with a bunch of other traders and on the principle that no one in an environment like that wants to see anyone else *failing*, you help each other out, and share information. Most firms also offer high leverage, anywhere between five to ten times your deposit. You get a better feel for the behaviour of the markets, as well,' – he was getting back into his stride here – 'because it's often just a question of being able to gauge the collective mood, and then deciding either to go *with* it or . . . I don't know' – he shrugged his shoulders – '*against* it.'

I asked him if he could recommend one of these places.

'There are a couple of good ones I've heard about – actually on, or at least around, Wall Street itself. Though if you ask me, Eddie, it sounds like you're doing pretty good on your own.'

I wrote down the names he reeled off and thanked him anyway. Then we each took sips from our respective glasses.

'So . . . a quarter of a million in two days.' He whistled in admiration. 'What's your strategy?'

I was about to give him an edited version of events when two guys in suits came up behind us and one of them slapped Kevin on the back. 'Hey Doyle, you old dog, what's happening?'

These were money-scented financial-sector jocks, and when Kevin introduced me but didn't say that I was a managing director or an executive vice-president with this or that outfit, they more or less ignored me. During the ensuing conversation about the emerging markets of Latin America, and then about the tech stocks bubble, I could see Kevin struggling with his fear that I was going to start talking again about *day-trading on a PC* – and in front of these guys. So when I stood up to go, I think he was a little relieved.

I told him I'd phone him in a few days' time and let him know how I'd gotten on with *that thing* we'd been discussing.

Lafayette Trading was on Broad Street, just a few blocks down from the New York Stock Exchange. In the main room of a sparsely furnished suite of offices on the fourth floor, twenty tables were arranged in a large rectangle. Each table held enough terminals and PCs for at least three traders, and of the fifty or so traders I saw there on my first morning – all male, each seated in comfortable executive-style chairs – I'd say more than half of them were under thirty years old, and of those about half again were wearing jeans and baseball caps.

The deal was that you put down a minimum deposit of $25,000 and Lafayette then provided all the hardware and software you needed in order to trade. In return for this, they charged a commission of two cents a share on each trade you made. If you wanted it, and most people did, they also offered pretty high leverage on your deposit. I registered with them, paying a deposit of $200,000 and then arranged to leverage myself to two and a half times that amount – which meant, effectively, that I was starting off this new phase of my trading career with half a million dollars at my disposal.

I had to do a short induction course in the morning. Then I spent most of the early afternoon chatting to some of the other traders and more or less observing the room. The atmosphere at Lafayette was – as Kevin had said it might be in such a place – friendly and collaborative. There was a sense of us all being in this together, of us all working against the big marketmakers down the street. But it didn't take long to see that there *were* factions in the room, and some big personalities, and that the dynamics weren't always going to be so easy to read. There were different trading styles, as well, of course. The guy to my left, for example, was a manic keyboard-crusher who didn't seem to do any research or analysis.

'What's that stock?' I asked him, pointing to a symbol on his screen soon after I'd sat down.

'No idea,' he mumbled, not taking his eyes off what he was doing, 'it has a big spread and it's moving, and that's all I need to know.'

Other traders seemed more cautious and did quite a lot of research – by watching the TV sets bolted to the side-wall, or by running from their tables to a Bloomberg terminal at the top of the room, or just by poring over endless stock graphs on their own screens. In any case, when I felt I had the measure of the room, and its mood, I went to work at my allotted table-space, looking for some likely trades myself. But as it was my first day I took it fairly easy and when I closed out my positions before the final bell I was only about $5,000 up. Given my admittedly short track record, this didn't seem like all that much to me, but some of the other traders didn't agree. Clearly, as the new kid on the block, I had already aroused a certain amount of curiosity, not to say suspicion, in the room. Someone asked me rather tentatively if I wanted to join a group of them who were going for a drink to some place down at Pier 17 Pavilion, but I declined. I didn't want to form any new alliances just yet.

It had been a relatively slow day for me – at least in terms of mental activity and the amount of work I'd done – so when I got home I was feeling pretty restless, even a little frenzied. Unable to sleep that night, I stayed on the couch in the living-room, watching TV and reading. Against a background of cable movies, quiz shows and commercials, I ploughed through the financial sections of the day's papers, a biography of Warren Buffet and all the text, captions, advertising copy, mastheads and photo credits of half a dozen glossy business magazines.

On my second morning at Lafayette, a Tuesday, I spent a good deal of time nosing around the various financial websites. I eventually opened up more than a dozen major positions, eighty thousand shares in total, and then concentrated on tracking them carefully.

At about eleven-thirty, there was a slight commotion to my left. A few tables up, three of the guys in baseball caps, who appeared to be working very closely together, started punching the air and hissing *yessss* to each other. It took another few minutes for the 'tip' to filter down. The keyboard-cruncher beside me, whose name was Jay, pulled himself away from his screen for a brief moment and turned to face me.

'Think something's just come through on the wire about some biotech stock.'

He shrugged his shoulders and then went back to work, but the guy beside *him* wheeled his chair around and spoke to me as though we'd known each other since high school.

'Medical breakthrough, hasn't been announced yet. MEDX – that's Mediflux Inc., a Florida drug company, yeah? – seems they've got some anti-cancer protein in development. It's got the white-coats over at the National Cancer Research Foundation all excited.'

'And?'

He looked at me as if to say, *What – are you a moron?* Then, pausing uncertainly, he said, '*Buy* Mediflux!'

I could see that Jay, the guy beside me, was already doing just that. I nodded at the other guy and then went back to my screen to see what information might be available about this pharmaceutical company – Mediflux Inc. It was currently selling at $43^{1}/_{3}$, having moved up from an opening price of $37^{3}/_{4}$. Everyone was assuming it was going to continue this upward trend, and everyone – at least everyone in the room around me – seemed to be buying Mediflux on that basis. I spent a while looking at its fundamentals – historical earnings, growth potential, that kind of thing – and at one point during this Jay nudged me and said, 'How much did you buy?'

I looked at him and paused, quickly reviewing in my head everything I'd just read about Mediflux.

'I didn't buy any,' I said. 'In fact, I'm going to sell it short.'

This meant that, contrary to the prevailing wisdom in the room, I expected the Mediflux share price to fall. While they were all busy buying it, I would borrow Mediflux stock from my broker. I would then sell it, having committed to buying it back later at what I hoped would be a considerably lower price. The lower the price, of course, the greater the profit for me.

'You're going to *short* it?'

He said this quite loudly, and as the word *short* darted its way around the tables like an acute pain along a sciatic nerve, you could almost feel the whole room stiffen. There was a brief silence and then everyone started talking at the same time and checking their screens and looking across at my table. Over the next couple of minutes the tension in the room increased as the original Mediflux faction regrouped and began hurling comments in my direction.

'Feel sorry for *you*, buddy.'

'Margin call!'

'Loser!'

I ignored these taunts and got on with executing my short-sell strategy on Mediflux, as well as looking after my other positions. For the next while the Mediflux share price continued to rise, reaching 51 points, but then it seemed to stabilize. Jay nudged me again and shrugged his shoulders as if to say, *Talk to me, why did you short it?*

'Because it's all hype,' I said. 'What – a couple of mice with cancer in some laboratory somewhere sit up in bed and ask for tea and suddenly we're all into a *buying* frenzy?' I shook my head. 'And when is this new protein they're developing going to have a commercial application anyway? Five years? Ten years?'

Jay looked worried all of a sudden and seemed to recoil into himself.

'Besides,' I said, pointing at my screen, 'Eiben-Chemcorp pulled out of a takeover deal of Mediflux about six months ago, and it was never properly explained – doesn't anyone want to remember *that*?'

I could see him rapidly processing the information.

'This does *not* have legs, Jay.'

He turned to the other guy beside him and started whispering. Soon – as my analysis made its way around to all of the other traders – dark clouds of uncertainty descended on the room.

From the babble of muttering and clicking that ensued, it was obvious that two camps were emerging – some of the traders were going to hold on to their stock, while others were going to join me in shorting Mediflux. Jay, and the guy beside him, reversed their positions. The baseball caps held fast to theirs, but refrained from

120

making any comments about it – not aloud, at any rate. I remained huddled over my terminal, keeping a low profile, even though the atmosphere was electric, with a definite sense that in the ecosystem of the room I was an interloper who was making some kind of a bid for power. I hadn't intended it that way, of course, but the thing is, I *was* convinced that MEDX was a turkey – and so it was to prove.

Late in the afternoon, just as I had predicted, the stock collapsed. It started slipping at about 3.15 p.m., much to the consternation of about two thirds of the traders in the room. MEDX closed at $17^{1}/_{2}$ points, a drop of $36^{1}/_{2}$ points from its high, earlier in the day, of 54.

At the closing bell, a cheer went up from a small group sitting at the table directly opposite me. They came over afterwards to introduce themselves – and I realized that with them, Jay, the guy beside him, and one or two others, I had formed my own crew. It wasn't only because they were happy to have taken the tip from me, but it was also, I think, because of what they saw as the sheer, ballsy scale of my own trade. I had shorted 5,000 MEDX shares and come away with over $180,000. This was more in one trade than most of them could hope to make in a year, and they loved it – loved the sanction it gave to risk, loved how it confirmed that scoring big *was* possible.

One of the three baseball caps nodded at me from across the room, a gesture that I think was meant to indicate he was conceding defeat, but then he left quickly with the other two and I didn't get a chance to say to him – magnanimously, or, perhaps, patronizingly – that hey, they had come up with the stock in the first place. I still refused to go for a drink with anyone, but I did stick around for ages, chatting and trying to find out as much as I could about how day-trading firms like this one operated.

On my third morning at Lafayette I was the centre of attention. But I was also, undeniably, on trial. Was I a one-hit wonder – I'm sure they were all thinking – or did I actually know what the fuck I was doing?

As it turned out my period of probation only lasted a few hours. A position with a data-storage company, JKLS – not unlike the one of the previous day – soon presented itself, and I whispered to Jay that I was about to initiate coverage of the stock at its current price with an immediate short-sell. Jay, who had quietly assumed the role of my underboss, passed on this information to the next table up, and within less than a minute it seemed that the whole room was shorting JKLS. During the course of the morning, I fed out a few other tips that some people, but certainly not everyone, picked up on. Early in the afternoon, however, when the JKLS price began falling rapidly, and a cheer went up, a quick review of my other tips took place, and the doubters joined in.

By the closing bell at four o'clock, it was *my* room.

Over the next couple of days, the trading 'pit' at Lafayette was packed to capacity – with all of the regulars in attendance, as well as quite a few new faces. I stuck to my short-selling strategy and led an onslaught against a whole series of overhyped and overvalued stocks. My instinct for identifying these stocks appeared to be unerring and it was thrilling to watch them all behave exactly as I had predicted. In turn, people were watching *me* very closely and naturally wanted to know how I was doing it, but since these same people were also making a lot of money from my recommendations, no one had the temerity to come out straight and simply ask me. Which was just as well, because I wouldn't really have had an answer.

It did seem to me to be instinct, though – but informed instinct, instinct based on a huge amount of research, which of course, thanks to MDT-48, was conducted more rapidly and comprehensively than anyone at Lafayette would ever realize.

But that also wasn't enough to explain it – because there were plenty of well-resourced, well-financed research departments around, from the windowless backrooms of investment banks and brokerage houses throughout the country, stuffed full of pale, nameless 'quants' number-crunching till dawn, to places stuffed full of Nobel-prize winning mathematicians and economists, places like the Santa Fe Institute and MIT. For an individual, I was processing a huge amount of information – it was true – but I still couldn't compete with outfits like those.

So what was it?

After the first day of my second week at Lafayette, I tried to evaluate the various possibilities – maybe it was superior information, or heightened instinct, or brain chemistry, or some kind of mysterious synergy between the organic and the technological – but as I sat there at my table, staring vacantly at the screen, these ruminations slowly coalesced into an overwhelming vision of the vastness and beauty of the stock market itself. Grappling for understanding, I soon realized that despite its susceptibility to predictable metaphor – it was an ocean, a celestial firmament, a numerical representation of the will of God – the stock market *was* nevertheless something more than just a market for stocks. In its complexity and ceaseless motion the twenty-four-hour global network of trading systems was nothing less than a template for human consciousness, with the electronic marketplace perhaps forming humanity's first tentative version of a collective nervous system, a global brain. Moreover, whatever interactive combination of wires and microchips and circuits and cells and receptors and synapses was required to achieve this grand convergence of band-width and brain-tissue, it seemed to me in that moment that *I* had tumbled upon it – *I* was jacked in and booted up . . . *my* mind was a living fractal, a mirrored part of the greater functioning whole.

I was also aware – not to lose the run of myself here – that whenever an individual is on the receiving end of a revelation like this, addressed to himself alone (and written out, say, on the night sky, as Nathaniel Hawthorne would have it), the revelation can only be the result of a morbid and disordered state of mind, but surely *this* was somehow different, surely *this* was empirical, demonstrable – after all, at the end of my sixth day of trading at Lafayette, I had an unbroken chain of winners and over *a million dollars* in my brokerage account.

That evening I went for a drink with Jay and a few of the others to a place on Fulton Street. After my third beer and half a dozen cigarettes, not to mention a torrent of day-trading lore from my new colleagues, I resolved to set a few things in train – changes that I felt it was now time to make. I resolved to put a deposit down on an apartment – somewhere bigger than my place on Tenth Street, and in a different part of town, maybe Gramercy Park, or even Brooklyn Heights. I also resolved to throw out all my old clothes and furniture and accumulated *stuff*, and only replace what I absolutely needed. Most important, however, I resolved to move on from day-trading and into a wider playing field, to move up to money management maybe, or hedge funds or global markets.

I'd only been trading for little over a week, so naturally I didn't have much idea about how I was going to pull something like this off, but when I got back to my apartment, as though on cue, there was a message from Kevin Doyle on my answering machine.

Click.

Beeep.

'Hi Eddie, Kevin – what is all this stuff I've been hearing? Call me.'

Without even taking my jacket off, I picked up the phone and dialled his number.

'Hello.'

'So what have you been hearing?'

Beat.

'Lafayette, Eddie. Everyone's talking about you.'

'About *me*?'

'Yeah. I happened to be having lunch with Carl and a few other people today when someone mentioned they'd heard rumours about a day-trading firm on Broad Street – and some trader there who was performing phenomenally. I made a few enquiries after lunch and your name came up.'

I smiled to myself and said, 'Oh yeah?'

'And Eddie, that's not all. I was speaking to Carl again later and I told him what I'd found out. He was really interested, and when I said you were actually a *friend* of mine he said he'd like to meet you.'

'That's great, Kevin. I'd like to meet him. Any time that suits.'

'Are you free tomorrow night?'

'Yeah.'

He paused. 'Let me call you back.'

He rang off immediately.

I went over and sat on the couch and looked around. I was going to be getting out of here soon – and not a moment too soon, either. I envisaged the spacious, elegantly decorated living-room of a house in Brooklyn Heights. I saw myself standing at a bay window, looking out on to one of those tree-lined streets that Melissa and I, on our way from Carroll Gardens into the city, on summer days, had often walked along, and even talked about one day living on. Cranberry Street. Orange Street. Pineapple Street.

The phone rang again. I stood up and walked across the room to answer it.

'Eddie – Kevin. Drinks tomorrow night? At the Orpheus Room?'

'Great. What time?'

'Eight. But why don't you and I meet at seven-thirty, that way I can fill you in on some stuff.'

'Sure.'

I put the phone down.

As I stood there, with my hand still on the receiver, I began to feel light-headed and dizzy, and everything went dark for a second. Then, without consciously registering that I had moved – *and moved to the other side of the room* – I suddenly found myself reaching out to the edge of the couch for something to lean against.

It was only then that I realized I hadn't eaten anything in three days.

[12]

I ARRIVED AT THE ORPHEUS ROOM before Kevin and took a seat at the bar. I ordered a club soda.

I didn't know what I expected from this meeting, but it would certainly be interesting. Carl Van Loon was one of those names I'd seen in newspapers and magazines all throughout the 1980s, a name synonymous with that decade and its celebrated devotion to Greed. He might be quiet and retiring these days, but back then the chairman of Van Loon & Associates had been involved in several notorious property deals, including the construction of a gigantic and controversial office building in Manhattan. He had also been involved in some of the highest-profile leveraged buyouts of the period, and in countless mergers and acquisitions.

Back in those days, as well, Van Loon and his second wife, interior-designer Gabby De Paganis, had been denizens of the black-tie charity circuit and had had their pictures in the social pages of every issue of *New York* magazine and *Quest* and *Town and Country*. To me, he'd been a member of that gallery of cartoon characters – along with people like Al Sharpton, Leona Helmsley and John Gotti – that had made up the public life of the times, the public life we'd all consumed so voraciously on a daily basis, and then discussed and dissected at the slightest provocation.

I remember once being in the West Village with Melissa, for instance, about 1985 or 1986 – in Caffe Vivaldi – when she got up on her high horse about the proposed Van Loon Building. Van Loon had long wanted to regain the title of World's Tallest for New York, and was proposing a glass box on the site of the old St Nicholas

Hotel on Forty-eighth Street. It had been designed at over fifteen hundred feet, but after endless objections was eventually built at just under a thousand. 'What *is* this shit with skyscrapers?' she'd said, holding up her espresso cup, 'I mean, haven't we gotten over it yet?' OK, the skyscraper had once been the supreme symbol of corporate capitalism, indeed of America itself – what Ayn Rand referring to the Woolworth Building as seen from New York Harbour had called 'the finger of God' – but surely *we no longer needed it*, no longer needed people like Carl Van Loon coming along trying to imprint their adolescent fantasies on the city skyline. For the most part, in any case – she went on – the question of height had been irrelevant, a red herring, as skyscrapers had merely been commercial *billboards* for the likes of sewing-machine companies and retailers and car manufacturers and newspapers. So what was *this* one going to be? A billboard for fucking *junk bonds*? Jesus.

Melissa, on occasions such as this, had wielded her espresso cup with a rare elegance – suitably indignant, but never spilling a drop, and always ready if necessary to flip the axis and start laughing at herself.

'Eddie.'

She always calmed down in the same way, too – no matter how animated she'd become. She would lean her head slightly forward, maybe swirling whatever coffee was left in the cup, and go still and quiet, diaphanous strands of hair settling gently across her face.

'*Eddie?*'

I turned around in my seat, away from the bar. Kevin was standing there, staring at me.

I held out my hand.

'Kevin.'

'Eddie.'

'How are you?'

'Fine.'

As we shook hands, I tried to edge that image of Melissa from my mind. I asked him if he wanted a drink – an Absolut on the rocks – and he did. A few minutes of small talk followed, and then Kevin started priming me for the meeting with Van Loon.

'He's . . . mercurial – one day he's your best friend and the next he'll look right through you, so don't be put off if he's a little weird.'

I nodded.

'Oh, and – I'm sure I don't have to tell you this – but . . . don't pause or hesitate when you're answering him, he hates that.'

I nodded again.

'You see, he's really caught up at the moment in this MCL-Parnassus thing with Hank Atwood and . . . I don't know.'

One of the largest media conglomerates in the world, with cable, film studio and publishing divisions, MCL-Parnassus was the kind of company that business journalists liked to describe as 'a megalith' or 'a behemoth'.

'What's going on with Atwood?' I asked.

'I'm not sure exactly, it's all still under wraps.' Then something occurred to him. 'And *don't ask him* – what*ever* you do.'

I could see that Kevin was having second thoughts about setting this thing up. He kept looking at his watch, as if he were working to a deadline and time was running out. He drained the last of the vodka from his glass at about ten to eight, ordered another one, and then said, 'So, Eddie, just what exactly are you going to be telling him?'

'I don't know,' I answered, shrugging my shoulders, 'I suppose I'll tell him about my adventures in day-trading, and give him a run-down of all the major positions I've held.'

Kevin seemed to be expecting something more than this – but *what*? Since I couldn't offer him any satisfactory explanation for my success-rate, other than to refer to some *in*explicable ability I seemed to have developed, all I ended up saying was, 'I've been *lucky*, Kevin. I mean – don't get me wrong – I've worked at it, and I do a *lot* of research, but . . . yeah, things have gone my way.'

As far as Kevin was concerned, however, this kind of ill-defined bullshit clearly wasn't going to be enough – even if he couldn't bring himself to say as much out loud. It was then I realized that there was an underlying anxiety in everything he *had* been saying up to that point, a fear that unless he had some inside track on my trading strategy, and consequently some leverage with Van Loon, he was just going to end up handing me over to Van Loon – and that then, effectively, he would be out of the picture.

But there wasn't much I could do about that.

For my part, I felt pretty good. I'd eaten a plate of pasta *in bianco* after my disturbing spell of dizziness the previous evening. Then I'd taken some vitamin pills and diet supplements and gone to bed. I'd slept for about six hours, which was as much, if not more, than I'd managed in a month. I was still on two doses of MDT a day, but I now felt fresher and more in control – and more confident – than ever before.

Van Loon swept into the Orpheus Room as though he were being filmed in an elaborate tracking shot and this was just the last stage in a sequence that had taken him all the way from his limousine outside on the street. Tall, lean and a bit stooped, Van Loon was still quite an imposing figure. He was sixtyish and tanned, and the few wisps of hair he had left were a distinguished silvery-white. He shook my hand vigorously and then invited us both to join him over at his regular table in the corner.

I hadn't seen him ordering anything or even making eye contact with the barman, but a couple of seconds after we'd sat down – me with my club soda and Kevin with his Absolut – Van Loon was served what looked like the perfect Martini. The waiter arrived, placed the glass down on the table and withdrew, all with a lightness of touch – silence and near invisibility – that was clearly reserved by management for a certain . . . *class* of customer.

'So, Eddie Spinola,' Van Loon said, looking me directly in the eyes, 'what's your secret?'

I could feel Kevin stiffen beside me.

'Medication,' I said at once, 'I'm on special medication.'

Van Loon laughed at this. Then he picked up his Martini, raised it to me and said, 'Well, I hope it's a repeat prescription.'

This time *I* laughed, and raised my club soda to him.

But that was it. He didn't pursue the matter any further. To Kevin's obvious annoyance, Van Loon then went on to talk about his new Gulfstream V, and the problems he'd been having with it, and how he'd spent sixteen months on a waiting list just to get the damned thing. He addressed all of these remarks directly to me, and I got the impression – because it was too pointed to be accidental – that he was deliberately excluding Kevin. I took it for granted, therefore, that we wouldn't be going back to the subject of what my 'secret' might be, and we – or rather Van Loon – simply talked about other things . . . cigars, for example, and how he'd recently tried to buy JFK's humidor, unsuccessfully as it had turned out. Or cars – his latest being a Maserati that had set him back nearly 'two hundred large'.

Van Loon was brash and vulgar and conformed almost exactly to how I would have imagined him from his public profile of a decade before, but the strange thing was I liked him. There was a certain appeal in the way he focused so intently on money and on various imaginative, flamboyant ways of spending it. With Kevin, on the other hand, the emphasis seemed to be solely on ways of making it, and when a friend of Van Loon's joined us a while later from another table, Kevin – true to form – succeeded in veering the conversation around to the subject of the markets. Van Loon's friend was Frank Pierce, a fellow veteran from the 1980s who had worked for Goldman Sachs and was now running a private investment fund. None too subtly, Kevin mentioned something about using mathematics and advanced software programs to beat the markets.

I said nothing.

Frank Pierce, who was quite chubby and had beady eyes, said, 'Horseshit. If it could be done, you think someone wouldn't have done it by now?' He looked around, and then added, 'I mean, we all do quantitative analysis, we all do the *math*, but they've been going on about this other stuff for years, this black-box stuff, and it's crap. It's like trying to turn base metals into gold, it can't be done, you can't beat the markets – but there'll always be some jerk with too many college degrees and a pony-tail who thinks you can.'

'With respect,' Kevin said, addressing himself to Frank Pierce, but obviously trying to draw me out at the same time, 'there *are* some examples around of people who have beaten the markets, or appear to have.'

130

'Beaten the markets *how*?'

Kevin glanced over in my direction, but I wasn't going to rise to the bait. He was on his own.

'Well,' he said, 'we haven't always had the technology we have now, we haven't always had the capacity to process such huge amounts of information. If you analyse enough data, patterns *will* emerge, and certain of those patterns just may have predictive value.'

'*Horseshit*,' Frank Pierce boomed again.

Kevin was a little taken aback at this, but he soldiered on. 'I mean, by using complex systems and time-series analysis you can . . . you can identify pockets of probability. Then you patch these together into some mechanism for pattern-recognition . . .' – he paused here, less sure of himself now, but also in too deep to stop – '. . . and from there you build a model to predict market trends.'

He looked over at me imploringly, as if to say *Eddie, please, am I on the right track here? Is this how you're doing it?*

'Patterns my ass,' said Pierce. 'How do you think *we* made our money?' He leant his weight forward in the chair and with his stubby index finger rapidly identified himself and Van Loon. 'Huh?' Then he pointed to his right temple, tapped it slowly, and said, 'Un-der-stan-ding. That's how. Understanding how business works. Understanding when a company is overvalued, or undervalued. Understanding that you never make a bet you can't afford to lose.'

Van Loon turned to me, like a chat-show host, and said, 'Eddie?'

'Absolutely,' I said in a quiet voice, 'no one could argue with that . . .'

'*But?*' Pierce snorted sarcastically. 'There's always a *but* with these guys.'

'Yes,' I went on, sensing Kevin's obvious relief that I had deigned to speak, 'there *is* a but. It's a question of velocity' – I had no idea what was coming next – 'because . . . well, there's no time for human judgement anymore. You see a chance, you blink and it's gone. We are entering the age of decentralized, online decision-making, with the decisions being made by millions – and potentially *hundreds* of millions – of individual investors all around the world, people who have the ability to shift huge amounts of money around in less time

131

than it takes to sneeze, but without consulting each other. So, understanding doesn't come into it – or, if it does, it's not understanding how companies work, it's understanding how mass psychology works.'

Pierce waved a hand through the air. 'What – you think *you* can tell *me* why the markets boom or crash? Why today, let's say? And not tomorrow, not yesterday?'

'No, I can't. But these *are* legitimate questions. Why should data cluster in predictable patterns? Why should there *be* a structure to the financial markets?' I paused, waiting for someone to say something, but when no one did I went on, 'because the markets are the product of human activity, and humans follow trends – it's that simple.'

Kevin had gone pale by this stage.

'And of course the trends are usually the same . . . *one*, aversion to risk, and *two*, follow the herd.'

'*Pah*,' said Pierce.

But he left it at that. He muttered something to Van Loon that I didn't catch, and then looked at his watch. Kevin remained motionless, staring down at the carpet, almost in despair now. *Is that it*, he seemed to be thinking, *human fucking nature? How am I supposed to turn* that *to my advantage?*

What *I* was feeling, on the other hand, was acute embarrassment. I hadn't wanted to say anything in the first place, but I could hardly have ignored Van Loon's invitation to contribute. So what happens? I speak and end up being a patronizing asshole. *Understanding doesn't come into it?* Where did *I* get off lecturing two billionaires about how to make money?

After a couple of minutes, in any case, Frank Pierce muttered his excuses and left without saying goodbye to either Kevin or myself.

Van Loon then seemed happy enough to let the conversation drift on for a while. We discussed Mexico and the probable effects the government's apparently irrational stance was going to have on the markets. At one point, still fairly agitated, I caught myself reeling off a comparative list of per capita GDP figures for 1960 and 1995, stuff I must have read somewhere, but Van Loon cut me short and more or less implied that I was being shrill. He also contradicted a few things I said and was clearly right in each case to do so. I saw him looking at me once or twice, too – strangely – as if he were on the point of calling security over to have me ejected from the building.

But then, a bit later, when Kevin had gone to the bathroom, Van Loon turned to me and said, 'I think it's time we got rid of this clown.' He indicated back to where the bathrooms were, and shrugged his shoulders. 'Kevin's a great guy, don't misunderstand me. He's an excellent negotiator. But sometimes. *Jesus.*'

Van Loon looked at me, seeking confirmation that I agreed with him.

I half smiled, unsure of how to react.

So here it came again, that *thing*, that anxious, needy response I'd somehow triggered in all of the others – in Paul Baxter and Artie Meltzer and Kevin Doyle.

'Come on, Eddie, drink up. I live five blocks from here. We're going back to my place for dinner.'

As the three of us were walking out of the Orpheus Room, I was vaguely aware that no one had paid the check or signed anything or even nodded to anyone. But then something occurred to me. Carl Van Loon *owned* the Orpheus Room, in fact owned the entire building – an anonymous steel-and-glass tube on Fifty-fourth between Park and Lexington. I remembered reading about it when the place had first opened a few years before.

Out on the street, Van Loon summarily dismissed Kevin by telling him that he'd see him in the morning. Kevin hesitated, but then said, 'Sure, Carl. See you in the morning.'

We made eye contact for a second but both of us pulled away in embarrassment. Then Kevin was gone and Van Loon and I were walking along Fifty-fourth Street towards Park Avenue. He hadn't had a limousine waiting after all, and then I remembered reading something else, an article in a magazine about how Van Loon often made a big thing of walking – and especially walking in his 'quarter', as though that somehow meant he was a man of the people.

We got to his building on Park Avenue. The brief trip from the lobby up to his apartment was indeed just that, a trip, with all of the elements in place: the uniformed doorman, the swirling turquoise marble, the mahogany panels, the brass radiator-grills. I was surprised by how small the elevator-car was, but its interior was very plush and intimate, and I imagined that such a combination could give the experience of being in it, and the accompanying sensation of motion – if you were with the right person – a certain erotic charge. It seemed to me that rich people didn't think up things like this, and then decide to have them – things like this, little serendipitous accidents of luxury, just *happened* if you happened to have money.

The apartment was on the fourth floor, but the first thing that caught your attention as you stepped into the main hall was a marble staircase sweeping majestically up to what had to be the fifth floor. The ceilings were very high, and decorated with elaborate plaster-work, and there were friezes around the edges which took your eyes gradually downwards to the large, gilt-framed paintings on the walls.

If the elevator-car was the confessional box, the apartment itself was the whole cathedral.

Van Loon led me across the hallway and into what he called 'the library', which is exactly what it was – a dark, book-lined room with Persian rugs, an enormous marble fire-place and several red leather couches. There were also lots of expensive-looking 'pieces' of fine French furniture about the place – walnut tables you wouldn't ever put anything on and delicate little chairs you wouldn't ever sit in.

'Hi, Daddy.'

Van Loon looked around, slightly puzzled. He obviously hadn't expected anybody to be in here. On the far side of the room, barely visible against a wall of leather-bound books, there was a young woman holding open a large volume in her two hands.

'*Oh,*' Van Loon said, and then cleared his throat. 'Say *hello* to Mr Spinola, darling.'

'Hello Mr Spinola, darling.'

The voice was quiet but assured.

Van Loon clicked his tongue in disapproval.

'*Ginny.*'

I felt like saying to Van Loon, *That's OK, I don't mind your daughter calling me 'darling'. In fact, I kind of like it.*

My second erotic charge of the evening had come from Virginia Van Loon, Carl's nineteen-year-old daughter. In her younger and more vulnerable years, 'Ginny' had spent quite a bit of time on the front pages of the daily tabloids for substance abuse and poor taste in boyfriends. She was Van Loon's only child by his second wife, and had quickly been brought to heel by threats of disinheritance. Or so the story had gone.

'Look, Ginny,' Van Loon said, 'I've got to go and get something from my office, so I want you to entertain Mr Spinola here while I'm gone, OK?'

'Of course, Daddy.'

Van Loon turned to me and said, 'There are some files I want you to have a look at.'

I nodded at him, not having a clue what he was talking about. Then he disappeared and I was left standing there, peering across the dimness of the room at his daughter.

'What are you reading?' I said, trying not to remember the last time I'd asked someone that question.

'Not *reading* exactly, I'm looking something up in one of these books Daddy bought by the yard when he moved in here.'

I edged over to the centre of the room in order to be able to see her more clearly. She had short, spiky blonde hair and was wearing trainers, jeans and a pink sleeveless top that left her midriff exposed. She'd had her belly-button pierced and was sporting a tiny gold hoop that glistened occasionally in the light as she moved.

'What are you looking up?'

She leant back against the bookcase with studied abandon, but the effect was spoilt somewhat by the fact that she was struggling to keep the enormous tome open, and balanced, in her hands.

'The etymology of the word *ferocious*.'

'I see.'

'Yeah, my mother's just told me that I have a ferocious temper, and I *do* – so, I don't know, to cool down I thought I'd come in here and check out this dictionary of etymology.' She hiked the book up for a second, as though displaying it as an exhibit in a court room. 'It's a strange word, don't you think? *Ferocious*.'

'Have you found it yet?' I nodded at the dictionary.

'No, I got distracted by *feckless*.'

'*Ferocious* literally means "wild-eyed",' I said, moving around the biggest of the red leather couches in order to get even closer to her. 'It comes from a combination of the Latin word *ferus*, which means "fierce" or "wild", and the particle *oc*-, which means "looking" or "appearing".'

Ginny Van Loon stared at me for a second and then slammed the book closed with a loud *thwack*.

'Not bad, Mr Spinola, not bad,' she said, trying to suppress a grin. Then, as she struggled to get the dictionary back into its place on the shelf behind her, she said, 'You're not one of Daddy's business guys, are you?'

I thought about this for a second before answering. 'I don't know. Maybe I am. We'll see.'

She turned around again to face me and in the brief silence that followed I was aware of her eyeing me up and down. I became uncomfortable all of a sudden and wished that I'd gotten around to buying another suit. I'd been wearing this one every day for quite some time now and had begun to feel a bit self-conscious in it.

'Yeah, but you're not one of his *regular* guys?' She paused. 'And you don't . . .'

'What?'

'You don't look too comfortable . . . dressed like that.'

I looked down at my suit and tried to think of something to say about it. I couldn't.

'So what do you do for Daddy? What *service* do you provide?'

'Who says I provide a service?'

'Carl Van Loon doesn't have friends, Mr Spinola, he has people who do things for him. What do *you* do?'

None of this – strangely enough – came across as snotty or obnoxious. For a girl of nineteen, she was breathtakingly self-possessed, and I felt compelled simply to tell her the truth.

'I'm a stock-market trader, and I've been very successful recently.

So I'm here – I think – to provide your father with some . . . *advice*.'

She raised her eyebrows, opened her arms and did a little curtsey, as if to say *voilá*.

I smiled.

She reverted to leaning back against the bookcase behind her, and said, 'I don't like the stock market.'

'Why's that?'

'Because it's so profoundly *un*interesting a thing to have taken over so many people's lives.'

I raised *my* eyebrows.

'I mean, people don't have drug-dealers any more, or psychoanalysts – they have *brokers*. At least with getting high or being in analysis, it was about *you* – *you* were the subject, to be mangled or untangled or whatever – but playing the markets is like surrendering yourself to this vast, impersonal *system*. It just generates and then feeds off . . . *greed* . . .'

'I—'

'. . . and it's not as if it's your own individual greed either, it's the same greed as everyone else's. You ever been to Vegas, Mr Spinola? Ever seen those big rooms with the rows and rows of slot machines? *Acres* of them? I think the stock market today is like that – all these sad, desperate people planted in front of machines just *dreaming* of the big score they're going to make.'

'Surely that's easy for you to say.'

'Maybe so, but it doesn't make it any less true.'

As I was trying to formulate an answer to this, the door opened behind me and Van Loon came back into the room.

'Well, Eddie, did she keep you entertained?'

He walked briskly over to a coffee table in front of one of the couches and threw a thick folder of papers on to it.

'Yes,' I said, and immediately turned back to look at her. I tried to think of something to say. 'So, what are you doing, I mean . . . these days?'

'These days.' She smiled. 'Very diplomatic. Well, *these* days I suppose I'm a . . . recovering celebrity?'

'OK, sweetheart,' Van Loon said, 'enough. Skedaddle. We've got business to do here.'

'Skedaddle?' Ginny said, raising her eyebrows at me interrogatively. 'Now there's a word.'

'Hhmm,' I said, pantomiming deep thought, 'I would say that the word skedaddle is very probably . . . of unknown origin.'

She considered this for a moment and then, gliding past me on her way over towards the door, whispered loudly, 'A bit like yourself, Mr Spinola . . . darling.'

'*Ginny.*'

She glanced back at me, ignoring her father, and was gone.

Shaking his head in exasperation, Van Loon looked over at the library door for a moment to make sure that his daughter had closed it properly. He picked up the folder again from the coffee table and said he was going to be straight with me. He had heard about my circus tricks down at Lafayette and wasn't particularly impressed, but now that he'd had the chance to meet me in person, and talk, he was prepared to admit that he was a little more curious.

He handed me the folder.

'I want your opinion on these, Eddie. Take the folder home with you, have a look through the files, take your time. Tell me if you think any of the stocks you see there look interesting.'

I flicked through the folder as he spoke and saw long sections of dense type, as well as endless pages of tables and charts and graphs.

'Needless to say, all of this stuff is strictly confidential.'

I nodded *of course*.

He nodded back, and then said, 'Can I offer you something to drink? The housekeeper's not here I'm afraid – and Gabby's . . . in a bad mood – so dinner's a non-starter.' He paused, as though trying to think of a way out of this dilemma, but quickly gave up. 'Fuck it,' he said, 'I had a big lunch.' Then he looked at me, obviously expecting an answer to his original question.

'Scotch would be fine.'

'Sure.'

Van Loon went over to a drinks cabinet in the corner of the room and as he poured two glasses of single malt Scotch whisky, he spoke back at me, over his shoulder.

'I don't know who you are, Eddie, or what you're game is, but I'm sure of one thing, you don't work in this business. I know all the moves, and so far you don't seem to know any – but the thing is, I *like* that. You see, I deal with business graduates every day of the week, and I don't know what it is – they've all got this *look*, this business-school *look*. It's like they're cocky and terrified at the same time, and I'm sick of it.' He paused. 'What I'm saying is this, I don't care what your background is, or that maybe the nearest you've ever come to an investment bank is the business section of the *New York Times*. What *matters*' – he turned around with a glass in each hand, and used one of them to indicate his belly – 'is that you've got a fire in here, and if you're smart on top of that, then nothing can stand in your way.'

He walked over and handed me one of the glasses of Scotch. I put the folder down on to the couch and took the glass from him. He held his up. Then a phone rang somewhere in the room.

'*Shit.*'

Van Loon put his glass down on the coffee table and went back in the direction he'd just come from. The phone was on an antique writing desk beside the drinks cabinet. He picked it up and said, 'Yeah?' There was a silence and then he said, 'Yeah. Good. Yeah. Yeah. Put him through.'

He covered the phone with his hand, turned to me and said, 'I've got to take this call, Eddie. But sit down. Have your drink.'

I smiled briefly in acknowledgement.

'I won't be long.'

As Van Loon turned away again, and receded into a low-level murmur, I took a sip from the whisky and sat down on the couch. I was glad of the interruption, but couldn't figure out why – at least not for a few seconds. Then it occurred to me: I wanted time to think about Ginny Van Loon and her little rant about the stock market and how it had reminded me so much of the kind of thing Melissa might have said. It seemed to me that despite obvious differences between them, the two women shared something – a similar, steely intelligence, as well as a style of delivery modelled on the heat-seeking missile. By referring to her father at one point as 'Carl Van Loon', for instance, but at all other times as 'Daddy', Ginny had not only displayed a sophisticated sense of detachment, she had also made *him* seem silly and vain and isolated. Which – by extension – was precisely how I now felt, too.

I told myself that Ginny's comments could be dismissed as the cheap and easy nihilism of an overeducated teenager, but if that was the case, why was I so bothered by them?

I took a tiny plastic sachet from the inside pocket of my jacket, opened it and tapped a tablet out on to the palm of my hand. Making sure that Van Loon was facing away from me, I popped the tablet into my mouth and washed it down with a large gulp of whisky.

Then I picked up the folder, opened it at the first page and started reading.

The files contained background information on a series of small-to-medium sized businesses, from retail chains to software houses to aerospace and biotech companies. The material was dense and wide-ranging and included profiles of all the CEOs, as well as of other key personnel. There was technical analysis of price movements going back over a five-year period, and I found myself reading about peaks, troughs, points of resistance – stuff that a few weeks earlier would have been rarefied, incomprehensible fuzz, Mogadon for the eyes.

But just what did Carl Van Loon want? Did he want me to state the obvious, to point out that the Texas-based data-storage firm, Laraby, for example, whose stock had increased *twenty thousand* per cent over the last five years, was a good long-term investment? Or that the British retail chain, Watson's – which had just recorded its worst ever losses, and whose CEO, Sir Colin Bird, had presided over similar losses at a venerable Scottish insurance company, Islay Mutual – was not? Was Van Loon seriously looking to me, a freelance copy-writer, for recommendations about what stocks he should buy or sell? Again, I thought, *hardly* – but if that wasn't the case, then what did he want?

After about fifteen minutes, Van Loon covered the phone again with his hand and said, 'Sorry this is taking so long, Eddie, but it's important.'

I shook my head, indicating that he shouldn't be concerned, and then held up the folder as evidence that I was happily occupied. He went back to his low-level murmuring and I went back to the files.

The more I read, the simpler, and more simplistic, the whole thing seemed. He was testing me. As far as Van Loon was concerned I was a neophyte with a fire in my belly and a lip on me, and as such just might find this amount of concentrated information a little intimidating. He was hardly to know that in my current condition it wasn't even a stretch. In any case, and for something to do, I decided to divide the files into three separate categories – the duds, the obvious high-performers and the ones that weren't instantly categorizable as either.

Another fifteen minutes or so passed before Van Loon finally got off the phone and came over to retrieve his drink. He held it up, as before, and we clinked glasses. I got the impression that he was having a hard time suppressing a broad grin. A part of me wanted to ask him who he'd been on the phone to, but it didn't seem appropriate. Another part of me wanted to ask him an endless series of questions about his daughter, but the moment didn't seem right for that either – not, of course, that it ever would.

He glanced down at the folder beside me.

'So did you get a chance to look through any of that stuff?'

'Yes, Mr Van Loon, I did. It was interesting.'

He knocked back most of his drink in one go, placed the glass on the coffee table and sat down at the other end of the couch.

'Any initial impressions?'

I said yes, cleared my throat and gave him my spiel about eliminating the duds and the high-performers. Then I recited a shortlist I'd drawn up of four or five companies that had real investment potential. I especially recommended that he buy stocks in Janex, a California biotech company, not based on its past performance, but rather on what I described, in a breathless rush, as 'its telling and muscular strategy of pursuing intellectual-property litigation to protect its growing portfolio of patents'. I also recommended that he buy stocks in the French engineering giant BEA, based on the equally telling fact that the company seemed to be shedding everything except its fiber-optics division. I supported what I had to say with relevant data and quotes, including verbatim quotes from the transcripts of a lawsuit involving Janex. Van Loon looked at me in a curious way throughout, and it didn't occur to me until I was coming to the end that a possible reason for this was because I hadn't once referred back to the folder – that I had spoken entirely from memory.

Almost under his breath, and looking at the folder, he said, 'Yeah. Janex . . . BEA. They're the ones.'

I could see him trying to work something out – calculating, eyebrows furrowed, how much of the folder it might be possible to read in the length of time he'd been on the phone. Then he said, 'That's . . . *amazing.*'

He stood up and paced around the room for a bit. It was clear now that he was calculating something else.

'Eddie,' he said eventually, coming to a sudden halt and pointing back at the phone on the antique writing desk, 'that was Hank Atwood I was talking to there. We're having lunch on Thursday. I want you to come along.'

Hank Atwood, the Chairman of MCL-Parnassus, was routinely described as one of the 'architects of the entertainment-industrial complex'.

'*Me?*'

'Yes, Eddie, and what's more, I want you to come and work for me.'

In response to this I asked him the one question that I had promised Kevin I wouldn't ask.

'What's going on with Atwood, Mr Van Loon?'

He held my gaze, took a deep breath, and then said, clearly against his better judgement, 'We're negotiating a takeover deal with Abraxas.' He paused. '*By* Abraxas.'

Abraxas was the country's second-largest Internet service provider. The three-year-old company had a market capitalization of $114 billion, scant profits to date, and – of course – attitude to burn. Compared to the venerable MCL-Parnassus, which had assets stretching back nearly sixty years, Abraxas was a mewling infant.

I said, barely able to contain my disbelief, 'Abraxas buying out *MCL*?'

He nodded, but only just.

The kaleidoscope of possibilities opened up before me.

'We're mediating the deal,' he said, 'helping them to structure it, to engineer the financials, that kind of thing.' He paused. 'No one knows about this, Eddie. People are aware that I'm talking to Hank Atwood, but no one knows why. If this got out it could have a significant impact on the markets, but it'd also most likely kill the deal . . . so . . .'

He looked straight at me and let a shrug of his shoulders finish the thought.

I held up my hands, palms out. 'Don't worry, I'm not talking to *any*one about this.'

'And you realize that if you *traded* in either of these stocks – tomorrow morning down at Lafayette, say – you'd be contravening the rules as set down by the Securities and Exchange Commission . . .'

I nodded.

'. . . and could go to prison?'

'Look, *Carl*,' I said, deciding to use his first name, '. . . you can *trust* me.'

'I know that, Eddie,' he said, with a hint of emotion in his voice, 'I know that.' He took a moment to compose himself and then went on. 'Look, it's a very complex process, and right now we're at a crucial stage. I wouldn't say we're blocked exactly, but . . . we need someone to take a fresh look at it.'

I felt the rate of my heart-beat increase.

'I've got an army of MBAs working for me down on Forty-eighth Street, Eddie, but the problem is *I know how they think*. I know what they're going to tell me before they even open their mouths. I need someone like you. Someone who's quick and isn't going to bullshit me.'

I couldn't believe this, and had a sudden flash of how incongruous it all seemed – Carl Van Loon needing someone like me?

'I'm offering you a real chance here, Eddie, and I don't care . . . I don't care *who* you are . . . because I have a *feeling* about this.'

He reached down, picked up his glass from the coffee table and drained what was left in it.

'That's how I've *always* operated.'

Then he allowed the grin to break though.

'This is going to be the biggest merger in American corporate history.'

Fighting off a slight queasiness, I grinned back.

He held up his hands. 'So . . . Mr Spinola, what do you say?'

I struggled to think of something, but I was still in shock.

'Look, maybe you need a little time to think about it – which is OK.'

Van Loon then reached down to the coffee table, took my glass in his other hand and as he walked over to the drinks cabinet to get refills, I felt the strong pull of his enthusiasm – and the ineluctable pull of an unlooked-for destiny – and knew that I had no choice but to accept.

[13]

I LEFT ABOUT AN HOUR LATER. Disappointingly, there was no sign of Ginny in the hallway as Van Loon ushered me out of the apartment, but by that point I was in such a state of euphoria that if I'd had to talk to her – or, for that matter, to anyone else – I probably wouldn't have made much sense.

It was a cool evening, and as I strolled down Park Avenue I cast my mind back over the previous few weeks. It had been an extraordinary time in my life. I wasn't hindered by anything or inhibited in any way, and not since my early twenties had I been able to look to the future with such energy, and – perhaps more significantly – *without* that debilitating dread of the ticking clock. With MDT-48, the future was no longer an accusation or a threat, no longer a precious resource that was running out. I could pack in so many things between now and the end of next week, say, that it actually felt as if the end of next week might never come.

At Fifty-seventh Street, waiting for a 'Don't Walk' sign to change, a strong sense of gratitude for all of this welled up inside of me – though gratitude directed towards whom in particular I didn't know. It was accompanied by an acute sense of exhilaration, and was quite physical, almost like a form of arousal. But then moments later, when I was half-way across Fifty-seventh Street, something weird happened – all of a sudden these feelings surged in intensity and I was overcome with dizziness. I reached out for something to lean against, but there wasn't anything there and I had to stumble forward until I got to a wall on the other side of the street.

Several people skirted around me.

145

I closed my eyes and tried to catch my breath, but when I opened them again a few seconds later – or what seemed like a few seconds later – I jolted back in fright. Looking around me, at the buildings and at the traffic, I realized that I wasn't on Fifty-seventh Street any more. I was a block further down. I was on the corner of *Fifty-sixth* Street.

It was the same thing that had happened the previous evening in my apartment. I had moved, but without being conscious of it, without registering that I had moved. It was as if I'd suffered a minor blackout – as if I'd trip-switched forward in some way, or *click-clicked* forward like on a faulty CD.

The previous evening was because of not having eaten – I'd been busy, distracted, food had taken a back seat. At least, that was the assumption, the rationalization.

Of course, I hadn't eaten *since* then either, so maybe that *was* it. A little shaken, but not wishing to dwell too much on what had happened, I walked slowly along Fifty-sixth Street towards Lexington Avenue in search of a restaurant.

I found a diner on Forty-fifth Street and took a booth by the window.

'C'n I get you, hon?'

I ordered a Porterhouse steak, rare, french fries and a side salad.

'To drink?'

Coffee.

The place wasn't busy. There was a guy at the counter, and a couple in the next booth up, and an old lady putting on lipstick in the next one up from that.

When the coffee arrived, I took a few sips and tried to relax. Then I decided to concentrate on the meeting I'd just had with Van Loon. I found myself reacting to it in two different ways.

On the one hand, I was beginning to feel a little nervous about taking up his job offer – which involved a nominal starting salary and some stock options, with whatever real money I made being on commissions. These would be from any successful deals that I recommended, brokered, negotiated, or, in the gnarled syntax befitting my current thought processes, participated in any phase of the negotiating *of* – like the MCL–Abraxas deal, for instance. But on what basis, I asked myself, had Van Loon been able to offer me such a deal? On the entirely spurious basis, perhaps, that I even had the slightest notion of how to 'structure' or 'engineer the financials' of a big corporate deal? Hardly. Van Loon had seemed to understand pretty unequivocally that I was an impostor, so he couldn't be expecting that much from me. But what, precisely, *would* he be expecting? And would I be able to deliver?

The waitress arrived over with my steak and fries.

'Njoy your meal.'

'Thanks.'

Then – on the other hand – I had this clear vision in my mind of what a pushover Hank Atwood was going to be. I had read articles about him that used woolly terms such as 'vision', 'commitment', 'driven', and it just seemed to me that whatever the nature of that *thing* I had triggered in the others really was – I would have no difficulty in triggering the same thing in him. This, in turn, of course, would place me in a potentially very powerful position – because as the new CEO of MCL–Abraxas, Hank Atwood would not only have the ear of the President and of other world leaders, he would *be* a world leader himself. The military superpower was a thing of the past, a dinosaur, and the only structure that counted in the world today was the 'hyperpower', the digitalized, globalized English-language based entertainment culture that controlled the hearts, minds and disposable incomes of successive generations of 18 to 24-year-olds – and Hank Atwood, who I would shortly be making friends with, was about to be placed at the apex of that structure.

But then all of a sudden, without warning or reason, I'd swing back to thinking that Carl Van Loon was surely going to come to his senses and at the very least withdraw the job offer.

And where would that leave me?

The waitress approached my booth again and held up the coffee pot.

I nodded and she refilled my cup.

'What's the matter, hon? You don't like your steak?'

I glanced down at my plate. I'd barely touched the food.

'No, no, it's fine,' I said, looking up at her. She was a big woman in her forties, with big eyes and big hair. 'I'm a just little concerned about the future, that's all.'

'*The future?*' she repeated, laughing out loud and walking away with the coffee pot held up in mid-air. 'Get in line, honey, get in line.'

When I got home to the apartment, the little red light was flashing on my answering machine. I reached down and flicked the 'play' button and waited. There were seven messages – which was about five or six more than I had ever received on it before at any one time.

I sat on the edge of the couch and stared at the machine.

Click.

Beeep.

'Eddie, this is Jay. I just wanted to let you know – and I hope you won't be pissed at me – but I was talking to a journalist from the *Post* this evening, and I . . . I gave her your number. She'd heard about you and wanted to do a story, so . . . I'm sorry, I should have checked with you first, but . . . anyway . . . see you tomorrow.'

Click.

Beeep.

'It's Kevin.' Long pause. 'How was *dinner*? What did you guys *talk* about? Give me a call when you get in.' There was another long pause and then he hung up.

Click.

Beeep.

'Eddie, it's your father. How are you? Any *stock* tips for me? (*Laughter.*) Listen, I'm going on vacation to Florida next month with the Szypulas. Give me a call. I hate these goddamned machines.'

Click.

Beeep.

'Mr Spinola, this is Mary Stern from the *New York Post*. I got your number from Jay Zollo at Lafayette Trading. Erm . . . I'd like to speak with you as soon as possible. Erm . . . I'll try you again later, or in the morning. Thank you.'

Click.

Beeep.

Pause.

'Why you don't call me?' Shit, I'd forgotten about Gennady. '. . . I have some idea for that *thing*, so call me.'

Click.

Beeep.

'It's Kevin again. You're a real jerk, Spinola, do you know that?' His voice was slurred now. 'I mean, who the *fuck* do you think you are, eh? Mike fucking Ovitz? Well, let me tell you something about peop—' There was a muffled sound at that point, like something being knocked over. A barely audible *shhhiit* followed, and suddenly the line went dead.

Click.

Beeep.

'Look – just *fuck* you, OK? *Fuck* you, *fuck* your mother, *fuck* your sister.'

Click.

That was it. End of new messages.

I got up from the couch, went into the bedroom and took off my suit.

Kevin I could do nothing about. He would have to be my first casualty. Jay Zollo, Mary Stern, Gennady and my old man I could deal with in the morning.

I went into the bathroom, turned on the shower and stepped under the jet of hot water. I didn't need these distractions and I certainly didn't want to waste any time thinking about them. After my shower, I put on a pair of boxer-shorts and a T-shirt. Then I sat at my desk, took another MDT pill and started making notes.

In the dimly lit library of his Park Avenue apartment, Van Loon had sketched out the problem for me. The bottom line, predictably enough, was that the principals in the deal couldn't agree on a valuation. MCL stock was currently selling at $26 a share, but they were asking Abraxas for $40 – a 54 per cent premium, which way way above the average for an acquisition of this kind. Van Loon had to find a way of either reducing the MCL asking-price or of justifying it to Abraxas.

He'd said that he would have some material couriered down to my apartment in the morning, relevant paperwork that I really needed to have a look at ahead of Thursday's lunch meeting with Hank Atwood. But I decided that before any 'relevant paperwork' arrived I needed to do some research of my own.

I went online and skimmed through hundreds of pages of material relating to corporate financing. I learned the basics of structuring a takeover deal and examined dozens of case histories. I followed a trail of links throughout the night and at one point even found myself studying advanced, mathematical formulae for determining the value of stock options.

I took a break at 5 a.m. and watched some TV – re-runs of *Star Trek* and *Ironside*.

At around 9 a.m., the courier arrived with the material Van Loon had promised. It was another thick folder, containing annual and quarterly reports, analysts' assessments, internal management accounts and operational plans. I spent the day wading through all of this stuff and by late afternoon felt that I had reached some sort of a plateau. I wanted the lunch with Hank Atwood to be happening *now*, and not in twenty hours' time, but I had probably absorbed as much information as I was going to, so I figured that what I needed at this point was a little R & R.

I tried to get some sleep, but I couldn't settle down – not even enough to doze for a few minutes, and neither could I bring myself to watch any more TV, so I eventually decided to just go and sit on a bar-stool somewhere, and have a couple of drinks, and chill out.

Before leaving the apartment, I forced myself to take a handful of diet-supplement pills and to eat some fruit. I also phoned Jay Zollo and Mary Stern, who I'd been fielding calls from all day. I told a distraught-sounding Jay that I'd been unwell and hadn't felt like going in. I told Mary Stern that I didn't want to talk to her, no matter who the hell she was, and that she was to stop calling me. I didn't phone Gennady, or the old man.

On my way downstairs, I calculated that I hadn't slept in nearly forty hours, and had probably, in any case, only slept a total of six hours in the seventy-two previous to *that*, so although I didn't feel it and didn't look it, I realized that at some level I must have been in a state of complete and utter physical exhaustion.

It was early evening and traffic was heavy, just like on that first evening when I'd come out of the cocktail lounge over on Sixth Avenue. I walked, therefore, rather than taking a cab – floated, in fact – floated through the streets, and with a vague sensation of moving through a kind of virtual-reality environment, a screenscape where colours contrasted sharply and perception of depth was slightly muted. Any time I turned a corner the movements I made seemed jerky and angular and guided, so after about twenty-five minutes, when I found myself lurching sideways all of a sudden and entering a bar in Tribeca, a place called the Congo, it was as though I were entering a new phase of play in some advanced computer game, and one with pretty realistic graphics – there was a long wooden bar to the left, wicker stools, a railed mezzanine at the back and enormous potted plants everywhere that reached right up to the ceiling.

I sat at the bar and ordered a Bombay and tonic.

The place wasn't too crowded, though it would probably be filling up fairly soon. There were some people to my left, two women sitting at stools – but facing away from the bar – and three men standing around them. Two of these were doing the talking, with the others sipping drinks, pulling on cigarettes and listening carefully. The subject of conversation was the NBA and Michael Jordan and the huge revenues he'd generated for the game. I don't know at what point it started again, exactly, that trip-switching forward thing, or *click-clicking* forward like on a faulty CD, but when it did I had no control whatsoever and could only observe, *witness*, each segment and each flash, as though each segment and each flash – as well as the greater, unrevealed whole – were happening to someone else and not to me. The first jump was very abrupt and came as I was reaching out to pick up my drink. I'd just made contact with the cold, moist surface of the glass, when suddenly, without any warning or movement, I found myself on the other side of the group, standing

151

very close to one of the women – a thirtyish brunette in a short green skirt, not excessively slim, distinctive blue eyes . . . my left hand hovering somewhere in the airspace above her right thigh . . .

. . . *and* I was in mid-sentence . . .

'. . . yeah, but don't forget that ESPN was set up in 1979, and with $10 million of seed money from *Getty* Oil for Christ's sake . . .'

'What's that got—'

'It's got *every*thing to do with it. It changed *every*thing. Because of a shrewd business decision college basketball players were suddenly becoming household names *overnight* . . .'

For a split second I was aware that one of the men – a chubby guy in a silk suit – was glaring at me. He was tense and sweaty and his eyes were drawn irresistibly to my left hand – but then . . . *click, click, click* . . . the barman was in front of me, waving his arms around, blocking my view. He looked Irish and had tired eyes that said *pleeease, enough.* Meanwhile, behind him – and only partially visible now – the chubby guy in the silk suit was holding a hand up to his face, trying to stop the flow of blood from his nose . . .

'*Fuck* you, pal . . .'

'Fuck *you* . . .'

The cool evening air touched the hairs on the back of my neck as I staggered away from the barman and out on to the street. The woman in the short green skirt was there too, just inside the door, pushing away someone who was behind her. She said something I didn't catch and then quickly manoeuvred herself around the barman, dodging his arms, but half a second later – inexplicably – she was linking arms with *me* a couple of blocks down the street.

Then we were in a cubicle together, a stall in the bathroom of a nightclub or a bar, and I was pulling away from her, *withdrawing* – her legs spread out against a backdrop of chrome, and white porcelain, and black tiles . . . her green skirt torn and dangling from the toilet seat, her blouse open, beads of sweat glistening between her breasts. As I leant back against the door, hurriedly doing up my trousers, she remained in position, with her eyes closed and head swaying rhythmically from side to side. In the background, there was some kind of pulsating music, as well as the periodic roar of electric hand-dryers and raised voices and manic laughter, and from the next cubicle what sounded like the flicking of lighters followed by sharp, rapid inhalations of smoke . . .

I closed my eyes at that point, but when I opened them a second later I was moving across a crowded dance floor – pushing past people, elbowing them, snarling at them. In another few moments, I was out on the street again, negotiating my way through more crowds and through heavy streams of traffic. Soon after that I seem to remember climbing into the familiar comfort of a yellow cab, sinking into the cheap plastic upholstery of the back seat and gazing out at the tawdry streaks of neon that stretched the city out, pulled it this way and that, like so many strands of multi-coloured chewing-gum. I also remember being acutely aware of my right hand, which was sore, throbbing in fact, from having punched that guy back at the Congo – something, incidentally, I couldn't believe I'd done. At any rate, the next thing I knew I was in the lobby of an Upper West Side restaurant – a place I'd read about called Actium – insinuating, *pushing*, my way into another conversation with another set of complete strangers, this time half a dozen members of some local art-gallery crowd. Posing as a collector, I introduced myself as Thomas Cole. Like before, I perpetually seemed to be in mid-sentence – '. . . and already in eighteen hundred and four the Noble Savage has become the Demonic Indian, it's there in Vanderlyn's *Murder of Jane McCrea*, the dark, rippling musculature, the ogre's raised tomahawk ready to strike at the woman's head . . .' I was probably as surprised by what I was saying as anyone else, but I couldn't press *pause*, couldn't do anything except endure it, and *watch*. Then it was *click, click, click* again and all of a sudden we were sitting around a table together having dinner.

To my left was an intense guy with a salt-and-pepper beard wearing a carefully crumpled linen jacket, probably an art critic, and to my right was a Bernice-bobs-her-hair type of woman with bony bits sticking out of her every time she moved. Directly opposite me was a heavy Latino guy in a suit who was talking non-stop. He spoke in English, but it was *norteamericano* this and *norteamericano* that, and in a fairly disparaging tone. I realized after a few moments that

153

the man I was looking at was Rodolfo Alvarez, the celebrated Mexican painter who'd recently moved to Manhattan and undertaken to recreate, from notebooks, the destroyed Diego Rivera mural originally destined for the lobby of the RCA Building in 1933.

Man at the Crossroads Looking with Hope and High Vision to the Choosing of a Better Future.

The dark-haired and very beautiful woman in a black dress, sitting to his left, was the sultry Donatella, his wife.

I'd read a profile of them in *Vanity Fair*.

How the *fuck* had I ended up with these people?

'That's ironic,' the salt-and-pepper guy was saying to someone, 'the *choosing* of a better future.'

'What's so ironic about that?' I heard myself saying, and then sighing impatiently. 'If *you* don't choose your future, who the hell's going to do it for you?'

'Well,' said Donatella Alvarez, smiling across the table – and smiling directly at *me* – 'that is the North American way, isn't it, Mr Cole?'

'I beg your pardon?' I said, a little taken aback.

'Time,' she said calmly. 'For you it is in a straight line. You look *back* at the past, and can disregard it if you so wish. You look *towards* the future . . . and, if you so wish, can *choose* it to be a better future. You can choose to *become* perfect . . .'

She was still smiling, and all I could say was, 'So?'

'For us, in Mexico,' she said very deliberately, as though explaining something to a small child, 'the past and the present and the future . . . *they co-exist.*'

I kept staring at her, but in the next moment she seemed to be in the middle of a sentence to someone else.

From this point on things got more and more fragmented, disjointed – jagged. Most of it I can't remember at all – apart from a few strong sense impressions, the weird colour and texture of mussels in white wine, for instance . . . swirls of dense cigar smoke, thick, glistening daubs of colour. I seem to recall seeing hundreds of tubes and brushes laid out in lines on a wooden floor, and dozens of canvases, some rolled, others framed and stacked.

Soon, painted figures, lurid and bulging, were mingling with real people in a terrifying kaleidoscope, and I found myself reaching out for something to lean against, but quickly focusing instead – across a crowded loft space – on the deep, earthy pools that were the eyes of Donatella Alvarez . . .

Next, and in what seemed like a flash, I was walking down an empty corridor in a hotel . . . having been in a room, quite definitely *been* in a room, but with no recollection of whose room, or of what had happened in that room, or of how I'd wound up there in the first place. Then, another flash and I wasn't in a hotel corridor any more but walking across the Brooklyn Bridge, quickly, and in time to something – in time, I soon realized, to the suspension cables flickering in geometric patterns against the pale blue of the early morning sky.

I stopped and turned around.

I looked back at the familiar postcard view of downtown Manhattan, aware now that I couldn't properly account for the last eight hours of my life – but aware, too, that I was fully conscious again, and alert and cold and *sore* all over. I quickly decided that whatever reasons I'd had for walking to Brooklyn had surely atrophied by now, seized up, been lost to some fossilized energy configuration that could never be re-animated. So I headed back over the bridge towards downtown, and walked – *limped*, as it turned out – all the way home to my apartment on Tenth Street.

[14]

I SAY *LIMPED*, because I had obviously sprained my left ankle at some point during the night. And when I was getting undressed to take a shower, I saw that there was extensive bruising on my body. This explained the soreness – or partly explained it – but in addition to these leaden blue patches on my chest and ribs, there was something else . . . something that looked curiously like a cigarette burn on my right forearm. I ran a finger over the small reddish mark, pressed it, *winced*, then circled it slowly – and as I did so, I felt a deep sense of unease, an incipient terror, tightening its grip around my solar plexus.

But I resisted, because I didn't want to think about this – didn't want to think about what may or may not have gone on in some hotel room, didn't want to think about *any* of it. I had a meeting with Carl Van Loon and Hank Atwood in a few hours' time and what I needed more than anything else – certainly more than I needed a debilitating panic attack – was to get myself organized.

And focused.

So I took two more pills, shaved, got dressed and started going over the notes I'd made the previous day.

The arrangement with Van Loon was that I'd show up at his office on Forty-eighth Street at around 10 a.m. We'd have a talk about the situation, compare notes and maybe devise a provisional gameplan. Then we'd go to meet Hank Atwood for lunch.

In the cab on the way to Forty-eighth Street, I tried to concentrate on the intricacies of corporate financing, but I kept being appalled anew at what had happened and at the degree of recklessness I was clearly capable of.

An eight-hour *blackout*?

Might that not just have constituted a warning sign?

But then I remembered getting sick in a bathroom once, years ago – actually throwing up *blood* into the washbasin – and immediately afterwards going back out to the living-room, to the little pile of product in the centre of the table . . . and to the cigarettes and to the vodka and to the elastic, malleable, untrackable conversation . . .

And then – twenty minutes later – having it happen again.

And again.

So . . . obviously not.

I stopped the cab at Forty-seventh Street and walked the remaining block to the Van Loon Building. By the time I got into the lobby, I had just about managed to suppress my limp. I was greeted by Van Loon's personal assistant and taken up to a large suite of offices on the sixty-second floor. I noticed that in the general design of the place – in the corridors and in the enormous reception area – there was an impeccable though slightly bewildering blend of the traditional and the modern, the stuffy and the streamlined – a sumptuous, seamless fusion of mahogany, ebony, marble, steel, chrome and glass. This made the company seem, at once, like an august, venerable institution *and* a pared-down, front-line operation – staffed mostly, I have to say, by guys about fifteen years my junior. Nevertheless, I had a keen sense that nothing here was beyond me, that it was all for the taking, that the corporate structure of a place like this was delicate and gossamer-thin and would yield to the slightest pressure.

But as I sat down in the reception area, beneath a huge Van Loon & Associates company logo, my mood shifted again, lurched a little closer to the edge, and I was assailed by queasiness and doubt.

How had I ended up here?

How had I come to be working for a private investment bank?

Why was I wearing a *suit*?

Who was I?

I'm not sure I know the answers to these questions even now. In fact, a few moments ago – in the bathroom of the Northview Motor

Lodge – staring into the mugshot-sized mirror above the stained wash-basin, with the hum and occasional rattle of the ice-machine outside penetrating the walls, and my skull, I struggled to see even a trace of the individual that had begun to form and crystallize out of that mass of chemically-induced impulses and counter-impulses, out of that irresistible surge of busyness. I searched, too, in the lines of my face for any indications of the individual I might eventually have become – a big-time player, a destroyer, a spiritual descendant of Jay Gould – but all there was in my reflection, all I recognized, with no real indications of anything the future might have held, was *me* . . . the familiar face of a thousand shaves.

I waited in the reception area for nearly half an hour, staring at what I took to be an original Goya on a wall opposite where I was sitting. The receptionist was extremely friendly and smiled over at me every now and again. When Van Loon finally arrived, he strolled across reception with a broad smile on *his* face. He slapped me on the back and ushered me into his office, which was about half the size of Rhode Island.

'Sorry for the delay, Eddie, but I've been overseas.'

Flicking through some documents on his desk, he then explained that he'd flown in direct from Tokyo on his new Gulfstream V.

'You've been to Tokyo and back since *Tuesday evening*?' I asked.

He nodded and said that having waited sixteen months to *get* the new jet, he'd wanted to make sure that it was worth its not inconsiderable price tag of $37m and change. His delay in arriving this morning, he added after a pause, had had nothing to do with the jet, but was rather the fault of gridlocked Manhattan traffic. It seemed to matter to him that I understood this.

I nodded, therefore, to show him that I did.

'So, Eddie,' he said, sitting down behind the desk, and indicating that I should sit down too, 'did you have a chance to look at those files?'

'Yes, of course.'

'And?'

'They were interesting.'

'*And?*'

'I don't think you should really have much difficulty justifying the price that MCL is asking,' I began, shifting in the seat, aware suddenly of how tired I was.

'Why not?'

'Because there are some very significant options embedded in this deal, strategic stuff that isn't evident in the existing numbers.'

'Such as?'

'Well, the biggest option value lies in the build-out of a broadband infrastructure, which is something Abraxas really needs . . .'

'Why?'

'To defend itself against aggressive competition – some other portal that might be in a position to develop faster downloads, streaming video, that kind of thing.'

As I spoke – and through the almost hallucinatory quality of my exhaustion – I was becoming conscious of how large a gap there was between information and knowledge, between the huge amount of data I'd absorbed in the last forty-eight hours and the arrangement of that data into a coherent argument.

'The thing is,' I went on, 'building-out broadband is a big cash drain and highly risky, but since Abraxas has a leading portal brand already, all it really needs is a credible *threat* to develop its own broadband.'

Van Loon nodded his head slowly at this.

'So, by buying MCL, Abraxas *gets* that credibility, without actually having to complete the build-out, at least not straightaway.'

'How's that?'

'MCL owns Cableplex, yeah? That puts them directly into twenty-five million homes, so even though they might need to upgrade their systems they're ahead of the game. Meanwhile, Abraxas can slow down MCL's spend on the broadband build-out, thereby delaying any negative cashflow, but retaining the option to develop it later should they need to . . .' I was having a sensation I'd had a couple of times before on MDT – one of walking on a verbal tightrope, of speaking to someone and clearly making sense, but at the same time *of having no idea at all what I was talking about.* '. . . and remember, Carl, the ability to delay an investment decision like that can have enormous value.'

'But it still remains risky, doesn't it? I mean, developing this broad-band thing? Regardless of whether you do it now or later?'

'Sure, but the new company that comes out of this deal probably won't have to make the investment in any case, because I think they'd actually be better off negotiating a deal with another broadband player, which would have the added advantage of reducing potential overcapacity in the industry.'

Van Loon smiled.

'That's pretty fucking good, Eddie.'

I smiled too.

'Yeah, I think it works. It's basically a win-win situation. And there are other options as well, of course.'

I could see Van Loon looking at me and wondering. He was obviously unsure of what to ask me next . . . in case it all fell apart and I somehow revealed myself to be an idiot. But he eventually asked me the only question that made any sense in the circumstances.

'How do the numbers add up?'

I reached out and took a legal pad from his desk, and a pen from my inside jacket pocket. I leant forward and started writing. After I'd gotten a few lines down on the page, I said, 'I've used the Black–Scholes pricing model to show how the option value varies as a percentage of the underlying investment . . .' – I stopped, flipped over the page and continued writing at the top of the next one – '. . . and I've done it over a range of risk profiles and time-frames.'

I wrote furiously for the next fifteen minutes or so, copying from memory the various mathematical formulae I'd used the previous day to illustrate my position.

'As you can see here,' I said, when I'd finished, pointing to the appropriate formulae with my pen, 'the value of the broadband option together with these other options easily adds an extra $10 a share in value to the MCL stock.'

Van Loon smiled again.

Then he said, 'This is just great work, Eddie. I don't know what to say. This is just great. Hank's going to love this.'

* * *

At about twelve-fifteen, after we'd gone through all the figures carefully, we wrapped up and left the office. Van Loon had booked a table for us at the Four Seasons. We made our way over towards Park Avenue and then strolled the four blocks uptown to the Seagram Building.

I had floated along during most of the morning in an icy and exhausted state of awareness – on automatic pilot in a way – but when I arrived with Van Loon at the Fifty-second Street entrance to the Four Seasons restaurant, and passed through the lobby, and saw the Miró tapestries and the leather seats designed by Mies van der Rohe himself, I began to feel energized again. More than being able to speak Italian, or read half a dozen books in a night, or even second-guess the markets, more than the fact that I had just outlined the financial structure for a huge corporate merger, it was being *here*, at the base of the Seagram Building, the holy of architectural holies, that brought the unreality of my entire situation home to me – because under normal circumstances I would never have found myself in a place like this, would never have found myself swanning into the legendary Grill Room, with its suspended bronze rods and French walnut panelling, would never have found myself gliding past tables occupied by ambassadors and cardinals and corporation presidents and entertainment lawyers and network anchormen.

And yet, strange as it seemed, here I was . . . happy to be swanning and gliding . . .

The *maître d'* led us to one of the tables under the balcony, and just as we'd settled down and ordered some drinks Van Loon's cellphone went off. He answered it with a barely audible grunt, listened for a couple of moments and then flicked it closed. As he was putting it away, he looked at me with a thin, slightly nervous smile.

'Hank's running a little late,' he said.

'But he's coming, right?'

'Yes.'

Van Loon fiddled with his napkin for a moment, and then said, 'Listen, Eddie, there's something I've been meaning to ask you about.'

I swallowed, unsure of what was coming next.

'You know that we have a small trading floor at Van Loon & Associates?'

I shook my head.

'Well, we have, and I was thinking – that run of trades you made at Lafayette?'

'Yeah?'

'That was pretty impressive, you know.'

A waiter arrived over with our drinks.

'I didn't really think so when Kevin told me about it at first, but I've looked into it since, and well . . .' – he held my gaze as the waiter laid out two glasses on the table, plus two half-bottles of mineral water, a Tom Collins and a vodka Martini – '. . . you certainly seem to know what you're doing.'

I took a sip from the Martini.

Still staring at me, Van Loon added, 'And how to pick them.'

I could see that he was burning to ask me how I'd done it. He kept shifting in his seat and glancing directly at me, unsure of what he had in his possession, tantalized at the prospect that maybe I did have some system after all, and that the Holy Grail was right here in the Four Seasons restaurant, sitting at *his* table. He was tantalized, and at the same time a little apprehensive, but he held off, skirted around the issue, tried to act as if the whole thing wasn't that big a deal. There was something pathetic and awkward about the way he did this, though – it was ham-fisted, and I began to feel a mild contempt for him stirring inside me.

But if he *had* asked me straight out, what would I have said? Would I have been able to bluff my way through some yarn about complexity theory and advanced mathematics? Would I have leant forward in my chair, tapped my right temple and whispered *un-der-stand-ing, Carl*? Would I have told him that I actually *was* on special medication, and that I had occasional visions of the Virgin Mary, to boot? Would I have told him the truth? Would I have been able to resist?

I don't know.

I never got the chance to find out.

❖   ❖   ❖

A few moments later, a friend of Van Loon's appeared from across the room and sat at our table. Van Loon introduced me and we all engaged in small talk for a few moments, but pretty quickly the two older men got to discussing Van Loon's Gulfstream, and I was happy to fade into the background. I could see that Van Loon was agitated, though – torn between not wanting to let me out of his immediate sphere of attention and not wanting to disengage from the conversation with his billionaire crony. But I was already gone, my mind drifting into a contemplation of the impending arrival of Hank Atwood.

From the various profiles I'd read of him, something had become clear to me about the Chairman of MCL-Parnassus. Even though he was a 'suit', a grey corporate executive who mainly concerned himself with what most people thought of as the tedious business of numbers and percentage points, Henry Bryant Atwood was a glamorous figure. There had been larger-than-life 'suits' before him, of course – in newspapers, and in the early days of Hollywood, all those cigar-toting moguls who couldn't speak English, for example – but it hadn't taken long, in the case of Hollywood, for the ivy-league accountants on the East Coast to step in and take the reins. What most people didn't understand, however, was that since the full-steam-ahead corporatization of the entertainment business in the 1980s, the centre of gravity had shifted again. Actors and singers and supermodels were still glamorous, sure, but the rarefied air of *pure* glamour had quietly wafted its way back in the direction of the grey-suited moneymen.

Hank Atwood was glamorous, not because he was good-looking, which he wasn't, and not even because the product he pedalled was the very stuff of people's dreams – the genetically modified food of the world's imagination – Hank Atwood was glamorous because of the unimaginably huge amounts of money he made.

And that was the thing. Artistic content was dead, something to be decided by committee. True content now resided in the numbers – and numbers, *large* numbers, were everywhere. Thirty-seven million dollars for a private jet. A lawsuit settled for $250 million. A $30 billion leveraged buyout. Personal wealth amounting to something in excess of *$100 billion* . . .

And it was at that point – while I was in the middle of this reverie of infinite numerical expansion – that things started to unravel.

For whatever reason, I suddenly became aware of the people sitting at the table behind me. They were a man and a woman, maybe a real-estate developer and an executive producer, or two trial lawyers – I didn't know, I wasn't focused on what they were saying – but there was something in the tone of the man's voice that cut through me like a knife.

I leant backwards a little in my chair, simultaneously glancing over at Van Loon and his friend. Set against the walnut panelling, the two billionaires looked like large, predatory birds perched deep in some arid canyon – but ageing ones, with drooping heads and rheumy eyes, old buzzards. Van Loon was involved in a detailed explanation of how he'd been driven to sound-proofing his previous jet, a Challenger something-or-other, and it was during this little mono-logue that a curious thing happened in my brain. Like a radio receiver automatically switching frequencies, it closed out Carl Van Loon's voice, '. . . you see, to avoid undue vibrations, you need these isolator things to wrap around the bolts that connect the interior to the air-frame – silicone rubber isolators, I think they're called . . .' and started receiving the voice of the guy behind me, '. . . in a big hotel downtown somewhere . . . it was on a news bulletin earlier . . . yeah, Donatella Alvarez, the painter's wife, found on the floor of a hotel room, she'd been attacked apparently, blow to the head . . . and now she's in a *coma* – but it seems they've got a lead already – a cleaner at the hotel saw someone leaving the place early this morning, someone with a limp . . .'

I pushed my chair back a little.

. . . someone with a *limp* . . .

The voice behind me droned on, '. . . and of course her being Mexican doesn't help with all of this *stuff* going on . . .'

I stood up, and for a split second it felt as if everyone in the restaurant had stopped what they were doing, had put their knives and forks down and were looking up, expecting me to address them – but they hadn't, of course, and weren't. Only Carl Van Loon was looking up at me, a mild flicker of concern in his eyes suddenly lurching into overdrive. I mouthed the word *bathroom* at him, turned away and started walking. I went quickly, moving between tables, and around tables, looking for the nearest exit.

But then I noticed someone approaching from the other side of the room – a short, balding man in a grey suit. It was Hank Atwood. I recognized him from magazine photographs. A second later we were passing each other, shuffling awkwardly between two tables, grunting politely. For a brief moment we were so close that I could smell his cologne.

I got outside on to Fifty-second Street and took in huge gulps of air. As I stood there on the sidewalk, looking around me, I had the sense that by joining the busy crowds out here I'd forfeited my right to be in the Grill Room, and that I wouldn't be allowed back inside.

But right now I had no intention of going back inside, and about twenty minutes later I found myself wandering aimlessly down Park Avenue South, consciously suppressing my limp, racking my memory to see if I could recall anything. But there was nothing . . . I *had* been in a hotel room and could even see myself walking down an empty hotel corridor. But that was it, everything else was a blank.

I didn't *really* believe, though . . . I mean . . . I didn't . . . I *couldn't* . . .

For the next half-hour, I walked – cutting left at Union Square, then right on First – and arrived back at my building in a complete daze. I walked up the stairs, holding on to the notion that perhaps I'd been hearing things in the restaurant, that I'd imagined it – that it had simply been another blip, a *glitch*. In any case, I was going to find out pretty soon, because if this thing really had happened, it would still be on the news, so all I had to do was tune in to the radio, or switch on one of the local TV channels . . .

But the first thing I noticed when I got into the apartment was the little red light flashing on my answering machine. Almost glad of the distraction, I reached down at once and flicked the 'play' button. Then I just stood there in my suit, like an idiot, staring out across the room, waiting to hear the message.

There was the low hum as the tape rewound, and then – click.

Beeep.

'Hi . . . Eddie. It's Melissa. I've been meaning to call you, I really have, but . . . you know how it is . . .' Her voice was a little heavy, and a little slurred, but it was still Melissa's voice, still *Melissa*, disembodied, filling up my living-room – 'Then something occurred to me, my brother . . . was he *giving* you anything? I mean – I don't want to talk about this over the phone, but . . . *was he*? Because . . .' – I heard ice-cubes clinking in a glass – '. . . because if he was, you should know something . . . that stuff . . .' – she paused here, as though composing herself – 'that *stuff* – MDT-whatever – is really, *really* dangerous – I mean, you don't know *how* dangerous.' I swallowed, and closed my eyes. 'So look, Eddie, I don't know, maybe I'm wrong – but . . . just call me, OK . . . *call me.*'

PART THREE

PART THREE

[15]

A TV NEWSCAST AT TWO O'CLOCK confirmed that Donatella Alvarez, the wife of the Mexican painter, had received a severe blow to the head and was now in a coma. The incident had taken place in a room on the fifteenth floor of a midtown hotel. There were few details given, and no mention was made of any man with a limp.

I sat on the couch, in my suit, and waited for more, *anything* – another bulletin, some footage, analysis. It was as if sitting on the couch with the remote control hanging limply in my hand was actually doing something, but what else was I going to do that would be any better? Phone up Melissa and ask her if this was the kind of thing she'd had in mind?

Dangerous?

What – as in severe blow to the head dangerous? Hospitalization dangerous? Coma dangerous? Death dangerous?

Obviously, I had no intention of phoning her up with questions like these, but a part of me was riddled with anxiety none the less. Had I really done it? Was the same thing – or something like it – going to happen again? Did Melissa's 'dangerous' mean dangerous to others, or simply dangerous to *me*?

Was I being hugely irresponsible?

What the *fuck* was going on?

As the afternoon progressed, I concentrated intently on each news bulletin, as though by sheer force of will I could somehow alter a key detail in the story – have it not be a hotel room, or have Donatella Alvarez not be in a coma. Between the bulletins, I watched cookery shows, live courtroom broadcasts, soaps, commercials, and was aware of myself – unable to help it – processing and storing random bits of useless information. Lay the chicken strips flat on a lightly oiled baking tray and sprinkle with sesame seeds. Call toll-free NOW for a 15 per cent markdown on *The GUTbuster 2000* home work-out system. On several occasions during the afternoon, I glanced over at the phone and considered calling Melissa, but each time some override mechanism in my brain kicked in and I immediately found myself thinking about something else.

By six o'clock, the story had begun to flesh out considerably. After a reception at her husband's Upper West Side studio, Donatella Alvarez had made her way to a midtown hotel, the Clifden, where she received a single blow to the head with a blunt instrument. The instrument had not as yet been identified, but a key question that remained unanswered was this: what had Señora Alvarez been doing in a hotel room in the first place? Detectives were interviewing all the guests who'd attended the reception, and were especially interested in speaking to an individual named Thomas Cole.

I stared at the screen for a couple of seconds, perplexed, barely recognizing the name myself. Then the report moved on, and so did I. They gave personal information about the victim, as well as photographs and interviews with family members – all of which meant that before long a very human picture of the 43-year-old Señora Alvarez had begun forming itself in the viewer's mind. Here, apparently, was a woman of rare physical and spiritual beauty. She was independent, generous, loyal, a loving wife, a devoted mother to twin baby girls, Pia and Flor. Her husband, Rodolfo Alvarez, was reported to be distraught and at a complete loss for any explanation as to what might have happened. They showed a black-and-white photograph of a radiant, uniformed schoolgirl attending a Dominican convent in Rome, circa 1971. They also showed some home-movie footage, flickering images in faded colour of a young Donatella in a summery dress walking through a rose garden. Other images included Donatella on horseback, Donatella at an archeological dig in Peru, Donatella and Rodolfo in Tibet.

The next phase in the reporting consisted of political analysis. Was this a racially motivated attack? Was it connected in some way to the current foreign policy débâcle? One commentator expressed the fear that it could be the first in a series of such incidents and blamed the attack squarely on the President's bewildering failure to condemn Defense Secretary Caleb Hale's intemperate remarks – or alleged remarks, since he was still denying that he'd actually made them. Another commentator seemed to feel that this was collateral damage of a kind we were simply going to have to get used to.

All through the afternoon, as I watched these reports, I clocked up a bewildering number of reactions – chief among them disbelief, terror, remorse, anger. I vacillated between thinking that maybe I *had* struck the blow and dismissing the idea as absurd. Towards the end, however – and after I'd taken a top-up of MDT – the only discernible thing I could feel was mild boredom.

By mid-evening, I was quite detached from everything and whenever I heard a reference to the story, my impulse was to say *enough, already*, as though they were talking about a new mini-series on a cable channel, something adapted from an over-hyped magic-realist pot-boiler . . . *The Dreadful Ordeal of Donatella Alvarez* . . .

A little after 8.30, I called Carl Van Loon at his apartment on Park Avenue.

Although the disbelief, terror, etc. of earlier had been uppermost in my mind for a good deal of the afternoon, another part of me had been riddled with anxiety of a different kind – anxiety about having blown my chances with Van Loon, about the extent to which this glitch, this operational malfunction, was going to interfere with my plans for the future.

As a result – and waiting for Van Loon to come to the phone – I was quite nervous.

'Eddie?'

I cleared my throat. 'Mr Van Loon.'

'Eddie, I don't understand. What *happened*?'

'I got sick,' I said – the excuse coming to me automatically – 'there was nothing I could do about it. I had to leave like that. I'm sorry.'

'You got *sick*? What are you, in first grade? You rush off without saying a word? You don't come back? I'm left there looking like a jerk, making excuses to Hank fucking *Atwood*?'

'I have a condition, a stomach condition.'

'Then you don't even bother to call?'

'I needed to see a doctor, Carl. In a hurry.'

Van Loon was silent for a moment.

Then he sighed. 'Well . . . how are you *now*?'

'I'm fine. It's taken care of.'

He sighed again. 'Are you . . . what? . . . I don't know . . . are you getting proper treatment for this thing? You want the names of some top consultants? I can . . .'

'I'm fine. Look, it was a once off. It's not going to happen again.' I paused for a moment. 'How did the meeting go?'

This time Van Loon paused. I was out on a limb now.

'Well it was a little awkward, Eddie,' he said eventually, 'I'm not going to lie to you. I wished you'd been there.'

'Did he seem convinced?'

'In outline, yeah. He says he feels it's something he can bring to the table, but you and me are going to have to sit down with him and go over the numbers.'

'Great. Sure. Of course. Whenever.'

'Hank's gone to the coast, but he'll be back in town on . . . *Tuesday* I think, yeah, so why don't you come into the office some time on Monday and we can set something up.'

'Great – and listen, Carl, I'm sorry again, I really am.'

'You sure you don't want to see *my* doctor? He's—'

'No, but thanks for the offer.'

'Think about it.'

'OK. I'll see you on Monday.'

I remained standing by the phone for a couple of minutes after the call to Van Loon, staring down at an open page of my address book.

I had a nervous, jumpy feeling in my stomach.

Then I picked the phone up and dialled Melissa's number. As I waited for her to answer I could have been back in Vernon's apartment – up on the seventeenth floor, still at the beginning of all of this, still in those last shining moments before I recorded a message on her answering machine and then went rooting around in her brother's bedroom . . .

'Hello.'

'Melissa?'

'Eddie. Hi.'

'I got your message.'

'Yeah. Look . . . erm . . .' – I got the impression that she was composing herself – '. . . what I said on the message, that just occurred to me today. I don't know. My brother was an asshole. He'd been dealing this weird designer thing for quite a while. And it occurred to me about *you*. So I started worrying.'

If Melissa had been drinking earlier on in the day, she seemed subdued now, hungover maybe.

'There's nothing to worry about, Melissa,' I said, having decided on the spot that this was what I was going to do. 'Vernon didn't give me anything. I'd met him the day before he . . . er . . . the day before it happened. And we just talked about stuff . . . nothing in particular.'

She sighed, 'OK.'

'But thanks for your concern.' I paused for a moment. 'How are you?'

'I'm fine.'

Awkward, awkward, awkward.

Then she said, 'How are *you*?'

'I'm fine. Keeping busy.'

'What have you been up to?'

This was the conversation we would be having in these circumstances – here it was – the inevitable conversation we would be having in these circumstances . . .

'I've been working for the last few years as a copywriter.' I paused. 'For Kerr & Dexter. The publishers.'

It was the truth, technically, but that's all it was.

'Yeah? That's great.'

It didn't feel great, though – *or* like the truth, my days as a copywriter for Kerr & Dexter suddenly seeming distant, unreal, fictional.

I didn't want to be on the phone to Melissa any more. Since we'd renewed our acquaintance – however fleetingly – I felt that I had already entered into a consistent pattern of lying to her. Going on with the conversation could only make that worse.

I said, 'Look, I wanted to call you back and clear that up . . . but . . . I'm going to get off the phone now.'

'OK.'

'It's not that—'

'Eddie?'

'Yes?'

'This isn't easy for me either.'

'Sure.'

There wasn't anything else I could think of to say.

'Goodbye then.'

'Bye.'

In need of immediate distraction, I flicked through my address book for Gennady's cellphone number. I dialled it and waited.

'Yeah?'

'Gennady?'

'Yeah.'

'It's Eddie.'

'Eddie. What you want? I busy.'

I stared at the wall in front of me for a second.

'I've got a treatment done for that thing. It's about twen—'

'Give me this in the morning. I look at it.'

'Gennady . . .' He was gone. '*Gennady?*'

I put the phone down.

Tomorrow morning was Friday. I'd forgotten. Gennady was coming for the first repayment on the loan.

Shit.

The money I owed wasn't the problem. I could write him out a cheque straightaway for the whole amount, plus the vig, plus a bonus for just being Gennady, but that wouldn't do it. I'd told him that I had a treatment ready. Now I had to come up with one, had to have one for the morning – or else he'd probably stab me

174

continuously until he developed something akin to tennis elbow.

I wasn't exactly in the mood for this sort of thing, but I knew it would keep me busy, so I went online and did some research. I picked up relevant terminology and worked out a plot loosely based on a recent mafia trial in Sicily, a detailed account of which I found on an Italian website. By some time after midnight – with suitable variations – I'd knocked out a twenty-five-page, scene-by-scene treatment for *Keeper of the Code*, a story of the Organizatsiya.

After that, I spent a good while searching through magazines for real estate ads. I had decided that I was going to phone some of the big Manhattan realtors the following morning and finally kickstart the process of renting – maybe even of buying – a new apartment.

Then I went to bed and got four or five hours of what passed for sleep these days.

Gennady arrived at about nine-thirty. I buzzed him in, telling him I was on the third floor. It took him for ever to walk up the stairs, and when he finally materialized in my living-room he seemed exhausted and fed up.

'Good morning,' I said.

He raised his eyebrows at me and looked around. Then he looked at his watch.

I had printed out the treatment and put it in an envelope. I took this from the desk and handed it to him. He held it up, shook it, seemed to be estimating how much it weighed. Then he said, 'Where the money?'

'Er . . . I was going to write you a cheque. How much was it again?'

'A *cheque*?'

I nodded at him, suddenly feeling foolish.

'A *cheque*?' he said again. 'You out of your fucking mind? What you think, we are a financial *institution*?'

'Gennady, look—'

'Shut up. You can't come up with the money today you in serious *fucking* trouble, my friend – you *hear* me?'

'I'll get it.'

'I cut your *balls* off.'

'I'll *get* it. *Jesus*. I wasn't thinking.'

'A *cheque*,' he said again, with contempt. 'Unbelievable.'

I went over to my phone and picked it up. Since those first couple of days at Lafayette, I had developed extremely cordial relations with my obsequious and florid-faced bank manager, Howard Lewis, so I phoned him and told him what I needed – twenty-two five in cash – and asked if he could possibly have it ready for me in fifteen minutes.

Absolutely no problem, Mr Spinola.

I put the phone down and turned around. Gennady was standing over at my desk, with his back to me. I mumbled something to get his attention. He then turned to face me.

'Well?'

I shrugged my shoulders and said, 'Let's go to my bank.'

We took a cab, in silence, to Twenty-third and Second, where my bank was. I wanted to make a reference to the treatment, but since Gennady was obviously in a very bad mood, I judged it better not to say anything. I got the cash from Howard Lewis and handed it over to Gennady outside on the street. He slipped the bundle into the mysterious interior of his jacket. Holding up the envelope with the treatment in it, he said, 'I look at this.'

Then he took off up Second Avenue without saying goodbye.

I crossed the street, and in line with my new strategy of trying to eat at least once a day, I went into a diner and had coffee and a blueberry muffin.

Then I wandered over to – and up – Madison Avenue. After about ten blocks, I stopped outside a realtor's office, a place called Sullivan, Draskell. I went inside, made some enquiries and got talking to a broker by the name of Alison Botnick. She was in her late forties and was dressed in a stylish navy-blue silk dress with a matching Nehru coat. I realized pretty quickly that even though I was in jeans and a sweater, and could easily have been a clerk in a wine store – or a freelance copywriter – this woman had no idea who I was and consequently had to be on her guard. As far as Ms Botnick was concerned, I could have been one of those new dot-com billionaires on the look-out for a twelve-room spread on Park. These days you never knew, and I kept her guessing.

Walking up Madison, I had been thinking in the region of $300,000 for a place – $500,000 tops – but it occurred to me now that given my standing with Van Loon and my prospects with Hank Atwood there was no reason why I shouldn't be thinking bigger – $2 million, $3 million, maybe even more. As I stood in the plush reception area of Sullivan, Draskell, thumbing through glossy brochures for luxury condos in new buildings called things like the Mercury and the Celestial, and listening to Alison Botnick's pitch, with its urgent lexical hammer-blows – high-end, liquid, snapped-up, close, close, *close* – I felt my expectations rising by the second. I could also see Alison Botnick, for her part – as she morphed fifteen years off my frame and mentally dressed me in a UCLA T-shirt and baseball cap – convincing herself that I *was* a dot-com billionaire. The flames were stoked further when I casually shrugged off her suggestion that, given the storm of paperwork required these days to pass the average co-op board's screening procedure, I would probably want to avoid a co-op apartment.

'The boards are getting very picky,' she said, 'not that—'

'Of course not, but who wants to be excluded without a fight?'

She assessed this.

'OK.'

Our manipulation of each other into these respective states of acquisitive and professional arousal could only have led to one thing: viewings. She took me first to see a four-bedroom prewar co-op in the East Seventies between Lexington and Park. We went by cab, and as we chatted about the market and where it was 'at' right now, I had that pleasant sensation of being in control – and of being *at* the controls, as though I had designed the software for this little interlude myself and everything was running smoothly.

The apartment we went to view on Seventy-fourth was nothing special. It had low ceilings and didn't have much natural light. It was also cramped and quite fussy.

'A lot of these prewar co-ops are like this, you know,' Alison said, as we made our way back down to the lobby. 'They've got leaks and need to be rewired, and unless you're prepared to just gut them and start over, they're not worth the money.'

Which in this case was $1.8 million.

Next we went to see a 3,200-square-foot converted loft space in the Flatiron District. It had been a textile factory of some kind up until the '50s, had lain vacant for most of the '60s and from the way the place was decorated it didn't look as if its present owner had made it much past the '70s. Alison said he was a civil engineer who'd probably paid very little for it, but was now asking $2.3 million. I liked it, and it certainly had potential, but it was huddled a little too anonymously in a part of town that was still relatively dull and unexciting.

The last place Alison took me to see was on the sixty-eighth floor of a condominium skyscraper that had just been built on the site of the old West Side rail yards. The Celestial, along with other luxury residential developments, was – in theory – to be the centrepiece of a new urban rejuvenation project. This would roughly cover the area between West Chelsea and Hell's Kitchen.

'If you take a look at it, there's a *ton* of empty lots there,' Alison said, sounding like a latter-day Robert Moses, 'from Twenty-sixth Street up to Forty-second Street, west of Ninth Avenue – it's ripe for redevelopment. And with the new Penn Station you'll have a huge increase in traffic – thousands more people pouring in every day.'

She was right, and as our cab cruised west along Thirty-fourth Street, down towards the Hudson River, I could see what she was talking about, I could see the great potential there was for gentrification, for a huge bourgeois-boho makeover of the entire neighbourhood.

'Believe me,' she went on, 'it's going to be the biggest land grab this city has seen in fifty years.'

Rising up out of the wasteland of disused and neglected warehouse buildings, the Celestial itself was a dazzling steel-frame monolith in a seamless casing of reflective bronze-tinted glass. As the cab pulled up alongside a huge plaza at the foot of the building, Alison started reeling off stuff that she obviously felt I should know. The

Celestial was 715 feet tall, had 70 storeys and 185 apartments – also several restaurants, a health club, a private screening room, dog-walking facilities, a 'smart garbage' recycling system . . . wine-cellar, walk-in humidor, titanium-sided roofdeck . . .

I nodded at all of this, as though mentally jotting it down for later scrutiny.

'The guy who designed this place,' she said, 'is even thinking of moving in *himself*.'

The vast lobby area had pink-veined marble columns supporting a gold-toned mosaic ceiling, but little in the way of furniture or art works. The elevator took us up to the sixty-eighth floor in what felt like ten seconds, but must have been longer. The apartment she was showing me still had some work to be done on it, so I wasn't to mind the bare light bulbs and exposed wiring. '*But . . .*' she turned to me and said in a whisper as she was putting the key in the door, '. . . check out the views . . .'

We stepped into an open, loft-style space, and although I was aware of various corridors going off in different directions, I was immediately drawn to the full-length windows on the far side of this bare, white room. There was plastic sheeting on the floor, and as I walked across it, Alison following just behind me, the whole of Manhattan rose dizzyingly up into view. Standing there at the window, I gaped out at the cluster of midtown skyscrapers directly ahead, at Central Park huddled up to the left, at the financial district over to my right.

Seen here from an angle that had a dreamlike quality of the impossible to it, all of the city's land-mark buildings were in place – but they appeared to be facing, even somehow *looking*, in this direction.

I sensed Alison at my shoulder – smelled her perfume, heard the gentle swish of silk against silk as she moved.

'Well,' she said, 'what do you think?'

'It's amazing,' I said, and turned to look at her.

She was nodding in agreement, and smiling. Her eyes were a vivid green and glistened in a way that I hadn't noticed before. In fact, Alison Botnick suddenly seemed a lot younger than I had imagined her to be.

'So, Mr Spinola,' she said, holding my gaze, 'do you mind if I ask you what line of work you are in?'

I hesitated, and then said, 'Investment banking.'

She nodded.

'I work for Carl Van Loon.'

'I see. That must be interesting.'

'It is.'

As she processed this information, maybe slotting me into some real estate client category, I glanced around at the room with its bare walls and incomplete grid of ceiling panels, trying to imagine how it might look fully furnished, and lived in. I thought about the rest of the place, as well.

'How many rooms are there?' I asked.

'Ten.'

I considered this for a moment – an apartment with *ten* rooms – but the scale of it defeated me. I was drawn irresistibly back to the window and gazed out again at the city – rapt as before, taking it all in. It was a clear, sunny day in Manhattan and just standing there made me feel utterly exhilarated.

'What's the ask price?'

I had the impression she was only doing it for effect, but Alison consulted her notebook, flicking through several pages and humming in concentration. After a moment, she said, casually, 'Nine point five.'

I clicked my tongue and whistled.

She consulted another page in her notebook and then stepped a little over to the left, as though she were now positively lost in concentration.

I went back to looking out of the window. It was a lot of money, sure, but it wasn't necessarily a prohibitive amount. If I continued trading at my current levels, and managed to play Van Loon the right way, there was no reason why I shouldn't be able to put some kind of a financial package together.

I glanced back at Alison and cleared my throat.

She turned around, and smiled politely.

Nine and a half million dollars.

There'd been a certain amount of wattage in the air between us, but apparently the mention of money had somehow defused this and for the next while we wandered in silence through the other rooms of the apartment. The views and angles in each one were slightly different from those in the main room, but they were equally as spectacular. There seemed to be light everywhere, and space, and as I passed through what would be the bathrooms and the kitchen, I had swirling visions in my head of onyx, terracotta, mahogany, chrome – elegant living in a kaleidoscope of floating forms, parallel lines, designer curves . . .

At one point, I contrasted all of this with the cramped atmosphere and creaking floorboards of my one-bedroom apartment on Tenth Street and I immediately began to feel light-headed, constricted in my breathing, a little panicky even.

'Mr Spinola, are you all right?'

I was leaning against a doorway now, with one hand pressed against my chest.

'Yeah, I'm fine . . . it's just . . .'

'What?'

I looked up, and around, to get my bearings . . . unsure that I hadn't had another momentary blackout. I didn't think I'd moved – didn't remember moving – but I couldn't be 100 per cent certain that . . .

That *what*?

That from where I was standing, the *angle* wasn't different . . .

'Mr Spinola?'

'I'm fine. I'm fine. I have to go now, though. I'm sorry.'

I started walking swiftly along the corridor towards the main entrance. With my back to her, I waved a hand in the air and said, 'I'll be in touch with your office. I'll phone. Thank you.'

I got out into the hallway and straight over to one of the elevator cars.

I was hoping, as the doors whispered closed, that she wouldn't follow me, and she didn't.

[16]

I WALKED OUT OF THE CELESTIAL and across the plaza towards Tenth Avenue, keenly aware of the colossal rectangular slab of bronze-tinted glass shimmering in the sun behind me. I was also aware of the possibility that Alison Botnick was still up on the sixty-eighth floor, and maybe even staring down at the plaza – which of course made me feel like an insect, and more so with each step I took. I had to walk several blocks along Thirty-third Street, past the General Post Office and Madison Square Garden, before finding a taxi. I never once looked back, and as I got settled into the cab I kept my head down. There was a copy of the *New York Post* lying folded on the seat beside me. I picked it up and held it tightly in my lap.

I still wasn't sure if anything had happened back there, but the merest hint of that *clicking* business starting up again absolutely terrified me. I sat still and waited, gauging each flicker of perception, each breath, ready to isolate and assess anything out of the ordinary. A couple of minutes passed, and I seemed to be OK. I then relaxed my grip on the newspaper, and by the time we were turning right on to Second Avenue, I had calmed down considerably.

I flipped open the *Post* and looked at the front page. The headline was FEDS PROBE REGULATORS. It was a story about goings-on at the New York State Athletic Commission and was accompanied by extremely unflattering photos of two NYSAC officials. As usual in the *Post*, across the top of the front page, above the masthead, there were three boxed headlines with page references for the articles inside. The middle one, white type on a red background,

182

immediately caught my eye. It said, MEX PAINTER'S WIFE IN BRUTAL ATTACK, page 2. I paused for a second, staring at the words, and was about to flick over to the story when I noticed the headline beside it. This one – white on black – said, MYSTERY TRADER CLEANS UP, page 43. I fumbled with the paper, trying to get it open, and when I eventually got to the article, which was in the business section, the first thing I saw was Mary Stern's by-line.

My stomach started churning.

I couldn't believe she'd gone ahead and written something about me, and especially after the way I'd spoken to her on the phone – but then maybe that was *why*. The text of the article took up half a page and was accompanied by a large photo of the Lafayette trading room. There were Jay Zollo and the others, swivelled around on their chairs, staring into the camera.

I started reading.

> Something unusual has been going on in one of the day-trading houses down on Broad Street. In a room with fifty terminals and as many baseball caps, guerrilla marketmakers shave and scalp their way to tiny profit margins – an eighth of a point here, a sixteenth of a point there. It's a hard graft at Lafayette Trading and the atmosphere is undeniably tense.

I was named in the second paragraph.

> But last week all of that changed as new kid on the block, Eddie Spinola, walked in off the street, opened an account and launched straight into an aggressive short-selling spree that left seasoned traders in the Lafayette pit gasping for breath – and reaching for their keyboards, as they followed his leads and swept up profits unheard of in the day-trading world. But get this – undisputed King Rat by the end of his first week, mystery trader Eddie Spinola has since gone AWOL . . .

I couldn't believe it. I skimmed the rest of the paragraph.

> refuses to speak . . . cagey with fellow-traders . . . evasive . . . elusive . . . hasn't been seen for days . . .

The article went on to speculate about who I was and what I might be up to, and included quotes from, among others, a baffled Jay Zollo. A sidebar gave details of trades I'd made and of how various Lafayette regulars had benefited – one guy making enough for a down-payment on an apartment, another booking himself in for some long overdue dental surgery, a third catching up on alimony arrears.

It was a strange feeling, being written about like this, seeing my name in print, in a newspaper, especially in the business section of a newspaper. It was even stranger that it should be in the business section of the *New York Post*.

I looked out at the traffic on Second Avenue.

I didn't know what any of this meant – in terms of my privacy, or of my relationship with Van Loon, or of anything – but there was one thing I was sure of: I didn't like it.

The cab pulled up at my building on Tenth Street. I was so distracted by the *Post* article that as I paid the driver and got out, I didn't notice the small group of what I would soon realize were photographers and reporters gathered on the sidewalk. They didn't know me, didn't know what I looked like, presumably only knew where I lived – but when I got out of the cab and stood there, staring at them in disbelief, it must have been obvious who I was. There was a brief moment of calm before the penny dropped, a two-second delay at most, and then it was *Eddie! Eddie! Here! Here! Click! Whirr! Click!* I put my head down, got my key out and surged forward. *When are you going back to Lafayette, Eddie? Look this way, Eddie! What's your secret, Eddie?* I managed to get inside the door and to slam it closed behind me. I rushed upstairs into my apartment and went straight over to the window. They were still down there, about five of them, clustered around the door of the building. Was this a result of the story in the *Post*? Everyone wanting to know about the guy who'd beaten the markets? The mystery trader? Well if *that* was news, I thought, it was just as well no one realized *I* was the Thomas Cole the police were so anxious to interview in connection with the Donatella Alvarez situation.

I turned back in towards the room.

The red light was flashing on my answering machine. I walked over to it, wearily, and pressed the 'play' button.

Seven messages.

I sat on the edge of the couch and listened. Jay Zollo, pleading with me to get in touch with him again. My father, puzzled, wanting to know if I'd seen that thing in the paper. Gennady, pissed, declaring that if I was yanking his chain he'd cut my fucking head off, and with a *bread* knife. Artie Meltzer, all pally, inviting me out to lunch. Mary Stern, telling me it'd be so much easier if I would just *talk* to her. A recruitment company, offering me an executive position in a major brokerage house. Someone from David Letterman's office – a booking agent – saying if I agreed I could be on the show *tonight*.

I flopped back on to the couch and stared up at the ceiling. I had to stay calm. I certainly hadn't wanted any of this attention or pressure, but if I was going to come through it in one piece, I really needed to keep my wits about me. I rolled off the couch, got up and went into the bedroom to lie down properly. Maybe if I could just sleep for part of the afternoon, for an hour or two, I might be able to think a bit more clearly. But the moment I lay down on the bed and stretched out I knew I wasn't going to be able to do it. I was wide awake and my mind was racing.

I got up again and went into the living-room. I paced back and forth for a while – from the desk to the phone, from the phone to the desk. Then I went into the kitchen. Then out again. Then into the bathroom, then out again to the living-room. Then over to the window. Then back again. But that was it, there was nowhere else to go – just these three rooms. Standing near my desk, I surveyed the apartment and tried to imagine what the place would be like with ten rooms, and high ceilings, and bare white walls. But I couldn't do it, not without getting dizzy. Besides, that was somewhere else – the sixty-eighth floor of the Celestial – and I was here now, in my apartment . . .

I stepped back from the desk, a little unsteadily, and leant against the bookshelves behind me. I felt queasy all of a sudden, and light-headed.

I closed my eyes.

After a moment, I found myself floating – moving along an empty, brightly lit corridor. Sound was distant and increasingly muffled. The forward motion seemed to continue for ages, the pace slow and dreamy. But then I was gliding around a broad curve, moving into and across a room, towards a wide, full-length window. I didn't stop at the window, but floated on – arms outstretched – *through* the window and out above the vast microchip of the city, while behind me, after a brief but inexplicable delay, the huge plate of bronze-tinted glass shattered deafeningly into a million pieces . . .

I opened my eyes – and jolted backwards, recoiling in fright from the unexpected aerial view I was now getting of the sidewalk down on Tenth Street, of the trash cans and parked cars and photographers' heads milling around like bacteria in a lab dish. I pulled myself in from the window ledge, struggling to keep my balance, and slumped down on to the floor. Then, taking deep breaths and rubbing the top of my head – which I had banged against the upper section of the window – I stared over in amazement at where I had been a moment before . . . and still *should* have been . . .

I got up slowly and walked back across the room towards the bookshelves, closely observing each step. I reached out to touch things as I passed them, to reassure myself – the side of the couch, the table, the desk. I looked back at where I had come from, and couldn't believe it. It didn't seem real that I had been leaning out of that window, and leaning out so *far* . . .

With my heart still thumping, I went into the bathroom. If this thing was going to start up again, and develop, I had to find some way to stop it. I opened the medicine cabinet above the washbasin and quickly searched through all the bottles and packets and sealed containers, the accumulated toiletries, shaving things, soap products, non-prescription painkillers. I found a bottle of cough syrup I'd bought the previous winter but had never used. I scanned the label and saw that it contained codeine. I opened the cap, pausing for a second as I glanced at myself in the mirror, and then started chugging the stuff down. It was horrible, sickly and viscous, and I gagged between swallows, but at least I knew that whatever synaptic short-circuiting in my brain was causing these blackouts, the codeine would slow me down and make me drowsy, and probably sufficiently drowsy to keep me here, passed out on the couch or on the floor – I didn't mind which, just so long as I wasn't outside somewhere in the city, out and about and on the loose . . .

I emptied the bottle of its last drop, put the cap back on and threw it into the little basket beside the toilet. Then I had to steel myself against throwing up. I sat on the edge of the bathtub for a while, clutching the sides of it tightly, and stared at the wall opposite, afraid even to close my eyes.

Over the next five minutes, before the codeine kicked in, there were two more occurrences, both brief as flickers in a slideshow, but no less terrifying for that. From the edge of the bathtub, and with no conscious movement on my part, I found myself standing in the middle of the living-room. I stood there, swaying slightly, trying to act unfazed – as if ignoring what had happened might mean it wouldn't happen again. Soon after that – *click, click* – I was half-way down the stairs, sitting on the bottom step of the first landing with my head in my hands. I realized that another trip-switch forward like that and I'd be outside on the street, being mobbed by photographers and reporters – maybe in danger, maybe a danger to others, certainly out of control . . .

But I could feel the onset now of a heaviness in my limbs and a kind of general spaciness. I stood up, grabbing on to the banisters for support, and turned around. I made my way slowly back up to the third floor. Walking now was like wading through treacle and by the time I got to the door of my apartment, which was wide open, I knew I wouldn't be going anywhere.

It then took me a couple of moments, standing in the doorway, to realize that the ringing sound I was hearing wasn't just in my head. It was the telephone, and before I'd had time to reason that I shouldn't be answering the telephone, given my present state, I was watching my hand floating down to pick up the receiver and then floating back up again towards my head.

'Hello.'

'Eddie?'

I paused for a moment, in shock. It was Melissa.

'*Eddie?*'

'Yeah, it's me. Sorry. Hi.'

My voice felt heavy, slack.

'Eddie, why did you lie to me?'

'I didn't . . . wh-what are you talking about?'

'MDT. Vernon. You know what I'm talking about.'

'But—'

'I've just been reading the *Post*, Eddie. Short-selling stocks? Second-guessing the markets? *You?* Come on.'

I didn't know what to say. Eventually, I came up with, 'Since when do you read the *New York Post?*'

'These days the *Post*'s about all I *can* read.'

What did that mean?

'I don't under—'

'Look, Eddie, forget the *Post*, forget the fact that you lied to me. MDT is the problem. Are you still taking it?'

I didn't answer. I could barely keep my eyelids open.

'You've got to stop taking it. *Jesus.*'

I paused again, but had no clear sense this time of how long the pause went on for.

'Eddie? Talk to me.'

'OK . . . let's meet.'

Now *she* paused, and then said, 'Fine, when?'

'You tell me.'

When I spoke, my tongue felt thick and swollen.

'Tomorrow. In the morning. I don't know – eleven-thirty, twelve?'

'OK. In the city?'

'Fine. Where?'

I suggested a bar on Spring Street.

'Fine.'

That was it. Then Melissa said, 'Eddie, are you OK? You sound strange. I'm *worried.*'

I was staring down at a knot in one of the floorboards. I rallied all of my strength and managed, 'I'll see you tomorrow, Melissa.'

Then, without waiting for an answer, I put the phone down.

I staggered over to the couch and lowered myself on to it. It was the middle of the afternoon and I'd just drunk a whole bottle of cough syrup. I laid my head on the armrest and stared up at the ceiling. Over the next half an hour or so, I was aware of various sounds drifting in and out of my consciousness – the door-buzzer, possibly someone *banging* on the door, voices, the phone ringing, sirens, traffic. But none of it was clear enough, or compelling enough, to rouse me from the torpor I was in, and gradually I sank into the deepest sleep I'd had for weeks.

[17]

OUT COLD UNTIL FOUR O'CLOCK the next morning, I spent a further two hours struggling to emerge from the other side of this paralysing blanket of drowsiness. Some time after six, aching all over, I dragged myself off the couch and slouched into the bathroom. I had a shower. Then I went into the kitchen and put on a large pot of coffee.

Back in the living-room, smoking a cigarette, I found myself glancing continually over at the ceramic bowl on the shelf above the computer. But I didn't want to get too close to it, because I knew that if I went on taking MDT, I would just end up having more of these mysterious and increasingly scary blackouts. On the other hand, I didn't really believe that I'd had anything to do with putting Donatella Alvarez into a coma in the first place. I was prepared to accept that *something* had happened, and that during these blackouts I continued functioning on one level or another, moving about, doing stuff, but I refused to accept that this extended to me striking someone over the head with a blunt instrument. I'd had a similar thought a few minutes earlier in the bathroom, while I was having my shower. There were still bruises on my body, as well as that small circular mark, fading now, of what had seemed to be a cigarette burn. This was incontrovertible evidence, I'd concluded, of *something*, but hardly of anything to do with *me* . . .

I wandered reluctantly over to the window and looked out. The street was empty. There was no one around – there were no photographers, no reporters. With any luck, I thought, the mystery trader of the tabloids had already become yesterday's news. Besides, it was Saturday morning and things were bound to be a little quieter.

I sat on the couch again. After a couple of minutes, I got back into the position I'd been in all night, and even started to doze a little. I felt pleasantly drowsy now, and kind of lazy. This was something I hadn't felt for ages, and although it took me a while, I eventually linked it in with the fact that I hadn't taken an MDT pill in nearly twenty-four hours, my longest – and only – period of abstinence since the beginning. It had never occurred to me before to just stop, but now I thought – well, why not? It was the weekend, and maybe I deserved a break. I would need to be charged up for the meeting with Carl Van Loon on Monday, but until then there was no reason why I shouldn't be able to chill out like a regular person.

However, by eleven o'clock I didn't feel quite so relaxed about things, and as I was getting ready to go out a vague sense of disorientation crept over me. But since I'd never really given myself the chance to let the drug wear off properly, I decided to stick to my plan of temporary abstinence – at least until I'd spoken to Melissa.

Down on Spring Street I left the sunlight behind me and stepped into the dim shadows of the bar where we'd arranged to meet. I looked around. Someone gestured to me from a booth in the corner, a raised hand, and although I couldn't see the person clearly from where I was standing, I knew that it had to be Melissa. I walked over towards her.

On my way to this place from Tenth Street, I'd felt very weird indeed, as if I *had* taken something after all and was coming up on it. But I knew it was actually the reverse, that it was more like a curtain being lifted on raw, exposed nerves, on feelings that hadn't seen the light of day for some time. When I thought about Carl Van Loon, for example, or Lafayette, or Chantal, I was first struck by how unreal they seemed, and then by a kind of retrospective terror at my involvement with them. When I thought about Melissa, I was overwhelmed – *blinded* by a pixel-storm of memories . . .

She half got up as I arrived and we kissed awkwardly. She sat back down on her side of the booth. I slid into the opposite side to face her.

191

My heart was pounding.

I said, 'How are you doing?' and it immediately seemed odd to me that I wasn't commenting on how she looked, because she looked so different.

'I'm OK.'

Her hair was short and dyed a kind of reddish brown. She was heavier – generally, but especially in the face – and had lines around her eyes. These made her look very tired. I was one to talk, of course, but that didn't make it any less of a shock.

'So, Eddie, how are *you*?'

'I'm OK,' I lied, and then added, 'I suppose.'

Melissa was drinking a beer and had a cigarette on the go. The place was almost empty. There was an old man reading a newspaper at a table near the door and there were two young guys on stools at the bar. I caught the eye of the barman and pointed at Melissa's beer. He nodded back at me. The normality of this little routine belied how strange and unsettled I was feeling. A few weeks earlier I'd been sitting opposite Vernon in a booth of a cocktail lounge on Sixth Avenue. Now, thanks to some unaccountable dream-logic, I was sitting in a booth opposite Melissa in *this* place.

'You look good,' she said. Then, holding up an admonitory finger, she added, 'And don't tell me *I* look good, because I know I don't.'

It occurred to me that despite the changes – the weight, the lines, the weariness – nothing could eradicate the fact that Melissa was still beautiful. But after what she'd said I couldn't think of any way to tell her this without sounding patronizing. What I said was, 'I've lost quite a bit of weight recently.'

Looking me straight in the eyes, she replied, 'Well, MDT will certainly do that to you.'

'Yeah, I suppose it will.'

In as quiet and circumspect a voice as I could muster, I then asked, 'So, what do you know about all of this?'

'Well,' she said, taking a deep breath, 'here's the bottom line, Eddie. MDT is lethal, or can be, and if it doesn't kill you, it'll do serious damage to your brain, and I'm talking about permanently.' She then pointed to her own head with the index finger of her right

192

hand, and said, 'It fucked *my* brain up – which I'll go into later – but the point I want to make now is, I was one of the lucky ones.'

I swallowed.

The barman appeared with a tray. He placed a glass of beer down in front of me and exchanged the ashtray on the table with a clean one. When he'd gone, Melissa continued. 'I only took nine or ten hits, but there was one guy who took a lot more than that, over a period of weeks, and I know *he* died. Another unfortunate shmoe ended up as a vegetable. His mother had to sponge him down every day and feed him with a *spoon*.'

My stomach was jumping now, and a mild headache had started up.

'When was this?'

'About four years ago.' She paused. 'Vernon didn't tell you any of this stuff?' I shook my head. She seemed surprised. Then, as though great physical effort were required for what she was doing, she took a deep breath. 'OK,' she went on, 'so about four years ago Vernon was hanging out with a client of his who worked at some pharmaceutical plant and had access that he shouldn't have had to a whole range of new drugs. One of them in particular, which didn't have a name yet and hadn't been tested, was supposed to be . . . *amazing*. So, in order to test it, because of course they were too goddamned shrewd to test it themselves, Vernon and this guy started getting people – their friends basically – to take it.'

'Even *you*?'

'Vernon didn't want me to take it at first, but he talked it up so much that *I* insisted. You know what I was like, curious to a fault.'

'It wasn't a fault.'

'Anyway, a few of us found ourselves in on this – I don't know – let's call it an *informal* trial period.' She paused and took a sip from her beer. 'So what do you want, I took it and it *was* amazing.' She paused again, and looked at me for confirmation. 'I mean, you've taken it, you know what I'm talking about, right?'

I nodded.

'Well. I did it a few more times and then I got scared.'

'Why?'

'*Why?* Because . . . I wasn't stupid. I knew no one could maintain that level of mental activity for very long and survive. It was nonsense. Let me give you an example, one day I read Brian Greene's *The Elegant Universe* . . . superstring theory, yeah? I read it in forty-five minutes, and *understood* it.' She took a last drag from her cigarette. 'Don't ask me about it now, though.' She stubbed the cigarette out in the ashtray. 'Then I had this thing I was supposed to be working on at the time, a series of articles about self-organizing adaptive systems – the research that's been done into them, their wider applicability, whatever. My work-rate increased *ten*-fold overnight, I'm not kidding you. My boss at *Iroquois* magazine thought I was pitching for his job as Features Editor. So I guess I just chickened out. I panicked. I couldn't handle it. I stopped taking it.'

She shrugged her shoulders a couple of times.

'And?'

'And – *eh* – I started getting sick, after a few weeks, headaches, nausea. Talk about panic. I went back to Vernon to see if I maybe shouldn't take another hit, or half a hit, see if *that* would make any difference. But that was when he told me about this other guy who'd just died.'

'How had he died?'

'Rapid two-day deterioration – headaches, dizziness, loss of motor skills, blackouts. Boom. He was dead.'

'How much had he taken?'

'One hit every day for about a month.'

I swallowed again and closed my eyes for a second.

'How much have *you* been taking, Eddie?'

She was looking directly at me now, with those remarkable deep brown eyes. She was biting on her lower lip.

'I've been taking a *lot*.' I clicked my tongue. 'More than *that* guy.'

'*Jesus.*'

There was a long pause.

'So you must still have a supply, then,' she said eventually.

'Not exactly, I've got some left, a stash, but . . . I got it *from* Vernon. *He* supplied it to me and now he's gone. I don't know anyone else.'

She looked at me, slightly puzzled. Then she said, 'That guy I told you about died because they didn't know what they were doing, they had no idea about dosage or strength, or anything – and as well, people reacted to it differently. But it didn't take them long to work all of that stuff out.' She paused, took in another deep breath, and continued. 'Vernon was making a lot of money dealing MDT, and I haven't heard of anyone else dying since the early days, so presumably whatever he gave you or told you was right for *you*. I mean, the dosage was worked out, right? You *do* know what you're doing?'

'Hmm.'

Did I tell her at this point that Vernon had only given me a sampler, and that he hadn't had a chance to tell me *anything*?

What I said was, 'So what happened with *you*, Melissa?'

She lit up another cigarette and seemed to be considering for a moment whether or not she was going to let me sidetrack her.

I took a cigarette, too.

Then she began. 'Well, naturally after me getting sick and that guy dying I didn't go near it again, I didn't touch it. But I was really scared. I mean I was married and had *two small kids*.' When she said this, she almost flinched, as though reacting to a threatened slap in the face – as though she felt that articulating this level of irresponsibility should instantly have provoked a violent reaction from *someone*. After a moment, she went on. 'Anyway, it never seemed to get much worse than bad headaches and occasional nausea. But over a period of months I noticed a pattern. I couldn't concentrate on anything for longer than ten minutes at a stretch without getting a migraine. I missed deadlines. I became sluggish, lazy. I put on *weight*.' She pulled contemptuously at her sweater. 'My memory was shot to bits. That series of articles? Forget it – the whole thing just disintegrated. *Iroquois* magazine let me go. The marriage fell apart. Sex? Get out of here.' She leant back and shook her head. 'That was four years ago and I haven't been the same since.'

'And now?'

'*Now* I live in Mahopac and waitress four nights a week at a place called Cicero's. *Now* I can't read any more – I mean, what, the fucking *New York Post*?'

I felt as though sulphuric acid were being secreted into the pit of my stomach.

'I can't deal with stressful or emotional situations any more, Eddie. I'm wired up now because I'm seeing *you*, but after this meeting I'm going to have a headache for three days. Believe me, I'm going to pay dearly for this.'

She half stood up and eased her way out of the booth.

'*And* I've got to pee. Which is another thing.' She stood there, looking down at me, one hand scratching the back of her head. 'But Jesus, you don't need to know about *that*, right?'

Waving an arm dismissively, Melissa walked off towards the bathroom.

I gazed out across the bar now, reeling from what she'd told me, barely able to comprehend it. First of all, it seemed incredible to me that we were actually in the same place together, sharing a drink, talking – and that right now she was over there in the bathroom, in jeans and a baggy sweater, peeing. Because any time I'd thought of her over the past ten years, the person I'd automatically visualized had been the thin shiny Melissa of circa 1988, the one with long black hair and prominent cheekbones, the Melissa I'd seen hike up her skirt a thousand times and pee and continue talking about whatever she'd been talking about. But the Melissa of those days, apparently, had unravelled in time and space and was a ghost now. I was never going to see *her* again, never going to bump into *her* in the street. She'd been supplanted by the Melissa I hadn't kept up with, the one who'd gotten married again and had kids, who'd worked for *Iroquois* magazine, the one who'd allowed her teeming, tumultuous brain to be damaged, and permanently so, by some untried, untested and previously unknown pharmaceutical product . . .

Before long, tears were gathering behind my eyes and I could feel a rawness in my throat. Then my hands started shaking. What was happening to me? It'd only been something like twenty-four hours since I'd taken my last dose of MDT and already it seemed that small cracks were appearing on the hard chemical shell that had formed around me in recent weeks. Seeping through these cracks, in turn, were some strong emotions, and I wasn't sure how well I

196

was going to be able to handle them. I pictured myself crying, sobbing, crawling across the floor, *climbing up the walls*, all of which seemed to make perfect sense for a while, as though it would be an exquisite relief. But then in the next moment Melissa was on her way back from the bathroom and I had to make some kind of an effort to pull myself together.

She sat down opposite me again and said, 'You OK?'

I nodded, 'I'm fine.'

'You don't *look* fine?'

'It's just . . . I'm happy to see you again, Melissa, I really am. But I feel so bad about . . . you know . . . I mean, I can't believe that you've . . .'

The tears I'd been trying to hold back came into my eyes at this point. I clenched my fists and stared down at the table. 'Sorry,' I said, after a moment, and then smiled – but the expression on my face was probably so demented that it didn't come across as a smile. I said 'sorry' again and as I wiped my eyes with one hand, I ground the knuckles of the other one into the surface of the wooden bench I was sitting on.

Without looking directly at her, I could tell that Melissa was now engaged in a damage limitation exercise of her own, one which involved taking deep breaths and whispering the word *shit* to herself every couple of seconds.

'Look, Eddie,' she said eventually, 'this isn't about me anymore, or about us – it's about *you*.'

That statement had a steadying effect on me and I tried to focus on the implications of it for a moment.

She went on, 'The reason I called you was because I thought . . . I don't know, I thought if you were doing MDT, or *had* done it, that you should at least know what had happened to me. But I'd no idea you were so . . .' she shook her head, '. . . *involved*. And then when I read that thing in the *Post* . . .'

I looked down into my glass of beer. I hadn't touched it and didn't think I was going to.

'I mean, day-trading? Short-selling biotech stocks? I just couldn't believe it. You must be doing a *lot* of MDT.'

I nodded, in tacit agreement.

'But what happens when your supply runs out, Eddie? That's when the real trouble's going to start.'

Almost thinking aloud, I said, 'Maybe I could stop taking it *now*. Or I could try weaning myself off it.' I paused briefly to consider these options, but then said, 'Of course there's no guarantee that by doing either of those things I'd be doing the *right* thing, right?'

'No,' she said, looking quite pale and tired all of a sudden, 'but I wouldn't just *stop*. Not outright. That's what I did. You see, it's about dosage – how much you take, when you take it. That's what they worked out after I started getting sick, and after that other guy died.'

'So I should cut down? I should cut *back*?'

'I don't know. I think so. Jesus, I can't believe that Vernon didn't *tell* you about any of this stuff.'

I could see that she was puzzled. My story – or what she knew of it so far – obviously made very little sense.

'Melissa, Vernon never told me anything.'

As I said this, I realized that for my story to *make* sense – without being the full truth – I was going to have to lie to her, and in a fairly elaborate way. Certain obvious and very awkward questions naturally posed themselves at this point, and I was dreading her asking them – questions such as: How many times had I actually seen Vernon? How had I come to have such a large supply of MDT? Why hadn't I bothered to find out more about it? But to my surprise, Melissa didn't put any of these questions to me, or any others for that matter, and we both fell silent for a while.

I studied her face as she lit up another cigarette. I would have expected the Melissa I'd known ten years before to pursue me on every point here, to seek clarification, to have me piece it all together for her. But the woman sitting opposite me now had clearly run out of that kind of steam. I could see that she was curious, and wanted to know why I wasn't being straight with her, but on another level it was also plain that she didn't have the time or energy for this sort of thing any more. Vernon was dead. She'd said her piece to me about MDT. She was undeniably concerned about my predicament.

But what else could she do or say? She had two kids at home and a life to cope with that was radically different from anything she might ever have envisaged for herself, or felt entitled to. She was *tired*.

I was on my own.

Melissa looked up at me. 'I'm sorry, Eddie.'

'One question,' I said, 'that client of Vernon's you mentioned? The one who worked for the pharmaceutical plant? I suppose I should be talking to him? That would make sense, wouldn't it?' But I immediately saw from the expression on her face that she wasn't going to be able to help me out.

'I only met him once, Eddie – four years ago. I don't remember his name. Tom something – or *Todd*. That's the best I can do. I'm really sorry.'

I began to feel panicky now.

'What about the police investigation?' I said, 'No one ever got back in touch with me after that first day. Did they get in touch with you? I mean – did they find out who killed Vernon, and why?'

'No, but they knew he'd been a coke-dealer at one point, so I guess they're working on the assumption that it was . . . a coke thing.'

I paused here, a little thrown by the phrase, 'a coke thing'. After a moment of reflection, and with the merest hint of sarcasm in my voice, I repeated it, 'a coke thing'. This was a phrase Melissa had once used to describe our marriage. She picked up on the reference immediately and seemed to deflate even further.

'That still rankles, does it?'

'Not really, but . . . it *wasn't* a coke thing—'

'I know that. Me making the comment was.'

I could have said a hundred different things in response to that, but all I could come up with was, 'It was a strange time.'

'That's true.'

'Whenever I look back on it now – I don't know – it feels . . .'

'What?'

'It's futile thinking about it, but there's so much of it that I would do differently.'

The obvious follow-up question – *like what?* – hung in the air between us for a moment or two. Then Melissa said, 'So would I.'

She was visibly drained now, and my headache was getting worse, so I decided it was time to extricate us both from the embarrassment and pain of a fraught conversation we'd wandered into carelessly, and which, if we didn't watch it, could lead us into messy and very complicated territory.

Bracing myself, I then asked her to tell me something about her children. It transpired that she had two daughters, Ally, eight, and Jane, six. They were great, she said, I'd love them – quick-witted, strong-willed tyrants who didn't miss a trick.

That was it, I thought, *enough* – I had to get out of there.

We spent a few more minutes chatting and then we brought it to a close. I promised Melissa that I'd keep in touch, that I'd let her know how I was getting on and that maybe I'd even come up someday to see her and the girls in Mahopac. She wrote down her address on a piece of paper, which I looked at and put into the pocket of my shirt.

Seeming to draw on some final reserve of energy, Melissa then held my gaze and said, 'Eddie, what are you going to do about this?'

I told her I wasn't sure, but that I'd be OK, that I had quite a few MDT pills left and consequently had plenty of room to manoeuvre. I would cut down gradually and see how that worked out. I'd be fine. Since I hadn't mentioned anything to her about the blackouts, however, this felt like a lie. But I didn't think that under the circumstances Melissa would notice.

She nodded. Maybe she had noticed – but again, even if she had, what could she do?

Outside on Spring Street we said goodbye and embraced. Melissa got a taxi to Grand Central Station and I walked back to Tenth Street.

[18]

THE FIRST THING I DID when I got into the apartment was take a
couple of Extra-Strength Excedrin tablets for my headache. Then
I lay on the couch and stared up at the ceiling, hoping that the pain
– which was concentrated behind my eyes and had got steadily worse
on the walk home from Spring Street – would subside quickly and
then fade away altogether. I didn't often get headaches, so I wasn't
sure if this one had come about as a result of my conversation with
Melissa, or if it was a symptom of my sudden withdrawal from MDT.
Either way – and both explanations seemed plausible at the time –
I found it extremely unsettling.

In addition to this, the cracks that had been appearing and multiplying since morning were now being prised apart even wider, and
left exposed, like open wounds. Again and again, I went over
Melissa's story, my thoughts vacillating between horror at what had
happened to her and fear about what might be happening to me. I
was haunted by the notion of how easily and irreversibly a careless
decision, a mood, a whim, can change the direction of a person's
life. I thought about Donatella Alvarez and found it harder than
before to simply dismiss the idea that I'd been in any way responsible for what had happened to *her* – for the easy, irreversible way
her life had changed. I thought about my time with Melissa, and
worried, agonized, about those things I might have done differently.

But this was clearly an intolerable situation. I had to take some
action soon, or before I knew it I'd be getting *sick* – sliding into a
clinical swamp, developing a whole syndrome of conditions, passing
some awful point of no return. So at the very first glimmer of relief

from the Excedrin – and this was only the merest dulling of the pain – I got up from the couch and started walking around the apartment, vigorously, as though in some literal sense trying to shake myself into good health.

Then I remembered something.

I went into the bedroom and over to the closet. Trying to ignore the throbbing in my head, I bent down and pulled out the old shoe-box from under the blanket and the pile of magazines. I opened it and lifted out the big brown envelope where I'd hidden the cash and pills. I put my hand into the envelope and felt around, ignoring the sealed plastic bag containing the more than 350 pills that were still left. What I was searching for was the other thing I'd hidden in the envelope – Vernon's tiny black notebook.

When I found it, I started thumbing my way through it page by page. There were dozens of names and phone numbers in it, quite a few of which had been crossed out, sometimes with new numbers written in above or below the old ones. I recognized Deke Tauber's name this time, and I vaguely recognized a few other names, but annoyingly – and I checked several times – I didn't find anyone listed in the notebook whose name was Tom or Todd.

But still, there had to be someone in amongst all these names who could help me, someone I could contact and maybe get some information from.

After all, I thought, who *were* these people?

Obvious as it was, and even though I'd had the notebook lying in my closet for weeks, it only dawned on me now – this, of course, had been Vernon's list of clients.

The realization that these people had all used MDT at one time or another, and were maybe still using it, came as quite a shock to me. It also bruised my ego a little, because although it was clearly irrational to think that no one besides myself had ever experienced the amazing effects of MDT, I nevertheless felt that my experience of it was in some way unique and more authentic than that of anyone else who might have tried it. This slightly indignant sense of ownership lingered in my mind as I read through the names in the notebook one more time, but then something else of significance occurred to me. If all of these people were on MDT, then surely that meant it had to be possible to *do* MDT without succumbing to headaches or blackouts, not to mention permanent brain damage.

I took another two Excedrin tablets and continued studying the notebook. The more I looked at the names the more familiar some of them seemed, until eventually about half of them had emerged from their earlier obscurity and I started being able to place them. A lot of the names that I recognized were from the business world, people who worked for new or medium-sized companies. There were several writers and journalists, and a couple of architects. Apart from Deke Tauber, none of these people was particularly well-known to the public at large. They all enjoyed some small measure of celebrity, but would be much better-known in their specific fields, so I decided it might be useful to do a little background research into some of them. I booted up my computer and went online.

Deke Tauber was the obvious one to start with. He had been a bond salesman on Wall Street in the mid-1980s – making lots of money, but spending considerably more. One or other of the Gants had known him in college, so he was often around, at parties, in bars, at openings, wherever there was premium quality blow to be had. I'd met him once or twice and found him to be arrogant and fairly objectionable. After the crash in 1987, however, he lost his job, moved out to California and that appeared to be the end of him.

Then about three years ago Tauber showed up in New York again, leading a dubious self-improvement cult – Dekedelia – that he had set up in LA. After a slow start, Dekedelia's membership grew dramatically and Tauber started producing best-selling books and videos. He set up his own software company, opened a chain of cybercafés and moved into real estate. Soon, Dekedelia was a multi-million dollar business, employing over two hundred people, most of whom were also cult members.

When I trawled through what information I'd managed to find

on other people named in Vernon's client list, I saw the first of two distinct patterns emerging. In each case I looked at, there was – over the previous three or four years – a sudden and unexplained leap forward in the career of the person concerned. Take Theodore Neal. After two decades of churning out unauthorized showbiz biographies and hack magazine work, Neal suddenly produced a brilliant and compelling life of Ulysses S. Grant. Described as 'a breathtaking and original work of scholarship', it went on to win the National Book Critics Circle Award. Or Jim Rayburn, the chief of struggling record-label, Thrust, who in one six-month period discovered and signed up hip-hop artists J. J. Rictus, Human Cheese and F Train – and then within another six months had a full mantelpiece of Grammy and MTV awards to his name.

There were others – middle management grunts fast-tracking it to CEO, defence attorneys mesmerizing juries to achieve unlikely acquittals, architects designing elaborate new skyscrapers over lunch, on the backs of cocktail napkins . . .

It was bizarre, and through the band of pain pulsating behind my eyes I had only one thought: MDT-48 was *out there in society*. Other people were using it in the same way that I'd been using it. What I didn't know was how much they were taking, and how often. *I'd* been taking MDT indiscriminately, one, two, occasionally even three at a pop, but I had no idea if I really needed that many, and if taking that many actually rendered the hit more intense or made it last any longer. It was like with cocaine, I supposed, in that after a while it was just a question of gluttony. Sooner or later, if the drug was there, gluttony became the controlling dynamic in your relationship to it.

So the only way I was going to find out about dosage was to contact someone on the list – just phone them up and ask them what they knew. It was when I did this that the second and more disturbing pattern began to emerge.

I put it off until the following day – because of my headache, because I was reluctant to call up people I didn't know, because I was scared of what I might find out. I kept popping Excedrin tablets every few hours, and although they took the edge off the pain, there was still a dull and fairly constant thumping sensation behind my eyes.

I didn't imagine I'd have any luck getting through to Deke Tauber, so the first name I selected from the list was that of a CFO in a medium-sized electronics company. I remembered his name from an article I'd read in *Wired*.

A woman answered the phone.

'Good morning,' I said, 'may I speak to Paul Kaplan, please?'

The woman didn't respond, and in the brief silence that followed I considered the possibility that we'd been disconnected. To check, I said, 'Hello?'

'Who is this, please?' she said, her tone both weary and impatient.

'I'm a journalist,' I said, 'from *Electronics Today* magaz—'

'Look . . . my husband died three days ago.'

'Oh—'

My mind froze. What did I say now? There was silence. It seemed to go on for ever. I eventually said, 'I'm very sorry.'

The woman remained silent. I could hear muffled voices in the background. I wanted to ask her how her husband had died, but I was unable to form the words.

Then she said, 'I'm sorry . . . thank you . . . goodbye.'

And that was that.

Her husband had died three days ago. It didn't necessarily mean anything. People died all the time.

I selected another number and dialled it. I waited, staring at the wall in front of me.

'Yes?'

A man's voice.

'May I speak to Jerry Brady, please?'

'Jerry's in . . .' He paused, and then said, 'who's this?'

I'd chosen the number at random and realized now that I didn't know who Jerry Brady was – or who *I* should be, calling him up on a Sunday morning like this.

'It's . . . a friend.'

The man hesitated, but then went on, 'Jerry's in the hospital . . .'
– there was a slight shake in his voice – '. . . and he's *really* sick.'

'Oh my god. That's awful. What's wrong with him?'

'That's just it, we don't know. He started getting these *headaches*
a couple of weeks ago? Then last Tuesday – no . . . Wednesday –
he collapsed at work . . .'

'*Shit.*'

'. . . and when he came to he said he'd been having dizzy spells
and muscular spasms all day. He's been in and out of consciousness
ever since, trembling, throwing up.'

'What have the doctors said?'

'They don't know. I mean, what do you want, they're *doctors*. All
the tests they've done so far have been inconclusive. I'll tell you
something, though . . .'

He paused here, and clicked his tongue. I got the impression
from his slightly breathless tone that he was dying to talk to someone
but at the same time couldn't quite ignore the fact that he had no
idea who I was. For my part I wondered who *he* was – a brother?
A lover?

I said, 'Yeah? Go on . . .'

'OK, here's the thing,' he said, obviously judging it immaterial at
this stage of the proceedings who the fuck I was, 'Jerry'd been weird
for weeks, even before the headaches. Like he was really preoccu-
pied with something, and *worried*. Which wasn't Jerry's style at all.'
He paused for a beat. 'Oh my god I said *wasn't*.'

I felt faint and put my free hand up to lean against the wall.

'Look,' I said quickly, 'I'm not going to take up any more of your
time. Just give Jerry my best, would you?' Without saying my name,
or anything else, I put the phone down.

I staggered back towards the couch and fell on to it. I lay there
for about half an hour, horrified, replaying the two conversations
over and over in my mind.

I eventually got up and dragged myself back to the telephone.
There were between forty and fifty names in the notebook and so
far I'd only called two of them. I picked another number – and then
another one, and then another one after that.

But it was the same story each time. Of the people I tried to contact, three were dead and the remainder were sick – either already in the hospital, or in varying states of panic at home. In other circumstances, this might have constituted a mini-epidemic, but given that these people displayed quite a wide range of symptoms – and were spread out over Manhattan, Brooklyn, Queens and Long Island – it was unlikely that anyone would make a connection between them. In fact, the only thing that did connect them, as far as I could see, was the presence of their phone numbers in this little notebook.

Sitting on the couch again, massaging my temples, I stared up at the ceramic bowl on the wooden shelf above the computer. I had no choice now. If I didn't go back on MDT, this headache would intensify and soon be joined by other symptoms, the ones I'd repeatedly heard described on the telephone – dizziness, nausea, muscular spasms, impairment of motor skills. And then, apparently, I would die. It certainly looked as if all the people on Vernon's client list were going to die, so why should I be any different?

But there *was* a difference, and a significant one. I could go back on MDT if I chose to. And they couldn't. I had a fairly substantial stash of MDT. And they didn't. Forty or fifty people were out there suffering severe and very probably lethal withdrawal symptoms because their supply had dried up.

And mine hadn't.

In fact, mine had only started, because clearly *their* supply – or what would have been their supply if Vernon hadn't died – was the stuff *I'd* been taking for the past few weeks. I had dreadful guilt feelings about this, but what could I do? There were over three hundred and fifty pills left in my closet, which gave me considerable breathing space, but if I were to share these out among fifty other people no one would benefit. Instead of us all dying this week, we'd all die next week.

In any case I decided that if I drastically reduced my own intake of MDT, it would have the effect of prolonging my supply, and might also, possibly, stop the blackouts, or at least curtail them.

❖   ❖   ❖

I got up and went over to the desk. I stood for a moment, gazing at the ceramic bowl on the shelf, but before I even reached out to touch it I knew that something wasn't right. I had a sense of fore-boding, of alarm. I took the bowl in my left hand and looked into it. The alarm quickly turned to panic.

Unbelievably, there were only *two* tablets left in the bowl.

Very slowly, almost as if I'd forgotten how to move, I sat down in the chair at my desk.

I'd put *ten* tablets into the bowl a couple of days before, and I'd only taken three of them out since then. So where were the other five?

I felt dizzy, and gripped the side of the chair to steady myself.

Gennady.

When I'd finished on the phone with my bank manager the other day, Gennady had been standing here at the desk, with his back to me.

Could he have taken some of the tablets?

It didn't seem possible, but I racked my brains trying to visualize what had gone on, what the exact sequence of movements had been. And then I remembered – when I'd picked up the phone to call Howard Lewis, I'd turned my back on him.

A couple of minutes drifted by, during which the mind-bending notion of Gennady on MDT sank in. How long would it be, I thought, before the stuff made its way on to the streets, before someone worked out just what it was, reproduced it, gave it a marketable name and started dealing it in clubs, in the backs of cars, on street corners . . . micro-doses cut with speed at ten bucks a pop . . . ? I didn't really imagine things would go that far, I suppose – not yet, not if Gennady only had five doses. But given the nature of the MDT hit, it would be safe to assume that once he'd tried it out the first time he'd be unlikely to exercise much restraint with the rest of it. He'd also be unlikely to forget where he'd come across the stuff in the first place.

I took one of the two tiny pills out of the bowl and using a blade divided it neatly in half. I swallowed one of the halves. Then I just sat at the desk, thinking about how my situation had changed so

208

radically over the previous three or four days, how it had started to fall apart at the seams, to convulse and haemorrhage and slip towards the recurring, the chronic, the terminal.

Then, about twenty minutes after that again, in the slipstream of this downward moodswing, I noticed out of the blue that my headache had lifted completely.

[19]

FOR THE NEXT FEW DAYS, therefore, I only took half a pill each morning with breakfast. This dosage brought me as close to 'normal' as it was probably possible to get under the circumstances. I was apprehensive at first, but when the headaches didn't come back, I relaxed somewhat and allowed myself to think I might have found a way out, or, at the very least – with a stash of nearly seven hundred such doses in prospect – plenty of time in which to *look* for a way out.

But of course it wasn't that simple.

I slept until nine o'clock on the Monday morning. I had oranges, toast and coffee for breakfast, followed by a couple of cigarettes. Then I had a shower and got dressed. I put on my new suit – which wasn't that new any more – and stood in front of the mirror. I had to go into Carl Van Loon's office, but all of a sudden I felt extremely uncomfortable about having to go anywhere dressed like this. I thought I looked strange. A while later, as I made my way into the lobby of the Van Loon Building on Forty-eighth Street, I was so self-conscious that I half expected someone to tap me on the shoulder and tell me it had all been a terrible mistake, and that Mr Van Loon had left instructions to have me escorted from the building if I happened to show up.

Then, in the elevator to the sixty-second floor, I started thinking about the deal I was supposed to be brokering with Van Loon – the Abraxas buyout of MCL-Parnassus. I hadn't given any thought to it for days – but now, as soon as I tried to recall any of the specifics, the whole subject became a blur. I kept hearing the phrase 'option value pricing-model' in my head, hearing it over and over – option value pricing-model, option value pricing-model – but I had only the vaguest notion any more of what this meant. I also knew that 'the build-out of a broadband infrastructure' was important, but I couldn't quite figure out why. It was like waking up after a dream in which you've been speaking a foreign language only to find out that you don't speak the language at all, and barely even understand a word of it.

I stepped out of the elevator and into the lobby area. I walked over to the main desk and stood for a moment, waiting to catch the receptionist's attention. It was the same woman who'd been here the previous Thursday, so when she turned to me, I smiled. But she didn't show any sign of recognition.

'May I help you, sir?'

Her tone was formal and quite chilly.

'Eddie Spinola,' I said, 'for Mr Van Loon.'

She consulted her diary and then started to shake her head. She seemed to be about to tell me something – maybe that Mr Van Loon was out of the country, or that she had no record of my appointment – but just then, walking slowly from a corridor to the left of the reception desk, Van Loon himself appeared. He looked sombre and as he put a hand out to greet me I noticed that his stoop was more pronounced than I'd remembered.

The receptionist went back to what she'd been doing before I interrupted her.

'Eddie, how are you?'

'I'm fine, Carl. Feeling much better.'

We shook hands.

'Good. Good. Come on in.'

I was struck again by the size of Van Loon's office, which was long and wide, but decorated very sparely. He went over to his desk and sat behind it. He indicated that I should sit as well.

He sighed, and shook his head for a moment. 'OK, look Eddie,' he said, 'that thing in the *Post* Friday was not good, not the kind of publicity we want associated with this deal, yeah?'

I nodded, unsure about where this might lead. I'd half hoped that the article might escape his notice.

'Hank doesn't know you, and the deal is still under wraps, so there's nothing to worry about, yet. I just don't think you should show your face down at Lafayette any more.'

'No, of course not.'

'Keep a low profile. Trade here. Like I said, we have our own trading room. It's discreet and private.' He smiled. 'No fucking base-ball caps.'

I smiled at this, too – but I actually felt quite uncomfortable, and nervous, as if I could very easily throw up.

'I'll have someone show you around the floor later.'

'Yeah.'

'The other thing I wanted to tell you, and maybe this is a good thing, is that Hank won't be here tomorrow. He's been delayed in LA, so we're not going to have that meeting until . . . probably until the middle or even the end of . . . *next* week.'

'Yeah, OK,' I mumbled, finding it hard to look Van Loon in the eye, 'it's probably . . . like you say, it's probably a *good* thing, no?'

'Yeah.' He picked a pen up from his desk and fiddled with it. 'I'm going to be away, too – until the weekend at least, so it gives us a little breathing space. We were rushed on Thursday in my opinion, but we can go at our own pace now, hone the figures, put a really air-tight package together.'

I looked up and saw that Van Loon was handing me something. I reached across the desk to take it. What he was handing me was the yellow legal pad that I'd used the previous Thursday to write out the option values on.

'I want you to expand these projections and do them up on the computer.' He cleared his throat. 'By the way, I've been looking at them and I've got a couple of questions I want to ask you.'

I sat back now and stared at the dense rows of figures and math-ematical symbols on the first page of the legal pad. Even though it was all in my own handwriting, I had difficulty making any sense of it and felt that I was looking at some strange form of hieroglyphics. Gradually, however, what was on the page reconfigured itself before my eyes into something vaguely familiar, and I saw that if I could only concentrate on it for an hour or two I'd probably be able to decode it.

But with Carl Van Loon sitting directly opposite me now, and ready to ask questions, a couple of hours wasn't really an option. This was the first serious indication I'd had that my strategy of minimum dosage was only going to be good for one thing: keeping the headaches at bay. Because none of the other stuff was happening, and I was becoming increasingly aware of what it meant to feel 'normal'. It meant not being able to influence people and make them anxious to do things for you. It meant not being able to run with your instincts and invariably be right. It meant not being able to recall minute details and make rapid calculations.

'I can see a couple of inconsistencies here,' I said, in an attempt to head off Van Loon's questions. 'And you're right, we *were* rushed.'

I flicked over to the second page and then got up from my chair. Pretending to be focused on the projections, I walked around for a bit and tried to think of what I was going to say next – like an actor who's forgotten his lines.

'I wanted to ask you,' Van Loon said from his desk, 'why is the life of the . . . third option there different from the others?'

I looked around at him for a second, mumbled something and then went back to the legal pad. I stared at it intently, but my mind was blank and I knew that nothing was going to suddenly pop into it that would rescue me.

'The *third* one?' I said, stalling for time, flipping the pages over.

Then I just flipped all the pages back again and put the pad under my arm. 'You know what, Carl?' I said, looking at him directly now, 'I'm going to have to go over these carefully. Let me do them up on the computer at home like you said and then maybe we can—'

'*The third option, Eddie,*' he said, raising his voice suddenly, '*what's the big fucking deal? You're not going to let me ask you a simple question?*'

I was standing about five yards now from the desk of a man who had appeared on dozens of magazine covers – a billionaire, an entrepreneur, an icon – and he was shouting at me. I didn't know how to respond. I was out of my depth. I was *afraid*.

And then, luckily, his telephone rang. He picked it up and barked, '*What?*'

I waited a second before turning around and moving away to let him speak. My hands were shaking slightly and the nauseous feeling I'd had earlier came back.

'Don't send those ones,' Van Loon was saying into the phone behind me. 'Check with Mancuso before you do anything – and listen, about the delivery dates . . .'

Relieved to be off the hook for a while, I drifted further down this huge room, towards the windows. These were full-length, with a west-facing view that was partially obscured by hanging blinds. I would tell Van Loon when he got off the phone that I had a migraine or something and that I couldn't focus properly. He'd seen me write the stuff out on Thursday and we'd talked about it in detail, so he could hardly doubt my command of the material. The important thing now, for me, was just to get out of there.

As I waited, I glanced around at the office. The top part was dominated by Van Loon's enormous desk, but the rest of it had the airy and austere feel to it of a waiting–room in an Art Deco railway station. By the time I got to the windows, I had the impression that Van Loon was far behind me, and that if I were to turn around he'd be a figure in the distance – his voice barely audible, droning on about delivery dates. At this end of the room there were some red leather couches and low glass tables with business magazines scattered on them.

As I stood at the windows, peering through the hanging blinds, one of the first things I noticed – in among the familiar cluster of midtown skyscrapers – was a glimmering shard of the Celestial Building over on the West Side. From this perspective, it seemed to be huddled in among a dozen other buildings, but if you looked closely you could see that it was further back than the others, and that it actually stood alone. It seemed incredible to me that I'd been in the Celestial a couple of days before, and had even contemplated buying an apartment in it – and one of the costlier units at that . . .

Nine and a half million dollars.

'*Eddie!*'

I turned around.

Van Loon was off the phone and approaching from the other end of the room.

I braced myself.

'Something's come up, Eddie. I have to go. I'm sorry.' His tone was all friendly now, and when he arrived at where I was standing, he nodded at the yellow legal pad under my arm. 'Do up that stuff and we'll talk. As I said I'm away until the weekend, so that should give you enough time.' He clapped his hands together suddenly. 'OK, you want to have a look at our trading floor? I'll call Sam Welles and have him show you around.'

'I think I'll head home and just get stuck into this, if you don't mind,' I said, and nudged my arm forward.

'But it'd only take—' Van Loon paused and stared at me for a moment. I could see that he was puzzled, and probably felt a mild antagonism towards me, just as he had earlier, but he clearly didn't understand why this was happening to him and wasn't sure how to handle it.

Then he said, 'What's the matter with you, Eddie? You're not going soft on me, are you?'

'No, I—'

'Because this shit isn't for the faint-hearted.'

'I know that, I just—'

'And I'm out on a limb here, Eddie. *No* one knows about this. You fuck up on me, you *talk* about this – my credibility is blown.'

'I know, I know.' I indicated again to the pad under my arm, '. . . I just want to get this right.'

Van Loon held my gaze for a moment and then sighed, as if to say, 'Well *that's* nice to know.' Then he turned around and started walking back towards his desk. I followed him.

'Call me when you're done,' he said. He had his back to me now, and was standing at the front of the desk, consulting something, a diary or a notebook. 'And make it no later than Tuesday or Wednesday of next week.'

I hesitated, but then realized I'd just been dismissed. I walked out of the office without saying another word.

On my way home, I stopped off at a Gristede's and bought a few large packs of potato chips and some beers. Back in the apartment, I sat at my desk, got out the thick folder of stuff Van Loon had sent me the previous week and assembled my notes. I thought if I could come to grips with all of this material, I'd be OK. I'd be as informed and up-to-date as I had been when I'd impressed Van Loon with my proposal for structuring the buy-out deal.

I kicked off with the set of MCL-Parnassus quarterly reports in the folder. I laid them out on my desk, opened the first pack of chips and bottle of beer, and started reading.

It took me about two hours of assiduous page-turning before I could admit to myself that not only was this material stultifyingly boring, it was also largely incomprehensible to me. The problem was simple: I couldn't remember how to interpret this kind of stuff. I had a look at some of the other documents, and although these were slightly less dense and impenetrable than the quarterly reports, they were no less boring. But I persevered, and made sure that I read everything – or, at least in the sense that my eye passed over every word and every line, didn't *miss* anything.

I finished all of the chips and beer and ordered up Chinese at about ten o'clock. Shortly after midnight, I finally caved in and went to bed.

The next morning I made a quick and terrifying calculation. It had taken me eight hours the day before to read what previously I'd read in about forty-five minutes. I then tried to recall some of it, but could only summon up fragments, generalities. Previously I'd been able to remember all of it, back to front, inside out.

The temptation at this stage to take a couple of MDT pills was very strong indeed, but I persevered. If I went back full-thrust on MDT, I would only end up having more blackouts, and where would that leave me? So the pattern remained the same over the next couple of days. I stayed at home and waded through hundreds of pages of material, only leaving the apartment to get stuff like potato chips and cheeseburgers and beer. I watched a good deal of TV, but studiously avoided newscasts and current affairs shows. I kept my phone unplugged. I suppose at some level I created the illusion for myself that I was coming to grips with the material, but as the days passed I had to admit that very little of it was sinking in.

On the Wednesday evening I detected the onset of another headache. I wasn't sure what had caused it, maybe it was all the beer and junk food I'd been consuming, but when it hadn't gone away by Thursday morning I decided to up the minimum dosage of MDT to one pill a day. Of course, within about twenty minutes of taking this higher dosage my headache had lifted, and – of course – I started worrying. How long would it be before I had to increase the dosage again? How long would it be before I was chugging down three or even four pills each morning just to keep the headaches at bay?

I took out Vernon's little notebook again and examined it. I had no desire to go through the same routine as before, but I nevertheless felt that if there was any hope left in this situation it had to lie somewhere in among these numbers. I decided to call a few of the ones that had been crossed out and didn't have replacements written in above or below them. Maybe I would discover that they belonged to people who were still alive, and weren't even sick, people who would talk to me, ex-clients. Or maybe – more likely – I would find out that the reason they were ex-clients was because they *were* dead. But it was worth a try.

I called five numbers. The first three were no longer in service. The fourth number didn't reply or have an answering machine. The fifth one picked up after two rings.

'Yep?'

'Hello. May I speak to Donald Geisler please?'

'Speaking. What do you want?'

'I was a friend of Vernon Gant's. I don't know if you know but he was killed a while back and I was—'

I stopped.

He'd hung up.

It was a response, though. And clearly the guy wasn't dead. I waited ten minutes and called again.

'Yep?'

'Please don't hang up. *Please*.'

There was a pause, during which Donald Geisler didn't hang up. Or say anything.

'I'm looking for some help,' I said, 'some information maybe. I don't know.'

'Where did you get this number?'

'It was . . . among Vernon's things.'

'*Shit!*'

'But there's noth—'

'Are you a *cop*? Is this an investigation of some kind?'

'No. Vernon was an old friend of mine.'

'I don't like this.'

'In fact, he was my ex-brother-in-law.'

'That doesn't make me feel any better.'

'Look, this is about—'

'Don't say it on the phone.'

I stopped again. He *knew*.

'OK, I won't. But is there any way that I could talk to you? I need your help. I mean, you obviously know—'

'*You* need *my* help? I don't think so.'

'Yes, because—'

'Look, I'm going to hang up now. So *don't* phone me back. In fact, don't *ever* try to contact me again, and—'

'Mr Geisler, I might be dying.'

'Oh, *Christ*.'

'And I need—'

'*Leave me alone, all right?*'

He hung up.

My heart was thumping.

If Donald Geisler didn't want to talk to me, there wasn't much I could do about it. He mightn't have been able to help in any case, but it was still frustrating to make such brief contact with someone who obviously knew what MDT was.

Not in the mood any more to go on with this, I put the black notebook away. Then, in an effort to distract myself, I returned to my desk and picked up a document that I'd printed out earlier from a financial website.

I opened it and started reading.

The document was a highly technical article about anti-trust legislation and by page three my attention had already drifted. After a while I stopped reading, put the article down and lit up a cigarette. Then I just sat there for ages, smoking, staring into space.

Later, in the afternoon, I made a trip to the bank. Gennady was coming the next morning for the second payment on the loan and I wanted to be ready for him. I withdrew over $100,000 in cash, my intention being to pay off the whole loan straightaway – the repayments, the vig, everything. That way I could get him off my back. If Gennady had taken the five MDT pills – and that was the only plausible explanation for the fact that they were missing – I certainly didn't want him coming around to my apartment every Friday morning.

As I was waiting for them to get the cash ready, my balding and overweight bank manager, Howard Lewis, invited me into his office for a little chat. This walking heart-attack seemed to be concerned that after my initial flurry of activity with Klondike and Lafayette – resulting, admittedly, in some fairly substantial deposits – things had been, '. . . well, *quiet.*'

I looked across the desk at him in disbelief.

'. . . and then there are these rather large cash withdrawals, Mr Spinola.'

'What about them?' I said, my tone adding, *as if it's any of your fucking business.*

'Nothing in themselves, Mr Spinola, of course, but . . . well, in the light of that piece in last Friday's *Post* about—'

'What about—?'

'Look, it's all very . . . *irregular.* I mean, these days you can't be too—'

'In the *light* of my time at Lafayette, Mr Lewis,' I said, barely able to contain my irritation, 'I am currently in negotiations for a position as a senior trader at Van Loon & Associates.'

He looked back at me, breathing out slowly through his nose, as if what I'd said confirmed his worst fears about me.

His phone rang, and he scooped it up, a muscle on his face quivering slightly by way of apology. As he dealt with the call, I glanced around. Until that point, I'd been feeling quite indignant, but this cooled somewhat when I saw my reflection in the back panel of a silver photo-frame on Lewis's desk. It was a partially distorted image, but nothing could conceal how scruffy I looked. I hadn't shaved that morning and I was wearing old jeans and a T-shirt – implausible for a senior trader at Van Loon & Associates, even on a day off.

Howard Lewis finished his call, pressed another button on his phone, listened for a moment and then looked at me with a blank expression on his face.

'Your withdrawal is ready, Mr Spinola.'

Gennady arrived at nine-thirty the following morning. I'd just woken up about twenty minutes before he arrived and I was still feeling groggy. I'd intended to be up earlier, but from about seven on I'd kept waking and then falling back to sleep again, slipping in and out of dreams. When I finally managed to get out of bed, the first thing I did was take my MDT pill. Then I removed the bowl from the shelf above the computer. After that, I put on a pot of coffee and just stood around in boxer shorts and a T-shirt, waiting.

There were two possibilities. Either Gennady had done the pills – and if he'd done one he'd have done them all. Or, for some reason, he hadn't done the pills. I reckoned that when I saw him I would know fairly quickly which one it was.

'Morning,' I said, studying him closely as he made his way in from the hallway.

He nodded, but didn't say anything. Then I watched him as he silently surveyed my apartment. At first, I thought he was looking for the missing ceramic bowl, but then I realized that he was just registering how different the place was from the last time he'd been here. Looking around with him, following his eye, I registered the changes for myself. The apartment was a mess. Papers and documents and folders were strewn about the place. There was an empty pizza box on the couch and there were a couple of Chinese take-out cartons on my desk beside the computer. There were beer cans and coffee mugs everywhere, and full ashtrays and CDs and empty CD covers and shirts and socks.

'You some kind of fucking pig?'

I shrugged my shoulders. 'You can't get decent help these days.'

He furrowed his brow at this, slightly puzzled, and I knew straight-away that he wasn't on MDT – not right now at any rate.

'Where the money?'

After he said this I noticed him glancing over at the shelf above the computer. When he didn't see what he was looking for, he stepped a little closer to the desk and continued his discreet search.

'I want to pay off the whole thing now,' I said.

This caught his attention, and he turned to look at me. I'd left a bag with all the cash in it on top of one of the bookshelves. I reached up now and got it down.

Gennady shook his head when he saw the bag.

'What?' I said.

'Twenty-two five.'

'But I want to pay it *all* off.'

'You can't.'

'But—'

'*Twenty-two five.*'

I was going to say something else, but there was no point. I sighed and took the bag over to the table, made a space and started counting out the twenty-two five. When I'd finished, I handed the wad of cash to Gennady and he put it into his inside jacket pocket.

'Did you get a chance to read that treatment?' I said.

He sighed and shook his head.

'No time. Too busy.'

He glanced over once more at the desk.

'Maybe next time,' he said, and then left.

I made an effort to clean the place up after Gennady had gone, but quickly lost interest. Then I sat on the couch and tried to read an article in the latest issue of *Fortune* magazine, a survey of 'hot' developments in e-commerce, but when I'd made it a paragraph or two in, I started dozing and let the magazine drop from my hand and fall to the floor. In the late afternoon, I had a shower and shaved. I got dressed, took a handful of cash from the bag I'd left on the table in the dining area and headed out – not having *been* out, except to get food, for nearly a week. I wandered over to the West Village and stopped off at a couple of bars I occasionally went to and started drinking vodka Martinis.

Towards the end of the evening I found myself, fairly trashed, in a quiet place on Second Avenue and Tenth. I was sitting at the bar, and a bit further down there was a television set above where the cash register was, on wall-brackets. A movie had been playing – something, judging by the hair and clothes, from 1983 or 1984. The volume had been turned right down, but now a news bulletin came on and the barman turned it up.

The sudden intrusion of sound from the TV killed off any conversation in the bar, and everyone – dutifully, drunkenly – gazed up at the screen to listen to the headlines.

'Middle East peace-talks at Camp David break down after two weeks of intensive negotiations. Hurricane Julius arrives off the south coast of Florida, leaving a trail of devastation in its wake. And Donatella Alvarez, who has been in a coma for two weeks after a brutal attack in a Manhattan hotel room, dies this afternoon – police say they are now conducting a full-scale murder investigation.'

I stared in shock at the screen as the newscaster went back to the details of the peace-talks story. I grabbed on to the side of the bar, and held it tightly. After a couple of seconds, I mumbled something – maybe audibly, maybe not – and swung around to get off my stool.

I stood there for a moment, swaying from side to side, very unsteadily. The room then began to spin, and I moved, staggering the few yards over to the door. I just about made it out into the street before splatting an evening's worth of vodka, vermouth and olives up on to the sidewalk.

[20]

I CONTINUED DRINKING OVER the weekend, mostly vodka, and mostly at home. After all, what else was there to do? I'd just become the subject of a full-scale murder investigation – albeit, and very conveniently, under an assumed name – so surely, in the circumstances, a little drinkie or two could hardly be seen as anything other than appropriate. I wasn't making any further pretense at reading 'the material' either, so I gave in for a while and went back to watching the news on TV. This quickly became all I wanted to watch and again I found myself wading through hours of mindless crap, shouting drunken abuse at the screen as I waited for the next bulletin to come on.

There wasn't much for the media to say about Donatella Alvarez herself – the woman had died and that's all there was to it. What most of the reports were focusing on now was the political fall-out from her death. This came in the form of renewed calls for the Defense Secretary to resign. The brouhaha over Caleb Hale's original comments about Mexico had received a shot in the arm when the Alvarez story first broke, and another one now with her death. I hadn't followed the story too closely, but I'd been aware of it in the background – aware of it as one of those bizarre developments that takes on a life of its own and enters the news-chain like some kind of virus.

Six weeks or so earlier, Caleb Hale was reported to have said at a private gathering that Mexico had become a liability for the US and that 'we should just consider invading the damned place'. The source that leaked the story to the *Los Angeles Times* claimed that Hale had name-checked corruption, insurgency, the breakdown of

223

law and order, the debt crisis and drug-trafficking as the five points on 'the pentangle of Mexico's instability'. The source went on to claim that Hale had even cited John O'Sullivan on our 'manifest destiny to overspread the continent' and had mentioned an op-ed piece he'd once read called 'Mexico: The Iran Next Door'. Caleb Hale immediately issued a classic non-denial denial, but then proceeded, in an interview, to more or less justify precisely what he was claiming not to have said. The President was perceived to be weighing in behind Hale when he not only refused to demand the Secretary's resignation but also refused to condemn his alleged remarks – which of course opened the floodgates of comment and speculation. Everyone was initially shocked and incredulous, but as the days passed certain influential quarters appeared to warm to the idea, and early conclusions about the Defense Secretary being seriously out of touch softened a little, with some even transforming into a broad endorsement for, at the very least, a tougher line on foreign policy.

Now, with what was perceived as a racially motivated killing tossed into the mix, the debate had gone into overdrive. There were interviews, panel discussions, sound bites, one-liners, earnest reports from dusty border towns, aerial shots of the Rio Grande. I watched from my couch, glass in hand, and got caught up in it all as though I were watching a prime-time soap – continually forgetting in my alcoholic euphoria that I was perhaps just a fingerprint or DNA test away from full involvement in this myself, that I was perilously close to eye of the storm.

As the weekend progressed, however, and euphoria degenerated into numbness, and then anxiety, and then dread – my viewing patterns shifted. I cut down drastically on news shows, and towards Sunday evening found myself skipping them altogether. Increasingly, it was easier to switch over to channels where there were re-runs of *Hawaii Five-O* to be found – and *Happy Days* and *Voyage to the Bottom of the Sea*.

On the Monday I tried to stay sober, but didn't do too well. I had a few beers during the afternoon, and then opened a bottle of vodka in the evening. I spent most of the time listening to music, and eventually crashed out on the couch that night in my clothes. It had been getting steadily warmer over the previous week and I'd been leaving the window open most nights, but when I jolted awake from a confused dream at about 4 a.m., I noticed immediately that the temperature had dropped. It was a good deal chillier than when I'd fallen asleep, so I got off the couch, shivering, and went over to the window to close it. I sat back on the couch, but as I stared into the blue darkness of the night, the shivering continued. I realized, as well, that my heart was palpitating, and that the unpleasant tingling sensation I had in my limbs wasn't normal. I tried to identify what was happening to me. One possibility was that my system needed more alcohol, in which case I quickly scrolled down through the options – I could get dressed and go out to a bar, or I could go to a Korean deli down the street and buy a couple of six-packs, or I could just drink the cooking sherry I had in the kitchen. But I didn't really think booze was the problem, because the very idea now of going outside, to the street, to a neon-lit deli with other people in it, struck terror into me.

So that was it, I thought – I was having *a fucking panic attack*.

I kept taking deep breaths, and hitting one of the sofa cushions beside me with the back of my hand. It was four o'clock in the morning. I couldn't call anyone. I couldn't go anywhere. I couldn't sleep. I felt like a cornered rat.

I sat it out, though – on the couch. It was like having a massive heart attack that went on for an hour but didn't kill you, or even leave you with any physical after effects, nothing that a doctor might find if he were to subject you to a whole battery of tests.

The next day, I decided I had to do something. I'd slipped too far and too fast, and knew that if I slipped any further I'd be in danger of losing everything – although quite what 'everything' now meant was clearly open to interpretation. In any case, I had to do something – but the problem was, *what?* The most immediate and pressing concern was the Donatella Alvarez situation, but that was out of my control. Then, of course, there was Carl Van Loon. But frankly, my whole association with him was beginning to seem a little remote to me. I found it hard to accept that I had actually 'worked' with him, especially on something so improbable as the 'financials' of a corporate takeover deal. In memory, our various sessions together – in the Orpheus Room, in his apartment, in his office, in the Four Seasons – felt more like dreams now than recollections of real events, and seemed, as well, to have the twisted logic of dreams.

But at the same time I couldn't just ignore the situation. Not any longer. I couldn't ignore the reality that leapt up at me every time I looked at my own handwriting on Van Loon's yellow legal pad. Remote as it all might seem now, I *had* been involved with him, and I *had* helped to shape the MCL–Abraxas deal. So if I wanted to salvage anything from the experience, I would have to confront Van Loon, and as soon as possible.

I took a shower and shaved. I still felt fairly lousy as I went into the bedroom to get my suit out of the closet, but it was nothing to what I felt when I tried to put it on. I hadn't worn it in over a week and now all of a sudden I was struggling at the waist to get the trousers closed. It was my only presentable suit, though – so I had no choice but to wear it.

I took a cab to Forty-eighth Street.

As I walked across the main lobby of the Van Loon Building and rode the elevator up to the sixty-second floor, a sense of dread grew within me. Stepping out into the now familiar reception area of Van Loon & Associates, I identified this feeling, correctly, as the onset of another panic attack.

I hung around for a few moments in the middle of the reception area and pretended to be consulting something on the back of a large brown envelope I was carrying – a name, or an address. The envelope contained Van Loon's yellow legal pad, but there was nothing written on it. I glanced over at the receptionist, who glanced back at me and then picked up one of her telephones. My heart was beating rapidly now and the pain in my chest had become almost unbearable. I turned around and headed in the direction of the elevators. What had I been proposing to do in any case – confront Van Loon? But how? By returning the projections exactly as we'd left them? By showing him I was on a crash diet of cheeseburgers and pizza?

It had been reckless of me to come in here like this. I obviously hadn't been thinking straight.

The doors finally opened, but the relief of getting away from the reception area was short-lived, because I now had to contend with the elevator car, the interior of which, with its reflective steel panels, its controlled climate and relentless humming, felt as if it had been custom-built to induce and fuel panic attacks. It was a physical environment that seemed to ape the very symptoms of anxiety – the sinking feeling, the uncontrollable fluttering in the stomach, the ever-present threat of nausea.

I closed my eyes, but then couldn't help picturing the dark elevator shafts above and below me . . . couldn't help imagining the heavy steel cables snapping as the car and its counterweights accelerated rapidly in opposite directions, the car naturally hurtling downwards, free-falling to ground level . . .

Instead it came to a barely perceptible halt near the foot of this concrete tube, and the door slid gently open. To my surprise, standing there – waiting to step inside – was Ginny Van Loon.

'Mr Spinola!'

When I didn't respond immediately, she stepped forward and stretched a hand out to take me by the arm, 'Are you all right?'

I got out of the elevator car and moved with her into the lobby area, which was crowded and busy, and almost as terrifying – though for different reasons – as the elevator car. I was in a cold sweat now and had started shivering again. She said, 'My God, Mr Spinola, you look—'

'Like shit?'

'Well,' she replied after a moment, 'yeah.'

We made our way across the lobby and stopped by a large copper-tinted window that looked out on to Forty-eighth Street.

'What . . . what's the matter? What happened?'

I focused on her properly now and saw that her concern was genuine. She was still holding on to my arm and for some reason this made me feel slightly better. Once I acknowledged that, there was a knock-on effect and I managed to calm down considerably.

'I was . . . up on sixty-two,' I said, 'but I didn't—'

'You couldn't take the heat, right? I knew you weren't one of Daddy's business guys. Anyway, they're nothing but a bunch of automatons.'

'Automata. I think I was having a panic attack.'

'Good for you. Anyone who doesn't have a panic attack up there has something seriously wrong with them. And you can say automa-*tons* if you want.' She paused. 'You can say referen*dums*.'

'Yeah,' I said, trying to catch my breath, 'referen*dums*, sure, but you wouldn't say phenome*nons*, would you?'

She was wearing black jeans and a black sweater and was carrying a small leather doctor's bag.

'Not if I was talking to *you*, obviously. Anyway, one's from Latin and the other's from Greek, the rules are different, so fuck you. How are you feeling now?'

I took a few deep breaths and held my chest.

'A little better, thanks.'

Aware, suddenly, of my newly acquired girth, I tried to stand up a little straighter and to breathe in.

Ginny studied me for a while.

'Mr Spi—'

'Eddie, call me Eddie. Jesus, I'm only thir—'

'Eddie, are you sick?'

'Hhn?'

'I mean, are you *unwell*? Because you really *look* unwell. You've . . .' – she struggled to find the right words – '. . . you've . . . since that time I saw you in the apartment, you've put on some, well . . . some *weight*. And—'

'My weight fluctuates.'

'Yeah, but that was, what, only two weeks ago?'

I held up my hands. 'Hey, can't a fellah have a couple of cream-cakes once in a while?'

She smiled, but then said, 'Look, I'm sorry, I know it's none of my business, but I just think you should look after yourself better.'

'Yeah, yeah. I know. You're right.'

My breathing was more regular now and I felt a good deal better. I asked her what she was doing.

'I'm going up to see Daddy.'

'You want to get some coffee instead?'

'I can't.' She made a face. 'Anyway, if you've just had a panic attack, I think you should probably be avoiding coffee. Drink juice, or something wholesome that won't exacerbate your stress levels.'

I straightened up again and leant back against the window.

'Come and have a wholesome juice with me then.'

She looked directly into my eyes. Hers were bright blue – sparkling, cerulean, celestial.

'I can't.'

I was going to push it, ask her why not, but then I didn't. I got a flickering sense that she was a little uncomfortable all of a sudden, which in turn made me uncomfortable. It also struck me that feelings of panic probably came in waves, and that while an attack might abate, it might just as easily come back. I didn't want to be around here if that happened, even *with* Ginny.

'OK, look,' I said, 'thank you very much. I'm really glad I bumped into you.'

She smiled. 'Are you going to be OK?'

I nodded.

'You sure?'

'Yeah, I'm fine. Absolutely. Thanks.'

She patted me on the shoulder and said, 'OK, so long, Eddie.'

A second later she was walking away from me across the lobby, her little doctor's bag swinging by her side. Then – enveloped suddenly into the crowd – she was gone.

I turned to face the huge window behind where I was standing and saw myself reflected in its bronze-tinted glass, people and cars outside on Forty-eighth Street passing right through me as though I were a ghost. In addition to everything else, I now found myself in the inappropriate position of being disappointed that Van Loon's daughter apparently refused to see me as anything other than a genial associate of her father's – and a pedantic, panic-stricken, overweight one at that. I left the building, made my way over to Fifth Avenue and started walking downtown. Despite these grim thoughts, I somehow managed to keep things under control. Then, as I was crossing Forty-second Street, something else occurred to me, and I shoved my hand out, on impulse, to hail a cab.

Twenty minutes later I was taking another elevator, this time up to the fourth floor of Lafayette Trading on Broad Street. This had been the scene of earlier triumphs – days of excitement and success – and I figured now there was no longer anything to stop me from trying to re-create *that*. I didn't have the advantage of being full-thrust on MDT, OK, but neither did I care any more. My confidence had taken a bruising, and I just wanted to see how well I could do on my own.

There was a mixed reaction when I walked into the room. Some people, including Jay Zollo, went out of their way to ignore me. Others couldn't help smiling and doffing their baseball caps in my direction. Even though I hadn't been there for a while and didn't have any positions open, my account was still active. I was told my 'usual' spot was taken, but that others were available and I could start trading immediately if I wanted to.

As I took my place at one of the terminals and got ready, I could feel a curiosity growing in the room about what I intended to do. There was a definite buzz now, with some people looking over my shoulder, and others keeping a close eye on things from the opposite side of the 'pit'. It was a lot of pressure to be under and when I found that I wasn't quite sure how to proceed, I had to admit to myself that perhaps I'd been a little hasty in coming here. But it was too late to pull out.

I spent a while studying the screen, and gradually it all came back to me. It wasn't such a complicated process – but what *was* complicated, of course, was choosing the right stocks. I hadn't been following the markets of late and didn't really know where to look. My previous strategy of short-selling, which had been heavily dependent on research, wasn't much use to me either, so I decided to play it safe on my first day back – I decided to go with the prevailing wisdom and buy tech stocks. I bought shares in Lir Systems, a risk-management services company, in KeyGate Technologies, an Internet security outfit, and in various dot-coms, Boojum, Wotlarks!, @Ease, Dromio, PorkBarrel.com, eTranz, WorkNet.

Once I started I couldn't stop, and thanks to a combination of recklessness and fear, I ended up emptying my bank account, spending everything I had in the space of a couple of hours. Matters weren't helped by the artificial, game-like nature of electronic trading, nor by the dangerous sense I increasingly had that the money involved wasn't real. Naturally, this storm of activity attracted a lot of attention in the room, and even though my 'strategy' was about as unoriginal and mainstream as you could get, the rate and scale of my trading obviously gave it a curious shape – a colour, a character – of its own. Before long, as a result, people started following my lead, watching my every move, channelling 'tips' and 'information' out from my workstation. There was an urgency about the whole thing – no one wanted to get left behind – and I soon had the impression that lots of the traders around me were borrowing heavily or renegotiating leverage on their deposits.

The dizzying Net stocks boom still had the power, apparently, to disorient and whipsaw anyone who dared to get near it – and this included *me*, because although I'd landed here today on the back of my reputation, of my previous performance, I was now beginning to realize that *this* time around not only did I not know what I was doing, I didn't know how to stop . . .

Eventually, however, the pressure became too much for me. It kick-started another panic attack, and left me no choice but to just grab the envelope and *go* – without even closing out my positions. This caused some degree of consternation in the room, but I think most of the Lafayette traders had come to expect the unexpected from me and I managed to get away without too much hassle. A good number of the stocks I'd bought had already gone up by tiny margins, so no one was worried or nervous – they were just unhappy at letting what they saw as an *über*trader escape from their midst. On my way down in the elevator, my heart started palpitating again and when I got out on to the street I felt really horrible. I walked down Broad Street to the South Ferry Terminal and then over to

Battery Park, where I sat on a bench, undid my tie and gazed out at Staten Island.

I remained there for about half an hour, taking deep breaths and fielding dark, unsettling thoughts. I wanted to be at home, on my couch, but I didn't want to go through what was required to get there, which was negotiate the streets again, and the people, and the traffic. But after another while I just stood up and started walking. I went over to State Street and managed to get a taxi at once. I slumped into the back seat, clutching the envelope, and as the cab inched its way forward through the traffic, up past Bowling Green on to Broadway, and then past Beaver Street and Exchange Place and Wall Street itself, I had a fleeting impression that something quite odd was happening. It was difficult to put my finger on what it was exactly, but there was a very jittery atmosphere in the streets. People were stopping and talking, some whispering conspiratorially, others shouting across cars, or from the steps of buildings, or into cellphones – and in that curious way people have when some dire public event has taken place, like an assassination or an upset in the World Series. Then there was a break in the traffic and we surged forward out of the financial district, leaving behind whatever it was I'd picked up on. Soon we were crossing Canal Street and then a few moments later turning right on to Houston, where it was business as usual.

When I got home, I made straight for the couch and flopped down on to it. The taxi ride had been unbearable and once or twice I'd come close to having the driver stop and let me out. Lying on the couch wasn't *that* much better, but at least I was in a familiar, controlled environment. For the next hour or so, I vacillated between thinking that the attack would pass, and thinking that . . . *no*, I was going to *die* – here, *today*, right now, on this fucking couch . . .

But when, eventually, I didn't die, and had started to feel a bit less awful, I reached down from the side of the couch to pick up the remote control panel, which was lying on the floor. I zapped the main TV into action and surfed through the channels. It took me a few moments to focus, and to realize that something was going on. I went to CNNfn, then to CNBC, and then back again to CNNfn. I looked at the corner of the screen to check the time.

It was 2.35 p.m. and since about 1 p.m. – apparently – the markets had been in freefall. The Nasdaq had already dropped 319 points, the Dow Jones 185 points, and the S & P 93 points, with none of them showing any signs of halting, let alone bouncing back. Both CNNfn and CNBC were providing minute-by-minute coverage from the floor of the New York Stock Exchange, as well as from their respective studios – the main thrust of the story being that the tech-stocks bubble appeared to be bursting in slo-mo before our very eyes . . .

I went over to my desk and switched on the computer. I was curiously calm, but when I saw the quotes, and saw how far the share prices had plunged, I began to feel dizzy. I put my head in my hands and tried not to panic – and just about succeeded . . . probably by sparing a thought for all those traders down in Lafayette who as a consequence of following my leads would almost certainly have been wiped out as well. Though I was ready to bet that none of them had lost as much as I had, which was now more than likely somewhere in the region of a million dollars . . .

[21]

THE NEXT MORNING I WENT OUT to get the papers – as well as to do a provisions run to Gristede's and the liquor store. The headlines ranged from things like OUCH! and NIGHTMARE ON QUEASY STREET to INVESTOR CAUTION AFTER MARKETS TUMBLE. The Nasdaq had rallied somewhat in the late p.m. – after a staggering lowest-point drop of 9 per cent – and was continuing to recover this morning. This was thanks to a few brokerage houses and mutual funds who'd seen the bottom coming and started buying on the dip. Some commentators were hysterical, talking about a repeat of Black Monday – or even of 1929 – but others took a more sanguine approach, saying that recent speculative excess in technology stocks had now been purged . . . or that what we had witnessed wasn't so much a wide-spread correction as a cleansing action in the frothier parts of the Nasdaq. This was all very reassuring for the long-haul players, but not much consolation to the millions of small-time investors who'd bought on margin and then been annihilated by the big sell-off.

Poring over opinion pieces in the newspapers, however, wasn't going to change anything. It wasn't going to change the fact – for example – that my bank account had been cleaned out, or that I wouldn't be able to trade any more at Lafayette.

Putting the newspapers aside, I looked at the bag of cash on the cluttered dining table and reminded myself, for the fiftieth time, that what was in that bag was the sum total of what I had left in the world – *and that I owed it all to a Russian loanshark* . . .

⁕　⁕　⁕

234

Gennady's visit on Friday morning was going to be the next event of any significance in my life, but I certainly wasn't looking forward to it. I spent the couple of days in between drinking and listening to music. At one point during this time – and more than half-way through a late-night bottle of Absolut – I got to thinking about Ginny Van Loon, and what a curious girl she was. I went online and searched through various newspaper and magazine archives for any references there might be to her. I found quite a lot of stuff, quotes from 'Page Six' and the 'Styles' section of the *New York Times*, clippings, profiles and even some photos – a sixteen-year-old Ginny out of her head at the River Club with Tony De Torrio, Ginny surrounded by models and fashion designers, Ginny with Nikki Sallis at a party in LA sipping from a bottle of Cristal. A recent piece in *New York* magazine repeated the story about her parents reining her in with threats of disinheritance, but the same piece also quoted friends saying that she had calmed down a lot anyway and was no longer 'much fun to be around'. Ginny herself was quoted in an article as saying that she'd spent most of her teens wanting to be famous and now only wanted to be left alone. She'd done some acting and modelling, but had left all of that behind – fame was a disease, she'd said, and anyone who craved it was a moron. I read these articles over several times – and printed out the photos, which I stuck on my notice-board.

Large chunks of time seemed to be drifting by now, during which I did nothing but idly surf the Net or sit on the couch and drink – becoming maudlin, confused, cranky.

When Gennady showed up on Friday morning, I was hungover. The mess in my apartment had gotten worse and I'm sure it didn't smell too good either – though at the time that aspect of things wasn't anything I was actually aware of. I was too miserable and sick to notice.

When Gennady arrived at the doorway and stood looking in at the chaos, my worst fear – or *one* of them, at any rate – was realized. I knew straightaway that Gennady was on MDT. I could tell from the alert expression on his face and even from the way he was standing. I knew, too, that my suspicion would be confirmed as soon as he opened his mouth.

'What's your problem, Eddie?' he said, with a mirthless laugh, 'are you depressed or something? Maybe you need some medication.' He sniffed and made a face. 'Or maybe you just need to get an air-conditioning unit in this place.'

It was clear even from those few sentences that his spoken English had improved dramatically. His accent was still quite strong, but his grasp of structures – grammar and syntax – had obviously undergone some rapid transformative process. I wondered how many of the five pills he'd already taken.

'Hello, Gennady.'

I went over to the dining table, sat down and extracted a wad of cash from the brown paper bag. I started counting $100 bills, sighing wearily every couple of seconds. Gennady came into the room and wandered about for a while, surveying the mess. He came to a stop right in front of me.

'That's not very safe, Eddie,' he said, 'keeping all your money in a fucking paper *bag*. Someone might come in and steal it.'

I sighed again and said, 'I don't like banks.' I handed him up the twenty-two five. He took it and put it into the inside pocket of his jacket. He walked over to my desk, turned around and leaned back against it.

'Now,' he said, 'I want to talk to you about something.'

Here it came. I felt a sinking feeling in my stomach. But I tried to play dumb.

'You didn't like the treatment,' I said, and then added, 'It was just a draft.'

'*Fuck* that,' he said, with a dismissive gesture of the hand, 'I'm not talking about *that*. And anyway, don't pretend you don't *know* what I'm talking about.'

'What?'

'Those pills I stole. Are you going to tell me you didn't notice?'

'What about them?'

'What do you think? I want more.'

'I don't have any.'

236

He smiled, as though we were playing a game – which of course we were.

I shrugged my shoulders and said, 'I *don't*.'

He pushed himself up from the desk and walked over towards me. He stopped where he'd stopped before and slowly reached his hand back into the inside pocket of his jacket. I was scared, but didn't flinch. He took out something which I couldn't see properly. He looked at me, smiled again and then with rapid a motion of his hand released the blade of a long flick-knife. He placed the tip of the blade at the side of my neck and moved it up and down, scraping it gently against my skin. 'I *want* some *more*,' he said.

I swallowed. 'Do I *look* like I have any more?'

He paused for a moment and stopped moving the knife, but didn't withdraw it. I went on, 'You've taken it, right? You know what it's like, and what it *does* to you.' I swallowed again, louder than before. 'Look around you, does this strike you as the place of someone who's taking the drug *you* took?'

'Well, where did you get it from then?'

'I don't know, some guy I met in a—'

He jabbed the knife sharply against my neck and withdrew it quickly.

'*Ow!*'

I put my hand up to the point where he'd jabbed me and rubbed it. There wasn't any blood, but the jab had really hurt.

'Don't lie to me, Eddie, because – and make sure you understand this – if I don't get what I want I'm going to kill you anyway . . .' Then he set the point of the knife to just under my left eye, and pressed it in, gently but firmly. 'And in stages.'

He continued pressing the knife, and when I could feel my eyeball starting to protrude, I whispered, '*OK*.'

He held the knife in place for a moment and then withdrew it.

'I can get them,' I said, 'but it'll take a few days. The guy who deals them is very . . . security conscious.'

Gennady clicked his tongue, as if to say *go on*.

'I phone him, and he arranges a pick-up.' I paused here and rubbed my left eye, but it was really to give me a moment to work

237

out what I was going to say next. 'If he catches a whiff of someone else getting involved in this, by the way – someone he doesn't know – that's it, we'll never hear from him again.'

Gennady nodded.

'And another thing,' I said, 'they're *expensive*.'

I could tell that he was excited at the prospect of scoring. I could also tell that despite his heavy-handed tactics he would go along with whatever I proposed, and would pay whatever I asked.

'How much?'

'Five hundred a pop . . .'

He whistled, almost with glee.

'. . . which is why I'm out of them. Because we're not talking dime bags here.'

He looked at me, and then pointed at the money on the table. 'Use that. Get me . . . er . . .' – he paused, and seemed to be doing some calculations in his head – '. . . get me fifty or sixty of them. For starters.'

If I did end up giving him any, they would have to come from my stash, so I said, 'The most I can get in one go is ten.'

'Fuck that—'

'Gennady, I'll *talk* to the guy, but he's very paranoid. We've got to take this slowly.'

He turned around and walked over to the desk, and then back again.

'OK, when?'

'I should be able to get them by next Friday.'

'Next fucking Friday? You said a few days.'

'I leave him a message. It takes a few days for him to get back to me. Then another few days to set it up.'

Gennady held the knife out again and pointed it directly in my face. 'If you fuck with me, Eddie, you'll be sorry.'

Then he put the knife away and walked over to the door.

'I'm going to phone you Tuesday.'

I nodded.

'OK. Tuesday.'

Standing in the doorway, and as though it were an afterthought, he said, 'So what *is* this shit anyway? What's in it?'

'It's a . . . smart-drug,' I said, 'I don't really know what's in it.'

'It makes you smart?'

I held out my hands. 'Well, yeah. Hadn't you noticed?' I was going to say something to him about his English and how it had improved, but I decided against it. He might get offended at the idea that I hadn't thought his English was good to start with.

'Sure,' he said, 'it's *amazing*. What's it called?'

I hesitated. 'Er . . . MDT. It's called MDT. It's a chemical name, but . . . yeah.'

'*MDT?*'

'Yeah. You know, score some MDT. Do some MDT.'

He looked at me for a moment, dubiously, and then said, 'Tuesday.'

He went out into the hallway, leaving the door open. I remained sitting in the chair and listened to him clumping down the stairs. When I heard the door of the building banging closed I stood up and went over to the window. I looked out and saw Gennady pacing along Tenth Street towards First Avenue. From the little I knew of him, the lightness in his step seemed, to say the least, uncharacteristic.

Looking back now – from the dead stillness of this room here in the Northview Motor Lodge – I can see that Gennady's intrusion into my life, his attempt to muscle in on my supply of MDT, had quite an unsettling effect on me. I had lost nearly everything and I resented the idea that someone could so easily destroy what little there was left. I hadn't wanted to take MDT at full throttle any more because I was scared of surrendering myself to another blackout, scared of being open again to that same level of darkness and unpredictability. But neither did I want to just give up and leave everything behind – and especially not for a circling vulture like Gennady to pick at and tear apart. Besides, the idea of Gennady on MDT seemed a complete waste to me. Suddenly the guy was able to speak comprehensible English? Big fucking deal. He was still a bonehead, a *zhulik*. MDT wasn't going to change someone like *him*. Not the way it had changed me . . .

❉   ❉   ❉

On foot of this realization, I decided I had to make one last effort. Maybe I could salvage something from the situation. Maybe I could even reverse it. I'd make another call to Donald Geisler and plead with him to talk to me.

What harm could it do?

I rooted out Vernon's black notebook, found the number and dialled it

'Yep?'

I paused for a second and then rushed into it.

'This is Vernon Gant's friend again, don't hang up, *please* . . . five minutes, all I want is five minutes of your time, I'll *pay* you . . .' – this came to me on the spur of the moment – '. . . I'll pay you five thousand dollars, a thousand dollars a minute, just *talk* to me . . .'

I stopped, and there was silence. As I waited, I stared over at the brown paper bag on the table.

He released a long sigh. '*Jeesus!*'

I didn't know what this meant, but he hadn't hung up on me. I decided not to push it. I remained silent.

Eventually, he said, 'I don't want your money.' He paused again, and then said, 'Five minutes.'

'Thank you . . . very much.'

He gave me the address of a café on Seventh Avenue in Park Slope in Brooklyn and told me to meet him there in an hour. He was tall and would be wearing a plain yellow T-shirt.

I had a shower and shaved, knocked back a quick cup of coffee and some toast, and got dressed. I picked up a cab straightaway out on Tenth Street.

The café was small and dark and nearly empty. Sitting alone at a table in the corner was a tall man wearing a plain yellow T-shirt. He was drinking an espresso. Beside his cup, neatly stacked, he had a pack of Marlboros and a Zippo lighter. I introduced myself and sat down. From his greying hair and the lines around his eyes, I reckoned that Donald Geisler was about fifty-five years old. He had the tired, gruff demeanour of someone who's been around the block a few times, and probably a few different blocks at that.

'OK, then,' he said, 'what do you want?'

240

I gave him a quick and heavily edited version of events. At the end I said, 'So what I really need to know about is dosage. Or, failing that, if you've heard of an associate of Vernon's called Tom, or Todd.'

He nodded his head, pensively, and then stared at his espresso cup for a few moments. As I waited for him to gather his thoughts, or whatever it was he was doing, I took out my pack of Camels and lit one up.

I'd smoked more than half of the cigarette before Geisler spoke. It occurred to me that if we were supposed to be sticking to the five-minute rule, we were already way over time.

'About three years ago,' he said, 'three and a half maybe, I met Vernon Gant. I was an actor at the time, with a small company I'd co-founded five years before that. We did Miller and Shepard and Mamet, that kind of thing. We had some success – especially with a production of *American Buffalo*. And we toured a lot.'

I knew immediately from the tone in his voice, as well as from the languid narrative route he appeared to be taking, that despite his earlier protests, he was in this for the long haul.

I discreetly ordered two more espressos from a passing waitress and lit up another cigarette.

'Around the time I met Vernon was also when the company decided to change direction and mount a production of *Macbeth* – which I was going to take the lead in. And direct.' He cleared his throat. 'At the time, meeting Vernon seemed like a piece of really good luck – because here I am scared shitless at the prospect of doing Shakespeare and this guy is offering me . . . well, you know what he was offering me.'

Geisler's delivery was slow and deliberate, his voice like gravel. It was an actor's voice. I also got the impression, as he went on, that he had never spoken about this stuff to anyone before. His account of the early days of MDT was much fuller than Melissa's had been but was essentially the same. In his case, he'd received the pitch from Vernon, been unable to resist and after a couple of 15mg doses had memorized the entire text of *Macbeth* – thoroughly intimidating his cast and crew in the process. He'd then gone on, over the early rehearsal period, to take a further dozen pills, an average of about three a week. The pills were unmarked, but Vernon's partner, a guy called Todd, had shown up one day with Vernon and explained the dosage and something about what was in MDT and how it worked. This Todd character had also asked Geisler questions about how he was responding to the drug and if he'd been experiencing any adverse side-effects. Geisler had said that he hadn't.

Two weeks before opening, and under intense pressure, Geisler had cleaned out what he had in the bank and upped his intake to six pills a week – 'Nearly one a *day*,' he said.

I wanted to ask him more about Todd and what he'd had to say about dosage – but at the same time I could see that Geisler was concentrating really hard and I didn't want to interrupt his train of thought.

'Then, in the few days before we were due to open, it happened – my life fell apart. From a Tuesday to a Friday. It just . . . fell apart.'

Up to this point, Geisler had kept both his hands under the table and out of view. I hadn't thought anything of it, but now as he moved his right hand up and reached out to take his espresso cup, I saw that his hand had a slight but noticeable tremor. I thought at first that it might be a symptom of alcoholism, a morning-after shake, something like that, but when I saw him leaning forward, gripping the cup to make sure he got it up to his lips without spilling any of the coffee, I realized that he was probably suffering from some neurological disorder. He replaced the cup, very carefully, and then put himself through the laborious process of lighting a cigarette. He did this in silence, pointedly making no comment about the diffi-culty he was having. He knew I was watching, which almost turned it into a kind of performance.

Once he had his cigarette on the go, he said, 'I was under a lot of pressure, rehearsing fourteen, fifteen hours a day . . . but then . . . before I know it, and out of the fucking blue, I'm having these periods of memory loss.'

I stared at him, nodding my head.

'I lost track of what I was doing for hours at a time.'

Barely able to contain myself, I kept saying, 'Yeah, yeah, go on, go on.'

'I still don't know what I got up to, exactly, during these . . . *black-outs*, I suppose you'd call them . . . all I know is that between the Tuesday and Friday of that week – and as a *result* of what I got up to – my girlfriend of ten years left me, the production of *Macbeth* was cancelled and I was thrown out of my apartment. I also ran over and nearly killed an eleven-year-old girl on Columbus Avenue.'

'*Jesus.*'

My heart was racing.

'I went to Vernon to try and find out what was happening to me, and at first he didn't want to know, he was scared, but then he contacted Todd and we met up. Todd was the technical one – he worked for a pharmaceutical company. I could never figure out what their story was, but it soon became clear that Todd was siphoning this stuff out of the labs where he worked and that Vernon was just the front man. It also emerged that Vernon had mixed up a batch of tablets and had been dealing me 30- instead of 15mg pills, which meant that my dosage had shot up dramatically without me knowing it. Anyway, I told Todd what had happened and he said that I needed to combine the MDT with something else, another drug, something to counteract the side-effects. That's what he called these blackouts – *side-effects* . . .'

'What was the na—'

'. . . but I told him I wasn't taking *anything* else, that I wanted to stop, and to get back to normal. I asked him if I could do that, if I could just stop – without there being any *other* adverse side-effects, and he said he didn't know, he wasn't the FDA, but that since I'd been on such a high dosage he wouldn't recommend stopping outright. He said I should probably reduce my intake gradually.'

I nodded.

'Which is what I did. But not systematically, not according to any known clinical procedure.'

'And what happened?'

'I was fine for a while, but then *this* started . . .' – he held up his hands – '. . . and then . . . insomnia, nausea, chest and sinus infections, loss of appetite, constipation, dry mouth, *erectile* dysfunction.'

243

He threw his hands up, this time in a gesture of despair.

I didn't know what to say to him, and we were both silent for a while. I still wanted answers to my original two questions, but at the same time I didn't want to be insensitive.

After a moment, Geisler said, 'Look, I'm not blaming anyone but myself. No one forced me to take MDT.' He shook his head, and went on. 'I guess I was a guinea pig, though, because I bumped into Vernon about a year later and he told me they'd sorted out any dosage problems they'd been having, that dosage had to be individually adjusted – *customized*, he said.' A sudden look of anger came into his face. 'He even suggested I might like to try it again, but I told him to go *fuck* himself.'

I tried to nod sympathetically.

I also waited to see if he was going to say anything else. When it appeared that he wasn't, I said, 'This Todd guy, do you know his surname? Or anything about him? Which company he worked for?'

Geisler shook his head.

'I only ever met him two or three times anyway. He was very circumspect, very careful. He and Vernon were some act, I'll tell you – but Todd was definitely the brains.'

I fiddled with the pack of Camels on the table beside my espresso cup.

'One more question,' I said. 'When Todd told you that you needed to combine the MDT with something else, with another drug, to counteract the side-effects, the memory loss . . . did he say what that drug might be?'

'Yes.'

My heart jumped.

'What was it?'

'I actually remember it very well, because he kept on about it, telling me that it would take care of the problem, that he'd just worked it out. It was a product called Dexeron. It's an antihistamine and is used for treating certain allergies. It contains some . . . *thing*, some agent, that reacts with a specific receptor complex in the brain and in a way, *he* claimed, that would prevent the blackouts from happening. I don't know exactly. I don't remember the details of what he said. I don't think I understood it at the time. But apparently you can get it over the counter.'

'*You* didn't ever use it, though?'

'No.'

'I see.'

I nodded my head, as though I were considering this – but all I was thinking about now was getting out of there as fast as possible and getting to a pharmacy.

'. . . anyway, then, after Janine left me and I was kicked out of the company,' Geisler went on, 'I tried to pick up the pieces, but that wasn't so easy, because of course . . .'

I drained my coffee and desperately tried to formulate an exit strategy in my head. Even though I felt sorry for Geisler, and was horrified at what had happened to him, I *really* didn't need to hear this part of the story – but I couldn't just stand up and leave, either, so I ended up smoking two more cigarettes before I found the courage to say that I had to go.

I told him *thanks* and said I'd get the check on the way out. He looked at me, as if to say *C'mon, sit down, have another cigarette, drink some more coffee*, but then a second later he waved a hand at me, dismissively, and said, 'Oh, go on, get out of here. And good luck. I suppose.'

I found a pharmacy on Seventh Avenue, a few doors up from the café, and bought two packs of Dexeron. I then took a cab home.

Once in the apartment I made straight for the bedroom closet and took out the MDT pills. I wasn't sure how many to take, and I deliberated on it for quite a while. I eventually decided to take three. This was my last chance and it would either work or it wouldn't.

I went into the kitchen and got a glass of water. I swallowed the three MDT pills in one go, and then took two of the Dexeron. After that, I went in and sat on the couch, and waited.

Two hours later, my CDs were back in alphabetical order. There were also no more crushed pizza-boxes to be seen in the apartment, or empty beer cans, or dirty socks . . . and every single inch of surface space was polished and gleaming . . .

PART FOUR

PART FOUR

[22]

OVER THE WEEKEND, I stuck to this new dosage regime, and monitored my progress fairly closely. I decided not to go out, just in case anything went wrong – but nothing did go wrong. There were no clicks or jumps or flashes, and it appeared that whatever was in the Dexeron actually worked – which wasn't to say that I was in the clear, of course, or that I wouldn't ever be having another blackout again, but it definitely felt good to be *back*. All of a sudden, I was confident, and clear-headed, and buzzing with ideas and energy. If the Dexeron went on working, my future path was laid out in front of me, brick by brick, and the only thing that I had to do was follow it, undistracted, unrepentant. I would re-acquaint myself with the MCL–Abraxas material and then I'd go and smooth things over with Carl Van Loon. I'd get trading again and make some money, and move into the Celestial Building. I'd eventually extricate myself from involvement with people like Van Loon and Hank Atwood and set up an independent business structure of my own – the Spinola Corporation, SpinolaSystems, Edinvest, whatever.

I couldn't get Ginny Van Loon out of my mind as I entertained these thoughts, and I tried now to slot her in at some appropriate point along the way. She resisted, however – or the *idea* of her resisted – and the more resistance there was the more agitated I became. Eventually, I put these feelings aside, compartmentalized them, and moved on to the MCL–Abraxas material.

I read through all of the documents, and marvelled at how I hadn't been able to understand them before. It certainly wasn't the most exciting material in the world, but it was still relatively

249

straightforward. I re-acquainted myself with how the Black–Scholes pricing model worked and did up the projections on the computer. I ironed out any difficulties there'd been, including the discrepancy in the third option that Van Loon had pointed out to me that day in his office.

The other thing I did over the weekend – apart from a hundred sit-ups each morning and evening – was to get back into some serious news consumption. I read the papers online and watched all the major current affairs shows on TV. There was very little mention of the Donatella Alvarez murder investigation, other than a brief appeal for anyone who might have witnessed anything to come forward – which meant, presumably, that the police had come up with no leads on Thomas Cole and were now clutching at straws.

There was quite a lot of coverage of the Mexico story. A number of high-profile attacks had taken place – on tourists, and on US citizens, chiefly businessmen, living in Mexico City. One company director had been shot dead and two others had been kidnapped and were still missing. These incidents were being directly linked to the foreign policy debate that was raging in the press – and in which the 'i' word was now routinely being used. What had yet to be plausibly constructed in the public mind, despite talk of safety concerns for US citizens, not to mention threatened Mexican expropriation of foreign investments, was a rationale for any invasion that might take place – but they were clearly working on it.

I also looked at how the markets had been performing since the big drop in tech stocks the previous Tuesday, and did some preliminary research for the coming Monday morning – which was when I planned to re-activate my account with Klondike.

Late on the Sunday evening, I was restless and decided to go out for a while. It was only when I hit the warm night air, and started walking, that I understood just how much better I really felt. Unlike before, I now had a strong physical sense of MDT, an almost buzz-like tingling in my limbs and head. At the same time, I didn't feel intoxicated in any way. I just felt fully in control of my faculties – stronger, more awake, sharper.

I went to a few different bars, drank soda water and *talked* all night long. In each place I went to, it only took me a few minutes to start up a conversation with someone and then a few more after that to attract a circle of listeners around me – these people apparently fascinated by what I had to say, as I talked about politics, history, baseball, music, anything that found its way into the conversation. I had women coming on to me, too, and even some men, but I had no sexual interest in these people and tactfully deflected their advances by raising the polemical temperature of whatever discussion we were involved in. I am aware that this might make me sound obnoxious and manipulative, but it really didn't play that way at the time, and as the night marched on and *they* all got drunker, or more wired, and eventually started dropping out, *I* felt more invigorated, and – frankly – like some kind of minor god.

I got home at about 7.30 in the morning and immediately started sweeping through the financial websites. I'd shifted all of my funds out of the Klondike account on signing up with Lafayette – except for the deposit, which it had been necessary to leave in order to keep the account open. I was glad now that I'd done this, but as I eased my way back into trading throughout the course of the day, I found that I missed the company of other traders and the atmosphere of a 'room'. Nevertheless, it was remarkable how quickly I regained the confidence to make big trades and to take considerable risks, and by Tuesday afternoon – when Gennady phoned – I had already notched up about $25,000 in my account.

I'd forgotten that Gennady would be phoning and I was in the middle of devising a complicated trading strategy for the following day when the call came. I was in quite a buoyant mood and didn't want any trouble, so I told him I'd have the ten pills ready for him on Friday. He immediately wanted to know if I'd have them any time before then and if he could come and collect them. Slightly irritated by this, I said that no, I wouldn't, and he couldn't – and that I'd see him on Friday morning. When I put the phone down, I gave some thought to how I was going to deal with the Gennady situation. It had the potential to become a very serious problem indeed, and although I had no choice but to give him the ten pills this time, I didn't like the idea that he'd be out there, probably scheming his way up the Organizatsiya ladder – and also possibly even scheming against *me*. I would have to come up with something – a scheme of my own – and soon.

On the Wednesday, I went out shopping to get a couple of new suits. Thanks to a combination of not eating and doing hundreds of sit-ups, I'd lost a little weight over the previous five days – so I figured it was now time, finally, to inject some new life into my wardrobe. I got two wool suits, one of them a steel grey and the other a midnight blue – both by Boss Hugo Boss. I also got cotton shirts, silk ties, pocket squares, boxers, socks and shoes.

Sitting in the back of a cab on the way home from midtown, surrounded by scented, post-modern shopping bags, I felt exhilarated and ready for anything – but when I got upstairs to the third floor of my building I experienced again that sense I'd often had on MDT of being hemmed in, of not having enough space. My apartment, quite simply, was too small and cramped, and I was going to have to address that issue, as well.

Later on that evening, I wrote a lengthy and carefully phrased note to Carl Van Loon. In the note, I apologized for my recent behaviour and attempted to explain it by referring obliquely to a course of medication I'd been on but had now completed. I ended by asking him to let me come and talk to him, and enclosed the note in a folder with the revised projections I'd drawn up. I'd originally been going to have the package couriered to his office the following morning, but then I decided to deliver it in person. If I bumped into him in the lobby or in the elevator, well and good – if not, I'd wait and see how he responded to the note.

I spent the rest of the evening, and most of the night, studying an 800-page textbook I'd bought a few weeks earlier on corporate financing.

The next morning I did my sit-ups, drank some juice and had a shower. I chose the blue suit, a white cotton shirt and a plain ruby tie. I got dressed in front of the full-length mirror in the bedroom, and then took a cab to the Van Loon Building on Forty-eighth Street. I felt fresh and confident as I entered the lobby and strode over to the elevators. People were whizzing by in all directions and I had the sensory impression of cutting my way through a dense fuzz of commotion. As I waited for the elevator doors to open, I glanced over at the section of the enormous bronze-tinted window where I had stood wheezing in panic with Ginny the previous week, and found it hard to relate to the scene in any meaningful way at all. Neither was there the slightest hint in the elevator car, as it hurtled up to the sixty-second floor, of my earlier fear and anxiety. Instead, I eyed my reflection in the steel panels of the car's interior and admired the cut of my new suit.

The lobby area of Van Loon & Associates was quiet. There were a few young guys standing around chatting and letting off occasional volleys of boisterous laughter. The receptionist was looking at something on her computer screen, and seemed to be engrossed in it. When I reached her desk, I cleared my throat to attract her attention.

'Good morning, sir. May I help you?'

She showed a flicker of recognition, but also of confusion.

'Mr Van Loon please.'

'I'm afraid Mr Van Loon is out of the country at the moment. We don't expect him back until tomorrow. If you would . . .'

'That's OK,' I said, 'I'd like to leave this package for him. It's very urgent that it be brought to his attention as soon as he returns.'

'Of course, sir.'

She smiled.

I nodded, and smiled back.

Stopping short of clicking my heels, I then spun around and headed over towards the elevators again.

I went home and traded online for the rest of the day, adding a further ten grand to my pile.

So far, the combination of MDT and Dexeron had worked really well for me, and I kept my fingers crossed. I'd been on it for nearly a week now and I hadn't had the merest hint of a blackout. But for

Gennady's visit I decided to mess up my apartment a little, deliberately. I wanted to play down the intensity of high-dosage MDT and try to convince him that taking more than one pill every couple of days was actually dangerous. That way I could slow him down and give myself a little breathing space. However, I really had no idea what I was going to do about him.

When he came in the door on Friday morning, I could see that he had regressed a little. He didn't say anything, but just held out his hand and shook it in a *gimme* motion.

I took a tiny plastic container with ten MDT pills in it out of my pocket and gave it to him. He opened it immediately, standing there, and before I could launch into my spiel about dosage, he had popped one of the pills into his mouth.

He closed his eyes and remained still for a few moments – during which time I stood still as well, and said nothing. Then he opened his eyes and glanced around. I had tried to make the place look untidy, but it hadn't been easy – and there was certainly no comparison at all between how the place looked now and how it had looked the previous week.

'You get some, too?' he said, nodding his head at the general tidiness.

'Yes.'

'So you get more than ten? You tell me only ten.'

Shit.

'I got twelve,' I said, 'I managed to get twelve. Two extra for me. But that was a thousand bucks. I can't afford any more than that.'

'OK, next week, you get *me* twelve.'

I was going to say *no.* I was going to say *fuck you.* I was going to run at him and see if the physical kick of a triple dose of MDT would be enough to let me overpower him and maybe choke him to death. But I did nothing. I said, 'OK.'

Because what if it went wrong and *I* got choked to death – or, at best, I drew the attention of the police? And was finger-printed, booked, keyed into the system? I needed a safer and much more efficient way to get myself out of this situation. And it had to be permanent.

Gennady held his hand out again, and said, 'The seventeen-five?'

I had the money ready and just gave it to him without saying anything.

He put it into his jacket pocket.

As he was going out the door, he said, 'Next week, *twelve*. Don't forget.'

Carl Van Loon phoned me at seven o'clock that evening. I hadn't been expecting such a quick response, but I was glad – because now, one way or the other, I could proceed. I'd been getting restless, prickled by an increasing need to be involved in something that would consume all of my time and energy.

'Eddie.'

'Carl.'

'How many times are we going to have to do this, Eddie?'

I took a relatively subdued comment like that as a good sign, and launched into a defensive broadside that culminated in a plea to let me get involved again in the MCL–Abraxas deal. I told him that I was fired up and brimming with new ideas and that if he took a good look at the revised projections he'd see just how serious I was.

'I *have* looked at them, Eddie. They're terrific. Hank's here and I showed them to him earlier. He wants to meet you.' He paused. 'We want to get this thing off the ground.'

He paused again, longer this time.

'Carl?'

'But Eddie, I'm going to be straight with you. You pissed me off before. I didn't know who – or *what* – I was talking to. I mean, whatever it is you've got, some kind of bipolar shit, I don't know – but that degree of instability is just not on when you're playing at this level. When the merger is announced there's going to be a lot of pressure, wall-to-wall media coverage, stuff you can't imagine if you haven't already been there.'

'Let me come and talk to you, Carl, face to face. If you're not satisfied after that, I'll back off. You won't hear from me again. I'll sign confidentiality agreements, whatever. Five minutes.'

Van Loon paused for a full thirty seconds. In the silence, I could hear him breathing. Eventually, he said, 'I'm at home. I've got something on later, so if you're coming round, come round *now*.'

I had Van Loon back onside within ten minutes. We sat in his library, drinking Scotch, and I spun out an elaborate tale for him of an entirely imaginary condition I was supposed to be suffering from. It was easily treatable with light medication, but I had reacted adversely to a certain element in the medication and this had resulted in my erratic behaviour. The medication had been adjusted, I'd completed the course and now I was fine. It was a thin enough story, but I don't think Van Loon was actually listening very closely to what I was saying – he seemed, rather, to be mesmerized by something in the timbre of my voice, by my physical presence, and I even had the feeling that what he wanted more than anything else was just to reach over and touch me – and be, in a sense, electrified. It was a heightened version of how people had reacted to me before – Paul Baxter, Artie Meltzer, Kevin Doyle, Van Loon himself. I wasn't complaining, but I had to be careful about how I dealt with this. I didn't want it to cause any interference, or to unbalance things. I figured the best way to harness it was to keep busy, and to keep whoever I was exerting an influence over busy as well. With this in mind I swiftly moved the conversation on to the MCL–Abraxas deal.

It was all very delicate, Van Loon said, and time was of the essence. Despite a number of hitches, Hank Atwood was anxious to proceed. Having devised a price structure to bring to the table, the next step was to propose who should get the top jobs, and what shape the new company should have. Then it would be on to meetings, negotiations, bull sessions – the MCL-Parnassus people with the Abraxas people – '. . . and *us* in the middle.'

Us?

I took a sip from my Scotch. 'Us?'

'Me, and if it works out, *you*. Jim Heche, one of my senior vice-presidents knows what's going on, my wife knows – and that's about it. Same thing with the principals. Hank's just brought in a couple of advisers, he's being very cautious. That's why we want this thing wrapped up in a couple of weeks, a month tops.' He drained the whisky from his glass and looked at me. 'It's not easy keeping the lid on something like this, Eddie.'

We chatted for another half hour or so and then Van Loon said he had to go out. We arranged to meet the following morning at his office. We'd have lunch with Hank Atwood and then set the ball rolling in earnest.

Van Loon shook my hand at the door and said, 'Eddie, I sincerely hope this works out. I really do.'

I nodded.

On the way from the library to the main door of the apartment, I'd glanced around, hoping to catch sight of Ginny . . .

'Just don't let me down, Eddie, OK?'

. . . if she was at home.

'I won't, Carl. I'm *on* this, believe me.'

But there was no sign of her.

'Sure. I know that. I'll see you tomorrow.'

The lunch with Hank Atwood went very smoothly. He was impressed by my command of the material relating to the deal, but also by my wide-ranging knowledge of the business world in general. I had no problems answering the questions he asked me, and I even deftly managed to turn a few of them back on Atwood himself. Van Loon's relief that things were finally working out was palpable, and I could also sense he was pleased that my performance was reflecting well on Van Loon & Associates. We'd gone to the Four Seasons again, and as I sat looking out over the room, fiddling with the stem of my empty wine glass, I tried to recall the details of what had happened the last time I'd been there. But I soon had the weirdest feeling that what I was conjuring up, like a misremembered dream, was unreliable. It even occurred to me that I *hadn't* been there before, not really, but had constructed this memory from what someone had told me, or from something I'd read. However, the sense of distance from that other time which this created was welcome – because I was here *now*, and that was all that counted.

I was enjoying it, too – though I only picked at the food and didn't have anything to drink. Hank Atwood relaxed quite a bit as the lunch progressed, and I even saw in him a little flicker of that needy reliance on my attention that had become such a feature of earlier, similar relationships. But that was fine. I sat there in the Four Seasons and revelled in the heady atmosphere, reflecting occasionally – when I reminded myself who these men were – that what I was experiencing could well have been the prototype for an extremely sophisticated virtual reality game.

In any case, this lunch was to be the start for me of a busy, strange and exciting period in my life. Over the following two or three weeks I got caught up in a constant round of meetings, lunches, dinners, late-night confabulations with powerful, tanned men in expensive suits – all of us in search of what Hank Atwood kept referring to as 'vision lock', that moment when the two parties could agree on a basic outline for the deal. I met with various sorts of people – lawyers, financiers, corporate strategists, a couple of congressmen, a senator – and was able to hold my own with all of them. In fact, somewhat to the alarm of Carl Van Loon, I became, in a couple of respects, pivotal to the whole thing. As we approached the critical mass of vision lock, the few of us who were actually in on the deal became quite pally, in a corporate, cliquey kind of way, but I was the one who provided the social glue. I was the one who was able to paper over the cracks between the two markedly different corporate cultures. In addition to this, I became utterly indispensable to Van Loon himself. Since he couldn't bring in his usual teams of people to work on the deal, he increasingly relied on me to monitor what was going on and to digest and process huge amounts of information – from Federal Trade Commission regulations to the intricacies of broadband, from appointment times to the names of people's wives.

While all of this was going on, I managed to do other stuff as well. I made it most days to the Van Loon & Associates gym to burn off some of my excess energy, spending time on different machines and trying to do an all-round work-out. I managed to keep track of my Klondike portfolio and even got a little action in on the company trading floor that Van Loon had told me about. I bought a cellphone, which was something I'd been meaning to do for ages. I bought more clothes, and wore a different suit every day – or, at least, rotated six or seven suits. Since the act of sleeping didn't feature too prominently in my life any more, I also got to read the papers and do research, sitting at my computer – late at night, and often deep into the night . . .

Another part of my life, and one that I couldn't ignore – unfortunately – was Gennady. Given that I was so busy in this increasingly blurred continuum of waking time, I slipped into an easy routine of supplying him with a dozen tablets each Friday morning, telling myself as I handed them over that I'd address the issue before the next time, that I'd take steps to contain the situation. But how? I didn't *know* how.

Each time he came, too, I was shocked by how much he'd changed. That smack addict's pallor had gone and there was a healthy glow to his skin now. He'd had a haircut, and had started wearing suits as well – though they weren't anywhere near as nice as mine. He'd also taken to arriving by car, a black Mercedes something or other, and had guys waiting for him downstairs. He had to let me know this, of course, and more or less directed me to look out of the window and down at his entourage, waiting on Tenth Street.

Another thing Gennady did which annoyed me, was to shake one of the pills out into his hand the moment he got them, and then pop it into his mouth – right there in front of me, as though I were a coke-dealer and he was checking out the product. He also used to dispense the rest of the pills into a little silver pillbox he had, which he kept in the breast-pocket of his jacket. He'd pat this part of his jacket and say, 'Always be prepared.' Gennady was an asshole and I physically couldn't bear to have him in the room. But I was powerless to stop him, because he obviously *had* moved up in the Organizatsiya, so how did I even begin to deal with *that*?

What I did was compartmentalize it, deal with it at the time and then move swiftly on.

I seemed to be doing a lot of that these days.

Mostly, though, my time was spent huddled in various offices and conference rooms of the Van Loon Building on Forty-eighth Street, with Carl and Hank Atwood and Jim Heche, or with Carl and Jim and Dan Bloom, the chairman of Abraxas, and *his* people.

Late one night, however, I found myself alone with Carl in one of the conference rooms. We were having a drink, and since we were close to agreeing a deal, he brought up the subject of money, something he hadn't mentioned since that first night in his apartment on Park Avenue. He passed a comment about the commission rate we'd be getting for brokering the deal, so I decided to ask him outright what my share would be. Without batting an eyelid, and distractedly consulting a folder on the table, he said, 'Well, given the scale of your contribution, Eddie, it won't be anything less than forty. I don't know, say, forty-five.'

I paused, and waited for him to go on – because I wasn't sure exactly what he meant. But he didn't say anything else, and just continued staring at the folder.

'Thousand?' I ventured.

He looked at me, and furrowed his eyebrows. He seemed slightly confused.

'*Million*, Eddie. Forty-five million.'

[23]

I HADN'T ANTICIPATED earning that kind of money so quickly – not
having imagined, in the first place, that the MCL–Abraxas deal would
be so lucrative for Van Loon & Associates. But when I thought about
it, and looked at other deals, and at the way these things were struc-
tured, I realized that there was nothing unusual about it at all. The
combined value of the two companies concerned would be somewhere in the region two hundred *billion* dollars. Based on that, our
brokerage fee – point something of a per cent – would yield, well
. . . handsomely.

I could do plenty, I thought, with that kind of money. I devoted
quite a while to thinking about it, in fact, but it didn't take me long,
either, to feel aggrieved that I wasn't in possession of any of the
money *now*. It took me even less time to get working on Van Loon
for an advance.

When he put the folder aside and I had his attention again, I
explained to him that I'd been living on Tenth Street and Avenue A
for about six years, but that I felt it was time for a change. He smiled
awkwardly at this, as if I'd told him I lived on the moon – but he
perked up considerably when I added that I'd been looking at a
place in the Celestial Building over on the West Side.

'Good. That sounds more like it. No disrespect, Eddie – but I
mean Avenue A, what the fuck is *that* all about?'

'Income levels, Carl. *That's* what it's about. I've never had enough
money to live anyplace else.'

Obviously thinking he'd put me in an awkward position, Van Loon mumbled something and looked uncomfortable for a moment. I told him I *liked* living down on Avenue A and Tenth Street, and that it was a great neighbourhood, full of old bars and weird characters. Five minutes later, however, I had him telling me not to worry, that he'd arrange financing immediately so I could buy the apartment in the Celestial Building. It'd be a routine company loan that I could settle later, further down the line, whenever. Sure, I thought, nine and a half million dollars – a routine loan.

I phoned Alison Botnick the next morning at Sullivan, Draskell, the realtors on Madison Avenue.

'Well, Mr Spinola, how *are* you?'

'I'm fine.'

I told her I was sorry for having run off that day, making a joke out of it. She said, oh, not even to *mention* it. Then I asked her if the apartment was still on the market. It was, she said, and all the work on it had just been completed. I told her I'd be interested in seeing it again, that day if possible, and in talking to her about entering a bid.

Van Loon had also said he'd write a reference letter for me, which would probably make it unnecessary for Sullivan, Draskell to pry into my tax returns and credit history – and would mean, if everything went well, that I could sign the contracts almost immediately and move in.

This had now become the controlling dynamic in my life – immediacy, acceleration, *speed*. I shifted rapidly from scene to scene, from one location to another, with little sense of where the joins met. For example, I had to see several people that morning, and in different places – the office on Forty-eighth Street, a hotel uptown, a bank down on Vesey Street. Then I had a lunch appointment with Dan Bloom at Le Cirque. I squeezed in seeing the apartment again after lunch. Alison Botnick was waiting for me when I arrived up on the sixty-eighth floor – almost as though she hadn't left since my last visit and had been waiting patiently for me to return. Barely recognizing me at first, she was then all over me, but within about five minutes, probably even less, I had put in a bid at a small but strategic amount over the ask price and was gone – back to Forty-eighth

Street and another meeting with Carl and Hank and Jim, to be followed by cocktails at the Orpheus Room.

As this last meeting was wrapping up, Van Loon took a call at his desk. We were now very close to announcing the deal, and everyone was in an upbeat mood. The meeting had gone well, and even though the hardest part lay ahead – seeking Congressional, FCC and FTC approval – there was a real sense of collective accomplishment in the room.

Hank Atwood stood up from his chair and strolled over to where I was sitting. He was in his early sixties, but looked trim and wiry and very fit. Even though he was short, he had a commanding, almost threatening presence. Landing a gentle punch on my shoulder, he said, 'Eddie, how do you do it?'

'What?'

'That extraordinary recall you've got. The way your mind processes everything. I can *see* it working.'

I shrugged my shoulders.

He went on, 'You're on top of this thing in a way that I find almost . . .'

I was beginning to feel uncomfortable.

'. . . almost . . . I mean I've been in business for forty years, Eddie, I've headed up a food-and-drinks conglomerate, I've run a movie studio, I've seen it all, every trick in the book, every kind of deal there is, every kind of guy you can meet . . .'

He was looking directly into my eyes now, standing over me.

'. . . but I don't think I've ever met anyone quite like you . . .'

I wasn't sure if this was meant as a declaration of love or an accusation, but just then Van Loon got up from his desk, and said, 'Hank . . . someone here to say hello.'

Atwood turned around.

Van Loon had stepped away from his desk and was walking across the room towards the door. I stood up from my chair and moved behind Atwood. Jim Heche had wandered about half-way down the room and taken out his cellphone.

I turned to face the door.

Van Loon opened it and motioned to whoever was there to come in. I could hear voices outside, but not what they were saying. There was a brief exchange, followed by a short burst of laughter, and then – a couple of seconds later – Ginny Van Loon appeared in the room.

I felt a quickening in my chest.

She pecked her father on the cheek. Then Hank Atwood raised his arms, '*Ginny*.'

She came towards him and they embraced.

'So, you had a good time?'

She nodded, and smiled broadly.

'I had a blast.'

Where had she been?

'Did you try that *osteria* I told you about?'

Italy.

'Yeah, it was *great*. That stuff, what was it called, *baccalà*? – I loved it.'

The north-east.

They went on chatting for the next minute or so, Ginny focusing all her attention on Atwood. As I waited for her to disengage and – I suppose – *notice* me, I watched her closely, and realized something that should have been obvious to me before.

I was in love with her.

'. . . and it's really cool how they name streets after *dates* . . .'

She was wearing a short grey skirt, a dusty blue cardigan, matching top and black leather pumps, all stuff she'd probably bought in Milan on her way back from Vicenza or Venice, or wherever she'd been. Her hair was different, too – not spiky any more, but straight, and with a bit at the front that kept falling into her eyes, and that she kept having to flick back.

'. . . Twentieth of September Street, Fourth of November Street, it *resonates* . . .'

She looked over and saw me, and smiled – surprised and not surprised.

Van Loon said, 'I guess history is pretty important to them over there.'

'Oh, and what are we,' Ginny said, turning suddenly to her father, 'one of those happy nations that hasn't got any history?'

'That's not what—'

'We just *do* stuff and hope no one notices.'

'What I—'

'Or we make it up to suit what people *did* notice.'

'And in Europe that's not what happens?' said Hank Atwood. 'Is that what you're telling us?'

'No, but . . . well, I don't know, take this Mexico shit that's going on at the moment? People over there can't believe we're even *talking* about invading.'

'Look, Ginny,' Van Loon said, 'it's a complicated situation. I mean, this is a *narco*-state we're dealing with here . . .' He went on to paint what had been in a dozen newspaper editorials and op-ed pieces recently: a vast fevered mural depicting instability, disorder and impending catastrophe . . .

Jim Heche, who had drifted back up the room, and had been listening closely, said, 'It's not only in *our* interests, Ginny, you know, it's in *theirs*, too.'

'Oh, invade the country to save it?' she said, in exasperation, 'I can't believe I'm hearing this.'

'Sometimes that's—'

'What about the nineteen-seventy UN injunction,' she said, her voice accelerating rapidly, 'that no state has the right to intervene, directly or indirectly, for any reason whatever, in the internal affairs of any other state?'

She was standing in the centre of the room now, ready to fend off attacks from any quarter.

'Ginny, listen to me,' Van Loon said patiently. 'Trade with Central and South America has always been crucial to—'

'Oh, *Jesus*, Daddy, that's all *spin*.'

Looking like his daughter had just kick-boxed him, Van Loon threw his hands up.

'You want to know what *I* think it's about?' she went on, 'I mean *really* about?'

Van Loon looked dubious, but Hank Atwood and Jim Heche were obviously interested, and waiting to hear what she had to say. For

265

my part, I had retreated to the oak-panelled wall behind me and was watching the scene with mixed feelings – amusement, desire, *confusion*.

'There's no grand plan here,' she said, 'no economic strategy, no conspiracy. It wasn't thought out in any way. In fact, I think it's just another manifestation of irrational . . . *something* – not exuberance exactly, but . . .'

Losing patience a little now, Van Loon said, 'What does *that* mean?'

'I think Caleb Hale had a couple of drinks too many that night, or was maybe mixing booze with his Triburbazine pills, or whatever, and he just lost the run of himself. And now they're trying to gloss over what he said, cover their tracks, make out as if this is a real policy. But what they're doing is *entirely irrational* . . .'

'That's ridiculous, Ginny.'

'We were talking about history a minute ago – I think that's how most history *works*, Daddy. People in power, they make it up as they go along. It's sloppy and accidental and *human* . . .'

The reason I was confused during those few moments, as I stared over at Ginny, was because in spite of everything – in spite of how different they looked and how different they sounded – I could so easily have been staring over at Melissa.

'Ginny's starting college in the fall,' Van Loon said to the others. 'International studies – or is that *irrational* studies? – so don't mind her, she's just limbering up.'

Tapping out a quick timestep in her new shoes, Ginny said, 'Up yours, Mr Van Loon.'

Then she turned and walked over in my direction. Hank Atwood and Jim Heche converged, and one of them started speaking to Van Loon, who was back sitting at his desk.

As Ginny approached where I was standing, she threw her eyes up, dismissing everything – and every*one* – behind her. She arrived over and poked me gently in the stomach, 'Look at *you*.'

'What?'

'Where's all the weight gone?'

'I told you it fluctuates.'

She looked at me dubiously, 'Are you bulimic?'

'No, like I said . . .'

I paused.

'Or maybe schizophrenic then?'

'What is this?' I laughed, and made a face. 'Sure it's not *medical* school you're going to? I'm fine. That was just a bad day you caught me on.'

'A bad day?'

'Yeah.'

'Hhmm.'

'It *was*.'

'And today?'

'Today's a good day.'

I felt the impulse to add some sappy comment like *and it's even better now that you're here*, but I managed to keep my mouth shut.

A brief silence followed, during which we just looked at each other.

Then, from across the room, 'Eddie?'

'Yeah?'

It was Van Loon.

'What was that thing we were talking about earlier? Copper loops and . . . AD-something?'

I bent slightly to the left and looked around Ginny, over at Van Loon.

'ADSL,' I said. 'Asynchronous Digital Subscriber Loop.'

'And . . . ?'

'It permits transmission of a single compressed, high-quality video signal, at a rate of 1.5 Mbits per second. In addition to an ordinary voice phone conversation.'

'Right.'

Van Loon turned back to Hank Atwood and Jim Heche and continued what he was saying.

Ginny looked at me and raised her eyebrows.

'Ex*cuse* me.'

'Let's get out of here and go somewhere for a drink,' I said, all at a rush. 'Come on, don't say no.'

She paused, and that flicker of uncertainty passed over her face again. Before she could answer, Van Loon clapped his hands together and said, 'OK, Eddie, let's go.'

Ginny immediately turned around and moved off, saying to her father, 'So where are you lot going?'

I slumped back against the oak-panelled wall.

'The Orpheus Room. We've got more business to discuss. If that's OK with you.'

She made a dismissive puffing sound and said, 'Knock yourselves out.'

'And what are *you* doing?'

As she looked at her watch, I looked at her back, at the soft dusty blue of her cashmere cardigan.

'Well, there's something I've got to do later, but I'm going home now.'

'OK.'

The next short while was taken up with *goodbyes* and *see you laters*.

Ginny drifted over to the door, waved at me, smiled, and then left.

On our way down to the Orpheus Room a couple of minutes later, I had to shake off an acute sense of disappointment and refocus my attention on the business at hand.

My bid for the apartment in the Celestial Building was accepted the following day, and I found myself signing all of the documents the day after that again. Van Loon's letter had silenced any enquiry into my tax affairs, and with the financing arrangements equally discreet, I have to say I had a very easy time of it. Less easy was deciding how I wanted the place to look. I called a couple of interior designers and visited some furniture showrooms and read various glossy magazines, but I remained undecided and fell into an obsessive cycle of plan and counter-plan, colour scheme and counter-colour scheme. Did I want it all spare and industrial, for example, with gunmetal-grey surfaces and modular storage units – or exotic and *busy*, with Louis XV chairs, Japanese silk screens and red lacquer tables?

When Gennady arrived at the apartment on Tenth Street that Friday morning, I had already started packing some of my stuff into boxes.

I should have expected trouble, of course, but I hadn't been letting myself think about it.

He came in the door, saw what was happening and lost his temper almost immediately. He kicked a couple of boxes over and said that was *it*. 'I've had enough of you and your two-faced guinea *shit*.'

He was wearing a baggy, cream-coloured suit with a swirling pink and yellow tie. His hair was slicked back and he had steel-rimmed, reflective sunglasses resting on the tip of his nose.

'I mean, what the *fuck* is going on here?'

'Take it easy, Gennady. I'm just moving to a new apartment.'

'*Where?*'

This was going to be the hard bit. Once he understood where I was moving to, he'd never be happy to go on with the arrangement as it was. I'd paid off all of the loan by that stage, so essentially the arrangement between us was *me* dealing *him* twelve MDT pills a week. I didn't want to go on with this arrangement either, of course, but clearly there'd be a difference of opinion about the nature of any changes we might make.

'A place in the West Thirties, on Twelfth Avenue.'

He kicked another box.

'When are you moving?'

'Early next week.'

The new place wasn't ready in terms of décor and furnishings, but since it had a shower and phonelines and cable, and since I didn't mind eating delivery food for a while – and since I *really* wanted to get out of Tenth Street – I was prepared to just move into it straightaway, as it was.

Gennady was now breathing through his nose.

'Look,' I said to him, 'you've got my social security number and my credit-card details. It's not like you'll be losing track of where I am. Besides it's only across town and up a bit.'

'You think I'm worried about losing *track* of you?' He threw a hand up in the air dismissively. 'I'm tired of *this* . . .' – he pointed to the floor – '. . . coming *here*. What I want is to meet your dealer. I want to buy this shit in *bulk*.'

I shook my head and clicked my tongue.

'Sorry, Gennady, that's just not going to be possible.'

He stood still for a second, but then lunged forward and punched me in the chest. I fell backwards, over a full box of books, arms outstretched, and whacked my head on the floor.

It took me a few moments to sit up, and a few more to rub my head and look around in bewilderment, and then to get up on my feet again. I thought of a hundred things to say to him, but didn't bother with any of them.

He had his hand out.

'Come on, where are they?'

I stumbled over to the desk and got the pills from a drawer. I went back and handed them to him. He swallowed one of the pills and then spent the next couple of minutes carefully transferring the rest of them from the little plastic container I'd given him to his silver pillbox. When he'd finished doing this, he discarded the plastic container and put the pillbox into the breast pocket of his jacket.

'You shouldn't take more than one of those a day,' I said.

'I don't.' Then he looked at his watch, and sighed impatiently. 'I'm in a hurry. Write down the address of this new place.'

I went over to the desk again, still rubbing the back of my head. When I found a piece of paper and a pen, I considered giving him a false address, but then thought what would the point be – he *did* have all my details.

'Let's go. I've got a meeting in fifteen minutes.'

I wrote down the address and handed him the piece of paper.

'A *meeting*?' I said, with a hint of sarcasm in my voice.

'Yeah,' he smirked, obviously missing the sarcasm, 'I'm setting up an import-export company. Or trying to. But there's so many fucking laws and regulations in this country. You know how much shit you have to go through just to get a licence?'

I shook my head, and then asked him, 'What are you going to be importing? Or exporting?'

He paused, leant forward a little and whispered, 'I don't know, you know . . . *stuff*.'

'Stuff?'

'Hey, what do you want, this is a complicated scam I'm working on – you think I'm going to tell a cocksucker like *you* about it?'

I shrugged my shoulders.

'OK, Eddie,' he said, 'so listen. I'm giving you until next week. Set up a time with this person and we'll meet. I'll cut you in for a commission. But fuck with me, and I'll rip your heart out with these two hands and fry it up in a skillet. Do you understand me?'

I stared at him. 'Yes.'

His fist came from out of nowhere, like a torpedo, and landed in my solar plexus. I doubled up in pain and staggered backwards again, just avoiding the box of books.

'Oh, *I'm* sorry, did you say *yes*? My mistake.'

As he was walking down the stairs, I could still hear him laughing.

When I was able to breathe normally again, I went over to the couch and lowered myself on to it. I stretched out and stared up at the ceiling. For some time now, Gennady's personality had been threatening to spiral out of control. I was going to have to do something about it, and *soon* – because once he saw the apartment in the Celestial Building there'd be nothing I *could* do. Not any more. It'd be too late. He'd want in. He'd want everything.

He'd *ruin* everything.

However, a bit later – when I thought matters through more fully – I came to the conclusion that the real crisis wasn't with Gennady at all. The real crisis had to do with the fact that my supply of MDT was haemorrhaging – and at an alarming rate. Over the past month or so, I'd been dipping into it several times a week, indiscriminately, without ever bothering to count how many pills were left – thinking each time that I'd count them the *next* time. But I never did. I never got around to it. I was too caught up in things, too caught up in the relentless drumbeat inside my own head – the MCL–Abraxas deal, the Celestial Building, *Ginny Van Loon* . . .

I went into the bedroom. I opened the closet, took out the big brown envelope and emptied its contents on to the bed. I counted the pills. There were only about two hundred and fifty of them left. At the current rate of consumption – plus Gennady's regular supply – they'd all be gone in a couple of months. Even if I eliminated Gennady from the equation, that would still only add a few more weeks to the total. So ultimately . . . a few weeks, a few months – what difference did it make?

This was the real crisis I was facing, and in the end, it came back – again – to Vernon's little black notebook. Somewhere in that list of names and telephone numbers there had to be someone who knew about MDT, about its origins, and about how dosage levels worked, and maybe even about how to get a new supply line up and running. Because if I was to have any chance of fulfilling this great, unlooked-for destiny that was stretching out before me, I had to address these issues – either or both of them, dosage and supply, and I had to do it *now*.

I took out the notebook and went through it again. Using a red pen, I crossed out the numbers I'd already tried. On a separate piece of paper, I made a fresh list of selected numbers I hadn't tried. The first number on this new list was Deke Tauber's. I'd been reluctant to call him before, because I hadn't imagined there'd be much chance I'd get through to him. In the 1980s he'd been a bond-salesman, a Wall Street jock, but now he'd recreated himself and was the reclusive leader of an eponymous self-improvement cult – Dekedelia.

The more I thought about it, however, the more sense it made for me to call him. Regardless of how weird or reclusive he'd become, he would still know who I was. He'd known Melissa. I could invoke *the old days*.

I dialled the number and waited.

'Mr Tauber's office.'

'Hello, could I speak to Mr Tauber please.'

Suspicious pause.

Shit.

'Who may I ask is calling?'

'Erm . . . tell him it's an old friend, Eddie Spinola.'

Another pause.

'How did you get hold of this number?'

'I don't think that's any of your business. Now, may I speak to Mr Tauber, please?'

Click.

I really didn't like people hanging up on me – but I knew it was probably going to keep happening.

I looked at the list of numbers again.

Who is this?

What do you want?

How did you get hold of this number?

The thought of going through the list and crossing each number out, one after the other, was too demoralizing, so I decided to persist with Tauber for a while. I visited the Dekedelia website and read about the courses they offered and about the selection of books and videos they sold. It all seemed very commercial and had clearly been designed to attract new recruits.

I surfed around for a bit, and found links to a wide range of other sites. There was a directory of fringe religions, an awareness network called CultWatch, various 'concerned parents' organizations and other sites dealing with issues such as mind control and 'recovery facilitation'. I ended up at the homepage of a qualified exit counsellor in Seattle, someone who had lost his son fifteen years previously to a group called the Shining Venusians. Since this person had mentioned Dekedelia on his homepage, I decided to find his number and give him a call. We spoke for a few minutes and although he wasn't much help he did give me the number of a concerned parents group in New York. I then spoke to the secretary of this group – a concerned and clearly deranged parent – and got the name, in turn, of a private investigation agency which was conducting surveillance of Dekedelia on behalf of some members of the group. After several attempts and a lot of dissembling, I got to speak to one of the agency's operatives, Kenny Sanchez.

I said I had some information about Deke Tauber that might be of interest to him, but that I was looking for some information in

273

return. He was cagey at first, but eventually agreed to meet me – at the skating rink in Rockerfeller Plaza.

Two hours later we were pacing up and down Forty-seventh Street. Then we drifted on to Sixth Avenue, past Radio City Music Hall and up towards Central Park South.

Kenny Sanchez was short and paunchy and wore a brown suit. Although he was serious and obviously very circumspect when it came to his work, he started to relax after about ten minutes and even became quite chatty. Exaggerating slightly, I told him I'd been a friend of Deke Tauber's for a while in the 1980s, but that we'd lost touch. This seemed to fascinate him, and he asked me a few questions about it. By answering these freely, I created the impression that I was willing to share any information I had – which meant that by the time I started asking *him* questions, I had pretty much won him over.

'The basic tenet of this cult, Eddie,' he told me, in confidential tones, 'is that each individual needs to escape the inherent dysfunction of the family matrix, and – get this – to *re-create* themselves independently in an alternative environment.'

He stopped for a moment and shrugged his shoulders, as if to distance himself from what he'd just said. Then he continued walking.

'When it started up, Dekedelia was no more, or less, flaky than any of a dozen other of these outfits – you know, with lectures and meditation sessions and newsletters. Like all the others, too, it had an aura of cheap, second-hand mysticism about it – but things changed pretty quickly, and before you knew it the leader of this quote-unquote spiritual movement was producing best-selling books and videos.'

I took an occasional sidelong glance at Kenny Sanchez as he spoke. He was articulate and this stuff was obviously vivid in his mind, but I also felt he was anxious to let me know that he was on top of his brief.

'The problems started soon after that. A succession of people – always young, usually stuck in dead-end jobs – seemed to just *disappear* into the cult. But there was nothing illegal about it, because the members were always careful to write "goodbye" letters to their

274

families, thus . . .' – he held up the index finger of his right hand – '. . . cleverly pre-empting any missing-person investigations by the police.'

He was focusing on three individual cases, he said, young people who had disappeared within the past year, and he gave me a few details about each of them – stuff I didn't particularly need to hear.

'So, how are your investigations going now?' I asked.

'Erm . . . not so well, I'm afraid.' He clearly hadn't wanted to say it, but it didn't look as if there'd been much choice. Then, as though to compensate, he added, 'But there seems to be something strange going on at the moment. Within the past week or two, rumours have been circulating that Deke Tauber has taken ill. He hasn't been seen, hasn't given any lectures, hasn't done any book-signings. He can't be reached. He's effectively incommunicado.'

'Hhmm.'

I felt the time had now come for me to show my hand.

I said I had reason to believe that Deke Tauber was taking a strange, physically addictive designer drug and that if he was ill it might be because the only known supplier of the drug had . . . disappeared recently, leaving all of his clients high and dry – as it were. Kenny Sanchez was naturally very interested in this, though I did keep it quite vague and told him almost immediately what *I* needed – which was information on an associate of Tauber's, a Todd-something. I told him that if he helped me out with this, I'd pass on any further information I managed to uncover about the drug thing.

In trying to impress me, Kenny Sanchez had lost his professional bearings somewhat, but he still managed to balk convincingly at the notion of revealing, to a third party, information he had learned during the course of an investigation.

'Information on an associate of Tauber's? I don't know, Eddie – that's not going to be easy. I mean, we're bound by rules of confidentiality . . .' – he paused – '. . . and ethics . . . and stuff . . .'

I stopped on the corner of Sixth and Central Park South and turned to face him. He stopped as well. I looked directly into his eyes.

'How do you get information in the first place, Kenny? It's a commodity, like anything else, no? A currency? This would simply be an exchange . . .'

'. . . I suppose . . .'

'I mean, what *are* sources anyway?'

'Yeah, but . . .'

'There has to be some give and take, surely.'

I kept on at him like this until he eventually agreed to help me out. He said he'd see what he could do, and added – sheepishly – that if he tried he could probably get access to Tauber's phone records.

I spent the weekend packing up the remainder of my stuff and having most of it moved into the Celestial. I got to know the main guy, Richie, at the desk in the lobby. I checked out a few more furniture showrooms, as well as having a look at the latest in kitchen appliances and home entertainment systems. I bought a complete set of Dickens, something I'd been meaning to do for ages. I also learned Spanish – something else I'd been meaning to do for ages – and read *One Hundred Years of Solitude* in the original.

Kenny Sanchez called me on Monday morning. He asked if we could meet, and suggested a coffee shop on Columbus Avenue in the Eighties. I was going to object, and suggest somewhere a little closer to midtown, but then I didn't. If this was to be one of his little private investigator *things* – meeting in public places, like skating rinks and coffee shops – then so be it. I made a few calls before going out. I set up an appointment for later with my Tenth Street landlord to hand over the keys. I made an unsuccessful attempt to set another one up with the guy who was going to be tiling my bathroom. I also spoke to Van Loon's secretary and scheduled a couple of meetings for the middle part of the afternoon.

Then I went down to First Avenue and hopped in a cab.

That was last Monday morning.

As I sit now in the eerie quiet of this room in the Northview Motor Lodge, it seems incredible to me that *that* was only five days ago. Equally incredible, given all that's happened since, is what I was doing – setting up business meetings, worrying about bathroom tiles, taking what I imagined were sensible steps to address the MDT situation . . .

Outside there has been a subtle shift in the light. The darkness has lost its edge, and it won't be long now before a blue tinge starts seeping up from the horizon. I am tempted to put the laptop down, to go outside and look at the sky, and feel the vast stillness that surrounds this small clearing on the edge of a Vermont highway.

But I stay where I am – inside, in the wicker armchair – and continue writing. Because the truth is, I don't have that much time left.

In the cab on the way to the coffee shop, we passed Actium, on Columbus Avenue – the restaurant where I'd sat opposite Donatella Alvarez. I caught a glimpse of the place as we sped by. It was closed and looked strangely flat and unreal, like an abandoned movie set. I allowed my head to replay what I could remember of the dinner there and of the reception in Rodolfo Alvarez's studio afterwards – but soon those painted figures, lurid, bulging, *multiplying*, were all I could see, and I had to stop. I blocked it out by reading the charter of passenger's rights on the back of the seat in front of me.

When I got to the coffee shop, Kenny Sanchez was sitting in a booth, eating a plate of ham and eggs. There was a large brown envelope on the table beside his coffee cup. I sat down opposite him and nodded a suitably discreet *hello*.

He wiped his mouth with his napkin and said, 'Eddie, how are you? You want something to eat?'

'No, I'll just have a coffee.'

He nabbed a passing waitress and ordered the coffee.

'I've got something for you,' he said and tapped the envelope.

I felt my heart beat a little faster.

'That's great. What is it?'

He took a sip from his coffee.

'We'll come to that, Eddie – but first, you've got to be straight with me. This designer drug thing – how real is it? I mean, how do you even *know* about it?'

Obviously – having gone off and had himself a little think – he'd concluded that I was trying to put one over on him, to finagle the information out of him without giving anything substantial in return.

'It's real all right,' I said, and paused. Then the waitress arrived with the coffee, which gave me a moment to think. But there was nothing *to* think. I needed the information.

When the waitress had gone, I said, 'You know all these performance-enhancing drugs you read about in the papers, and that are tainting sport – swimming, track-and-field, weight-lifting? Well, this is like one of those, except it's for the brain – a kind of steroid for the intellect.'

He stared at me, unsure of how to react, waiting for more.

'Someone I knew was dealing them to Tauber.' I nodded at the envelope. 'If those are Tauber's phone records, then this guy's name is probably on there, too. Vernon Gant.'

Kenny Sanchez hesitated. But then he picked up the envelope, opened it and pulled out a sheaf of papers. I could see straightaway that it was a print-out of telephone numbers, along with names, times and dates. He riffled through them, looking for something specific.

'There,' he said after a moment, and held a page out, pointing at a name, 'Vernon Gant.'

'So is there a Todd listed on there, as well?'

'Yes. Just three or four calls, all around the same time, a period of a couple of days.'

'And after which there are no more calls from Vernon Gant either.'

He looked back at the pages, flicking them over, one by one, checking what I'd said. Eventually, he nodded and said, 'Yeah, you're right.' He put the sheaf of papers down on the envelope. 'So what does that mean? He disappeared?'

'Vernon Gant is dead.'

'Oh.'

'He was my brother-in-law.'

'Oh.' He sighed. 'I'm sorry.'

'Don't be. He was a jerk.'

We were both silent for a few moments after that. Then I took a

278

calculated risk. I picked up the sheaf of papers, and when they were firmly in my hand, I raised my eyebrows at him interrogatively.

He nodded his assent.

I studied the pages for a few moments, flicking through them randomly. Then I came across the 'Todd' calls. His surname was Ellis.

'That's a New Jersey number, isn't it?'

'Yeah. I checked. The calls were to a place called United Labtech, which is somewhere near Trenton.'

'United Labtech?'

He nodded, and said, 'Yeah. You want to take a drive out there?'

His car was parked just up the street, so within a few minutes we were heading down the Henry Hudson Parkway. We took the Lincoln Tunnel to New Jersey and then got on to the Turnpike. Kenny Sanchez had given me the envelope to hold when we got into the car, and after a few minutes on the road I'd taken the pages out and had started examining them. It was obvious that Sanchez was a little uncomfortable about this, but he didn't say anything. I managed to keep things ticking over by talking, and asking him questions – about cases he'd worked, about anomalies in the law, about his family, whatever. Then, suddenly, I was asking him questions about the list. Who were these people? Had he tracked all of the calls? How did that work?

'Most of the numbers,' he said, 'are connected to the business end of Dekedelia – publishers, distributors, lawyers. We can account for them, and for that reason have eliminated them. But we've also isolated a list of about twenty-five other names that don't check out, that we can't account for.'

'Who are they to? Or from?'

'To *and* from – and fairly regularly, as well. They're all individuals living in major cities throughout the country. They hold executive positions in a wide range of companies, but none of them seems to have any connection to Dekedelia.'

'Like . . . er,' I said, homing in on one of the few out-of-state numbers I could find, 'this . . . Libby Driscoll? In Philadelphia?'

279

'Yeah.'

'Hmm.'

I looked out of the window, and as the gas stations, factories, Pizza Huts and Burger Kings flitted past, I wondered who these people could be. I tried a few theories out for size. But I soon became distracted by the fact that Kenny Sanchez now seemed to be looking in his rearview mirror every couple of seconds. For no apparent reason, he also changed lanes – once, twice, and then a third time.

'Anything wrong?' I said eventually.

'I think we're being followed,' he said, switching lanes again and then accelerating.

'Followed?' I said. 'By who?'

'I don't know. And maybe we're not. I'm just being . . . cautious.'

I craned my neck around. The traffic coming from behind was flowing across three lanes, the whole busy highway winding back serpent-like over a hilly, industrial landscape. I found it hard to imagine how Sanchez could have isolated one car from all of these and thought it was following us.

I didn't say anything.

A few minutes later, we took the exit for Trenton and after driving around for what seemed like ages finally arrived at an anonymous single-storey building. It was low and long, and looked like a warehouse. There was a large parking area in front of it that was about half-full. The only identifying mark in the whole place was a small sign at the main entrance to the car park. It had the name 'United Labtech' on it, and underneath a logo that strained for scientific effect – a kind of multiple helix set against a curving blue grid. We drove in and parked.

It suddenly occurred to me how close I might be to meeting Vernon Gant's partner, and I felt a rush of adrenalin.

I went to open the door, but Sanchez put a hand on my arm and said, 'Whoa there – where are *you* going?'

'What?'

'You can't just walk in there. You need some kind of a cover.' He reached across me and opened his glove compartment. 'Let me do it.' He took out a handful of business cards, flicked through them and selected one. 'Insurance is always good for this type of thing.'

Undecided about what to do, I chewed for a moment on my lower lip.

'Look, I'm just going to establish that he's *in* there,' Sanchez said, 'It's the first step.'

I hesitated.

'OK.'

I watched Sanchez get out of the car, walk over to the entrance of the building and disappear inside.

He was right, of course. I would have to approach Todd Ellis very carefully indeed, because if I blurted out something inappropriate as soon as I met him – especially if this was where he worked – I might easily scare him off, or blow *his* cover.

As I sat there waiting in the car, my cellphone rang.

'Hello.'

'Eddie, Carl.'

'What's up.'

'I think we're there. Vision lock. Hank and Dan. I've asked them both to dinner in my place this evening, and it looks like we could be getting a final handshake.'

'Great. What time?'

'Eight-thirty. I've cancelled your meetings for this afternoon, so . . . where are you, by the way?'

'New Jersey.'

'What the—'

'Don't ask.'

'Well haul your ass back in here as quick as you can. We've a lot to go over before this evening.'

I looked at my watch.

'Give me an hour.'

'OK. See you then.'

My head was reeling as I put the phone away. Too many things were happening at once now – locating Todd Ellis, the deal, the new apartment . . .

Just then Kenny Sanchez re-appeared. He walked briskly over to the car and got in.

I looked at him, silently screaming *well*?

'They say he doesn't work there any more.'

He turned to face me.

'Left a couple of weeks ago. And they don't have any forwarding address, or number where he can be reached.'

[24]

WE DROVE BACK TO THE CITY in almost total silence. I had a jumpy, nauseous feeling in my stomach at the thought that Todd Ellis had just disappeared into thin air. I also didn't like the fact that he no longer worked at United Labtech, because if that's where they produced MDT, what chance would I stand of getting any more without an inside connection? When we were about half-way through the Lincoln Tunnel, I said to Sanchez, 'So, do you think you'll be able to trace him?'

'I'll try.'

I sensed from his tone that he was a little fed up. But I didn't want to leave him like that. I needed him on my side.

'You'll try?'

'Yes, but I wish . . .'

He stopped and sighed impatiently. He didn't want to say it, so I said it for him.

'You wish you had more to go on than just my frankly implausible story.'

He hesitated, but then said, 'Yes.'

I thought about this for a moment, and when we were coming out of the tunnel, I said to him, 'These people on the list, the twenty-five or so names you can't account for? Have you spoken to any of them?'

'A few of them, when we first started tracking his calls.'

'When was that?'

'About three months ago. But it was a dead end.'

I took out my cellphone and started dialling a number.

'Who are you calling?'

'Libby Driscoll.'

'But, how did—'

'I have a good memory . . . Libby Driscoll, please.'

A couple of moments later, I put the phone down in my lap.

'She's out sick. Has been for a week.'

'So?'

I took the pages out of the envelope and went through them. I found another of the out-of-state numbers, checked it with Sanchez and then called it.

It was the same story.

We were on Forty-second Street now and I asked Sanchez if he could drop me off at Fifth Avenue.

'It's just a guess,' I said, 'but if you call every name on that short-list, I think you'll find that they're *all* sick. Furthermore, you'll also probably find that the three people you're looking for – the missing cult members – are, in fact, people *on* that list—'

'*What?*'

'—living out successful new identities, fuelled up on MDT-48 supplied by Deke Tauber.'

'*Jesus.*'

'But the supply has run out and that's why they're getting sick.'

Sanchez pulled up just before Fifth Avenue.

'My guess,' I went on, 'is that everyone on the list is really someone else. Like you said, they re-create themselves in an alternative environment.'

'But—'

'They probably don't even know they're taking it. He gives it to them – I don't know, *somehow* – but the most likely pay-off is that he gets a percentage of their fat executive salaries.'

Kenny Sanchez was staring straight ahead now and I could almost *hear* his mind working.

'Look, I'll get on this straightaway,' he said, 'and I'll call you as soon as I have anything.'

I got out of the car, still feeling mildly nauseous. But as I walked up Fifth Avenue towards Forty-eighth Street, I also felt vaguely satisfied at how deftly I'd managed to keep Kenny Sanchez onboard.

I spent the afternoon with Carl Van Loon going over stuff we'd gone over a hundred times before, especially our public relations strategy for dealing with the announcement. He was very excited about finalizing the deal, and didn't want to leave anything to chance. He was also excited about having it happen at his apartment on Park Avenue, which – although he'd forgotten it now – had been my idea. In all the hectic activity of the past few weeks, Hank Atwood and Dan Bloom had only met face to face twice – fairly briefly and in formal business settings. I had suggested, therefore, that a casual dinner in Van Loon's apartment might be a better setting for this next and most crucial meeting, on the basis that a congenial, clubby atmosphere with brandy and cigars would more easily facilitate the one thing that remained to be done in this whole affair – which was the two principals eyeballing each other across a table and saying, *Fuck it, let's merge.*

I left the office at around 4 p.m. and went to Tenth Street, where I'd arranged to meet my landlord. I handed over the keys and took away the remainder of my things – including the envelope of MDT pills. It was strange closing the door for the last time and walking out of the building, because it wasn't just that I was leaving an apartment behind, a place I'd been in for six years – I felt at some level that I was leaving *myself* behind. Over the past few weeks, I had shed much of who I was, and even though I'd done this with considerable abandon, I think I'd unconsciously felt that as long as I was still living in the apartment on Tenth Street I would always have the option, if it became necessary, to reverse the process – as though the place contained a part of me that was ineradicable, some form of genetic sequencing embedded in the floorboards and the walls that could be used to reconstitute my movements, my daily habits, *all* of who I was. But now, climbing into the back seat of a cab on First Avenue – with the last few items from the apartment stuffed in a holdall – I knew for sure, finally, that I was cutting myself adrift.

A little over an hour later I was gazing out at the city from the sixty-eighth floor of the Celestial Building. Surrounded by unpacked boxes and wooden crates, I was standing in the main living area, wearing only a bathrobe and sipping a glass of champagne. The view was spectacular and the evening that lay ahead promised, in its own way, to be equally spectacular. And I remember thinking at the time that, well, if this was what being adrift was like, then I reckoned I could probably get used to it . . .

I got to Van Loon's place on Park Avenue for eight o'clock and was shown into a large, chintzy reception room. Van Loon himself appeared after a few minutes and offered me a drink. He seemed a little agitated. He told me that his wife was away and that he wasn't very comfortable entertaining without her. I reminded him that apart from ourselves, the dinner was just going to be Hank Atwood, Dan Bloom and one adviser apiece from their respective negotiating teams. It wasn't some extravagant society bash he was throwing. It would be simple, casual, and at the same time we'd get a little business done. It would be discreet, but with far-reaching implications.

Van Loon slapped me gently on the back ' "Discreet, but with far-reaching implications." I like that.'

The others arrived in two shifts, about five minutes apart, and soon we were all standing around, glasses in hand, pointedly *not* discussing the MCL–Abraxas merger. In line with the casual dress-code for the evening, I was wearing a black cashmere sweater and black wool trousers, but everyone else, including Van Loon, was in chinos and Polo shirts. This made me feel slightly different – and in a way it reinforced the notion that I was taking part in some super-sophisticated computer game. I was identified as the hero by being dressed differently, in black. The enemy, in chinos and Polo shirts, were all around me and I had to schmooze them to death before they realized that I was a phony and froze me out.

This mild feeling of alienation lingered through the early part of the evening, but it wasn't actually unpleasant, and it occurred to me after a while just what was going on. I'd done this. I'd done the merger negotiations thing. I'd helped to structure a huge corporate deal – but now it was over. This dinner was only a formality. I wanted to move on to something else.

As if they somehow sensed this in me, both Hank Atwood and

Dan Bloom, separately, discreetly, intimated that if I was interested – down the line, of course – there might be some . . . *role* I could play in their newly formed media behemoth. I was circumspect in how I responded to these overtures, making out that loyalty to Van Loon was my first priority, but naturally I was flattered to be asked. I didn't know what I would want from such an arrangement in any case – except that it would have to be different from what I'd been doing up to that point. Maybe I could run a movie studio, or plot some new global corporate strategy for the company.

Or maybe I could branch out altogether, and diversify. Go into politics. Run for the Senate.

We drifted into an adjoining room and took our places at a large, round dining table, and as I elaborated mentally on the notion of going into politics, I simultaneously engaged with Dan Bloom in a conversation about single malt Scotch whiskies. This dreamy, distracted state of mind persisted throughout the meal (tagliatelle with jugged hare and English peas, followed by venison sautéed in chestnuts), and must have made me seem quite aloof. Once or twice, I even saw Van Loon looking over at me, a puzzled, worried expression on his face.

When we were about half-way through the main course – not to mention all the way through two bottles of 1947 Château Calon-Ségur – the conversation turned to the business at hand. This didn't take long, however, because once the subject had been raised, it quickly became clear that the details and the fevered number-crunching of recent weeks were largely cosmetic and that what counted more than anything else right now was agreement in principle. Van Loon & Associates had facilitated this, and that was where the real brokering skill lay – in orchestrating events, in making it happen. But now that the thing was virtually on auto-pilot, I felt as if I were watching the scene from a distant height, or through a pane of tinted glass.

When the plates had been cleared away, there was a tense pause in the room. The conversation had been manoeuvring itself into position for some time, and it seemed now that the moment was right. I cleared my throat, and then – almost on cue – Hank Atwood and Dan Bloom reached across the table and shook hands.

There was a brief flurry of clapping and air-punching, after which a bottle of Veuve Clicquot and six glasses appeared on the table. Van Loon stood up and made a show of opening the bottle, and then there was a toast. In fact, there were several toasts – and at the end there was even one to *me*. Choosing his words carefully, Dan Bloom held up his glass and thanked me for my keen focus and unstinting dedication. Hank Atwood added that I had been the lifeblood of the negotiations. Van Loon himself said he hoped that he and I – having together helped to broker the biggest merger in the history of corporate America – would not feel that our horizons had in any way been limited by the experience.

This got a hearty laugh. It also eased us out of the main order of business and moved us safely on to the next stage of the evening – dessert (glazed almond brittle), cigars and an hour or two of untrammelled *bonhomie*. I contributed fully to the conversation, which was wide-ranging and slightly giddy, but just below the surface, thrumming steadily, my fantasy of representing New York in the US Senate had taken on a life of its own – even to the extent of my seeing it as inevitable that at some future date I would seek the Democratic Party's nomination for the presidency.

This *was* a fantasy, of course, but the more I thought about it, the more the fundamental notion of entering politics actually made sense to me – because getting people on my side, getting them energized and doing things for me, was precisely what I seemed to be good at. After all, I had *these* guys – billionaires in Polo shirts – competing with each other for my attention, so how hard could it be to woo the attention of the American public? How hard could it be to woo the attention of whatever percentage of registered voters would be required to get me elected? Following a carefully worked-out plan I could be sitting on sub-committees and select committees within five years, and after that, who knew?

In any case, a good five-year-plan was probably just what I needed – something to burn up the incredible energy and breath of ambition that MDT so easily engendered.

I was fully aware of the fact, however, that I didn't have a constant supply of MDT, and that the supply I did have was alarmingly finite, but I was nevertheless confident that one way or another, and sooner rather than later, I would be overcoming this problem. Kenny Sanchez would locate Todd Ellis. *He* would have a constant supply of the stuff. I would somehow gain permanent access to this supply. It would all – somehow – work out . . .

At around 11 p.m., there was a general movement to break up the proceedings. It had been agreed earlier that there would be a press conference the following day to announce the proposed merger. The story would be strategically leaked in the morning, and the press conference would take place in the late afternoon. The glare of media coverage would be intense, but at the same time everyone was looking forward to it.

Hank Atwood and I were still sitting together at the table, contemplatively swirling brandy around in our glasses. The others were standing, chatting, and the air was thick with cigar smoke.

'You OK, Eddie?'

I turned to look at him.

'Yeah. I'm fine. Why?'

'No reason. You just seem, I don't know, subdued.'

I smiled. 'I was thinking about the future.'

'Well . . .' He reached over and very gently clinked his glass against mine. '. . . I'll drink to *that* . . .'

Just then, there was rap on the door and Van Loon, who was standing nearby, went over to open it.

'. . . immediate *and* long-term . . .'

Van Loon stood at the door, looking out, and then made a motion to shoo in whoever was there – but whoever was there obviously didn't want to be shooed in.

Then I heard her voice, 'No, Daddy, I really don't think—'

'It's just a little cigar smoke, for godsakes. Come in and say hello.'

I looked over at the door, hoping that she *would* come in.

'. . . either way,' Atwood was saying, 'it's the promised land.'

I took a sip from my glass.

'What is?'

'The future, Eddie, the future.'

I looked back, distracted. Ginny was stepping tentatively into the room now. When she was just inside the door, she reached up to kiss her father on the cheek. She was wearing a strappy satin top and corduroy trousers, and was holding a suede clutch bag in her left hand. As she pulled away from her father, she smiled over at me, raising her right hand and fluttering her fingers – a greeting which I think was meant to take in Hank Atwood as well. She moved a little further into the room. It was only then I noticed that Van Loon had his arm stretched out to greet someone else who was coming in behind her. A second or two later – and after what looked like a vigorous handshake – a young man of about twenty-five or twenty-six appeared through the door.

Ginny shook hands politely with Dan Bloom and the other two men, and then turned around. She stood at the table and put a hand on the back of an empty chair that was positioned directly opposite where I was sitting.

The young man and Van Loon were talking now, and laughing, and although I found it hard not to look at Ginny, I kept glancing over at them. The young man was wearing a hooded zip-front thing, a black crew-neck T-shirt and jeans. He had dark hair and a little goatee beard. I wasn't sure, but I thought I recognized him. At any rate, there was something about him, something *around* him that I recognized. He and Van Loon seemed to know each other quite well.

I looked back at Ginny. She pulled out the chair and sat down. She placed her clutch bag on the table and joined her hands together, as though she were about to conduct an interview.

'So, gentlemen, what are we talking about?'

'The future,' said Atwood.

'The future? Well, you know what Einstein had to say about that?'

'No, what?'

'He said I never think of the future. It comes soon enough.' She looked at me directly, and added, 'I tend to agree with him.'

'*Hank.*'

Suddenly, Van Loon was waving an arm in our direction, and indicating for Atwood to come over.

'Excuse me, my dear,' he said, and made a strained face as he got up. He walked around the table, and it occurred to me then who the young man was – Ray Tyner. As movie stars reportedly often do, he looked a little different in real life. I'd read about him in the previous day's paper. He'd just come back from shooting a movie in Venice.

'So,' Ginny said, looking around, 'this is where the cabal meets, the secret movers and shakers, the smoke-filled back-room.'

I smiled. 'I thought we were in *your* dining-room.'

She shrugged her shoulders. 'Yeah, but *I* ain't never had dinner in here. I eat in the kitchen. This is the control centre.'

I nodded over at Ray Tyner. Atwood and Bloom and the others had all gathered around him now, and he seemed to be telling a story.

'So, who's running the control centre now?'

She turned around in her chair for a moment to look over at him. I stared intently at her profile, at the curve of her neck, at her bare shoulders.

'Oh, Ray's not like that,' she said turning back, 'he's sweet.'

'Are you two an item?'

She pulled her head back, a little surprised at my question.

'What are you, moonlighting for Page Six now?'

'No, I'm just curious. For future reference.'

'Like I said, Mr Spinola, I don't think of the future.'

'Is he why you wouldn't go for a drink with me?'

She paused. Then she said, 'I don't understand you.'

I was puzzled at this.

'What don't you understand?' I said.

'I don't know . . .' Her face changed, as she tried to think of the words. 'I'm sorry – it must be an instinctive thing – but I get the feeling that when you look at me, you're seeing someone else.'

I didn't know what to say to that. I stared uncomfortably at my brandy glass. Was it that obvious? Ginny resembled Melissa, it was true, but until that moment I hadn't realized what a deep impression the likeness they shared had made on me.

There was a sudden burst of laughter from the other side of the room, and the group started to break up.

I looked at her again.

'I don't think of the past,' I said, trying to be clever.

'And the present?'

'I don't think of that either.'

'Yeah, I suppose,' she said, and then laughed. 'It *goes* soon enough.'

'Something like that.'

Ray Tyner had come up behind her now. She turned slightly and twisted her arm up to reach him. He took her hand and she got out of the chair.

'Ray, this is Eddie Spinola, a friend of mine. Eddie, Ray Tyner.'

I reached over and we shook hands.

I was inordinately pleased that she had described me as a friend of hers.

Up close, Ray Tyner was almost preternaturally good-looking. He had amazing eyes and the kind of smile that meant he could probably work a room without even bothering to open his mouth.

Maybe I'd ask him to be my running mate.

I got back to the Celestial just after twelve. It was to be my first night in the new apartment, but I didn't have anything to sleep on. In fact, I didn't have any furniture at all, no bed, or sofa, or bookshelves, nothing. I had ordered some stuff, but none of it had been delivered yet.

I wasn't going to be doing much sleeping in any case, so it didn't really matter. Instead, I wandered from room to room, through the huge, empty apartment – trying to convince myself that I wasn't upset or jealous or in any way put out at all. Ginny Van Loon and Ray Tyner made a fabulous-looking couple – and next to a bunch of old business farts smoking cigars and talking percentages, they looked even better.

What was there to be upset about?

After a while I got my computer out of its box and put it on a wooden crate. I went online and tried to catch up with the day's financial news.

[25]

I WAS BACK IN FORTY-EIGHTH STREET the next morning at around seven-thirty, drafting speeches and making some final changes to the press release. Given that the announcement was only a couple of hours away and that secrecy was no longer an issue, Van Loon had been able to call some of his regular people in to get the PR machinery up and running. Although this was a great help, the place was now busier than Grand Central Station.

Before leaving the apartment, I had taken my usual dose of five pills – three MDT and two Dexeron – but then at the last minute I had gone back and rummaged in the holdall bag and taken two more, one of each. As a result, I was operating at full tilt, but I found that my accelerated work-rate was intimidating some of these Van Loon regulars – people who probably had a lot more experience than I had. To avoid any friction, therefore, I set up a makeshift office in one of the boardrooms and got some work done on my own.

At around ten-thirty, Kenny Sanchez called me on my cellphone. I was sitting at a large oval table with a laptop computer and dozens of pages spread out in front of me when he rang.

'I have some bad news, Eddie.'

I got a sharp, sinking feeling in my stomach.

'What?'

'Well, a couple of things. I've located Todd Ellis, but I'm afraid he's dead.'

Shit.

'What happened?'

'Hit-and-run accident, about a week ago. Around where he lived, in Brooklyn.'

Fuck.

This flooded in on me now – without Todd Ellis, what chance did I have? Where did I go? Where did I even *begin*?

I noticed that Kenny Sanchez was silent.

'You mentioned there were a couple of things,' I said. 'What else?'

'I've been re-assigned.'

'*What?*'

'I've been re-assigned, given another case to work on. I don't know why. I kicked up shit, but there's nothing I can do. It's a big agency. This is my *job.*'

'So . . . who's looking after it now?'

'I don't know. Maybe no one.'

'Is this normal – I mean, interference like this?'

'No.'

He sounded very pissed off.

'I worked the phones all yesterday afternoon when I left you, and even late into the evening. Then this morning I get called in to make a report and they tell me I'm needed on another case and to hand over all my paper-work.'

I thought about it for a second, but what could I say? Then I just said, 'What else did you manage to find out?'

He sighed, and I pictured him shaking his head.

'Well, you were right about the list,' he said eventually. 'It was incredible.'

'Why's that?'

'Those out-of-state numbers? You were right. They all seem to be cult members living under assumed names. Most are sick, but I got to speak to some of them.' There was a brief pause, during which I heard him sighing again. 'Of the three I was originally looking for, two are in the hospital and one is at home suffering from severe migraines.'

I could tell by his tone that despite having been reassigned he was excited at the progress he'd made.

'It took a while to get anyone to speak to me, but when I did, it was amazing. The longest conversation I had was with a girl called Beth Lipski. It seems the standard Dekedelia make-over involves a completely new identity – chemically-assisted alteration of metabolism, plastic surgery, new "designated" relatives, the lot. And just like you said, career advancement is the measure of a successful new identity, with 60 per cent of income going back into the organization. Shit, it's like a cross between the Freemasons and the Witness Protection Program.'

'Why did she talk?'

'Because she's afraid. Tauber has cut off all contact with her, and she feels nervous and lost. She has a permanent headache and can't work properly. She doesn't know what's happening to her. I don't even think she knows she's been taking a drug – and I didn't want to push her over the edge by bringing it up. She was paranoid about talking to me in the first place, but then once she started she couldn't stop.'

'So how do you think he gives them the drug?'

'Apparently, he has them all on a programme of vitamins and special diet supplements, so I guess he slips it in there somehow. And that's obviously the source of his power over these people, and of his supposed charisma.' He paused. I heard him stamping his foot, or banging his fist on something. Then he said, 'Damn! I really can't believe this shit. I've never worked on such an interesting case before.'

I didn't have time for this now – Kenny Sanchez having a career crisis down the phone at me. I felt a slight queasiness all of a sudden. I took a deep breath, and then asked him if he had come up with anything on United Labtech.

He sighed again.

'Yeah, I did,' he said, 'one thing anyway. It's owned by the pharmaceutical company, Eiben-Chemcorp.'

Soon after that, I told him I had to go, that I was at work. I thanked him, wished him luck, and got off the phone as quickly as I could.

I put the phone down on the table and stood up.

I walked across the room, slowly, and stood at the windows. It was a clear, sunny day in Manhattan and from up here on the sixty-second floor everything was visible, there to be seen, and picked out, every landmark, every architectural feature – including some less obvious ones, such as the Celestial Building over to my right, or the old Port Authority Terminal further down, on Eighth Avenue, where Kerr & Dexter had their offices. Standing at this window, in fact, I saw that my whole life was laid out in front of me, like a sequence of tiny incisions in the vast microchip of the city – street corners, apartments, delis, liquor stores, movie-theaters. But now, instead of a deeper and more permanent line being cut into the surface, these minute nicks were in danger of being smoothed over and levelled off.

I turned around and stared at the plain white walls on the other side of the room, and at the grey carpet and at the anonymous company furniture. I hadn't given in to panic yet – though it surely wouldn't be long in coming. The press conference was scheduled for the afternoon, and already the thought of it filled me with a sense of dread.

But then something else occurred to me, and with the single-mindedness of a condemned man, I latched on to it – and wouldn't let go.

Sanchez had mentioned Eiben-Chemcorp. I knew I'd heard that name somewhere quite recently, and after a couple of minutes I remembered where. I'd seen it at Vernon's that day – in the *Boston Globe*. Vernon had apparently been reading about an upcoming product liability trial in Massachusetts. As far as I could recall, a teenage girl who'd been taking Triburbazine had murdered her best friend and then killed herself.

I walked back over to the table and sat in front of the laptop. I went online and searched the *Globe* archives for more detail on the story.

The girl's family had filed a lawsuit looking for punitive damages against Eiben-Chemcorp. In the trial, the company would be defending charges that its anti-depressant drug had caused 'loss of impulse control' and 'suicidal ideation' in the girl. Dave Morgenthaler, a personal injury lawyer, was to be the lead counsel representing the plaintiffs, and according to one article I read, he had spent the last six months collecting depositions from expert witnesses – among them scientists who'd been involved in the development and production of Triburbazine, and psychiatrists who would be willing to testify that Triburbazine was potentially harmful.

My mind was racing now. I picked up a pen and started doodling on a piece of paper, trying to link all of this together.

Eiben-Chemcorp owned Labtech, which was where MDT seemed to have come from. That meant, in effect, that MDT had been developed and produced by an international pharmaceutical corporation. This corporation, in turn, was facing high profile – and potentially very damaging – litigation.

In fact – I turned back to the computer and went into one of the financial websites, and there it was – due to adverse publicity surrounding the case, Eiben-Chemcorp's stock had already suffered quite a lot, having apparently dropped to $69^7/_8$ from a high earlier in the year of $87^1/_4$. This growing public interest in the case would probably continue as the trial date approached. I found numerous articles that had already touched on what would surely be a key point in the trial: if human behaviour was all about synapses and serotonin, then where did free will fit into the picture? Where did personal responsibility end and brain chemistry begin?

Eiben-Chemcorp, in short, was in a very vulnerable position.

I was too, of course – but what I then wondered was how I could use my knowledge of MDT to leverage some advantage out of Eiben-Chemcorp. A supply of MDT in return for not talking to Dave Morgenthaler, perhaps?

I stood up and wandered around the room.

It seemed to me that information coming out in court about an Eiben-Chemcorp product that hadn't ever been tested, and had already caused numerous deaths, would have a devastating effect on the company's share price. It was a stark, high-risk option, but given the circumstances it was probably the only option I had left.

I passed by the window again, but didn't look out this time. After a good deal of thought, I decided that the most practical first step would be to establish contact with Dave Morgenthaler. I would have to be careful how I approached him, but to pose a credible threat to Eiben-Chemcorp, I would need to have Morgenthaler primed for the kill. I would need to be able to set him loose at a moment's notice.

I made some enquiries and found the number for his office in Boston. I called it immediately and asked to speak to him, but he was out of the office for the day. I left my cellphone number and a message: that I had some 'explosive' information about Eiben-Chemcorp and wanted to meet him as soon as possible to discuss it.

When I put the phone down again, I tried to get back to work, to redirect my attention to the MCL–Abraxas deal and to the press conference in the afternoon, but I found it very difficult. I kept reliving the past few weeks in my mind and wishing I'd done this or that – wishing, for instance, that I'd investigated Deke Tauber a little earlier, which might have meant reaching Todd Ellis before he left United Labtech . . .

I then wondered if there'd been any connection between his death and Vernon's. But what was the use? Whether Todd Ellis's death had been accidental or not, that route was now closed off to me. I'd had no choice but to come up with an alternative.

I went over to the window again and gazed at the buildings opposite – gazed down along these vast, vertical plates of steel and glass, all the way down to the streets below, and to the tiny rivulets of people and traffic. This city would be buzzing soon with news of the deal and I would be there when the news broke. But I felt removed from it all now. I felt as though I had entered a confused dream, knowing somehow as I did so that I wouldn't ever be coming out of it again . . .

This impression was reinforced almost at once, when I was called in to one of the other offices to go over the last-minute arrangements for the press conference. Organized at admittedly very short notice by one of Van Loon's staffers, the press conference was being held at five o'clock in a midtown hotel. This much I had been aware of, but when I saw now *which* hotel, I got a return of that sharp, sinking feeling in my stomach.

298

'Are you OK?'

This was one of the staffers. I glanced up and looked at him, simultaneously catching sight of my reflection in a mirror that was on a side wall of the office.

My face was deathly pale.

'Yeah,' I said, 'I'm fine, it's just . . . a . . . moment, I think—'

I turned around and rushed out of the office, into the men's room and straight over to one of the washbasins.

I threw some cold water on my face.

The press conference was going to be held at the Clifden Hotel.

Van Loon and I arrived at about three-thirty, and already there was quite a bit of commotion in the place. The first inkling for the media that something was up had come earlier in the day, after Van Loon had phoned a few carefully selected people and told them to cancel whatever they'd had on for the late afternoon. The names Atwood and Bloom were mentioned in the same breath and that had been enough to start a wild fire of rumour and speculation. We'd sent out the press release an hour later. Then the phones had started ringing and hadn't stopped since.

The Clifden was a forty-five-storey tower rising out of a restored landmark building on Fifty-sixth Street, just off Madison Avenue. It was a luxurious hotel with over 800 rooms, as well as full business and conference facilities. The lobby area led on to a glass-enclosed atrium lounge and beyond that again there was a reception room where we would be holding our press conference.

As Van Loon took a call on his cellphone, I looked around the lobby area very carefully, but I honestly didn't recognize anything. Even though I had a lingering sense of unease about the whole thing, I came to the confident conclusion that I had never been there before.

Van Loon finished his call. We walked into the atrium lounge, and in the time it took us to cross it Van Loon was approached three times by different journalists. He engaged them in a charming, bantering way, but told them nothing they wouldn't have heard already or read in the press release. Inside the conference room itself there was a lot of activity, as technical crews set up cameras and tested sound equipment at the back. A little further up the room, hotel staff were laying out rows of foldable chairs, and at the top there was a podium, with two long tables on either side of it. Behind these there were mounted stands displaying the respective logos of the two companies, MCL-Parnassus and Abraxas.

I stood at the back for a while, as Van Loon consulted with some of his regular people in the middle of the room. Behind me, I could hear two technicians talking as they fiddled with wires and cables.

'. . . I swear to god, whacked on the back of the head.'

'*Here?*'

'With a blunt instrument. You don't read the papers? She was Mexican. Married to some painter.'

'Yeah. I remember now. Shit. That was *this* place?'

I moved away, over towards the doors – so I couldn't hear them any more. Then I slowly drifted out of the conference room altogether and back into the atrium lounge.

One of the things I remembered quite clearly from that night – from near the end of it, at any rate – was walking along an empty hotel corridor. I could picture it in my mind's eye still – the low ceiling, the patterned crimson and navy carpet, the magnolia walls, the oak panelled doors flitting past me on either side . . .

I just didn't remember anything else about it.

I crossed the lounge and wandered into the lobby area. More people were arriving now and there was a heightened air of anticipation about the place. I saw someone I knew and wanted to avoid, so I slipped over towards the elevators, which were on the far side of the reception desk. But then, as though carried along by some irresistible force, I actually followed two women *into* an elevator. One of them pressed a button, and then looked at me expectantly, her finger hovering in front of the panel.

'Fifteen,' I said, 'thanks.'

Mingling freely and somewhat sickeningly in the air with my anxiety was the scent of expensive perfume, and the always charged but never acknowledged intimacy of an elevator ride. As we hummed upwards, I felt my stomach churning over and I had to lean against the side of the elevator car to steady myself. When the door slid open at fifteen, I stared out in disbelief at a magnolia-coloured wall. Brushing past one of the two women, I made my exit – stepping a little unsteadily out on to a crimson and navy carpet.

'Good evening.'

I turned back, and as the two women were being closed off from view, I mumbled some kind of reply.

Left alone now in this empty corridor, I experienced something close to real terror. I *had* been here before. It was exactly as I had remembered it – the low, wide corridor . . . richly coloured, luxurious, deep and long like a tunnel. But this was *all* I could remember. I walked a few paces and then stopped. I stood facing one of the doors and tried to imagine what the room inside was like – but nothing came to me. I walked on, passing door after door on either side, until near the end of the corridor I came to one that was slightly open.

I stopped, and my heart was thumping as I stood there, peering through the chink into what I could see of the room – the end of a double bed, drapes, a chair, everything bright and cream-coloured.

With my foot, I gently tapped the door open a little wider, and stepped back. Framed in the doorway, I could see more of the same, a generic hotel room – but then suddenly, passing across the frame from left to right I saw a tall, dark-haired woman in a long black dress. She was clutching her head and there was blood pouring down the side of her face. My heart lurched sideways and I stepped back, reeling, and fell against the magnolia wall. I got up, and staggered along the corridor, back towards the elevators.

A moment later, behind me, I heard a noise and I turned around. Coming out of the room I'd just been looking into, there was a man, and then a woman. They pulled the door closed and started walking in my direction. The woman was tall and dark-haired, and was wearing a belted coat. She was in her fifties, as was the man. They were chatting, and completely ignored me as they passed. I stood and watched as they walked the length of the corridor and then disappeared into an elevator.

A couple of minutes ticked by before I could do anything. My

301

heart still felt as if it had been dislodged and was in danger of stopping. My hands were shaking. Leaning against the wall, I stared down at the carpet. Its deep colours seemed to be pulsating, its pattern shifting and alive.

Eventually, I straightened up and made my way to the elevators, but my hand was still trembling as I reached out to press the 'down' button.

By the time I got back to the conference room, a lot of people had arrived and the atmosphere was fairly frenetic. I wandered up to the front, where some of the MCL people had gathered in a group and were talking animatedly.

Suddenly, I heard Van Loon approaching me from behind.

'Eddie, where have you been?'

I turned around. There was a look of genuine surprise on his face.

'Jesus, Eddie, what happened? You . . . you look like you've seen—'

'A ghost?'

'Well, yeah.'

'I'm a little stressed out here, Carl, that's all. I just need some time.'

'Look, Eddie, take it easy. If anyone's earned a break around here, it's you.' He clenched his fist and held it out in a gesture of solidarity. 'Anyway, we've done our work. For the moment. Am I right?'

I nodded.

Van Loon was then whisked off by one of his people to talk to somebody on the far side of the podium.

I floated through the next couple of hours in a kind of semiconscious daze. I moved around and mingled and talked to people, but I don't remember specific conversations. It all felt choreographed, and automatic.

When the actual press conference started, I found myself at the top of the room, standing behind the Abraxas people, who were seated at the table to the right of the podium. At the back of the room – and over a sea of about 300 heads – there was a phalanx of reporters, photographers and camera-men. The event was going out

302

live on several channels, and there was also a webcast and a satel-lite feed. When Hank Atwood took the podium, there was an imme-diate barrage of sound from the cameras at the back – clicking, whirring, popping flashbulbs – and this din continued uninterrupted throughout the whole press conference, and even intermittently during the question-and-answer session that followed. I didn't listen carefully to any of the speeches, some of which I had helped to write, but I did recognize occasional phrases and expressions – even though the relentless repetition of words such as 'future', 'transform' and 'opportunity' only added to the sense of unreality I now felt about everything that was happening around me.

Just as Dan Bloom was finishing at the podium, my cellphone rang. I quickly took it out of my jacket pocket and answered it.

'Hello, is this . . . Eddie Spinola?'

I could barely hear.

'Yes.'

'This is Dave Morgenthaler in Boston. I got your message from this morning.'

I covered my other ear.

'Listen . . . hang on a second.'

I moved to the left, along the side of the room and through a door about half-way down that led into a quiet section off the atrium lounge.

'Mr Morgenthaler?'

'Yeah.'

'When can we meet?'

'Look, who are you? I'm busy – why should I take the time out to see you?'

As briefly as I could, I pitched him the story – a powerful, untested and potentially lethal drug from the labs of the company he was about to go up against in court. I kept it unspecific and didn't describe the effects of the drug.

'You haven't said anything to convince me,' he said. 'How do I know you're not some nut? How do I know you're not making this shit up?'

The lights were low in this section of the lounge and the only other people nearby were two old guys engrossed in conversation. They were sitting at a table next to some huge potted palm trees. Behind me, I could hear voices resounding from the conference room.

'You couldn't make MDT up, Mr Morgenthaler. This shit is real, believe me.'

There was a pause, quite a long one, and then he said, 'What?'

'I said you couldn't—'

'No, the name. What name did you say?'

Shit – I shouldn't have said the name.

'Well, that's—'

'MDT . . . you said MDT.' There was an urgency in his voice now. 'What is this, a *smart* drug?'

I hesitated before I said anything else. He knew about it, or at least knew *something* about it. And he clearly wanted to know more.

I said, 'When can we meet?'

He didn't pause this time.

'I can get an early flight tomorrow morning. Let's meet, say . . . ten?'

'OK.'

'Somewhere outside. Fifty-ninth Street? In front of the Plaza?'

'OK.'

'I'm tall and—'

'I've seen your photo on the Internet.'

'Fine. OK. I'll see you tomorrow morning then.'

I put the phone away and wandered slowly back into the conference room. Atwood and Bloom were together at the podium now, answering questions. I still found it hard to focus on what was going on, because that little incident up on the fifteenth floor – hallucination, vision, whatever – was still fresh in my mind and was blocking everything else out. I didn't know what had happened between me and Donatella Alvarez that night, but I suspected now that as a manifestation of guilt and uncertainty, this was only the tip of a very large iceberg.

*   *   *

After the question-and-answer session had been wrapped up, the crowd began to disperse, but then the place became more chaotic than ever. Journalists from *Business Week* and *Time* were floating around looking for people to get comments from, and executives were slapping each other on the back and laughing. At one point, Hank Atwood passed and slapped *me* on the back. He then turned, and with an outstretched arm pointed an index finger directly at me.

'The future, Eddie, *the future.*'

I half smiled, and he was gone.

There was talk among the Van Loon & Associates people about going out somewhere for dinner, to celebrate, but I couldn't have faced that. With the events of the day so far, I had assembled the possible makings of a full-blown anxiety attack, and I didn't want to do anything stupid now that would actually precipitate one.

Without saying a word to anybody, therefore, I turned around and strolled out of the conference room. I crossed the atrium lounge and the lobby area and just walked right out of the hotel on to Fifty-sixth Street. It was a warm evening and the air was thick with the muffled roar of the city. I went over to Fifth Avenue and stood at the foot of Trump Tower, looking up the three blocks towards Fifty-ninth Street – at Grand Army Plaza and the corner of Central Park. Why did Dave Morgenthaler want to meet me there? Out in the open like that?

I turned and looked in the opposite direction, at the streams of traffic, dipping and rising, and at the parallel lines of the buildings, trailing towards some invisible point of convergence.

I started walking in this direction. It occurred to me that Van Loon might try to reach me, so I took out my cellphone and switched it off. I kept walking along Fifth, and eventually made a right on to Thirty-fourth Street. After a few blocks, I had reached what I supposed was my new neighbourhood – which was what? Chelsea? The Garment District? Who the fuck knew any more?

I stopped at a dingy-looking bar on Tenth Avenue and went inside.

I sat at the bar and ordered a Jack Daniel's. The place was nearly empty. The barman poured me the drink and then went back to watching the TV set. It was bracketed high on to a wall just over the door leading to the men's room, and there was a sitcom showing. After about five minutes – during which time he had laughed only once – the barman picked up the remote and started flicking through the channels. At one point I caught a sudden flash of the MCL-Parnassus logo, and I said, 'Wait, go back to that for a second.'

He flicked back and then looked at me, still aiming the remote up at the TV set. It was a news report of the announcement with footage of the press conference.

'Hold it there, for a minute,' I said.

'A *second*, now a *minute*, Jesus,' he said, impatiently.

I glared at him.

'Just this segment, *all right*? Thank you.'

He dropped the remote down on to the bar and held his hands up. Then we both turned our attentions back to the screen.

Dan Bloom was at the podium, and as the voice-over report described the scale and importance of the proposed merger, the camera panned slowly to the right, taking in all of the Abraxas executives sitting at the table. In the background, there was a clear view of the company logo, but that wasn't all you could see. There were also several people in the background, standing, and one of them was me. As the camera moved from left to right, I passed across the screen from right to left, and then disappeared. But in those few seconds, you could see me clearly, like in a police line-up – my face, my eyes, my blue tie and charcoal grey suit.

The barman looked at me, obviously registering something. Then he looked back at the screen, but they had already returned to the studio. He looked at me again, with a dumb expression on his face. I lifted my glass and drained it.

'You can change the channel now,' I said.

Then I put a twenty on the bar, got up off my stool and left.

[26]

THE NEXT MORNING I TOOK A CAB to Fifty-ninth Street, and on the way I rehearsed what I was going to say to Dave Morgenthaler. In order to keep him interested, and to buy some time, I would have to promise that he could have a sample of MDT. Then I'd be in a position to make my approach to someone in Eiben-Chemcorp. I was also hoping that by talking to Morgenthaler I might be able to get some idea about *who* in Eiben-Chemcorp I could approach. I got to Grand Army Plaza at ten minutes to ten and walked around, occasionally glancing up at the hotel. In my head, I had already left Van Loon and the merger behind – at least for the moment.

At five minutes past, a taxi pulled up at the kerb and a tall, thin man in his early fifties got out. I recognized him immediately from the photos I'd seen in archive articles on the Internet. I walked towards him, and although he saw me approaching, he surveyed the vicinity for any other possible candidates. Then he looked back at me.

'Spinola?' he said.

I nodded, and stuck my hand out. 'Thanks for coming.'

We shook hands.

'This better be worth my while.'

He had jet-black hair, quite a lot of it, and wore thick-rimmed glasses. He looked tired and had a kind of hangdog expression on his face. He was in a dark suit and a raincoat. It was an overcast day and there was a breeze blowing. I was about to suggest looking for a coffee shop, or even going into the Oak Room of the Plaza, seeing as how it was right there – but Morgenthaler had other ideas.

'Come on, let's go,' he said, and started crossing over towards the park. I hesitated, and then caught up with him.

'A walk in the park?' I said.

He nodded yes, but didn't say anything, or look in my direction.

Walking briskly, and in silence, we went down the steps into the park, around by the pond, up by Wollman Rink and eventually over to Sheep Meadow. Morgenthaler selected a bench and we sat down, facing the skyline of Central Park South. Where we were sitting was exposed and uncomfortably windy, but I wasn't about to start complaining now.

Morgenthaler turned to me and said, 'OK, what's this about?'

'Well, like I said . . . MDT.'

'What do you know about MDT and where did you first hear about it?'

He was very direct in his approach, and obviously intended to interrogate me as he would a witness. I decided that I would play along with this until I had him in a position where he couldn't just walk. In the way I answered his questions, I got several key ideas across to him. The first was that I knew what I was talking about. I described the effects of MDT in almost clinical detail. He was fascinated by this, and had pertinent follow-up questions – which also confirmed for me that *he* knew what he was talking about, at least in terms of MDT. I let it be known that I could supply the names of possibly dozens of people who had taken MDT, subsequently stopped and were now suffering acute withdrawal symptoms. There would be enough cases to establish a clear pattern. I let it be known that I could supply the names of people who had taken MDT and had subsequently *died*. Finally, I let it be known that I could supply samples of the actual drug itself for analysis.

When we got to this point, I could see that Morgenthaler had become quite agitated. All of the stuff I'd told him would be dynamite if he could bring it out in court – but of course at the same time I had been tantalizingly non-specific. If he walked away now, he'd be walking away with nothing more than a good story – and this was precisely where I wanted him.

'So, what next?' he said. 'How do we proceed?' And then added, with the merest hint of contempt in his voice, 'What's in this for *you*?'

I paused, and looked around. There were some people out jogging, others walking dogs, others pushing strollers. I had to keep him interested, without actually giving him anything – not yet, at any rate. I also had to pick his brains.

'We'll come to that,' I said, echoing Kenny Sanchez, 'but first, tell me how *you* know about MDT.'

He crossed his legs, folded his arms and leant backwards in the bench.

'I came across it,' he said, 'in the course of my research into the development and testing of Triburbazine.'

I waited for more, but that seemed to be it.

'Look, Mr Morgenthaler,' I said, 'I answered your questions. Let's build up a little confidence here.'

He sighed, barely able to hide his impatience.

'OK,' he said, assuming the role of expert witness, 'in taking depositions relating to Triburbazine, I spoke to a lot of employees and ex-employees of Eiben-Chemcorp. When they described the procedures for clinical trials, it was natural for these people to give me examples, to draw parallels with other drugs.'

He leant forward again, obviously uncomfortable about having to do this.

'Several people, in this context, made reference to a series of trials that had been done on an anti-depressant drug in the early Seventies – trials that had gone disastrously wrong. The man responsible for the administration of these trials was a Dr Raoul Fursten. He'd been with the company's research department since the late Fifties and had worked on LSD trials. This new drug was said to enhance cognitive ability – to some extent anyway – and at the time, it seems, Fursten had spoken endlessly about his great hopes for it. He'd spoken about the politics of consciousness, the best and the brightest, looking towards the future, all of that shit. Remember this was the early Seventies, which were still really the Sixties.'

Morgenthaler sighed again, and exhaled, seeming to deflate in the process. Then he shifted on the bench and got into a more comfortable position.

'Anyway,' he went on, 'there had been some serious adverse reactions to the drug as well. People had apparently become aggressive and irrational, some had even suffered periods of memory loss. One person intimated to me that there had been fatalities and that this had been covered up. The trials were discontinued and the drug – MDT-48 – was dropped. Fursten retired and apparently drank himself to death in the space of a year. None of the people I spoke to can prove any of this, no one will confirm anything. It has the status of hearsay – which of course, in terms of what *I'm* trying to do, is of absolutely no use.

'Nevertheless, I talked to some other people in the weird, wonderful world of neuropsychopharmacology – try saying *that* when you've had a couple of drinks – people who shall remain nameless, and it turns out that there were rumours floating around in the mid-Eighties that research into MDT had been taken up again. These were only rumours, mind . . .' – he turned and looked at me – '. . . but now, what, you're telling me this stuff is practically on the fucking *streets*?'

I nodded, thinking of Vernon and Deke Tauber and Gennady. Having been quite evasive about my sources, I hadn't mentioned anything to Morgenthaler about Todd Ellis, either, and the unofficial trials *he'd* been conducting out of United Labtech.

I shook my head.

'You said the mid-Eighties?'

'Yeah.'

'And these trials would be . . . unofficial?'

'Clearly.'

'Who's in charge of research now at Eiben-Chemcorp?'

'Jerome Hale,' he said, 'but I can't believe he'd have anything to do with it. He's too respectable.'

'*Hale?*' I said. 'Any relation?'

'Oh yeah,' he said, and laughed, 'they're brothers.'

I closed my eyes.

'He worked with Raoul Fursten in the early days,' Morgenthaler went on. 'He took over from him, in fact. But it's got to be someone working under him, because Hale's more of a front-office guy now.

Anyway, it doesn't matter, it's Eiben-Chemcorp – it's a pharmaceutical company withholding selective information in the interests of profit. That's the case we're making. They manipulated information in the Triburbazine trials, and if I can prove they did the same with MDT and show a pattern . . . then we're home free.'

Morgenthaler was allowing himself get excited about the possibility of winning his case, but I couldn't believe that in his excitement he had so easily passed over the fact that Jerome Hale and Caleb Hale were brothers. The implications of that seemed enormous to me. Caleb Hale had started his career in the CIA in the mid-1960s. In my own work for *Turning On*, I had read all about the CIA's Office of Research and Development, and of how its MK-Ultra projects had secretly funded the research programmes of various American drug companies.

The whole thing suddenly took on an unwieldy, headachy scale. I also saw just how far out of my depth I was.

'So, Mr Spinola, *I* need your help. What do *you* need?'

I sighed.

'Time. I need some time.'

'For what?'

'To think.'

'What's there to think? These bastards are—'

'I understand that, but it's not really the point.'

'So what *is* the point, money?'

'No,' I said emphatically, and shook my head.

He hadn't been expecting this, obviously assuming all along that I *had* wanted money. I sensed a growing nervousness in him now, as if he had suddenly realized that he might be in danger of losing me.

'How long are you staying in town?' I asked.

'I have to get back this evening, but—'

'Let me call you in a day or two.'

He hesitated, unsure of how to answer.

'Look, why don't—'

I decided to head him off. I didn't like doing it, but I had no choice. I *did* need to get away and think.

'I'll come up to Boston if necessary. With everything. Just . . . let me call you in a day or two, OK?'

'OK.'

I stood up, and then he did as well. We started walking back towards East Fifty-ninth Street.

This time I was the one stage-managing the silence, but after a few moments something occurred to me and I wanted to ask him about it.

'That case you're working on,' I said, 'the girl who was taking Triburbazine?'

'Yeah?'

'Did she . . . I mean, was she really a *killer*?'

'That's what Eiben-Chemcorp is going to be arguing. They're going to be looking for dysfunction in her family, abuse, any kind of background shit they can find and dress up as motivation. But the fact is, anyone who knew her – and we're talking about a nineteen-year-old girl here, a college student – anyone who knew her says she was the sweetest, smartest kid you could meet.'

My stomach started churning.

'So, basically, *you* say it was the Triburbazine, they say *she* did it.'

'That's what it comes down to, yeah – chemical determinism versus moral agency.'

It was only the middle of the day, and yet because the sky was so overcast there was a weird, almost bilious quality to the light.

'Do you believe that's possible?' I said. 'That a drug can override who we *are* . . . and can cause us to do things that we wouldn't otherwise do?'

'What I think doesn't matter. It's what the jury thinks. Unless Eiben-Chemcorp settles. In which case it doesn't matter what anyone thinks. But I'll tell you one thing for free, I wouldn't like to be on that jury.'

'Why not?'

'Well, you get called in for jury service and you figure, OK, a few weeks' break from my crappy job, and then you wind up having to make a decision on something of *this* magnitude? Forget it.'

After that we continued in silence. When we got back to Grand Army Plaza, I told him again that I'd phone him soon.

'A day or two, yeah?' he said. 'And please *do*, because this could really make a difference. I don't want to push you, but—'

'I *know*,' I said firmly, 'I know.'

'OK.' He held up his hands. 'Just . . . call me.'

He started looking around for a taxi.

'One last question,' I said.

'Yeah?'

'Why all this outdoor, park-bench stuff?'

He looked at me and smiled.

'Do you have any idea what kind of power structure I'm up against in Eiben-Chemcorp? And what kind of money is at stake for them?'

I shrugged my shoulders.

'Well, it's a lot, on both counts.' He stuck his arm out and hailed a taxi. 'I'm under constant surveillance from these people. They watch everything I do, my phones, e-mail, my travel itinerary. You think they're not watching us now?'

The taxi pulled up at the kerb. As he was getting into it, Morgenthaler turned to me and said, 'You know, Mr Spinola, you may not have as much time as you think.'

I watched the cab drive away and disappear into the flow of traffic on Fifth Avenue. Then I took off in that direction myself, walking slowly, still feeling a bit nauseous – not least now because I realized that my plan was unworkable. Morgenthaler may have been slightly paranoid, but it was nevertheless clear that threatening to play hardball with a huge pharmaceutical company was not a good idea. Who would I be approaching in any case? The Defense Secretary's *brother*? Apart from how complicated that made things, I couldn't see a company like Eiben-Chemcorp standing for black-mail in the first place, not with all of the resources they'd have at their disposal. This, in turn, made me think of how Vernon had died, and of how Todd Ellis had left United Labtech and then conve-niently been run over. What had happened there? Had Vernon and Todd's little scam siphoning off and dealing supplies of MDT been found out? Maybe Morgenthaler wasn't being paranoid after all, but if that was how things really were I was going to have to come up with another plan – something a little less audacious, to say the least.

I arrived at Fifty-seventh Street, and as I was crossing it I looked around. I remembered that one of my earliest blackouts had occurred here, after that first night in Van Loon's library. It'd been a couple of blocks over, on Park. I'd been overcome with dizziness, and had stumbled, and without any explanation found myself a block further down, on Fifty-sixth Street. Then I thought about the major blackout I'd had the following evening – punching that guy in the Congo down in Tribeca, then that girl in the cubicle, then Donatella Alvarez, then the fifteenth floor of the Clifden . . .

Something had gone seriously wrong that night, and just thinking about it now caused a stabbing sensation in the pit of my stomach.

But then it struck me . . . the whole sequence here – MDT, cognitive enhancement, blackouts, loss of impulse control, aggressive behaviour, Dexeron to counteract the blackouts, more MDT, more cognitive enhancement – it was all tinkering with brain chemistry. Maybe the reductionist view of human behaviour that Morgenthaler was going to pitch to his jury was right, maybe it *was* all down to molecular interaction, maybe we *were* just machines.

But if that was the case, if the mind was simply a chemical-software program running in the brain – and pharmaceutical products such as Triburbazine and MDT were simply rewrite programs – then what was to stop me from learning how all of that stuff worked? Using the supply of MDT-48 I had left, I could focus my powers of concentration for the next few weeks on the mechanics of the human brain. I could study neuroscience, and chemistry, and pharmacology, and even – goddammit – neuropsychopharmacology . . .

What would there then be to stop me from making my own MDT? There had been plenty of underground chemists in the old LSD days, people who had sidestepped the need to cultivate supply sources in the medical or pharmaceutical communities by setting up their own labs in bathrooms and basements all around the country. I was no chemist, for sure, but before I took MDT I hadn't been a stock-market trader, either – far from it, in fact. Excited now at the prospect of getting started on this, I quickened my pace. There was

314

a Barnes & Noble at Forty-eighth Street. I'd stop in there and pick up some textbooks and then get a cab straight back to the Celestial.

Passing a news-stand I saw a headline on a paper referring to the proposed MCL–Abraxas merger and remembered that I still had my cellphone powered off. As I walked along, I took it out and checked it for messages. There were two from Van Loon, the first puzzled, the second slightly irritated. I would have to talk to him soon and come up with some pre-emptive excuse for my absence over the coming weeks. I couldn't just ignore him. After all, I owed the man nearly ten million dollars.

I spent an hour in Barnes & Noble, browsing through college text-books – enormous tomes in fine print, with charts and diagrams and a blizzard of italicized Latin and Greek terminology. Finally, I picked out eight books with titles like *Biochemistry & Behaviour, Vol. 1.*, *Principles of Neurology* and *The Cerebral Cortex*, paid for them by credit card and left the store weighed down with two extremely heavy bags in each hand. I got a cab out on Fifth Avenue, just as it was starting to rain. By the time we pulled up at the Celestial, it had turned into a downpour, and in the ten or so seconds it took me to hobble across the plaza to the main entrance of the building, I got soaked. But I didn't care – I was excited and dying to get up to the apartment so I could make a start on these textbooks.

When I was inside, walking across the lobby, the guy on the desk, Richie, waved over at me.

'Mr Spinola. Hi. Yeah . . . I let those guys in.'

'What?'

'I let them in. They just left about twenty minutes ago.'

I walked over towards the desk.

'What are you talking about?'

'Those guys you said were delivering something. They were here.'

I put the bags down, and looked at him.

'I didn't say anything to you about any guys delivering . . . anything. What are you talking about?'

He swallowed and looked nervous all of a sudden.

'Mr Spinola, you . . . you called me about an hour ago, you said

315

some guys were coming to deliver something and that I was to give them a key . . .'

'*I* called you?'

'Yes.'

Water was dripping now from my hair down into the back of my shirt collar.

'Yes,' he repeated, as though to reassure himself. 'The line was bad, you said so yourself, it was your cellphone . . .'

I picked up the bags and started walking very quickly towards the elevators.

'Mr Spinola?'

I ignored him.

'Mr Spinola? Are . . . are we OK about this?'

I got into an elevator, pressed the button and as the car climbed up to the sixty-eighth floor, I could feel my heart beating so hard that I had to take deep breaths and bang my fist on the side panels of the car a couple of times to steady myself. Then I ran a hand through my hair and shook my head. Drops of water sprayed everywhere.

At sixty-eight, I picked up the two bags and slid out of the car before the elevator door was even fully open. I rushed along the corridor to my apartment, dropped the bags on the floor and fumbled in my jacket pocket for the key. When I got the key out, I had a hard time getting it into the keyhole. I eventually managed to get the door open, but the second I stepped inside the apartment I knew that everything was lost.

I'd known it downstairs in the lobby. I'd known it the second I heard Richie say the words, *I let those guys in . . .*

I looked around at the damage. The boxes and wooden crates in the middle of the living-room had been knocked over and smashed open, and everything was strewn about the place. I rushed over and searched through the mess of books and clothes and kitchen implements for the holdall bag where I'd been keeping the envelope with the stash of MDT pills in it. After a while I found the bag – but it was empty. The envelope with the pills in it was gone, as was Vernon's little black notebook. In the vain hope that the envelope was still around somewhere – that it had maybe just fallen out of the bag – I searched through everything, and then I searched through everything again. But it was no use.

The MDT was gone.

I went over to the window and looked out. It was still raining. Seeing the rain from this high an angle was weird, as though a couple more floors up and you'd be clear of it, looking down through sunshine at grey blankets of cloud.

I turned around and leant back against the window. The room was so large and bright, and there was such a small amount of stuff in it, that the mess in the centre wasn't even that much of a mess. The room hadn't been trashed, because there was so little in it to trash – just my few belongings from Tenth Street. They'd done a much better job on Vernon's place.

I stood there for quite a while – in shock, I suppose – not thinking anything. I glanced over at the open door. The two Barnes & Noble bags were still outside in the hallway, sitting on the floor next to each other, looking as though they were patiently waiting to be carried inside.

Then the phone rang.

I wasn't going to answer it, but when I noticed that they hadn't yanked the phone cable out of the wall, as they had with the computer and the TV, I went over to it. I bent down and picked it up. I said *hello*, but it went dead immediately.

I stood up again. I went over and edged the two bags inside the door with my foot. Then I shut the door and leant back against it. I took a few deep breaths, swallowed, closed my eyes.

The phone rang again.

I went over and answered it as before, but – as before – it went dead. Then almost immediately it rang again.

I picked it up but didn't say anything.

Whoever it was didn't hang up this time.

Eventually, a voice said, 'So, Eddie, this is it.'

'Who is this?'

'You went too far talking to Dave Morgenthaler. *Not* a good idea—'

317

'Who the fuck *is* this?'

'—so we've decided to pull the plug. But . . . just thought we'd let you know. Seeing as how you've been such a sport and all.'

The voice was very quiet, almost a whisper. There was no emotion in it, no hint of an accent.

'I shouldn't be doing this, of course – but at this stage, I almost feel that I *know* you.'

'What do you mean *pull the plug?*'

'Well, I'm sure you've noticed already that we've taken the stuff back. So, as of now, you can consider the experiment terminated.'

'*Experiment?*'

There was silence for a moment.

'We've been monitoring you ever since you showed up that day at Vernon's, Eddie.'

My heart sank.

'Why do you think you never heard back from the police? We weren't sure at first, but when it became obvious to us that you had Vernon's supply, we decided to see what would happen next, to conduct a little clinical trial, as it were. We haven't had that many human subjects, you know . . .'

I stared out across the room, trying to cast my mind back, trying to identify signs, tells . . .

'. . . and boy, what a subject you turned out to be! If it's any consolation to you, Eddie, no one has ever done as much MDT as you have, no one's ever taken it as *far* as you have.'

'Who are you?'

'I mean, we knew you really must've been hitting it hard when you cleaned up at Lafayette, but then when you moved in on Van Loon . . . that was amazing.'

'Who are you?'

'Of course, there *was* that little incident at the Clifden—'

'Who are you?' I repeated, dully now, almost mechanically.

'—but tell me, what exactly *did* happen there?'

I put the phone down, and kept my hand on it, hard, as though by pressing it like that, he – whoever *he* was – would go away.

When the phone rang again, I picked it up at once.

'Look, Eddie, no hard feelings, but we can't risk having you talking to private detectives – not to mention Russian loansharks. Just know that you've been . . . a *very* useful subject.'

'Come on,' I said, a sense of desperation welling up in me all of a sudden, 'is there no way . . . I mean, I don't have to . . .'

'Listen, Eddie—'

'I didn't give Morgenthaler anything, *I didn't tell him anything* . . .' – there was a crack in my voice now – '. . . couldn't I just get . . . some kind of supply, some . . .'

'Eddie—'

'I've got money,' I said, clutching the receiver tightly to stop my hand from trembling. 'I've got a *lot* of money in the bank. I could—'

The line went dead.

I kept my hand on the receiver, just like I had the last time. This time, however, I waited a full ten minutes. But nothing happened.

I finally lifted my hand away and stood up. My legs were stiff. I shifted my weight from one foot to the other, back and forth for a while. It felt like I was doing something.

Why had he hung up?

Was it because I had mentioned money? Would he be calling back in a while with a figure? Should I be ready?

How much *did* I have in the bank?

I waited another twenty minutes or so, but nothing happened.

Over the next twenty minutes again, I convinced myself that his hanging up on me had been some kind of a coded message. I'd offered him money, and now I was going to have to sweat it out until he called me back with a figure – which I'd better have ready.

I stared down at the phone.

I didn't want to use it, so I took out my cellphone and rang Howard Lewis, my bank manager. He was on another call. I left a message for him to call me back on this number. I said it was urgent. Five minutes later, he returned the call. Between what I'd made trading recently and money I'd borrowed from Van Loon for the decorating and furnishing of the apartment, there was just over $400,000 in the account. Since Van Loon had gotten involved in my financial affairs on a personal level, Lewis had reverted to his earlier obsequious mode, so when I told him that I needed half a million dollars in cash – and as quickly as possible – he was flustered but at the same time so eager to please that he promised to have the money ready for me first thing in the morning.

I said OK, I'd be there. Then I closed up the phone, switched it off and put it back in my pocket.

Half a million dollars. Who could turn that down?

I paced around the room, avoiding the mess in the centre. Every now and again, I glanced over at the phone on the floor.

When it started ringing again, I leapt towards it, bent down and picked it up in what seemed like a single movement.

'Hello?'

'Mr Spinola? It's Richie, down at the desk?'

Shit.

'*What?* I'm busy.'

'I just wanted to check that everything was all right. I mean, about that—'

'Yes, yes, everything's fine. There's no problem.'

I hung up.

My heart was pounding.

I stood up again and continued pacing around the room. I considered tidying up the mess, but decided against it. After a while I sat down on the floor, with my back to the wall and just stared out across the room, waiting.

I stayed in that position for the next eight hours.

Normally, I would have taken a dose of MDT in the afternoon, but since that hadn't been possible, I was overtaken with fatigue by late evening – something I identified as the earliest stage of the withdrawal process. As a result of this, I actually managed to get some sleep – even if it was fitful and disturbed. I had no bed, so I stacked up some blankets and a duvet on the floor and used that to sleep on. When I awoke – at about five in the morning – I had a dull headache and my throat was dry and raspy.

I made a cursory effort to tidy the mess up, just for something to do, but my mind was too clogged with anxiety and fear, and I didn't get very far.

Before I went to the bank, I took two Excedrin tablets. Then I rooted out my answering machine from one of the smashed wooden crates. It didn't look as if it had sustained too much damage, and when I connected it up to the phone on the floor, it appeared to be working. I got my briefcase from another crate, put on a coat and left – avoiding eye-contact with Richie at the desk down in the lobby.

In the cab on the way to the bank, with the empty briefcase resting on my lap, I experienced a wave of despair, a sense that the hope I was clinging to was not only desperate, but clearly – and absolutely – unfounded. As I looked out at the traffic and at the passing, streaming façade of Thirty-fourth Street, the notion that things could somehow be reversed, at this late stage, suddenly seemed, well . . . too much to hope for.

But then at the bank, as I watched an official stack my briefcase full with solid bricks of cash – fifty and hundred dollar bills – I regained a certain amount of confidence. I signed any relevant documents there were, smiled politely at the fawning Howard Lewis, bid him good morning and left.

In the cab on the way back, with the now full briefcase resting on my lap, I felt vaguely excited, as if this new scheme couldn't fail. When the guy phoned, I'd be ready with an offer – he'd have a proposal . . . we'd negotiate, things would slip neatly back into place.

As soon as I got up to the apartment, I put the briefcase down on the floor beside the telephone. I left it open, so I could see the money. There were no messages on the answering machine, and I checked my cellphone to see if there were any on that. There was one new one – from Van Loon. He understood I needed a break, but this was no way to go about taking one. I was to call him.

I powered off the phone and put it away.

By midday, my headache had become quite severe. I continued taking Excedrin tablets, but they no longer seemed to have any effect. I took a shower and stood for ages under the jet of hot water, trying to soothe the knots of tension out of my neck and shoulders.

The headache had started as a band across my forehead and behind my eyes, but by mid-afternoon it had worked its way out to every part of my skull and was pounding like a jackhammer.

I paced around the room for hours, trying to absorb the pain – glaring at the phone, *willing* it to ring. I couldn't understand why that guy hadn't called me back yet. I looked at the money. That was half a million dollars there, lying on the floor, just *waiting* for someone to come along and take it . . .

By early evening, I found that walking around didn't help much any more. I was having intermittent bouts of nausea now and was shivering all over, fairly constantly. It was easier, I decided, to lie on the makeshift bed of stacked blankets and a duvet, tossing and turning, and occasionally clutching my head in a vain attempt to ease the pain, As it got dark, I drifted in and out of a feverish sleep. At one point, I woke up retching – desperately trying to empty my already empty stomach. I coughed up blood on to the floor and then lay flat on my back again, staring up at the ceiling.

That night – Thursday night – was interminable, and yet in one sense I didn't want it to end. As the veil of MDT lifted further, my sense of horror and dread intensified. The torment of uncertainty gnawed away at the lining of my stomach and I kept thinking, *What have I done?* I had vivid dreams, hallucinations almost, in which I repeatedly seemed to come close to an understanding of what had happened that night at the Clifden Hotel – but then, since I was unable to separate what my fevered mind was concocting from what I was actually remembering, *it was never close enough*. I saw Donatella Alvarez calmly walking across the room, like before, in a black dress, blood pouring down the side of her face – but it was *this* room, not the hotel room, and I remember thinking that if she'd taken such a serious blow to the head, she wouldn't *be* calm, *or* walking around. I also dreamt that the two of us were on a couch together, entangled in each other's arms, and I was staring into her eyes, aroused, excited, engulfed in the flames of some nameless emotion – but at the same time it was my old couch we were on, the one from the apartment on Tenth Street, and she was whispering

322

in my ear, telling me to short-sell tech stocks now, now, *now*. Later, she was sitting across the table from me in Van Loon's dining-room, smoking a cigar and talking animatedly, '. . . because you *norteameri-canos* don't understand *any*thing, *no*thing . . .' – and then I seemed to be reaching out in anger for the nearest wine bottle . . .

Versions of this encounter passed through my mind continually during the night, each one slightly different – not a cigar, but a ciga-rette or a candle, not a wine bottle, but a cane or a statuette – each one like a shard of coloured glass hurtling in slow-motion through space after an explosion, each one vainly promising to form into a solid memory, into something objective and recollectable . . . and *reliable* . . .

At one point, I rolled off the duvet, holding my stomach, and crawled across the floor through the glistening darkness to the bath-room. After another fit of retching, this time into the toilet bowl, I managed to get up on to my feet. I leant over the wash-basin, strug-gled with the faucets for a moment and then threw some cold water on my face. When I looked up, my reflection in the mirror was ghost-like and barely visible, with my eyes – clear and moving – the only sign of life.

I dragged myself back into the living-room, where the dim shapes on the floor – the smashed boxes, the crumpled clothes, the open briefcase full of money – looked like irregular rock formations on some strange and dusky blue terrain. I slumped back against the wall nearest to the telephone and slid down into a sitting position on the floor. I stayed there for the next couple of hours, as daylight seeped in around me, allowing the room to reconstitute itself before my eyes, unchanged.

And I came to some accommodation with the pain in my head, as well – so long as I remained absolutely still, and didn't move, didn't flinch, it obligingly receded into a dull, thumping, mindless rhythm . . .

[27]

WHEN THE PHONE RANG BESIDE ME, just after nine o'clock, it felt like a thousand volts of electric current piercing my brain.

I reached over – wincing, my hand shaking – and picked up the receiver.

'Hello?'

'Mr Spinola? It's Richie, at the desk.'

'Hhhn.'

'There's a Mr . . . *Gennady* here to see you? Shall I send him up?'

Friday morning.

This morning. Well, yesterday morning by now.

I paused.

'Yeah.'

I put the phone down. He might as well see me – see what *he* would be in for shortly.

I struggled to get up off the floor – each movement I made like another charge of electric current through my brain. When I eventually got up I noticed that I was standing in a small pool of my own piss. There were blood and mucus stains on my shirt and I was trembling all over.

I looked down at the briefcase full of money, and then back at the phone. How could I have been so stupid, so vain? I looked over at the windows. It was a bright day. I walked over to the door, very slowly, and opened it.

I turned, and took a few paces back into the room, and then turned again to face the door. At my feet, there was a large, crushed box, its spilt contents – saucepans, pots, various kitchen implements – splayed out like intestines on the floor.

I stood there, an old man suddenly – feeble, stooped, at the mercy of everything around me. I heard the elevator opening, and then footsteps, and then a couple of moments later Gennady appeared in the doorway.

'Whoa . . . *fuck!*'

He looked around in shock – at me, at the mess, at the sheer size of the place, at the windows – obviously unable to decide if he was disgusted or impressed. He was wearing a pin-striped two-button suit, a black shirt and no tie. He'd shaved his head and was sporting a three-day stubble on his chiselled face.

He looked me up and down a couple of times.

'What the fuck's wrong with *you*?'

I mumbled something in response.

He came a little further into the room. Then, side-stepping the mess on the floor, he made his way over to the windows, irresistibly drawn to them, I suppose – just as I had been on that first visit here with Alison Botnick.

I didn't move. I felt nauseous.

'This is certainly a change from that shit-hole you had on Tenth Street.'

'Yeah.'

I could hear him behind me, pacing along by the windows.

'Shit, you can see everything.' He paused. 'I heard you'd found yourself quite a place, but this is amazing.'

What did *that* mean?

'There's the Empire State. The Chrysler Building. Brooklyn. I *like* this. You know, maybe I'll get a place here myself.' I could tell from his voice that he had turned around now. 'In fact, maybe I'll take *this* place, move in *here*. How'd that be, jerkoff?'

'That'd be great, Gennady,' I said, half turning around, 'I was going to look for a room-mate anyway, you know – to help with the repayments.'

'Listen to this, a comedian with shit stains on his pants. So, Eddie, what the fuck's going on here?'

He walked around the other side of the mess and came back into view. He stopped when he saw the briefcase of money on the floor.

'Jesus, you really *don't* like banks, do you?'

With his back to me, he bent down and started looking at the money, taking wads of it out and flicking through them.

'There must be three or four hundred thousand dollars here.' He whistled. 'I don't know what you're into, Eddie, but if there's much more where this came from, you might want to think of investing some of it. My import company's going to be up and running soon, so if you want in for some points . . . you know, we can talk about a price.'

Talk about a price?

Gennady didn't know it, but he was going to be dead soon – in a few days' time, after his supply of MDT had run out.

'Well,' he said, straightening up again and turning around, 'when am I going to meet this dealer of yours?'

I looked at him, and said, 'You're not going to meet him.'

'*What?*'

'You're not going to meet him.'

He paused, breathing out through his nose. Then he stood looking at me for about ten seconds. The expression on his face was like that of a thwarted child – but a thwarted child with a switchblade in his pocket. Slowly he took it out and flicked it open.

'I thought this might happen,' he said, 'so I did some homework. Found out a few things about you, Eddie. Been keeping an *eye* on you.'

I swallowed.

'You've been doing pretty well recently, haven't you? With your business associates and merger deals.' He turned and started pacing across the room. 'But I don't think Van Loon or Hank Atwood would be too happy to hear about your association with a Russian loanshark.'

I looked at him, starting to feel a little thwarted myself.

'Or about your history of substance abuse. Wouldn't play too well in the press either.'

My history of substance abuse? That *was* history. How could he know anything about that?

'It's incredible what you can find out about someone's past, isn't it?' he said, as though reading my thoughts. 'Employment records, credit history – even personal stuff.'

'Fuck you.'

'Oh, I don't think so.'

As he said this, he turned and walked quickly back to where I was standing. He held the knife up near my nose and waved it from side to side.

'I could re-arrange the elements of your face, Eddie, nicely, creatively, but I'd *still* want the answer to my question.' He stared into my eyes, and repeated it, this time in a whisper, *'When am I going to meet this dealer of yours?'*

I had nowhere to go, and very little to lose. I whispered back, 'You're not.'

There was a brief pause, and then he punched me in the stomach with his left hand — just as swiftly and efficiently as he'd done once before in my old apartment. I doubled up and fell back on to some boxes, wheezing and clutching myself with both arms.

Gennady then took off again, pacing back and forth across the room.

'You didn't think I was going to *start* with the face, did you?'

The pain was simultaneously awful and something I felt at a curious remove from. I think I was too concerned about how my privacy had been invaded, about how Gennady had managed to dig up my past.

'I've got a whole file on you. *This* thick. It's all out there, Eddie, information – for the taking, detail like you wouldn't believe.'

I looked up. He had his back to me now and was waving his hands about. Just then something caught my eye – something sticking out of the smashed box of kitchen implements in front of me.

'So what I want to know, Eddie, is this: how do you propose to explain all those years of mediocrity to your new friends at the top? Eh? Writing that turgid shit for K & D? Teaching English in Italy without a work permit? Fucking up the colour separations at *Chrome* magazine?'

As he was speaking, I reached over to the box. Sticking out of it

327

was the wooden handle of a long, steel carving knife. I took hold of it and eased it out of the box, my head pounding from the effort of trying to control the shake in my hand – to say nothing of having to lean across in the first place. I then struggled up on to my feet, being careful to keep the knife behind my back.

Gennady turned around.

'And you were married once, as well, weren't you?'

He came across the room towards me. I was dizzy now, seeing him in double as he approached, the background white and pulsating. But despite this unsteadiness, I seemed to know what I was doing – everything was clear and in place, anger, humiliation, fear. There was a logic to it all, an inevitability. Was this how it had been up on the fifteenth floor? I didn't see how it could have been, but I also knew that I would never find out.

'But that didn't work out either, did it?'

He stopped for a moment, and then came a few steps closer.

'What was her name again?'

He held the knife up and waved it in my face. I could smell his breath. My heart and head were pounding in unison now.

'Melissa.'

'Yeah,' he said. '*Melissa* . . . and she's got, what, *two* kids?'

I widened my eyes suddenly and looked over his shoulder. When he turned to see what I was looking at, I took a deep breath and brought the carving knife around. In a single, swift movement, I drove the point of it into his belly and grabbed the back of his neck with my other hand for leverage. I pushed the knife in as hard as I could, trying to direct it upwards. I heard a deep, gurgling sound and felt his arms flailing up and down, helplessly, as though they'd been cut adrift from the rest of his body. I gave a final shove to the knife and then had to let go. It had taken a huge effort to do this much and I just staggered backwards, trying to catch my breath. Then I leant against one of the windows and watched as Gennady stood in the same position, swaying, staring at me. His mouth was open and both his hands were clasping the wooden handle of the knife – the only part of it that was still visible.

The pounding in my head was so intense now that it short-circuited any sense of moral horror I might have felt at what I was watching, or at what I had *done*. I was also concerned about what was going to happen next.

Gennady took a couple of steps towards me. The look on his face was one of mingled incredulity and fury. I thought I was going to have to move aside to avoid him, but almost immediately he tripped on a torn box and came crashing forward on to a pile of large format art and photography books. The impact of this must have driven the knife in a little deeper – and fatally – because after he had fallen, he remained completely still.

I waited for a few minutes, watching and listening – but he didn't move or make any sound at all.

Eventually – and very slowly – I went over to where he had come down. I bent over him and felt for a pulse on the side of his neck. There was nothing. Then something occurred to me, and drawing on a final reserve of adrenalin I took him by the arm and rolled him over on to his back. The knife was lodged at a skewed angle in his stomach and his black shirt was now sodden with blood. I took a couple of deep breaths, and tried not to look at his face.

I lifted the right side of his jacket with one hand, raised it, and tentatively put my other hand into his inside breast pocket. I fished around for a moment, thinking I wasn't going to find anything – but then, folded in a flap of material I felt something hard. I got hold of it with the tips of my fingers and drew it out. I held it still for a moment – my heart thumping against the walls of my chest – and then shook it. The little silver pillbox made a small but very welcome rattling sound.

I got up and went back over to the window. I stood still for a few seconds in a vain attempt to ease the pounding in my head. Then I leant back against the window and slid down into a sitting position. My hands were still shaking, so in order to keep the pillbox steady I placed it on the floor between my legs. Concentrating really hard, I screwed the top off the box, put it aside and then peered down. There were five pills in the box. Again, working very carefully, I managed to get three of them out of it and on to the palm of my hand.

I paused, closed my eyes and involuntarily relived the previous couple of minutes in my mind – kaleidoscopically, luridly, but *accurately*. When I opened my eyes again, the first thing I saw – a few feet in front of me, like an old leather football – was Gennady's shaved head, and then the rest of him, splayed out on the flattened pile of books.

I raised my hand, took the three tablets into my mouth and swallowed them.

I sat there for the next twenty minutes, staring out across the room – during which time, like a cloudy, overcast sky breaking up and clearing to blue, the pain in my head slowly lifted. The shake in my hands faded, too, and I felt a gradual return – at least within the parameters of MDT – to some kind of normality. This was borrowed time, and I knew it. I also knew that Gennady's entourage was probably downstairs waiting for him, and that if much more time elapsed, they might get curious, or concerned even – and things might then get complicated.

I screwed the top back on to the pillbox and slipped it into the pocket of my trousers. When I stood up, I noticed the stains on my shirt again – as well as a couple of other signs of the general state of degradation I'd fallen into. I went over towards the bathroom, unbuttoning my shirt on the way. I took off the rest of my clothes and had a quick shower. Then I changed into some fresh clothes, jeans and a white shirt – making sure to transfer the pillbox into my jeans pocket. I went over to the telephone on the floor, called information and got the number of a local car-service. I then called the number and ordered a car for as soon as possible – instructing them to have me picked up at the back entrance to the building. After that, I gathered a few things into the holdall, including my laptop computer. I picked up the briefcase full of cash and closed it up. Then I carried both the briefcase and the holdall to the door, and opened it.

I stood there for a moment, looking back into the room. Gennady was almost lost from view in the general mess of things, *my* things

– boxes, books, clothes, saucepans, album covers. But then I saw a small trickle of blood making its way out on to a clear part of the floor. When I saw another one, I was overcome with a feeling of nausea and had to lean against the side of the door to keep my balance. As I was doing this, a sudden squeal sounded from the centre of the room. My heart jumped, but as the high-pitched, slightly muffled tone settled into an electronic rendition of the main theme from Tchaikovsky's Piano Concerto Number 1, I realized that it had to be Gennady's cellphone. The *zhuliks* downstairs were obviously getting restless, and would doubtless be on their way up soon. With no choice but to keep moving, therefore, I turned around and closed the door behind me.

I took the elevator down to the basement car park and walked the length of this huge interior space, past rows and rows of concrete pillars and parked cars. I made my way up a winding ramp to the concourse at the rear of the building. Fifty yards to the left of where I came out, a couple of trucks were making deliveries at a loading dock – probably to one or other of the Celestial's several restaurants. I waited around for about five minutes, staying out of view, until a black, unmarked car arrived. I signalled to the driver and he stopped. I got into the back, with the briefcase and the holdall, and paused for a moment. After I'd taken a couple of deep breaths, I told the driver to get on to the Henry Hudson Parkway, going north. He pulled around by the side of the building and then turned left. The traffic lights at the next block were red, and when the car stopped I turned around to look back. There was a Mercedes parked at the kerb of the plaza. A few guys in leather jackets were standing next to it on the sidewalk, smoking. One of them was looking up at the building.

The lights changed, and as we were pulling away – suddenly – three police cars appeared out of nowhere. They pulled up at the kerb of the plaza and within seconds – the last thing I could make out – five or six uniformed cops were running over towards the main entrance to the Celestial.

I turned back around. I didn't understand it. Since I'd left the apartment, there couldn't have been enough time for anyone to get up to it, get *into* it . . . call the cops and then for the cops to *arrive* . . .

It didn't make sense.

I caught the driver's eye in the rearview mirror. He held my gaze for a couple of seconds.

Then we both looked away.

[28]

WE CONTINUED NORTH.

As soon as we got on to Interstate 87, I felt a little less tense. I sat back in the car and stared out of the window, stared at the miles of highway flitting by and blending, slowly, into a continuous, hypnotic stream – a process which allowed me to smother any thoughts I was having about the last couple of days, the last couple of *hours*, and especially about what I had just done to Gennady. But after nearly forty minutes of this, I couldn't help turning my mind to what I had decided to do next, to the immediate future – the only kind of future I seemed to have left.

I told the driver to cut over and drop me off in someplace like Scarsdale or White Plains. He considered this for a couple of minutes, looked around at his options, and eventually took me into the centre of White Plains. I paid him – and in the vague hope that he might keep his mouth shut, I gave him a hundred-dollar tip.

Carrying the holdall and the briefcase – one in either hand – I wandered around for a while until I found a taxi on Westchester Avenue, which I then took to the nearest car-rental outlet. Using my credit card, I rented a Pathfinder. Then I immediately got out of White Plains and continued north on Interstate 684.

I passed Katonah and took a left at Croton Falls for Mahopac. Off the highway now and driving through this quiet, hilly, woodland area, I felt displaced, but at the same time strangely serene – as though I had already passed over into some other dimension. Shifts in perspective and velocity intensified my growing sense of unreality. I hadn't been behind the wheel of a car for ages – and not, in any case, out of the city, and at such speed, and never high up like this in one of these SUVs . . .

As I approached Mahopac itself, I had to slow down. I had to make an effort to refocus on what I was doing, and on what I was about to do. It took me a while to remember the address that Melissa had written down for me in the bar on Spring Street. It eventually came to me, and when I got into town, I stopped at a gas station to buy a map of the area so I could work out how to get to where she lived.

Ten minutes later I'd found it.

I cruised right on to Milford Drive and pulled up at the kerb in front of the third house on the left. The street was quiet and canopied with trees. I reached over to the back seat, where I'd put the holdall. I opened a side pocket of the bag and pulled out a small notebook and a pen. Then I took the briefcase from the passenger seat and placed it on my lap. I tore a page out of the notebook and wrote a few quick lines. I opened the briefcase, stared at the money for a moment and then secured the note inside so that it was clearly visible.

I got out of the car, pulling the briefcase after me and started walking along the narrow pathway towards the house. There was an area of grass on either side of the pathway and on one of them there was a small bicycle lying on its side. It was a single-storey, grey clap-board house, with steps leading up to it and a porch at the front. It looked like it could do with a lick of paint, and maybe a new roof.

I went up the steps and stood on the porch for a moment. I tried to peer inside, but there was a screen on the door and I couldn't see properly. I crooked my index finger and rapped it on the frame of the door.

My heart was thumping.

After a moment, the door opened and standing before me was a spindly little girl of about seven or eight. She had long, dark, straight hair and deep brown eyes. I must have shown how surprised I was because she furrowed her eyebrows and said, officiously, 'Yes?'

'You must be Ally,' I said.

She considered this for a moment and then decided to nod in the affirmative. She was wearing a red cardigan and pink leggings.

'I'm an old friend of your mother's.'

334

This didn't seem to impress her much.

'My name's Eddie.'

'You want to speak to my mom?'

I detected a slight impatience in her tone and in her body language, as though she wanted me to get on with it – to get to the point so she could get back to whatever it was she'd been doing before I came along to disturb her.

From somewhere in the background a voice said, 'Ally, who is it?'

It was Melissa. All of a sudden this began to seem a lot more difficult than I had anticipated.

'It's a . . . *man*.'

'I'll . . .' – there was a pause here, pregnant with momentary indecision, and maybe even a hint of exasperation – '. . . I'll be there in a minute. Tell him . . . to wait.'

Ally said, informatively, 'My mom's washing my kid sister's hair.'

'That'd be Jane, wouldn't it?'

'Yeah. She can't do it herself. And it takes ages.'

'Why's that?'

'Because it's so long.'

'Longer than yours?'

She made a puffing sound, as if to say, *Whoa, mister, you're nowhere near as informed as you think.*

'Well, listen,' I said, 'you're obviously all busy here.' I paused, and looked directly into her eyes, experiencing something like vertigo, but with both feet on the ground. 'So why don't I just leave this with you . . . and you can tell your mom I was here . . . and that I left *this* for her.'

Being careful not to seem in any way pushy, I leant forward a little and placed the briefcase on a rug just inside the door.

She didn't move as I did this. Then she looked down suspiciously at the briefcase. I took a couple of steps back. She glanced up at me again.

'My mom said you were to wait.'

'I know, but I'm in a hurry.'

She assessed this for plausibility, intrigued now – whatever she'd been doing before I arrived apparently forgotten.

335

'Ally, I'm coming.'

The urgency in Melissa's voice cut into me and I knew I had to get away before she appeared. I'd been going to tell her not to open the suitcase until I left. Now it would make no difference.

I backed down the steps.

'I've got to go, Ally. It was nice meeting you.'

She furrowed her eyebrows again, altogether unsure about what was going on now. In a small voice, she said, 'My mom's just coming.'

Stepping backwards, I said, 'Will you remember my name?'

In an even smaller voice, she said, 'Eddie.'

I smiled.

I could have stared at her for hours, but I had to break away and turn around. I got back to the car and climbed in. I started the engine.

Out of the corner of my eye, as I was pulling away, I was aware of a sudden movement at the door of the house. When I got to the first junction, and was about to turn left, I glanced into my rearview mirror. Melissa and Ally were standing – holding hands – in the middle of the street.

I made my way over towards Newburgh and then got back on to Interstate 87, heading north. I decided I would keep going until I got to Albany and then take it from there.

It was early afternoon as I arrived in the outskirts of the city. I drove around for a bit and then parked in a side street off Central Avenue. I sat in the car for twenty minutes, staring at the wheel.

But take *what* from here?

I got out and started walking, briskly, and not in any particular direction. As I moved, I replayed the scene with Ally over and over in my mind. Her resemblance to Melissa was uncanny and the whole experience had left me stunned – blinking at infinity, shuddering in sudden, unexpected spasms of benevolence and hope.

But as I moved, too, I could feel Gennady's silver pillbox lodged in the pocket of my jeans. I knew that in a few hours' time I would be opening the box, taking out the two tablets that were left in it, and swallowing them – a simple, banal sequence of movements that

336

was all too finite and bereft of anything even approaching benevolence or hope.

I wandered on, aimlessly.

After about half an hour, I decided there wasn't much point in going any further. It looked like it was going to start raining soon, and in any case the unfamiliarity of these busy commercial streets was becoming a little disconcerting.

I stopped and turned around to go back towards the car. But as I did so I found myself staring into the window of an electrical goods store in which there were fifteen TV sets banked up in three rows of five. On each screen, staring directly out at me, was the face of Donatella Alvarez. It was a headshot. She was leaning forward slightly, her eyes big and deep, her long, brown hair casting one side of her face into shadow.

I stood frozen on the sidewalk, people passing behind and around me. Then I stepped a little closer to the window and watched as the news report continued with exterior shots of Actium and the Clifden Hotel. I moved along the window and stepped inside the door so I'd be able to hear the report as well as see it – but the sound was quite low and with the traffic passing behind me all I could hear were fragments. Over a shot of Forty-eighth Street, I thought I caught something about '. . . a statement issued this afternoon by Carl Van Loon'. Then, '. . . a re-appraisal of the deal in the light of negative publicity'. And then – I was really straining to hear now – something like '. . . share prices adversely affected'.

I looked around in exasperation.

There was another display of TV sets tuned to the same channel in an alcove at the back. I quickly walked the length of the store, past VCRs and DVDs and stereos and ghetto-blasters, and just as I got to the other end, they were cutting to a piece of footage from the MCL–Abraxas press conference, the one with the camera gliding across the top of the room from left to right. I waited, my stomach jumping, and then after a couple of seconds . . . *there I was*, on the screen, in my suit, gliding from right to left, staring out. There was a curiously vacant look on my face that I didn't remember from the first time I'd seen this . . .

I listened to the report, but was barely able to take it in. Someone at Actium that night – probably the bald art critic with the salt-and-pepper beard – had seen the footage on the news, and it had jogged his memory. He'd recognized me as Thomas Cole, the guy who'd been sitting opposite Donatella Alvarez at the restaurant, and who'd later been speaking to her at the reception.

After the press-conference footage, they cut to a reporter standing in front of the Celestial Building. 'Following up this new lead,' the reporter said, 'police then came to Eddie Spinola's apartment here on the West Side to question him, but what they found instead was the body of an unidentified man, believed to be a member of a Russian crime organization. This man had apparently been stabbed to death, which means that Eddie Spinola . . .' – they cut back to the footage from the press conference – '. . . is now wanted by police for questioning in relation to *two* high-profile murders . . .'

I turned around and walked swiftly back to the other end of the store, avoiding eye-contact with anyone. I stepped out on to the sidewalk and turned right. As I passed along by the window-front, I was acutely aware of the multiple screens showing yet another re-run of the press-conference footage.

On my way to the car, I stopped at a pharmacy and bought a large container of paracetamol. Then I stopped at a liquor store and bought two bottles of Jack Daniel's.

After that, I got back on the road, still heading north, and left Albany as fast as I could.

I avoided the Interstate highways and took secondary roads, passing through Schenectady and Saratoga Springs and then up into the Adirondacks. I took a random, circuitous route, and wove my way towards Schroon Lake, oblivious of the natural beauty that was all around me, my head buzzing instead with an endless succession of garbled images. I veered over into Vermont, staying on secondary roads and worked my way up through Vergennes and Burlington, and then over towards Morrisville and Barton.

I drove for seven or eight hours, pulling in only once, for gas, at which point I also took the last two pills in the silver box.

I stopped at the Northview Motor Lodge at around ten o'clock. There was no point in driving any further. It was pitch dark now, and where was I going to go in any case? On up to Maine? New Brunswick? Nova Scotia?

I checked into the motel using a false name, and paid for the room in cash. In advance.

Two nights.

After I got over the initial shock of the décor and colour schemes in the room, I lay on the bed and stared up at the ceiling.

According to the TV news bulletin I'd seen earlier, I was now a wanted murderer. That wasn't quite how I saw myself, but given the circumstances I knew I'd have a pretty difficult time bringing anyone else around to my point of view.

It's a long story, I'd have to say.

And then I'd have to tell it.

Whether or not I had realized it at the time, I realized now that this was why I'd packed my laptop computer in the holdall. The last coherent thing I would ever do would be to tell my story, and leave it behind for someone else to read. I lingered on the bed for quite a while, thinking things through. But then I remembered that I didn't have that much time left in which to *be* coherent.

I got off the bed, therefore. I switched on the TV set, but kept the sound down. I took out the laptop from the bag, as well as one of the bottles of Jack Daniel's. I put the plastic container of paracetamol tablets on the little bedside table. Then I sat down here in this wicker armchair, and with the sound of the ice-machine humming in the background, I got started.

o   o   o

It's now Saturday morning, early, and I'm beginning to feel tired. This is one of the first signs of withdrawal from MDT – so it's just as well that I've more or less finished here.

But finished what?

Is this a true and honest account of how I came close to doing the impossible, to realizing the unrealizable . . . to becoming one of the best and the brightest? Is it the story of a hallucination, a dream of perfectibility? Or is it simply the story of a human lab rat, someone who was tagged and followed and photographed, and then discarded? Or is it – even more simply again – the last confession of a murderer?

I don't know any more, and don't even know that it matters.

Besides, I'm feeling drowsy, and a little weak.

I think I'm going to lie down for a while.

I've just slept for about five hours, fitfully, tossing and turning. For the whole time, it felt like I was having a continuous, full-on anxiety dream, and when I woke up I had a headache behind my eyes which quickly spread out to the rest of my skull. Disorientated, groggy, nauseous, I then got off the bed, came back over here to the wicker armchair and replaced the computer on my lap.

It's now around midday, and the TV is still on, tuned to CNN.

Clearly, something major has been happening since yesterday evening, or early this morning. I'm looking at shots of battleships stationed in the Gulf of Mexico, of ground troops being deployed along border areas, of Defense Secretary Caleb Hale in emergency session with the Chairman of the Joint Chiefs of Staff.

Along the bottom of the screen a band of text announces that a live presidential address from the Oval Office is about to commence.

I close my eyes for a while, and when I open them again the President is on the TV screen, sitting at his desk. I can't bear to turn the sound up, and as I study him closely, and see the alert, gorged MDT expression in his eyes, I realize that I can't bear to *look* at him any more either. I reach out for the remote control and flick over to another channel, cartoons.

I gaze down at the keyboard of the laptop. My head is pounding now, and getting steadily worse. It's time to shut off the computer and put it aside. I look over at the small table next to the bed, and at the plastic bottle on it containing 150 paracetamol tablets. Then I look at the keyboard once more and, wishing the command had a wider, smarter application – wishing it could somehow mean what it says – press 'save'.

Bloodland

(Autumn 2011)

Corruption. Collusion. Conspiracy.

A tabloid star is killed in a helicopter crash and three years later a young journalist is warned off the story.

A private security contractor loses it in the Congo.

In Ireland an ex-prime minister struggles to contain a dark secret from his time in office.

A dramatic news story breaks in Paris just as a US senator begins his campaign to run for office.

With echoes of John Le Carré, *24* and James Ellroy, Alan Glynn's follow-up to *Winterland* is another crime novel of and for our times – a ferocious, paranoid thriller that moves from Dublin to New York via Central Africa, as it explores the legacy of corruption in big business, the West's fear of China, the role of back-room political players and the question of who controls what we know.

Winterland

(available in paperback now)

'A dark edgy thriller packed with genuine suspense and a real sense of danger, diving into a world of crime, corruption and violence that is all too convincing.' *The Times*

'A page turner in the best sense of the word . . . the three set pieces of the story are as good as anything I've read in contemporary crime fiction.' John Boyne, *Irish Times*

'An enthralling and addictive read.' *Observer*

'Clever and intense; a dark and powerful slice of Dublin noir. I loved it!' R. J. Ellory

'A terrific read . . . completely involving.' George Pelecanos

'Timely, topical and thrilling.' John Connolly

'A resonant, memorable and uncomfortable read . . . *Winterland* is a book that speaks to absolutely now.' Val McDermid